DRAGON ASCENDING

VANIR DRAGON SERIES BOOK I

AMY BEATTY

Appropriate for Teens, Intriguing to Adults

Immortal Works LLC
1505 Glenrose Drive
Salt Lake City, Utah 84104
Tel: (385) 202-0116

Cover Art by Book Covers.io
www.bookcovers.io

Formatted by FireDrake Designs
www.firedrakedesigns.com

ISBN 978-1-7324674-2-2 (Paperback)
AISN B07FC1NLKM (Kindle Edition)

To Tom, who always said I could do anything.
And to Daniel and Elizabeth, my favorite distractions.

A NOTE FROM THE AUTHOR

Immerse yourself in *Dragon Ascending* on a whole different level! Hear the rush of the wind in the trees, the crackling campfire, water sloshing against the hull of the boat, and the sounds of the village marketplace as you travel through the world of the book.

I'm excited to offer a collection of custom soundscapes I developed for each chapter of my book. Listening to these sound generators as I write helps me more fully imagine the places my characters encounter. Now you can experience those places in the same way as you read.

Special thanks to sound engineer Dr. Ir. Stéphane Pigeon for his kind permission to share them with you.

Links are located on my website:

https://www.amybeatty.com/dragon-ascending-soundscapes.

CHAPTER 1

E drik landed belly down on the stone floor of the Shrike's Keep guardhouse hard enough to knock the air from his lungs. Probably just as well since, otherwise, he might have yelled when the guard's boot slammed into his back, gouging hobnails into the shallow sword wound just below his shoulder blade.

The ropes cut into his wrists behind his back as he writhed, and the sting of the iron mixing with his blood scorched through his body, drawing behind it a hot, twisting nausea that forced its way out of him in a violent retch. It wasn't enough for the humans that they'd built their filthy town on top of a massive deposit of iron ore, they had to grind the poison straight into his flesh as well.

His brawny captor laughed. "Burns a mite, do it?"

Edrik was too busy retching to answer.

Another voice said, "What you got there, Benit?"

"Dunno," said Edrik's captor. "Some mannish thing what don't take well to iron. Jumped Egil down by the delvers' quarters."

"Springing from the woodwork of late," muttered the newcomer. "Big fella this time, looks like. Give you much trouble?"

"Took three of us to knock 'im down."

Benit's friend prodded Edrik in the ribs with the haft of his spear like a little boy poking at a dead bird to see if it would move. "Sure looks to be down now." The man chuckled sourly. "Best clean 'im up. You know how the Mudge is about vermin."

Benit mashed his boot into Edrik's wound one more time before drawing his knife and crouching beside his prisoner. "Oh ach," he agreed. "I let a fella through with lice once, and I'm fair sure the Mudge picked ever one of 'em off and left 'em in my bed."

The iron blade of the knife skimmed across Edrik's skin, not cutting, but leaving a burning itch behind as the guard sliced Edrik's clothes off as efficiently as if he were skinning a kill. The smoldering coals in the watchmen's brazier woke up to lick at the shreds of linen tunic Benit tossed on top of them, sending flickers of firelight skittering across the floor.

A hawking snort, followed by a hiss as Benit's friend spat into the fire. "You got off easy. Mudge dosed Terren's dinner when he done it. Couldn't leave the privy for a week."

"You seen that scum the new night overseer took down there yesterday?"

More slicing.

"I seen 'im. Overseer says he's the monster as has been grabbing them women down by the river. Crawling with fleas at the very least."

"That's the one. Mudge ain't letting that slip by."

With Edrik stripped down to his breeks, Benit yanked the rope that stretched taut between his prisoner's shoulder blades, running from Edrik's bound wrists up around his throat. Edrik choked and struggled to his knees.

Benit grunted. "Best stand back from the overseer for a few days."

"Ach, I'll say." Sardonic laughter. "You want help with that one?"

"Meh." Benit grabbed a fistful of Edrik's hair and began shaving it off close to the scalp with his knife. "Fight's gone out of 'im. Think I can manage." He tossed the pale locks into the fire, and the gagging stench of burning hair rolled through the already musty room.

Edrik gritted his teeth and let the man do his job. Grabak had to be in Shrike's Hollow; they'd looked everywhere else that made any sense. And the only place in Shrike's Hollow they hadn't already looked was in the dungeon beneath the keep.

When Edrik had been suitably stripped, and shorn, and splashed with some vile herbal decoction, Benit yanked him to his feet and shoved him through a door on the far side of the guard room. Beyond, a short corridor led between two narrow holding chambers.

The room on the right contained three women: a ragged beggar and two women dressed in a manner that advertised both their profession and their wares. One of these smiled invitingly at Edrik, eying him up and down, and made a lewd gesture. Edrik winked back at her and tried to pretend that being paraded through a dungeon in his smallclothes didn't bother him at all.

On the left, several men in various stages of dishevelment and intoxication regarded Edrik suspiciously from behind the iron-barred gate. None of them had been given the same decontamination treatment Edrik had been subjected to. And none of them was Grabak. But that was to be expected; nobody in their right mind would keep someone like Grabak in a temporary holding pen. Edrik needed to find the cells where the Thane housed his more permanent prisoners.

When they reached the end of the corridor, Benit slid an iron-capped cudgel from his belt and used it to rap smartly on the heavy, iron-bound wooden door. A brief silence was followed by a rattling of locks and then a dour-faced guard pulled the door open from the other side.

The squat stone building that held the guardhouse and the temporary holding cells had been constructed with its back against the massive stone escarpment on which Shrike's Keep had been erected, overlooking the town. The corridor that waited for Edrik behind the iron-bound door had been carved into the scarp face itself, as had the cells, fronted with iron bars, that lined each side of the passageway, all of which would make escape more difficult.

Not for the first time, Edrik was glad of the invisible yot mark on the bottom of his foot that would allow Tait and Finn to track him.

Ten days: that was what they'd agreed on. Ten days to find Grabak, and then Tait and Finn would get them out. The yotun who'd made the yot mark for them claimed the magic was good for twelve days after the mark on the wafer-thin, waxy disk had been absorbed into the skin.

But two days had already passed. He gritted his teeth. Eight days left. He could handle eight days, even in an iron-plagued cell. If his friends hadn't come by then . . .

That wouldn't happen. They would come.

And they had the other yot mark—the wooden one that would burn through stone and metal. They'd get him out.

Benit gave him a shove, and the two of them started walking down the corridor as the other guard locked the door behind them.

Edrik peered more carefully into the cells in this gallery as he passed. Twelve cells, six on each side of the corridor. Five men—none of which were Grabak—settled in their cells for the long term.

Grabak had to be *somewhere!* They were running out of time. And Edrik could not fail. Not at this.

At the far end of the gallery, an open archway led to a small watch room where a guard sat whittling beside a glowing brazier. He looked up when Benit and Edrik approached, frowning as he took in Edrik's state of undress. "What's this? Another for the Mudge?"

Benit grunted an affirmative.

The guard rose, shaking his head. "Won't please 'im. Likes it quiet down there."

Benit grunted again and waited while the other guard unlocked yet another door at the back of the watch room.

The new passageway was more a narrow tunnel than a corridor. The stone was roughhewn and veined with the deep red of the iron ore that ran through the surrounding land like tainted blood. Edrik stumbled as Benit shoved him through the door, and his skin crawled when the rattle of the key in the lock behind them echoed back from the darkness ahead.

Something felt wrong.

Benit paused just inside the door, swearing softly, and Edrik realized the man must be waiting for his eyes to adjust. Edrik, whose eyes were better suited for darkness, could make out a faint glow coming from around a curve in the tunnel ahead.

Benit shoved, and Edrik moved toward the light, wincing when his shoulder brushed against an ore vein in the wall. The curve in the passageway turned out to be the top of a winding staircase that spiraled down into the heart of the stone beneath the keep. The light was a pale, reflected beam that made its way up the staircase by way of a series of bronze mirrors embedded into the stone walls.

Edrik sensed the weight of iron pressing in all around him, and the thought of going deeper made his stomach churn. But if Grabak really was in Shrike's Hollow, this was exactly the sort of place they would keep him. And Finn and Tait would come for him. Eight days.

Edrik drew a deep breath and ground the yot mark on his foot against the stone, just to be sure, then moved ahead down the stairs before Benit could shove him again. At the bottom of the stairway, Edrik froze, breath catching in his throat. The low archway that led into the next block of cells was covered, lintel, posts, and threshold, with dwarrow runes. And something smelled of death. He staggered back a step.

Benit had anticipated the move and prodded Edrik in the back, grinding the iron-clad end of his cudgel into Edrik's still seeping wound.

Edrik staggered and nearly fell as fire seared through his veins and bile rose in his throat. Benit shoved him again, and Edrik careened through the arch and crashed to the ground, unable to catch himself with his bound hands.

Benit laughed. "Can't run now. Door only goes one way for your kind. 'Less you're dead."

He caught hold of the rope that circled Edrik's neck and yanked him up to his knees, then bellowed, "Hoy, Mudge!"

While Benit waited for a response, Edrik took stock. He hadn't expected the runes. But Tait's yot mark would burn through stone; it would get them past the dwarrow work. It would have to—unless there was another way out. He scanned the room. There were four big cells, two on each side of a wide central aisle. Rough stone walls formed three sides of each cell, but the front walls consisted of iron bars running from floor to ceiling, spaced a hand-span or so apart. The light came from a glowing orb fastened to the ceiling in the center of the aisle—more dwarrow work.

One of the cells on the near end of the block was occupied by a leering bearded fellow who reeked of unwashed human. In the cell on the opposite side of the aisle, a well-muscled, dark-haired man wearing trousers and an unbuttoned shirt lounged comfortably on a stone ledge at the back of the cell, slowly turning the pages of a book. He looked up in annoyance at the interruption, and Edrik's heart surged in triumph. *Grabak!*

Edrik's exultation was short-lived, however. A movement in the cell beyond Grabak's caught his eye, and his heart froze in his chest.

Finn.

How could Finn be here?

Edrik stared. Even stripped and shaven, the man couldn't be mistaken for anyone but Finn. Edrik's mouth popped open, then closed when Finn frowned grimly. Edrik looked to the cell across from Finn and back again. Finn gave an almost imperceptible shake of his head and flicked his gaze toward the far end of the aisle.

There, another rune-carved archway opened into what appeared to be a workroom of some sort. Shelves lined the walls, filled with books, boxes, and jars. A fire burned cozily on a small hearth. A desk stood in the middle of the floor, cluttered with odds and ends. And off to one side, a robed figure straightened from bending over something that was laid out on a long work table. The robed figure was presumably the Mudge, whoever or *whatever* that was.

And the thing on the table, half flayed, with its innards pulled out and carefully arranged around it on an oilcloth was—or at least had been—Tait!

Kneeling on the cold stone floor and staring at what was left of his friend, Edrik worked to master himself enough to keep his expression neutral and assess the situation. His escape plan was in ruins. Tait was dead. They'd all be dead soon if he couldn't come up with another way out. What happened next was important; he had to focus. He shifted his gaze to the Mudge and forced himself to breathe.

Edrik didn't know what he'd expected a Mudge to be, but he was pretty sure it wasn't this. The Mudge was probably human. His softly bronzed skin, thin, angular face, and shrewd black eyes certainly looked human, though most of the humans in this town were fairer. Edrik thought the fellow smelled like a human too, but it was hard to tell through the stench of the human prisoner.

The Mudge seemed unaffected by all the iron, and that narrowed the possibilities. But he was too slight to be a dwarrow, too short to be a yotun, and not nearly elegant enough to be alfkin. Maybe some kind of hobgoblin. The tangled mess of black hair would certainly fit with such a creature, as would the dingy, shapeless garment the Mudge wore. But a thing as hairy as a hobgoblin would certainly not have smooth cheeks that looked as if they had never met a razor. No, the Mudge was human—but he must be a rather young one not to have a beard, still just a boy. Too young for this sort of work, surely.

The Mudge gave Edrik a quick once-over and then directed an impatient scowl at Benit. "Another one?"

Benit grunted and tugged the rope around Edrik's neck a little tighter.

The Mudge sighed and scrutinized Edrik more closely. "Almost pale enough for a draug, but that might just be from the iron. Bit lumpy in the face—more likely from rough handling than nature, though, I think." The boy frowned. "Three says he's another drake. What say you, Benit?"

"Meh. Could be, but we already got two dragons this week, what's the odds another drake would show? And the way it jumped Egil . . ." Benit paused, thinking. "Ach. I'll go two it's a troll. Look at the size of 'im."

The Mudge shrugged. "Big for a dragon, small for a troll, but I'll take it. What about you, Stig? I'll give you mutton to music he's a drake."

From the corner of his eye, Edrik saw Grabak slide off the stone ledge and move to the iron bars at the front of his cell. "That's not a wager I'll take," the old Drake said in a low rumble. "He looks too much like his father. But I'll play for you later if you like."

The Mudge grinned, a flash of even, white teeth. "Mutton tonight anyway. Spoke with Cook earlier."

Grabak grunted. "Remind me sometime to teach you how to lay a proper wager."

"Where's the fun in that?" Mudge shrugged and turned back to Edrik's captor. "You heard the man, Benit, he's a drake. Pay up."

"Pah!" Benit exclaimed. "You expect me to take that thing's word for it?"

Mudge rolled his eyes. "Fine, then, check his teeth."

"*You* check his teeth." Benit protested. "I ain't getting bit by a drake. Or a troll neither."

Mudge shrugged again. "Hold him."

Benit tucked his cudgel behind his belt. Then he cinched the rope so tight Edrik could hardly breathe, braced his hip against the back of Edrik's head, and placed his other beefy hand on Edrik's forehead. Mudge prodded Edrik under the chin. "Open up, drake."

When Edrik clamped his mouth more tightly closed, Mudge grabbed him firmly by the nose, cutting off his air. Edrik wriggled. He should have been able to throw the guard off easily, but between the ropes and the oppressive iron, he only succeeded in making Benit laugh at him before he had to open his mouth, gasping for breath.

Mudge's fingers deftly caught at Edrik's lips, pushing them out of the way. "Ha!" he exclaimed. "Double canines. Definitely a drake. Pay up."

Benit swore. "I'll bring it round tonight. You know I'm good for it. Where you want this baggage?"

Mudge shrugged and turned away, pulling a wad of keys from some pocket in the depths of his robe. Edrik thought he saw a rat poke its head up out of the robe's hood, which hung down the boy's back, but before he was certain, whatever it was disappeared into the nest of tangled hair that straggled over Mudge's shoulders.

"Only one cell empty," said the Mudge. "You bring any more in, and we'll have to start stacking them like cordwood."

Benit shifted back, tugging the rope to get Edrik to stand up. Instead, Edrik twisted and dropped. The rope wrenched his shoulders and clamped down on his neck, strangling him, but his sweeping leg knocked Benit's feet out from under him, and the rope slackened again as the guard crashed to the stone floor.

Edrik continued his motion into a somewhat awkward roll that still managed to put him in position to launch a kick at Mudge when the boy turned back.

The Mudge was quick and twisted aside in time. Unfortunately for the boy, his dodge brought him too close to the human prisoner's cell, and with a shrieking cackle, the filthy creature snagged a handful of the Mudge's robe. Mudge drew a breath to yell, but the prisoner slammed the skinny dungeon keeper against the iron bars and clamped a grubby hand over the boy's mouth. With a terrified squeak, something furry squirmed out of the Mudge's hair and landed, scrabbling, on the stone floor.

Edrik blinked, startled. It *had* been a rat.

Benit was cursing and scrambling to get up, so Edrik kicked the guard squarely in the face before squirming over to press his back against Finn's cell. His friend's nimble fingers went to work on the ropes as Edrik used the bars to lever himself to his feet, ignoring the burning itch of the iron against his skin.

"Hurry," Edrik said.

"What about the runes?" Finn muttered back.

"Sun and stars, Finn, one thing at a time!"

Benit was scraping himself off the floor again, face thunder dark, blood streaming from his nose.

Across the aisle, the Mudge thrashed frantically, trying to get free of the big hand that now covered both nose and mouth, suffocating him. Edrik almost felt sorry for the boy—until he remembered Tait.

One hand came free of the ropes, and Edrik rapidly worked the cramped muscles of his arm while Finn's fingers played over the knots that still bound Edrik's other wrist to the cord around his neck.

Benit was back on his feet.

"Too late," Edrik muttered.

Finn swore as the guard pulled his cudgel from his belt and started for Edrik.

Edrik dodged Benit's blow, and Finn leapt back as the cudgel struck sparks from the iron bars.

Edrik and Benit circled, watching each other warily, poised for the next attack. Behind Edrik, the human prisoner bellowed, and Benit's eyes refocused beyond Edrik's shoulder. Edrik took advantage of the guard's distraction and lunged—only to be brought up short as the rope around his neck snapped taut. The unexpected check threw Edrik off balance, and he landed flat on his back, staring up into the blood-smeared face of the Mudge.

The Mudge spat out blood—and something else that thumped softly against the stone. "Stay down," he suggested hoarsely, dropping the rope just before Benit's boot slammed into Edrik's ribs.

Edrik rolled again; pain lanced through his side as he scrabbled to get back on his feet, but Benit's boot landed between his shoulders, crushing him to the floor. The iron tip of Benit's cudgel mashed into the open wound on Edrik's back, sending the sickening burn of iron scorching through his body. Benit held him there until Edrik's convulsive retching had subsided into weak spasms, and Edrik found himself dimly grateful that he hadn't eaten properly for the past few days.

At last, Mudge's quiet voice said, "Enough, Benit."

The guard left the cudgel in place a moment longer, then backed off, leaving Edrik trembling on the floor. He lay there for a heartbeat, panting, then used his free arm to try to push himself to his feet. He barely made it to his knees.

The Mudge crouched down, keeping a safe distance, to look him in the face. "Finished?" he asked.

Edrik only glared back at the boy. He wouldn't be finished until he got out and took Finn and Grabak with him. But it didn't seem wise to say so.

"Have you got a name?" the boy asked.

Edrik glared.

Mudge shrugged. "Meh. Magic things never do. At least not that they'll answer to. I think I'll call you . . . Rolf." He turned to Grabak. "What do you think, Stig? Is Rolf a good name for him?"

Grabak chuckled but didn't answer.

A scrabbling sound off to one side announced the return of the rat. Mudge held out a hand, and the creature scampered up his arm to his shoulder, where it snuggled into the curve of his neck. The boy stroked the rat and made soothing noises. Then something on the floor caught his attention—the thing he'd spat out earlier. He picked it up and offered it to the rat, who took it and began to gnaw.

Edrik realized with horror that the thing was a man's finger, bitten off at the second joint. His gaze flew past Mudge to the cell behind him. The human prisoner huddled, rocking, in the back corner, clutching one hand in the other against his chest; blood seeped out between his fingers. So that was how the Mudge had gotten free. Edrik looked back up at the young dungeon keeper. Had he underestimated the boy?

Mudge grinned back and wiped the heel of one hand across his blood-smeared mouth. Then he rose and stretched. "Let's get Rolf into his new quarters, Benit," he said nonchalantly. "I don't think he's feeling well."

CHAPTER 2

A low moan escaped from the new drake as Mudge helped Benit drag him down the aisle to the last cell. Part of Mudge pitied the man. He was most likely guilty only of being in the wrong place at the wrong time and having the wrong reaction to being sliced open with an iron blade.

Still, a feral gleam lurked behind the exhaustion in the creature's pale green eyes as they followed Mudge, serving as a reminder that this was not just a man; it was a dragon. And letting an angry dragon run loose in Shrike's Hollow would be beyond foolish. The guards were right to bring him in.

The dragon made no sound as they tied him, spread-eagled, to the inside of the bars, but he twitched when his skin contacted the iron, and all his muscles went hard. He had the lean, ropy muscles of a fighter. And he was big. Bigger than the other dragons. Certainly bigger than Mudge.

Mudge was abruptly grateful for the strong ropes that now secured the dragon—by ankles, wrists, and elbows—to the iron bars, because it seemed extremely unlikely that this creature would hold politely still while a dungeon keeper worked him over.

But first things first. With the dragon secured, Mudge took Benit into the workroom and checked the guard's injuries before sending him off with a list of needed supplies for the quartermaster and a message for the cook.

As soon as Benit was gone, Mudge dumped Pip into his rat basket by the fire, drew water from the small well in the corner of the workroom and, fighting back the urge to vomit, scrubbed away every last trace of that filthy murderer's blood. If only scrubbing could wash away the memory of the horrible triumphant cackling while the man tried to snuff Mudge's life out, the sudden gush of blood, and the sickening pop of the finger joint giving way.

Mudge shuddered. One thing was certain: if any of the fleas that had been gnawing on that piece of human sewage turned up anywhere on Mudge's body, the new night overseer was going to have a lot more to worry about than the tincture of blister nettle that may or may not have already found its way into the odious man's wash water. New guards always seemed to think the rules didn't apply to them. And new overseers were even worse.

When even the taste of blood was thoroughly washed away, Mudge put a small copper pot filled with water on the fire to heat, then took a basin of cold water out to the aisle between the cells and scrubbed away the smears and spatters of blood the encounter had left on the dungeon floor. The drake's prolonged retching fit had resulted in only a few pitiful stains of bile mixed with blood. *How long had it been since he'd eaten?*

Mudge sluiced the whole mess down the small, grated drain in the middle of the floor and went back to fish the copper pot out of the fire, collect some rags and tools, and see about Rolf.

Rolf watched warily over his shoulder as Mudge set the pot on the stone floor, unrolled the leather toolkit, carefully laid out knives, needles, and other necessaries on one of the rags, and dipped another rag in the water. Rolf seemed younger than Stig, though Mudge wasn't sure exactly why; according to Grandfather, all adult dragons looked between about twenty and forty years old, and Mudge's experience was certainly bearing that out.

Perhaps it was because Stig had said he knew Rolf's father. Or maybe it was something in the way they moved. Stig's movements were always efficient and somewhat languid, as if he'd seen everything there was to see and didn't get too excited about much of anything. Even tied up, Rolf moved as if he were brimming with energy held carefully under control, but always on the verge of breaking free. Of course, that might be because he'd just been captured and thrown in a dungeon. Still, he seemed younger.

When Mudge reached between the bars to dab at the blood that had run down Rolf's back from the long laceration just below his shoulder blade, the drake flinched, but he stood rigid and silent while Mudge finished wiping away the blood and examined the wound itself. It was still bleeding, though not much, and seemed relatively shallow; if properly cleaned and stitched, it should heal well enough. Assuming the dragon lived that long—which was unlikely.

Mudge went back to the workroom for a collar and a pouch of herbs to put in the water. Then he took up a curved bone pick and began teasing bits of debris out of the injury.

Rolf drew a sharp breath, perhaps in pain, then let it out slowly and said, "What are you doing?"

"Cleaning your wound," Mudge answered quietly.

The drake thought that over, then cautiously asked, "Why?"

"Because if I stitch it up with all that dirt and grass in there, it's going to fester." Mudge sighed. "And because it will keep Benit from sticking his cudgel in it again. If he does that after I feed you, it'll make a mess."

The thick cords of muscle on Rolf's back shifted under Mudge's fingers as he twisted against the ropes, trying to see his keeper's face. "You're serious."

Mudge dug a small pebble out of the seeping gash. "About what?"

The muscles relaxed slightly and then began to spasm rhythmically as Rolf turned again to face forward. It took Mudge a moment to realize Rolf was laughing.

"Something's funny?"

The dragon's shoulders shook harder. "No." His voice had an edge of hysteria to it. "Not funny. It's just been a very long day and . . ." He gulped air and leaned his head back against the bars, trying to stop the manic reaction. "And . . ." He gasped through clenched teeth as his body stilled. He drew one more deep breath, and when he spoke this time, his voice had control in it again. "And with all those little blades and skewers, and me trussed up like this, I thought you had something different in mind."

Mudge worked in silence for a while, then said quietly, "Not today, Rolf. And not by my hand. But that will come. The Thane is away just now, and the Thanesson won't interfere with his father's prisoners. But when the Thane comes back, he'll want to know what brings three dragons to town in the same week. The Thane is a fair man, for the most part, but a hard one, and he knows better than to turn things like you loose once you've been in here. And his questioner is quite good at extracting information."

Rolf grunted as Mudge scraped out a bloody clump of dried mud and dung that looked as if it had come off the bottom of someone's boot.

Mudge ignored him and went on. "You have maybe two weeks until the Thane gets back. Maybe another week after that, depending on how well you fare under interrogation and whether you or your friend breaks first. And then you'll talk. And then they'll kill you."

"Then why are you fixing me?" Rolf asked, his voice now a low rumble.

Mudge snorted a bitter laugh and picked several blades of grass from the wound. "Practice. I like you, Rolf. You've got pluck. But don't get your hopes up. You're going to die. They put people in here to die. That's what this place is for."

"Stig seems healthy enough," Rolf pointed out. "And unless I'm mistaken, he's been here a good while; he has hair."

"And trousers," muttered the other dragon from the cell across the aisle.

Mudge laughed. "Yes, well, Stig is a special case. He was my first dragon, back when I was still an apprentice—how long has it been, Stig? Four years? Five?

"I bought Stig off the Thane with some money my mother left me. I pay half my salary to board him here. When the company is no longer worth more to me than the coin, I'll stop paying, and they'll kill him too; it wouldn't do to have a vengeful dragon roaming the countryside. But I can't afford two such pets."

Rolf snorted. "Five years in an iron dungeon? I think I'd rather die."

"You will." Mudge scraped the pick along the bottom of the laceration, gathering small bits of grit.

Rolf squirmed. There was a flap of tissue at one edge of the wound that would need to be trimmed so it didn't putrefy.

Mudge reached for the smallest of the knives. The blade was iron; nothing else held a proper edge. "This is going to hurt. Try to hold still."

The dragon's strong back muscles braced for the pain, but when the iron blade touched the exposed muscle tissue, Rolf convulsed anyway, straining against the ropes. Mudge worked quickly, but Rolf kept flinching, making it difficult to aim properly, and by the time the excision was complete, the dragon was retching again, and his skin was slick with sweat.

After a few panting moments, Rolf muttered, "Not today, Mudge?" A bitter chuckle. "I hope you'll at least have the decency to wait until I'm dead before you skin me."

Something in the tone of it made Mudge glance up. Rolf's grim gaze was fixed over his shoulder on something in the workroom. Turning, Mudge realized that from this cell Rolf had a clear view of the dissection on the table.

"Someone you know?" Mudge asked.

Rolf said nothing.

But the dead one had been brought in with the live one across the way—the one Rolf had gone to for help during his fight with Benit. Those two clearly knew each other, so the dead one was probably Rolf's friend too. Mudge worked for a few more minutes in increasingly heavy silence, then murmured, "He was already dead when they brought him in. There was nothing I could do for him. I'm sorry."

Rolf twisted slightly, apparently trying to get a better view of Mudge's face.

Mudge ducked down to get another wet rag and waited until Rolf turned away again before straightening and squeezing a trickle of water into the wound. "Sometimes I take the dead ones apart so I can figure out how to put the living ones back together. I've not had many dragons to work with."

The truth was, the dragon on the table was the first one Mudge had ever dissected. But Rolf didn't need to know that.

Mudge drenched the wound thoroughly with the herbed water and then prodded it with a finger, feeling for any remaining debris, before smearing on a thin layer of the liniment that helped stave off fever. "Hold still while I stitch this up.

"Stig? Earn your keep. Some music to pass the time. Or a story. We have dragons in the dungeon tonight; you never tell me any dragon stories."

"A dragon story." Stig was quiet for a moment.

When he spoke again, his voice held a soft, dreamlike quality that seemed somehow to penetrate even the stone of the dungeon. "'Twas in the long-ago times, before the fall of the faekind and the Breaking of the World."

Mudge sorted through the bone needles for one with the right curve to it. Was this how a dragon sounded when he used compulsion on a person—assuming there wasn't any iron around to stop his magic from working?

Stig's hypnotic voice went on. "The dark alfkin—the dwarrows—held peace in their mountain strongholds, and the bright alfkin lived quietly in their woodlands. The yotun dreamed in their rocky coves by the western sea, and the deadlands in the north and the firelands of the south were still.

"The kingdoms of men filled the plains, and the Free People, the Ratatosk, poled their barge-towns up and down the waters of the great river Drasil like squirrels dashing up and down the trunk of a tree. And beyond the Edge of the World, in the mountains north of the river, south of the ice, east of the sea, and west of the grasslands, dwelt the Vanir—the dragonfolk—and all save the faekind feared them, for the working of iron was not yet known."

The quiet in the dungeon had taken on a vibrating, breathless quality, and Rolf's muscles relaxed a bit under the spell, allowing Mudge to feel the faint trembling that betrayed the dragon's deep exhaustion.

"In the Westlands, out on the plains, old King Arech sat upon the throne, with his elder son Hartwen at his right hand and his younger son Lebewen at his left. Four daughters he had married to the princes of the kingdoms, but a fifth, the youngest and most beautiful, remained a maid. Suitors came from near and far to vie for the hand of Emelyn, but she would have none of them. At last, King Arech grew weary of love-struck princes wandering through his lands and decreed that Emelyn must choose a husband before the new moon, or she'd have a husband chosen for her."

Mudge frowned. "This doesn't sound like a dragon story."

Stig chuckled. "You must be patient, young Mudge."

Mudge heaved a long-suffering sigh, and Stig continued. "It was at about this time that a dragon came into the Westlands—a fearsome black beast with eyes the color of emeralds, and teeth as sharp as swords, and wings like the breath of nightmares."

"What color are you, Stig?" Mudge interrupted again. "When you're a real dragon, I mean."

Stig was silent a moment before answering. "I am always a real dragon, Mudge. And it hardly matters what I look like when I ascend, as that magic is lost to me here, where I will die, as you say, when you tire of my songs and stories."

Mudge didn't quite know what to say.

Stig didn't wait for a reply. "The prince of the Fengard Dunes went out to slay the beast, swearing an oath that when he returned he would lay its head at Emelyn's feet and thereby win her love. But the prince of the Fengard Dunes did not return. The prince of Kraggen Keep was known through all the kingdoms of men for his prodigious strength and his unquestionable bravery, and it was he who next rode out to challenge the black dragon. But the prince of Kraggen Keep did not return.

"Whispers began to circulate through the kingdom that this dragon was no ordinary young wilding seeking a territory of his own, but one of the Nine Dragonlords of the Vanir, come to waste the Westlands and carry its treasure off to his mountain lair. The king sent twelve of his best knights out to rid the kingdom of this plague beast. But the knights did not return."

Mudge threaded the needle with plied horsehair—the dragon wouldn't live long, so there was no use wasting good spider silk on him—and pushed the edges of the gash together.

Stig's voice grew softer, more intense. "On the night before the new moon, the king and his court heard a roaring voice calling from the courtyard like the sound of the churning ocean, 'Ho, King Arech! Show your face, you miserable wretch. You hide behind your stone walls and think they will keep you safe while you send your puny princes and knights out to fight your battles for you. If you would slay Grafoldaur the Drake you must face me yourself, king to king!' For the rumors were true; this was no ordinary dragon. Nor was he of the Nine. This was *the* Drake himself, king of all the dragonfolk, mightiest of his kind.

"King Arech knew he would die if he faced this dragon in battle, but what else was he to do? He must stand, and fight, and die like the king he was. Solemnly, he placed his crown upon the head of Hartwen, his heir, took up his spear and a shield he had of dwarrow make, and called for his squire to bring his armor."

"That doesn't sound very smart," said Mudge.

"He was a human." Stig paused and cleared his throat before he went on. "The black dragon crouched in the courtyard with the light from the last sliver of the waning moon glinting off his scales and gleaming from his emerald eyes. A deep chuckle rumbled in his throat, and his claws struck sparks from the paving stones. Dread settled in the king's royal heart."

The bone needle stuck in Rolf's skin, and the young drake hissed as Mudge forced it through.

Stig sighed. "I'm trying to tell a story, Mudge. Be gentle with the boy."

"Sorry. Please do go on."

Stig grunted and went on. "As the king stood in the courtyard waiting for death, another figure strode from the castle keep, small and slim and beautiful. The princess walked right up to the king of the dragons and looked him in the eye. 'I am Emelyn, youngest daughter of Arech, King of the Westlands. Are you truly Grafoldaur the Drake,' she demanded, 'Lord of the Vanir and High King Among the Mountains?'

"The dragon had been ready for a battle and was rather taken aback by this development. He leaned down to examine this woman who was so bold as to speak to a dragon. 'Oh yes, little princess, I most assuredly am.'

"'Ah, great king,' said Emelyn, 'then I must conclude that you have come, like the other kings and princes, to seek my hand in marriage. Your prowess in battle and your daring speech to my father have impressed me; for doubtless you have heard the tales of my father's skill as a warrior and know that should you face him, you must surely die. Therefore, I am prepared to consider your suit, and I offer terms upon which I shall be induced to accept you as my husband.'

"No woman had ever spoken to the Drake in this manner before. In those days, dragons mostly acquired their women by abducting them, or demanding them as sacrifice; they didn't bother speaking with them much beforehand. For a moment, he considered eating her before he killed her father, but her daring speech had surprised and amused him, and he was curious as to what terms she might offer for marriage to a dragon, so he decided to play along. 'I am prepared to hear your terms, little princess,' he announced, just to find out what she'd say.

"Emelyn did not hesitate, even for a moment. 'My terms are these,' she declared. 'First, you must never use your dragon charm on me; I will come to you willingly or not at all. Second, you must marry me before the court as befits a royal princess, and I must be your queen. You shall have no other women while I am your wife. Third, our sons will be heirs to your kingdom, but our daughters must be returned to the Westlands where I was born. These are my terms. Should you accept, my father shall call for a feast in honor of our betrothal. Should you decline, he shall chop off your head, for I have offered no terms to another king or prince, and he will not suffer refusal to go unanswered.'

"If Grafoldaur the Drake had never been accosted by a princess before, he had certainly never been threatened by one. Yet he found himself drawn to this small woman, whose hair gleamed black in the light of the dying moon, and whose eyes sparked with defiance. 'Very well, little princess.' He chuckled into the night. 'I accept your terms and shall return at noon tomorrow to claim my bride before your court.' And with that, he launched himself on ebon wings into the night sky, and the roars of his laughter rolled across the plains for leagues around.

"The next day, the dragon returned, and such a wedding you never did see. Grafoldaur honored the terms he'd agreed to and found that a willing wife was much more entertaining than charmed chattel. Emelyn bore no daughters, but she bore two sons, both with their father's strength of body and their mother's strength of will. They grew to take honored places among the Nine Dragonlords of the Vanir. And Emelyn was happy all her days with the husband she chose for herself."

Mudge mulled this over for a minute. "Did you know them, Stig?"

Stig sighed. "Did I know whom?"

"Grafoldaur and Emelyn and their sons. I thought dragons lived forever."

"It only seems that way some days." Stig's chuckle held an edge of bitterness. "A dragon does not age once he reaches maturity. And a woman who creates a true marriage with a dragon—not merely a superficial agreement born of mutual affection, mind you, but a catalytic relationship that awakens the deep magic in both of them and binds the two as one—that woman will draw life from her husband, as he draws strength from his wife, and she will not age either. So dragons and their wives can live a very long time. But not even the eldest of us goes back that far, and I am not the eldest. There are many things to die from that have nothing to do with age—illness, accident, farmers with iron pitchforks, the odd knight on a quest, battling with a rival over territory or mates." He sighed. "The boredom of a young dungeon keeper."

Clearly, Stig was working himself into one of his moods. But he so rarely talked about dragons that Mudge couldn't help pushing just a little more. "Do you have a wife, Stig?"

Stig's silence dragged on for so long that Mudge almost thought he wasn't going to answer.

But then he said softly, "I did have. Now . . . I don't know. She might be dead. I cannot feel the bond anymore, but I don't know if that is because of the iron, or because . . ." He sighed again. "We parted badly. I wish . . ." He stopped talking.

"Stig?" Mudge tested.

"I'd rather not talk about it." Stig retreated to the back of his cell, obviously wanting to be left alone.

Mudge tugged the last knot secure on the suture and severed the thread. "What about you, Rolf? Do you have a wife?"

"I don't want to talk about it either," said Rolf grimly. "Do you have a wife, Mudge?"

Mudge scoffed. "Who'd marry me? What about you, other dragon? You have a wife?"

After a moment of silence, the dragon across the aisle said, "Why does he get a name, and I don't?"

Mudge snorted a laugh. "He fought. I thought he deserved a name, even if it wasn't his own. But you can tell me your name if you want to."

"Give my name to an enemy?" He sounded appalled at the thought.

"Have it your way, Other Dragon." Mudge began cleaning minor scrapes and lacerations and poking at clusters of spreading bruises. Rolf had been thoroughly trounced by the guards who took him, but most of it would heal well enough on its own. If he lived long enough. A prod at the spot where Benit had kicked him in the ribs made Rolf wince and grunt.

The Other Dragon said, "I don't see any point in getting married. I can have any woman I want as a mate, for as long as I want her, and when I get tired of her, I can move on. Or I can have more than one mate at a time if I want. If I married a woman, I'd be stuck with just her until she died. Even if I didn't bond with her, I could still be tied to one woman for decades of my life, watching her get old and shriveled.

What if I met someone else I liked better, and the first one wouldn't agree to divorce? And if I did bond with her, she'd be able to sense where I was and what mood I was in—all the time. And I wouldn't be able to compel her anymore. And she would literally suck my life right out of me. Why would anyone in his right mind do that to himself on purpose?"

"Enough!" Stig's voice held a tone of command that not even Mudge wanted to argue with.

Silence thickened the air in the dungeon until Rolf asked, "Are you finished?"

Mudge frowned. "I think you may have a broken rib. It would be best if I checked your lungs, especially with all that retching you've been doing. But I'd have to go in there to do it properly, and . . . well . . . that seems unwise."

"I'm tied up."

"I'm sure that's what Benit thought, too, right before you knocked him down and smashed his nose."

Rolf chuckled softly. "I'll tell you what, Mudge. If you promise not to stick iron in me when you come in, I promise not to eat you."

Mudge thought about this. In the end, the enticement of actually listening to the inner workings of a living dragon's lungs won out. There would probably never be another opportunity. Stig would certainly never stand for such a thing. Locking a creature in a cage was not the same thing as domesticating it. Mudge collected a few things from the workroom and stopped by the dissection table to double check the correct size and positioning of the lungs—which was pointless since in this form dragons were virtually indistinguishable from humans, even on the inside. Cautiously, Mudge twisted the key in the lock and swung open the section of bars that formed the door to Rolf's cell.

For some reason, Rolf looked bigger without the bars between them, or Benit holding on to him. But if this thing was going to happen, it wouldn't do to show fear. Mudge set the supplies on the cell's stone ledge and moved to stand in front of Rolf. Several small scrapes had left trickles of blood down the drake's broad chest, and

Mudge began by cleaning those up—at least that procedure could be done at arm's length. Rolf watched without comment. Then Mudge prodded the dragon's ribs again. It had been hard to tell from the back how far around the bruising went. Rolf flinched.

Mudge nodded. "That one. Cracked at the very least."

More prodding. Rolf gritted his teeth.

After a moment, Mudge added, "Don't think it's broken through, but it's hard to tell sometimes."

Mudge showed Rolf the listening horn, set the wide end against the dragon's chest, stepped closer, and leaned down to listen at the narrow end. The heat of Rolf's skin warmed Mudge's cheek. The drake smelled of blood, and herbs, and drying sweat . . . and something richer and more wild. But the breath sounds Mudge heard were normal, as was the insistent beating of the dragon's heart.

The action felt, abruptly, far too intimate, as if these were sounds only the dragon's lover should hear. Mudge's heart pounded faster. This was much too close to get to a dragon. Best get this over with quickly. Shifting the horn down and to the side, Mudge bent to listen closer to the site of the injury. That was even worse. But the breath sounds were normal.

Mudge straightened, swallowed hard, and turned back to the stone ledge to avoid looking Rolf in the eye. "Does it hurt when you breathe?"

Rolf didn't answer, and at last, Mudge turned to look at him.

Rolf frowned. "You say I am to be questioned and expect me to tell you what hurts?"

"Right. Sorry. Well, I think you're going to be all right." Mudge looked down. "At least . . . until you're not."

"You're finished, then?" Rolf asked.

"Only one more thing." Mudge held up the iron collar. "Everybody gets one. It's the rules."

"Of course it is." Rolf's deep voice held bitter resignation.

"It would be easier to put it on from this side, but I can go back out and place it from the back if you think you'll feel obligated to smash my face in with your forehead or something."

Rolf thought this over. "If I hold still, will you untie me?"

"Yes," said Mudge. "But not until I'm back outside."

"Done," said Rolf.

Mudge stepped close again, heart thumping with fear and that unsettling sense of intimacy, and closed the dwarrow-worked collar around the dragon's neck, settling it against his collar bones like a torc. "It won't come off until I take it off. That's what the runes are for."

"And by then, I will be dead," Rolf said solemnly.

"Probably," said Mudge.

Rolf's lips drew back in a slow grin, showing double canine teeth on both sides. "You are an odd little man, Mudge."

Mudge swallowed hard and backed up. "That's a very popular opinion."

CHAPTER 3

Edrik was grateful Mudge had the sense to untie his feet first. He hadn't realized just how much of his weight was being supported by the ropes until his first arm came loose and he staggered, twisting, away from the bars. When Mudge freed his other arm, the pain that shot through Edrik's body as his ribs shifted stole his breath and buckled his knees. He caught himself with his other arm before he crumpled completely to the floor and knelt there, panting, while the stabbing pain drew back on itself and settled in his side. An itching burn seeped into his skin from the iron collar, and he sensed the heaviness of the iron ore all around him, but at least the bars weren't pressed against his back anymore. He drew a steadying breath.

Behind him, tools clicked and rattled as the skinny dungeon keeper gathered up his things.

Faintly, from the next cell, the human prisoner whined, "What about me? Ain't you gonna stitch me up too?"

"No." Mudge's voice was quiet and matter-of-fact, but it held an edge of stone.

"But—" the prisoner whined.

"I don't like you," Mudge interrupted conversationally. "You stink. You have fleas. You killed three women, and you tried to kill me."

"Aw," wheedled the prisoner, "I weren't gonna kilt ya, boy. I were jest keeping ya out a them other fellows' way. Ya see?"

Mudge snorted derisively. "Look on the bright side. Tomorrow, they'll hang you. After that, you won't care how many fingers you have, and I won't care if you tried to raise your victim count to four." The dungeon keeper's feet scuffed softly as he rose and started toward the workroom.

"Five!" barked the prisoner.

Mudge's footsteps stopped.

"I kilt five of 'em." The prisoner sounded smug this time. "Nobody care if a couple a wharf whores turn up in a gutter. Nobody care 'til it's respeckable girls gone missing. But I kin tell ya, them respeckable girls ain't no different from wharf whores under they clothes. Not even that fancy miss from the keep. They all the same under they clothes. All five of 'em."

Mudge halted. This time the boy's voice was veined with iron. "If you speak again, filth, I will stitch your lips shut for you."

After that, there was only silence, except for the soft sounds of Mudge shuffling back to the workroom and puttering about a bit before returning to shove a blanket between the bars of Edrik's cell.

The surge of adrenaline that had sustained Edrik through the fight had dissipated as he listened to Grabak's story, and a terrible, trembling lassitude had seeped in behind it. The blanket looked inviting, but the amount of effort he'd have to expend to retrieve it felt absurdly over-whelming, so he just stared listlessly at the crumple of thick wool.

He must have looked pitiful because after a long, silent pause, another blanket landed around his shoulders, startling him into a flinch. Pain stabbed through his side when his muscles tensed, and he gasped. Pathetic.

A furious rapping sound ruptured the quiet of the dungeon.

Mudge drew a deep breath and moved calmly to unlock a door at the back of the workroom. Edrik shifted, careful of his rib, closer to the bars for a better view, as a tall, spindly man with thinning hair burst into the workroom.

"This time you've gone too far, Mudge!" The man stuck a bony finger in the young dungeon keeper's face. That seemed unwise to Edrik, considering what had happened to the human prisoner.

Mudge, however, only bowed respectfully and spoke with controlled formality. "Master Steward, I'm quite astounded to see you. I regret to have caused you displeasure. Would you be kind enough to explain my offense?"

The steward huffed and began pacing back and forth across the room. "You know very well what I mean, boy. Gerd is blistered over half his face and both of his hands, as well as . . . in other sensitive areas of his person. This has got to stop."

"Gerd?" Mudge's eyebrows rose in puzzlement.

The steward's eyes narrowed. "The new night overseer, Mudge. Everyone knows it was you."

"Sir," Mudge said calmly. "I don't know what you've been told, but I've been down here all day working on that one." Mudge waved a hand at Tait's mutilated remains. "I haven't even seen Gerd since he brought his prisoner down last night."

The steward stopped pacing and rounded on Mudge.

"I know that," he grumbled. "You don't think I questioned the door guards? I can't prove it, but I know it was you. And it has to stop."

Mudge spread his hands in a helpless gesture. "If you'd like to send Gerd down here, I can try to determine the cause of the blisters and see if I have a salve that might—"

He cut off abruptly as the steward stuck his angry finger in Mudge's face again, tempting fate.

"Stop!" he snarled. "Just . . . stop."

A soft creaking noise edged into the tense silence, and both Mudge and the steward turned to look as a lad of perhaps ten or twelve years old peered around the edge of the workroom door.

"Mudge?" he said softly, and then stopped, looking back and forth between Mudge and the steward.

"What is it, Ket?" Mudge asked.

The boy shifted uncertainly from foot to foot. "Quartermaster's man is here. Needs your mark 'fore he can unload."

Mudge nodded. "Thank you, Ket. Please tell him I will be with him as soon as the master steward is finished with me."

The steward heaved an aggravated sigh. "I'm finished. Don't do it again, Mudge."

"As you say, sir." Mudge bowed again, and the steward swept back out through the door.

Ket waited while the steward's pounding footsteps receded, then cleared his throat.

"Something else, Ket?" asked Mudge.

"Cook says tell ya he dosed the sick pig like ya said, and the remedy is workin' fine."

A grin spread across the dungeon keeper's face. "I just heard. Shall we go see about the quartermaster's man?"

They went out, leaving the door slightly ajar.

Edrik gritted his teeth and twisted just enough to look for Grabak. The old Drake was still at the back of his cell where Edrik couldn't see him. Across the aisle, Finn paced back and forth behind the bars of his cell, muttering under his breath and scrubbing a hand over the dark, uneven stubble on his scalp.

"Finn!" Edrik kept his voice to a loud whisper, trying to catch his friend's attention without drawing the notice of anyone who might still be just outside the door.

Finn stopped pacing and glared at Edrik. Then the muscles of his jaw softened, and he asked just as quietly, "You all right?"

Edrik waved a dismissive hand. "What happened?"

Finn sank to the floor at the front of his cell and scrubbed his hands over his face. "They found our camp the night after you left. We were scouting for firewood and rabbits, and when we got back, they were waiting for us. Tait tried to ascend, but they caught him mid-change with an iron spear, and . . . and he reverted with the spear still inside him."

Edrik swallowed hard and looked away. If Tait had completed his transformation, the spear wouldn't have penetrated his scales, but caught mid-ascension—even if it hadn't killed him outright, the pain and shock of it would have paralyzed him long enough for the humans to finish him off.

29

They sat in silence for a few heartbeats. Then Finn said, "We have to get out of here. Now. The solstice—"

"I know," Edrik growled. "Thirty-two days. Don't you think I'm counting every one of them? We'll get out. It isn't as if we haven't broken out of a dungeon before. More than once."

"Before, we had Tait. And you had your belt and boots."

More specifically, Edrik knew, Finn meant they'd had the lock picks Edrik kept hidden in the seams of his boots and the wire saw he had threaded through his belt between the layers of leather. In *this* dungeon, they didn't have so much as a boot nail to dig with. And there were the dwarrow runes . . . and . . .

"We'll think of something," Edrik said grimly.

He glanced at the workroom door and raised one hand to examine his collar. The twisted band curved around his neck and rested heavily against his collar bones. His fingers skimmed the twining grooves of the dwarrow runes engraved on the surface and stopped to probe the latch point at the base of his throat. The ends of the band met in a complex pattern of interlocking spirals that seemed to be fused into each other. *"It won't come off until I take it off,"* Mudge had said. *"That's what the runes are for."* Edrik sighed his frustration and let his hand drop. Blasted, rimy dwarrow magic.

"What are you doing here in the first place?" Grabak had come to the front of his cell and was scowling at Edrik between the bars.

Edrik cleared his throat self-consciously. "Rescuing you."

"Foolish." The old Drake snorted. "What was your father thinking to allow it?"

Edrik steeled himself to answer. "My father has been dead these two years past."

A low hiss was all the response Grabak offered to that. The old dragon's voice was more solemn when he spoke again. "I take it your plan for getting out is no longer feasible."

"We'll think of something." Edrik leaned against the bars, letting the burn of the iron help focus his mind "What can you tell me that might help? Does the Mudge have a price? Or one of the other guards? Do they ever open the cells to clean them? Or take us out for exercise?

Do these drains go anywhere useful if we can enlarge the openings? What about the Thane, would he—"

Grabak's sardonic chuckle interrupted. "Five years I've been asking myself those questions. Nearly six. Do you think I'd still be here if I knew an easy way to get out?"

"We'll think of something," Edrik insisted. "Mudge said we have two weeks before the Thane returns. You seem friendly with the boy, what if you—"

"No!" It came out in a rumbling growl, and Grabak retreated to the back of his cell.

After another short silence, Finn cleared his throat and tried again. "We still need a plan."

"I know." Edrik glowered at his friend. "I suppose they took all the weapons? My father's sword?"

"I'm sorry." Finn hung his head. "There was no time to hide it."

Edrik swallowed a hiss. "And what happened to Tait's yot mark?"

"Burned it," Mudge said cheerily as he bustled in through the workroom door. "Can't have a thing like that sitting around down here, now can I?"

How much had he heard?

The dungeon keeper locked the door and settled at the desk, making careful notes in a large ledger.

No one in the dungeon said anything after that until the kitchen boy, Ket, returned with the supper kettle, and Mudge set a tin cup filled with water and a wooden bowl of mutton stew just inside the bars of Edrik's cell. There was no spoon—which he might have used to chip away at the stone at the base of the bars or to make a crude weapon with—but a heel of bread was wedged over one side of the bowl.

Edrik stared at the food for a long moment before he decided that Mudge wouldn't poison them since he was saving them for the questioner. He gritted his teeth and reached out to drag the bowl closer. The bread was easier on his empty stomach than the stew, so he ate that first, slowly, letting his body adjust.

He was still eating when Mudge returned to collect the bowls. The dungeon keeper frowned down at Edrik, evidently not liking what he saw. Edrik ignored him and kept eating.

Mudge went back into the workroom and returned a few minutes later to set another tin cup on the floor just outside the bars of Edrik's cell.

"It'll help with the pain," he said, "but it will also make you sleep a long time. You decide." The boy peered up at the white dwarrow light in the ceiling and shrugged. "It'll be dark soon anyway."

The light did seem to be dimming; it must be the kind that was tied to the sun. Steam drifted lazily off the dark liquid pooled in the bottom of the tin cup. Edrik's ribs hurt. The wound in his back hurt. His head hurt from all the iron pressing in on him. His whole body ached from the weeks of hard travel that had brought them here. He needed rest if he was going to be able to travel like that again once they got out—real rest, not the shallow, sporadic dozing he'd managed the last few days. And food; the stew sat in his unaccustomed stomach like a burning stone.

Time was short, though; Finn was right about that. The solstice was drawing ever closer. And their escape plan was as dead as Tait.

Edrik sighed and rubbed a hand over the uneven stubble on his scalp. Tait. That was his fault. He should never have gotten his friends involved in this.

He gritted his teeth and pushed himself to his feet, pretending to ignore the fireball of pain that lanced through his ribs when he moved. He paced the length of the bars, examining every inch of the dungeon that he could see in the dimming dwarrow light. He had to find a way out. Past the bars. Past the runes. Past the strange little human dungeon keeper. But he had no tools. Nothing to work with. And Grabak didn't seem inclined to help. Did he even *want* to go home?

Edrik couldn't think. He couldn't *think*. He leaned over slowly, biting down hard on a moan, to pick up the cup. It had stopped steaming. How long would he sleep if he drank it?

Finn saw him pick it up and leapt to his feet. "You can't!"

"I have to sleep."

"No." Finn peered into the workroom, where Mudge's head was bent over his ledgers, and whispered, "You have to get us out of here."

Edrik scowled at his friend. "We can't go anywhere tonight." He kept his voice low, glancing over at the dungeon keeper. "And I *have* to sleep, Finn." He raised the cup to his lips.

"No!" Finn slammed the heel of one hand hard against a bar, making the iron ring out.

Mudge raised his head and watched with interest as Edrik drained the cup and tossed it out through the bars before turning his back on Finn's disapproval.

Edrik tugged the blanket closer as he shuffled over to the ledge at the back of the cell. He had barely settled his aching, trembling body on the ledge, which was blessedly free of exposed ore veins, when the wave of muzzy darkness washed over him, pulling him along in its current down into a quiet place where the pain faded away and Lissara waited with her golden hair and sweet, secret smiles. He would see her again. Soon. They had found Grabak. Now they just needed to find a way out.

CHAPTER 4

Waves and eddies of sleep folded around Edrik, drawing him through gentle dreamscapes where Lissara laughed and kissed him, and churning him against the nightmare shoals of Tait ascending with iron in his blood.

Once, in the darkness, his awareness half surfaced, gasping, to find a slender arm supporting his head and a cup pressed to his lips. He swallowed reflexively as a thin broth trickled into his mouth and strained his eyes to see past the darkness and the tugging insistence of sleep. "Lissara?" he whispered—*but why would she be here?*

Gentle hands settled him back against the stone ledge and tugged at the blankets in a way that made Edrik realize how cold he'd been, just as the next wave of relentless sleep gulped him down again into the rolling depths.

He was pulled to the surface again by a series of piercing shrieks, followed by a long scuffle and the sound of muted voices. Figures moved in the dim gray light beyond the bars of his cell. The human prisoner was being dragged from the dungeon, pinned between two burly guards. A third guard trailed them, and a fourth lagged behind to speak with Mudge.

"Ya want this one back when the hangman's done with 'im?" The guard had to bellow to be heard over the cacophony echoing down the stairs that led up to the prison proper.

Mudge shook his head. "Meh. Leave him for the carrion crows. I've seen as much of that one as I ever care to. And I'm still working on the last one you brought me."

The guard shook his head. "Shame," he said, dropping his voice as the noise on the stairs dwindled. "I could use the coin, and the boys was looking forward to seeing that one get thoroughly mudged."

The young dungeon keeper laughed. "They'll have a better view if the crows do the job for me."

"Have it your way then." The guard clapped Mudge on the shoulder, nearly knocking the boy down, and stomped off after his fellows.

As Mudge turned toward the workroom, his eyes met Edrik's, and a grin flashed over the dungeon keeper's brown face. "Enough to wake the dead, eh Rolf?"

Edrik tried to open his mouth to answer, but his mind got caught in the undertow again and sucked back into the abyss.

The true awakening came gradually as the pain returned, stealing into his dreams and nudging him toward the surface. All was quiet and still in the dungeon, and the oppressive weight of the iron ore seemed augmented by the heavy darkness of night. The faint glow of the dwarrow light served more to emphasize the shadows than relieve them and did nothing at all to penetrate the blackness in the recesses of Finn's cell across the aisle.

Edrik eased himself up to a sitting position, leaning his back against the cool stone of the cell wall. His ribs still hurt when he moved, but the minor scrapes and bruises were already healing nicely, and the food and sleep had pushed back the marrow-deep exhaustion. Now he needed to figure out how they were all going to get out of here.

"You're awake." It was Grabak's deep voice that rumbled softly out of the darkness. He must have heard the rustle of Edrik's blankets when he moved.

Edrik drew a deep, careful breath. "Mostly. Is it safe to talk?"

"For now. Mudge has been called out, but there's no telling for how long. He sleeps in the workroom."

A scuffing sound came from Grabak's direction, and Edrik thought he could make out a dark shape moving against the deeper blackness at the front of the Drake's cell.

"How long was I out?"

"Two days."

Too long. Edrik mulled that over in silence for a few minutes.

Then Grabak said, "Tell me about . . . about home. My family." He sounded hesitant, as if he feared what Edrik might say.

So much had happened; Edrik wasn't sure where to even begin. "They miss you." Maybe this was the angle he needed to convince the Drake to help with the escape. "They need you."

Grabak let out a long sigh, as if he'd been holding his breath. "They're both alive then, my wife and daughter?"

Edrik cleared his throat. "They were both well when I left, but it has been nearly a year. Without my father to protect them, they are more vulnerable. We need to get back."

"You should have stayed." It was a low growl, but intense.

"Lissara asked me to find you. How could I deny her?"

"You should have *stayed*!" If Grabak hissed any louder, someone was going to hear them. But he choked down the emotion and asked more quietly, "Your father—how did that happen?"

Edrik was relieved when the need to answer was forestalled by the loud click of a lock. The creak of the workroom door covered any noise Grabak made as he retreated to the back of his cell. Mudge slipped somewhat furtively back into the dungeon, guided by a thin beam of light that leaked out through the gap of a shuttered lantern.

The boy stirred up the banked coals in the fireplace and added a log, sending warm firelight dancing across the workroom and down the aisle between the cells. He extinguished the lantern and knelt for a while staring into the reawakened fire. The pet rat crept from a basket near the fireplace, and Mudge held out one hand so the creature could climb to its accustomed perch on his shoulder.

Edrik drew back into the shadows of his cell. He didn't want to lie down again because of what the motion would do to his ribs, so he just sat back on the ledge and let the coolness of the stone soothe the ache in the stitched wound on his back. He must have made some sound, though, because Mudge came to the archway and peered down the aisle, blinking fire-dazzled eyes into the darkness.

"Stig?" he whispered tentatively. "Are you awake?"

Silence hung in the air so long that Edrik thought Grabak wouldn't answer, and Mudge started to turn back to the fire. But then the old dragon growled softly, "I'm here, Mudge."

The dungeon keeper tiptoed down the aisle. Edrik slid cautiously off his ledge and crept to the front of his cell to peer out. Mudge leaned against the bars of Grabak's cell, pressing his forehead against the cold iron. The shadow of the Drake loomed out of the blackness inside the cell, reaching for the boy. Edrik tensed. If Grabak could grab the dungeon keeper, maybe he could get the keys. And then . . . well, then there were the dwarrow runes. But the keys would be a good start.

Grabak, however, only laid his big hand on Mudge's shoulder and whispered, "What is it?"

Edrik had to strain to hear.

"Tell me I'm not a dangerous fool." Mudge breathed softly.

"You're young," Grabak whispered. "You do what you can. Mistakes will happen. You will learn from them."

"Some mistakes get people killed." The boy sighed and shifted in the darkness. "It wasn't just scrapes and bruises this time. Vivianne . . . she begged, Stig. On her knees, she begged me to get her out. I couldn't just stitch her up and leave her there. So I . . . made arrangements. But what if she changes her mind again? If she comes back and tells the Thanesson, he'll kill them all for helping her. And it will be my fault."

"You have a good heart, Mudge." Grabak moved closer to the boy, cupping one hand around the back of Mudge's head. "And you have a good head. You'll have measures in place."

"The only measures I can think of involve killing her before she talks. And she *will* talk . . . if she comes back. She can't help it. If my timing was off, if the Thanesson got to her first . . ." Mudge sighed again and shook his head, backing away from the bars. "I am a fool. A dangerous fool playing lethal games."

Grabak hesitated before replying. Then he said softly. "I wish you'd play one more."

Edrik's heart began to pound.

Mudge asked warily, "What do you mean?"

"His father was my friend—the one you call Rolf."

"Stig—"

"He was the closest thing I had to a brother. I can't just sit and watch his son die and do nothing."

"I can't." Mudge sounded shaken. "Don't ask that of me."

"Not for myself; I'll not leave you here alone. Just for Rolf. And for his friend."

"No." Mudge's whisper was adamant. "I can put something in their food to help with the pain when the questioner comes. I can hurry their deaths if you like. But I can't get them out. I can't. I'm sorry."

"I will beg on my knees if you like, Mudge."

"No. A courtesan is one thing—the Thane doesn't approve of his son's habits, and he would shield me for my grandfather's sake. But the dungeon is something else entirely. Nothing has ever escaped from here. Ever. If anyone gets out, they will know I helped, and they will kill me. Even the Thane couldn't shield me from that. I'm sorry." He whirled away from Grabak.

As Mudge stalked past, Edrik moved back from the bars, stepping silently into the long, black folds of shadow cast by the fire.

Nothing had ever escaped.

But the Mudge knew how to get people out. They just needed to find out the boy's price. Or his weakness.

CHAPTER 5

M udge dipped the carefully trimmed quill tip in ink and resumed sketching the dragon's dissected kidney as it lay, back side up, on the oilcloth. This specimen was getting old. Even with the blood drained and the preserving fluid carefully applied, the dragon's corpse had already lasted about as long as it was going to. The tissues were breaking down, and the smell was getting to be a real problem.

The pen scritched rhythmically against the parchment, making the only sound in the stillness of the dungeon. Ordinarily, Stig might have played his flute while Mudge worked, or the two of them might have talked over the current gossip from the keep. But Stig was becoming increasingly withdrawn as time wore on. Three days had passed since the old dragon asked Mudge to help his friends escape, and in that time, Stig had hardly spoken another word. When the other dragons were gone, would things go back to the way they had been between the two of them, or was this going to change their friendship—if it could be called that—forever?

Mudge's gaze wandered to where Rolf sat in his cell, stoically watching. He always watched when Mudge worked. He never said anything, just watched. Was he wondering if the same thing would happen to him when he was dead? Plotting revenge for his friend? It made Mudge jumpy.

Truth told, everything about Rolf made Mudge jumpy. Maybe it was just that he was bigger than the other two dragons. Maybe it was his quiet composure. Stig was moody, and Rolf's friend tended to impatience and agitation. But Rolf just watched, impassive, his intelligent green eyes taking everything in without giving anything away. Even entering Rolf's cell to feed him broth and check his wounds when the dragon was heavily drugged had made Mudge's heart pound and palms sweat. And when Rolf had opened his eyes and whispered that woman's name, Mudge had nearly dropped him and fled. It was ridiculous. Mudge had tended any number of dangerous creatures before without getting that spooked.

A loud rapping on the workroom door made Mudge start, blotching the drawing and marring the pen. The rapping came again, harder and more urgent. What could be worth all that noise? Mudge rose, stoppered the ink, and laid the parchment on the desk. Keys rattled, and the door creaked, and Ket burst, pale and wide-eyed, into the room.

"She's here!" the boy gasped frantically.

Something cold twisted in Mudge's gut. "Who's here?"

"Vivianne. She's here, and she's gone up! What if she tells?"

The cold knot climbed up and throttled Mudge's heart. "Where is she? Does *he* know?"

"Her rooms. Maid came to order water for a bath. Sent a footman to fetch him. What are we going to do?"

"*You* are going to do nothing. This is my mess, and I'll clean it up. Stay here. If anyone comes while I'm away, say I've gone to the herb woman."

The boy nodded, and Mudge drew a deep breath before hurrying through the door, pausing only long enough to hear the lock snick home. Outside the workroom, a staircase wound up toward a thick wooden door that opened into the back of a larder beneath the castle kitchens. As a child, Mudge had wondered whether this was to make it easier to feed the prisoners, or because some of the creatures who occupied the dungeon might, on occasion, find themselves headed for the stewpot. But Mudge wasn't a child anymore, and for this errand, it would be as foolish to exit the dungeon through the bustling kitchens as it would be to go up through the guardhouse.

Beneath the kitchen stairs, a storage area had been carved out of the stone and lined with sturdy shelves. It was cooler out there than in the workroom, and less damp, and Mudge used the space to store herbs, as well as bandages, blankets, and various other supplies.

Slipping a hand behind a crock of goose grease, Mudge tripped the latch at the back of the shelf. The whole section of shelving swung silently outward to reveal the narrow passageway hidden behind, twisting irregularly upward into darkness. Mudge stepped into the opening and pulled the hidden door closed, careful not to make a sound that might carry up the kitchen stairs.

What seemed a much too long, heart-pounding time later, the passage ended in the back of a broom closet in the lower level servants' living quarters. Down a dim hallway and up a flight of stairs, Mudge reached the above-ground portion of the massive stone keep, where it perched on the bluff overlooking the town. Deep voices echoed from the great hall, and one of the ladies of the keep plucked disconsolately at a lute in the small solar.

Staying in the stuffy servants' corridors, Mudge worked around to the other side of the keep and climbed another level before emerging into a broad, tapestry-hung hallway. The Thanesson kept most of his women in the guest chambers on the next story higher, but Vivianne had been moved to an apartment down the corridor from the Thanesson's last autumn.

The third tapestry down on the other side of the hall hid the sliding panel that led to the spy hole, and Mudge reached it without incident and without being seen. With the panel closed, the only light that illuminated the cramped space inside the wall came from the peephole. Standing on tiptoe, Mudge peered through the hole, which was hidden on the other side of the wall among some carved roses surrounding a floor-length mirror in Vivianne's private drawing room. It was one of several such places in the keep that Mudge had discovered as a child after being banished from the dungeon while the questioner worked.

Ket was right. Vivianne had returned. The Thanesson's favorite stood on the other side of the room with her back to Mudge, looking out the tall window into the courtyard and fidgeting with her long, silky dressing gown. With the sun gleaming in her golden hair, and her skin milk-pale against the deep red of the robe, she looked like a princess who'd wandered out of one of Stig's tales.

Three servants bustled around the ornate copper bathing tub that had been placed in the center of the room, finishing preparations for Vivianne's bath. Two of them left as soon as the bath was ready, leaving only the lady's maid to help her mistress slip free of the dressing gown and settle into the warm, scented water.

Mudge watched as the maid cleaned and combed Vivianne's wealth of curls and scrubbed the grime of travel from the courtesan's body, leaving her skin soft and rosy—except where the yellow and green of still healing bruises marred its perfection. And except for the angry line on the back of the woman's shoulder where Mudge had stitched up the gash left by the Thanesson's whip.

When the maid draped a towel over the tub to hold in the steam and went to arrange Vivianne's clothes in the next room, Mudge tripped the latch that made the mirror swing into the room and stepped through the opening it concealed.

Vivianne sat bolt upright in the tub, clutching the towel to her chest, and twisted toward the sound. "You!" she gasped, blue eyes wide and frightened.

Mudge didn't say anything, just walked across the thick rugs that covered the floor and crouched down next to the tub.

"I had to come back," Vivianne whispered urgently. "I had nowhere to go. I was hungry, and cold, and I didn't know what else to . . ."

Mudge frowned. "You were going to take work as a seamstress or a tavern maid."

"There was no work for seamstresses." Vivianne's delicate brows drew together. "The taverner wanted me to scour pans. Do you know what that does to a woman's hands? And I'm not emptying chamber-pots for *anyone*!"

Mudge's teeth clenched involuntarily. "Do you remember that kitchen boy who showed you the passageway out of the garden?"

Vivianne nodded, wide-eyed.

"He has a little sister who is too young to work. Their parents are both dead. What happens to the little girl if the kitchen boy is fed to the dogs for helping you leave when your lover wished you to stay?"

Vivianne stared at Mudge. "I won't tell."

Mudge shifted closer to the tub. "The man with the horse cart who took you to the docks has six children and another on the way."

Vivianne shook her head frantically, cringing back in the tub. "Please . . ."

"The dock worker who smuggled you onto the boat is to be married this autumn."

"I'll never tell a soul. I promise!"

"The boatman—"

"I won't tell!" She was nearly in tears now.

"He'll *make* you tell, Vivianne. You know he will. I won't let them die because you're too proud to empty chamberpots."

"You have my word! Please—"

"I had your word that you'd never come back." Mudge leaned forward, resting both elbows on the side of the copper tub. "I wish you had kept your word."

"Please, Mudge . . ." Vivianne reached a pale hand out to lay her long, slender fingers on Mudge's brown forearm and let the towel slip into the water, exposing more impossibly white skin and womanly curves. "I can make it up to you." She leaned forward, blue eyes pleading, pink lips inviting.

Mudge reached into the water to fish out the towel and wrapped its sopping bulk around Vivianne's shoulders. "I'm not the only one you betrayed."

Unsuspecting as the woman was, it was easy to twist the towel tight behind her back, trapping her arms. It was even easier to wind the other fist into her long, pale hair.

"And I keep my word. I'm sorry."

Vivianne opened her mouth in a startled gasp that began to turn into a scream when she realized what was about to happen; Mudge plunged the courtesan's head under the water before the scream was fully born and pinned her there, waiting grimly as the woman's thrashing intensified, then weakened, then stopped altogether.

And it was done. The mirror door clicked softly when Mudge went out again, leaving Vivianne for the maid to find.

Mudge managed to remain composed and keep a steady pace all the way back through the servants' corridors. As soon as the panel in the broom closet slid shut, however, and Mudge was alone in the darkness of the narrow passageway that led back to the dungeon storage shelves, the trembling began, and Mudge's knees gave out. It had been necessary. The others had trusted Mudge; they'd taken the woman on Mudge's assurance. It was Mudge's job to keep them safe. Mudge curled into a ball on the cold stone floor of the passageway and let the shuddering tears come.

When the worst of it had passed, Mudge returned to the workroom. Ket reported that no one had come to the dungeon while Mudge was gone, so Mudge sent the boy back up to the kitchens where he belonged. Ket could be trusted not to talk—and now, so could Vivianne. They were safe.

Mudge slumped onto the stool at the work table and poked at the dead dragon's kidney with one slightly trembling finger, trying to decide whether to attempt another sketch of it, or to pack up the whole specimen and be done with it. This had been a frustrating dissection from the start. Something should be different. There should be more than double canine teeth to distinguish human men from dragons— hidden wing buds or something in the throat to make fire—but there wasn't. At least, not that Mudge could find.

A soft scuffing sound came from the direction of the cells, and Mudge looked up to find Rolf standing at the front of his cell, arms folded across his bare chest, head tipped back and to one side as he studied Mudge appraisingly.

"You arranged for the woman to be silenced?" the dragon seemed skeptical.

Raising an eyebrow, Mudge said, "I don't know what you mean, Rolf. I haven't left the dungeon all afternoon."

From the end of the row, Stig emitted a loud, sardonic snort.

A slow, disconcerting grin spread across Rolf's face, and he looked as if he might say something else, but he just shook his head and went on watching Mudge without further comment. It made Mudge feel like a study specimen, as if the dragon were making his own sketches and notes.

What did Rolf know? How could he know anything?

Mudge picked up the kidney and carefully placed it back in the body cavity, then sighed and began painstakingly reassembling the entire specimen, checking each piece one last time for any features that might make it distinctly dragon. And the long afternoon wore on toward evening in nerve-racking silence. It would be nice when Stig decided to be friendly again—assuming that could ever happen now. He was angry that Mudge wouldn't get the other dragons out. How could he be less angry after they were dead because Mudge refused to help?

The dragon's torso was closed, the last few stitches had been put in to reattach the flayed skin, and Mudge was just finishing wrapping the corpse in the oilcloth when the click and creak of the upper dungeon door echoed faintly down the stairs, and the scuff of booted footsteps announced the arrival of a guard.

"Hoy, Mudge!" Benit's bellow dropped into the cold silence of the dungeon like hot iron into a quenching bucket. Mudge jumped, and a hissing rustle came from the cell block as all three dragons moved to stand at the bars so they could see whatever drama might occur to break the boredom of the long day. Mudge supposed they were wondering whether their strange little dungeon keeper had managed to get away with whatever had happened to Vivianne.

Without looking up, Mudge drew a steadying breath and called back, "Don't tell me someone found another one. Really, Benit, this has got to stop. There must be some ordinary criminals out there for you people to bully. Tell all the murderers and magical things to go home where they belong and leave me alone. I'm busy."

The big guard strode through the block and settled one shoulder against the rune-carved arch that separated the cells from the workroom. "Meh. Nothin' like that. Got paid today and brung down them two I owed you over that drake."

"About time." Mudge went to the basin to scrub away any residual dragon bits before holding out a hand for the guard's coin. "When you go back up, could you send someone down to cart this one off? It's too heavy for me, but I'm finished with it, and it's just going to start stinking up the place if I don't get it out of here. There's five in it for whoever is willing."

"Phaw. Already stinks if you ask me. Wasn't going to say nothing, but it ain't none too fresh down here." The guard straightened and took a step forward. "Now, you want fresh, I know where to get one. Girl this time. One of the Thanesson's. Drowned herself in her bath this afternoon."

So that's what they thought. Good; no inquiry, then.

Mudge frowned. "Human?" It wouldn't do to know too much without asking.

"Oh ach. But you don't get girls down here often—or this easy. Thanesson said just pitch her in the midden for burning. Shame, really. Deserves better. But no one will miss her, 'specially not with all the fuss over the Thane coming home early."

"Early?" Mudge's eyebrows rose. "When?"

"Few days. Hard to say. Know how it is." Benit stepped over to the work table and prodded the oilcloth shroud with one finger. "Tell you what. Take this one off your hands for five and bring down the other for five more."

The thought of having to see Vivianne again—of looking into her staring blue eyes and slicing open her milk white skin—was nauseating, but Mudge pretended to mull the offer over.

"Four each?" Benit offered. He must have other debts to pay off. The man was a little too fond of a good wager.

Mudge sighed. "Meh. Too much death around here lately. I'll tell you what, Benit. Five for carting this one up, and another ten to make sure he gets a proper pyre. Ten more to arrange a pyre for the girl. Only criminals should be burned in the midden. That'll leave you, what . . . nine or ten?"

"Done," said the big guard, with a grin.

Mudge pointed a threatening finger at him. "Do it right, Benit. I'll find out if you skimp to keep more coin for yourself."

Benit put a hand over his heart, and his face went solemn. "Wouldn't dream of it. I learnt my lesson."

"Good." Mudge eyed the man's face to make sure, then bent to finish tying up the oilcloth shroud.

Benit slung the long bundle over his shoulders, and Mudge preceded him up the stairs to open the door. On the way back down, a whisper of voices carried up the stairs, but the words were indistinct. The silence thumped into place again when Mudge reached the bottom of the steps and all three dragons turned to look. Stig's face was drawn down in a dark, worried scowl. Rolf gazed back at Mudge with his usual unnerving impassivity. And the Other Dragon looked fierce and impatient. Stars only knew what they might have been plotting. Mudge heaved a tired sigh and stepped into the aisle, careful to keep to the center and out of reach.

"Mudge."

Mudge stopped at the sound of Stig's soft voice but didn't look at the dragon. "We're back on speaking terms now?"

"Mudge, it's time. You heard Benit: the Thane will be back in a few days. You have to get them out now. If you wait for the questioner, neither of them will be fit to travel. And with the Thane in residence there'll be twice as many guards to get past."

"No."

"Mudge—"

"No!" Anger burbled up inside as Mudge turned toward the old dragon. "I said no, Stig, and I meant no. They would kill me. That might not mean much to you, but I hope you'll excuse me for preferring to avoid it."

"We could all go." Rolf interrupted the exchange, leaning casually against the bars. "You could come with us."

Mudge stared at him. The dragon actually looked as if he meant it. For a single breath, Mudge felt the lure of it—a new life with the dragons and the humans who lived among them. Perhaps a cottage in one of the villages nestled among the island mountains and work as a healer instead of a dungeon keeper. But the next breath stank of reality. "You'd kill me as soon as we were outside the town's walls."

"Mudge!" Stig interrupted sternly.

The dungeon keeper rounded on him. "If one of them didn't, you'd kill me yourself, and you know it. We might play at being friends, but this isn't one of your fae tales. There is no 'lived-in-happiness-all-their-days' ending in real life. It just doesn't work like that. Especially not for dungeon keepers."

"You can't stay here, Mudge. It isn't what your grandfather wanted for you. And look what it's turning you into. You killed that girl yourself, didn't you?"

Mudge snorted. "She drowned herself in her bath. You heard the man."

"Your sleeves were wet when you came back. Mudge—"

"Enough! It is what it is. Don't ask again." Mudge stalked back to the workroom.

Would Ket never come with the supper pot? This day needed an end.

But the dwarrow light hadn't even begun to dim. Mudge fetched a jug of strong vinegar from the storage shelves and began scrubbing down the work table. The pungent odor helped clear the smell of death from the air, and the vigorous activity burned off some of Mudge's anger and pent up tension. After a while, Pip crept out of his basket by the fire and scampered up Mudge's robe to his accustomed perch, winding his tail gently around Mudge's neck. It was strangely comforting. Pip, at least, could be counted on as a friend. Mudge went on scrubbing, focusing on the *scritch, scritch* of the brush against the wood and letting everything else drift away.

"Mudge?" It was Rolf, not Stig, who interrupted the hypnotic reverie.

Mudge looked up to find the dragon sitting, as usual, at the front of his cell, watching. But there was something different in his expression this time, as if a crack had opened in his wall of impassivity, offering a glimpse of what lay inside. It was somehow even more unsettling.

"Thank you." Rolf's voice was low and resonating. His compulsion voice?

Grateful for the protective embrace of the iron in the stone, Mudge scowled. "For what?"

"For the pyre. For putting him back together at the end. For—for not treating him like so much refuse." Rolf shrugged—and winced as the gesture shifted his ribs. "He was my friend."

Mudge stared back at the dragon. "I can't let you out, Rolf."

"I know. That's not why—" Rolf shook his head and shrugged again, this time hiding the wince. "Just . . . thank you."

He rose, careful of his ribs, and moved to the back corner of his cell where the stone wall blocked Mudge's view from the workroom. Looking at his retreating back, Mudge was reminded that Rolf's stitches should be taken out sometime in the next few days to avoid creating additional scarring. But of course, the questioner would arrive in a few days; then Rolf would be dead, so it hardly mattered.

Except increasingly, it did matter. It shouldn't, but it did.

CHAPTER 6

Edrik woke to a cheerful, lilting melody being played on a flute—a children's song he had danced to a thousand times growing up in the Vanir court. The words of the chorus twirled through his mind, following the insistent lead of the flute.

. . . Oh bow to the king,
And bow to the queen,
And bow to the blacksmith's daughter . . .

The song was entirely at odds with the gray stillness of the inescapable, iron-plagued dungeon. Morning again, if the dwarrow light was to be believed. Another day closer to torture and death without an escape plan. Twenty-five days until the solstice. And Grabak apparently thought it was time for a festival.

Edrik rolled off the stone ledge—rolling hurt less than trying to sit up—and padded to the front of his cell. Across the way, Finn rolled over on his own stone ledge and pulled his blankets over his head. In the workroom, the young dungeon keeper crouched in front of the fire, stirring a copper pot. Porridge, no doubt. There had been porridge every morning in the dungeon.

Edrik rubbed a hand over the stubble on his scalp. *When did I begin to think of daily porridge as a luxury?* Sometime before he stopped taking shirts and trousers for granted, he supposed.

He scratched at his bare chest and watched silently as Mudge rose from the hearth and walked slowly through the arch and down the aisle to stand in front of Grabak's cell with his skinny arms wrapped around himself.

. . . And bow to the blacksmith's daughter . . .

The flute trailed off. A grunt and a rustle, and the old dragon stood at the bars of his cell, facing the grubby dungeon keeper.

"I've been behaving badly," Grabak said quietly.

"You're my prisoner, Stig," Mudge said, his voice careful and flat. "I keep you locked up. I can't expect you to be my friend."

"You keep me alive. They'd kill me if I wasn't locked up. They would've killed me years ago if not for you. I do think of you as a friend, Mudge; it isn't a thing I'm just playing at." Grabak shook his head. "It wasn't fair of me to ask you to risk your life or to give up the only life you've known just because someone I know came poking around Shrike's Hollow and got caught at it. I'm sorry."

Edrik shifted closer to the bars, his face drawing into a dark scowl. Was Grabak giving up? Making nice with the keeper to save his own skin?

"I'm sorry, too." Mudge shook his head and looked at the floor. "It'll be over soon," he offered.

Grabak's face went grim. "I suppose it will."

Mudge didn't meet Edrik's eyes on his way back to the workroom.

Edrik began to pace. There had to be a way out of this rimy dungeon; there was always a way out. But Grabak had been here five years without finding one. And Edrik had nothing to work with. He couldn't chip stone with a blanket or a tin cup. He couldn't bend the iron bars, and they were all solidly anchored; he'd tested each one more than once. The drain in the center of his cell's floor was much too small to fit through, even if he could find something to use to pry up the iron grate that covered it. And stars alone knew where the drains went, anyway. Mudge rarely left the dungeon, and when he did, he left that kitchen boy in the workroom to report on anything the prisoners might say, which made it all but impossible to work together on a solution. Ket might be the weak point. But he was fastidious about staying on the far side of the dwarrow runes; Edrik had heard Mudge threaten to replace him with another kitchen boy if he ever went into the cell block, and apparently, Ket wanted the privilege all to himself. And of course, compulsion was out of the question with all this rimy iron.

Edrik had never felt so helpless.

The current of daily routine swept in, eating relentlessly away at the shrinking window of time he had to figure out an escape. Mudge ordered them all to the backs of their cells while he placed a basin of water and a rag outside each cell so the prisoners could clean themselves. He set the wooden bowls of porridge between the bars. Tidied up in the workroom. Settled at the desk to work.

Today's work, now that Tait's body had been disposed of, seemed to consist of painstakingly copying from one book into another. Mudge kept at it for several hours, during which Grabak played softly on his flute, and Finn paced back and forth in his cell, apparently trying to wear a groove.

Sometime in the middle of the day, a guard came down to consult with Mudge, who gave him a salve and told him to do better at keeping his boots dry. And later, Benit came to report that he'd seen to both pyres, making certain to explain that he'd hauled most of the wood himself instead of paying the cleric's man to do it, so Mudge wouldn't think he'd kept too much coin for himself.

Edrik wanted to scream.

It was well past midday when Grabak challenged Mudge to a game of Pips and Pennies, and Mudge accepted.

"I'm leaving the keys in the workroom, though," the dungeon keeper announced pointedly, "so don't get any ideas, Stig."

Grabak snorted.

Mudge toted a game board down the aisle and set it up in front of Grabak's cell, just out of the old dragon's reach—to be on the safe side, Edrik supposed. Grabak called out his turns, and Mudge moved the pips for him. When it became apparent that Mudge was going to win, Finn started calling out advice to Grabak—some of which was faulty because Finn couldn't see the board. Mudge obligingly moved the board to a spot opposite the wall between the cells so both dragons could see. Mudge still won handily.

Finn demanded a rematch, which Mudge lost. Then Finn played against Grabak and was thoroughly trounced, making Edrik wonder if the old dragon had let Mudge win the first game as a peace offering or some such nonsense. Mudge was setting up for another match when the upper door banged open and a clamor of voices echoed down the stairs.

Mudge started, scooped up the game, and headed for the work-room. He was seated studiously behind the desk by the time the cluster of men burst through the archway at the other end of the small dungeon.

Leading the group was a burly man with graying temples and a red face—whether from too much sun or too much wine was difficult to say. He wore expensive hunting clothes and walked with the swagger of ownership, impatiently tapping a riding whip against his thigh. Two other men with the air and attire of minor nobles flanked him.

Mudge rose from his seat and bowed. "My Lord Thanesson. What an unexpected honor."

The Thanesson barely looked at the dungeon keeper before snapping, "Keys, Mudge. Get this cage open before the thing bites somebody else."

The Thanesson turned his attention back to the commotion behind him. Four or five huntsmen wearing the Thane's livery maneuvered something down the stairs—something that emitted a soft, keening wail as it struggled against the ropes that bound it and the game bag that had been pulled over its head.

Mudge snatched the keys off the desk and headed for the cell next to Edrik's that had formerly housed the human prisoner. Halfway there, he froze, staring at the captive creature.

Edrik had never seen anything quite like it before. It was bigger than most men, and its body was vaguely man-like, with narrow hips and a broad, barrel chest, but it stood on all fours, moving with an awkward, hunching gait on stubby hind legs and the elbows of its over-sized forelimbs, while it held its oddly shaped hands with their long, hooked fingers up under its chin. Its skin, deep gray and textured like tree bark, was torn in places and hung loose, revealing a damp, pale underskin beneath.

"Take the bag off." Mudge ordered, his voice oddly tight and hollow.

The huntsmen hesitated, looking nervously to the Thanesson.

"Take it *off!*" Mudge demanded again, more sharply this time.

The Thanesson made an impatient gesture, and one of the huntsmen reached to pluck the bag gingerly off the creature's head. It had bulbous eyes, slitted nostrils, and a complex mouth that was more like an insect's than a man's.

Mudge gasped and moved back a step, blood draining from behind the brown of his face. "M-my lord," he said, "you can't bring that thing in here."

The Thanesson's face darkened, brows drawing together, lips pulling back from his teeth. "I can bring anything I want in here, boy. It's *my* dungeon."

Mudge gulped and moved another step away from the creature. "Apologies, my lord, but I don't think the cell would hold it. Alfkin are not affected by the iron or by the dwarrow runes. And they're very strong. As I'm sure you know."

The Thanesson snorted derisively. "That's no alfkin, boy. I've dined with the Woodland King, and his court, and not one of them looked anything like that." He jabbed a thick finger toward the creature, which had calmed somewhat now that it could see, and was tipping its chin up and moving its mouthparts as if tasting the air. It let out a low hiss and tensed, twisting its head toward Grabak.

"I understand, m-my lord." Mudge was clearly working to regain his composure. "Perhaps they don't allow their children to dine in company."

"*Children?*" the Thanesson scoffed.

"Y-yes, my lord." Mudge swallowed and drew a deep breath. "The alfkin look a great deal like humans as adults, but they don't reproduce the same way humans do. They lay eggs—not often, and not many, and most of the larvae don't survive to adulthood. The juveniles—nymphs —go through a number of growth stages, shedding their skin as each stage passes." Mudge's gesture indicated the strips of bark-like skin that hung loose from the creature's body. "Usually, the adults guard them fiercely and keep them close to home. I never thought to see one."

"And you know this *how*?" The Thanesson's voice still held mocking skepticism, but it was threaded through with a rising anger. He didn't like that the boy knew more than he did. And he didn't like being lectured in his own dungeon by one of his servants.

"My grandfather's notebooks." Mudge, now firmly in control of himself, moved a step closer to the alfkin, gazing at it with fascination. "From what he wrote, I'd guess this nymph is in its fourth or fifth instar and will pupate soon." He moved another step closer.

"Why are you not with your clan?" he asked it softly in the tone people reserve for animals and very small children.

The head swung toward the young dungeon keeper, mouthparts twitching. A low, chuckling sound ground out of its throat, and then it said, distinctly, "Sheeking."

Mudge jumped. He had not, evidently, expected an actual response.

"What did it say?" the Thanesson demanded. His voice held fear now, as well as anger. "It said something."

Mudge cleared his throat. "It said 'Seeking,' my lord. It's . . . um . . . a rite of passage. I don't know much about it. Grandfather only wrote that an alfkin elder tosses bones, or stones, or something, to choose a totem beast, and the young alfkin must slay that beast and read the future in its entrails. They call it 'the Seeking.'"

"That doesn't explain what it was doing in my apple orchard," the Thanesson growled, "especially if they keep them close to home as you claim."

"N-no, my lord." Mudge was back to stammering again. "Un-unless . . ."

He took another step toward the alfkin and asked it, "What is your totem animal? What are you hunting?"

The creature tipped its head from side to side, studying Mudge. Then it made that chuckling sound again and gurgled out, "Sheeking . . . shuman." Again, it tasted the air, swinging its head toward Grabak as if the dragon made it nervous, and then turned back to peer at Mudge. "Shuman . . ." it said again.

A flurry of murmurs burst out among the huntsmen, and one of the minor nobles exclaimed, "Moon and stars!" and dabbed at his neck with a silk handkerchief.

The Thanesson paled. *"It wants to kill a human?"*

Mudge shook his head. "It *has* to kill a human. It can't go home until it does. If it returns without a destiny, the other alfkin will kill it."

The Thanesson growled and said, "Then *I* will kill it! Somebody bring me a blade!" He held an impatient hand out toward his huntsmen.

"No!" Mudge cried out, clutching at the Thanesson's elbow. "You mustn't!"

The Thanesson's other hand flashed out to grip the skinny dungeon keeper by the throat. "Do not tell me what I must and must not do, boy," the Thanesson bellowed. "You live only by my leave!" Then he jumped, startled, and released his hold as the rat scurried down from the boy's shoulder.

Mudge cowered. "Y-yes, my lord," he murmured. "Only . . . the alfkin are very fond of their children; they don't have many. And they will know where it is. If it dies by our hands—"

"Bah!" The Thanesson started pacing up and down the aisle. At least he had the sense to understand that if he killed the thing, its relatives would tear Shrike's Hollow and everyone in it to rubble.

"Lock it up, then," he growled. "I will send an emissary to the Woodland King requesting that they take their human hunt somewhere else."

"Even if the cell holds it, which I doubt, it'll pupate while you're waiting for your answer," Mudge said darkly. "And if it pupates down here, it'll die. They need sunlight to develop properly."

"Then we'll feed it a human. There must be some miscreant upstairs that no one will miss."

Mudge shook his head. "It has to choose its own fate. If you interfere, you'll bring every alfkin in a hundred leagues down on our heads. You have to let it go."

Everyone jumped as the creature emitted another grating chuckle and shuffled a step forward, tilting its head to examine Mudge with its bulging, faceted eyes. "Clever shuman," it rasped, and edged forward again. "Knowsh thingsh . . ."

The Thanesson's face flushed a blotchy purple, and the muscles in his cheeks jumped as he clenched and unclenched his jaw. His hand flashed out once more in a backhand that sent the dungeon keeper sprawling. The keys skidded across the floor. Mudge rolled to his hands and knees, scrambling to get them, but the Thanesson was quicker and brought his riding whip down hard on the boy's back. The first blow laid open the back of the dungeon keeper's robe and left a pale-edged red welt across the boy's brown skin. The welt from the second blow seeped blood from several small ruptures. And the next two cut cleanly through the skin, leaving long, red gashes and spattering blood.

After that, Mudge lay still.

"You do not tell me what to do, boy!" the Thanesson snarled. He drew a few more heaving breaths and rubbed at the back of his neck, staring at the crumpled, bleeding figure of the boy dungeon keeper. Then he waved an imperious hand toward his huntsmen. "Take it back to the apple orchard and let it go." He stomped back toward the stairs with the two minor nobles trailing after him.

The dungeon keeper's string of keys had come to rest on the floor on Edrik's side of the aisle. He darted a hand between the bars, gasping at the stabbing pain in his side as he stretched. It was too far. Only by a couple of hands' breadths, but too far was too far.

Mudge moaned and pushed gingerly up to his hands and knees.

"Stig," he said through gritted teeth, "next time I ask you if I am a fool, you are to remind me of this."

Grabak chuckled darkly. "Your Thanesson is a greater fool."

A blanket, Edrik thought. *It would extend his reach.* He scrambled for the ledge, snatched a handful of thick wool, and headed back to the bars, already twisting the fabric in his hands.

"Who is the bigger fool," Mudge asked as he clambered shakily to his feet, "the fool or the fool who provokes him?"

Edrik stuffed the twisted blanket between the bars and flung one end at the keys. It landed a finger's width too far to the right. He flipped it just so, and it fell over the keys. He began drawing it back, not daring to look to see if Mudge had noticed what he was doing. The keys slid several handspans closer before the blanket slipped off. Close enough to reach. Edrik shoved his hand between the bars—and just missed the keys as Mudge's bare brown foot kicked the string out from under his fingers. The keys skittered across the runed threshold of the archway into the workroom, and Mudge danced out of Edrik's reach.

Edrik levered himself back to a sitting position, ribs protesting, and glared up at the dungeon keeper.

Mudge grinned sourly back and nodded a small salute. "It was worth a try." As the boy made his way into the workroom, the tear in the back of his robe gaped open, revealing the bleeding gashes in his skin and a swathe of pale bandaging that wound around his upper back. Apparently, the dungeon keeper made a regular practice of impudence toward his betters.

CHAPTER 7

The silence of the dungeon echoed in Edrik's head as Mudge filled the copper pot with water and put it by the fire to warm. Moving gingerly, the boy gathered rags and a basin, a small linen pouch, and the kit of knives and needles he'd laid out when working on Edrik's wound.

"You'll want stitches," Grabak called from his cell.

"I'll get Ket to do it," Mudge called back. "He needs the practice."

Grabak snorted. "You'll look like an old boot."

"Worried my lover won't want me anymore?" Mudge's voice was heavy with mocking sarcasm.

"Mudge." Grabak's voice was sober and sincere. "You're my friend. Let me help you."

The dungeon keeper's hands stilled, and his head bowed as he thought it over. Finally, he said, "I'm leaving the keys in the workroom."

"I know."

"And I'm going to want a story."

Grabak laughed. "You've heard all my stories. Maybe Rolf will tell one this time. A story about home, eh Rolf?"

Edrik turned sharply to look at the old dragon. Grabak hadn't had a chance to ask again about his family. Was that what he was doing now? Grabak gave him a piercing glare and nodded. He wanted information.

Good. Maybe if he knew the whole story, he'd stop pussyfooting around with the dungeon keeper and help them get out. Edrik drew a deep breath and nodded back.

When the water was hot, Mudge took his collection of tools down the aisle to Grabak's cell, wincing as he bent to set them on the floor in front of the seated dragon. Before handing over the rolled bundle that held the knives, Mudge said, "If you kill me . . ."

"I'll die next. I know. Turn around."

Mudge worked his way to a sitting position with his back to the old Drake. Grabak reached between the iron bars, pushed back the torn edges of the tattered robe, and started dabbing at the blood that had trickled down the dungeon keeper's back.

"Well, Rolf?" Grabak asked gruffly. "Have you a story for us?"

Edrik cleared his throat and began. "'Twas a time not long past. The Vanir of the valleys lived peacefully in their villages under the protection of the great drakes in their mountain fortresses, and all were ruled by a wise and just king and his queen, who was beautiful and kind. It was the queen's task to watch over the human Vanir and sit in judgment among them while the king ruled the dragonkind.

"The king and queen had a fair young daughter who delighted to play in the gardens of the Aerie, the palace of the Vanir lords. One of her favorite playmates was the son of the king's most trusted adviser. And as time passed, the princess and her playmate grew tall and strong and began to think of more than children's games."

Glancing up, Edrik found Mudge's black eyes fixed on him, weighing, evaluating, as if the boy were mentally taking him apart to see how he worked. Grabak didn't look at Edrik at all, only picked studiously through Mudge's assortment of needles.

Edrik cleared his throat and went on, trying to ignore the dungeon keeper's scrutiny. "One day, the king was called away on business of his own—what it was he told no one, except perhaps the queen. Not wishing to add to his wife's burden, the king placed the affairs of the dragons in the hands of his trusted adviser and took to his wings, journeying out into the lands of men.

"The first year, all went smoothly. The queen ruled over the humans, and the adviser sat in the king's stead, ruling over the dragons; the kingdom flourished.

"The princess grew ever more enchanting, and both dragons and men began to vie for her favor. Her mother, the queen, encouraged her to choose a dragon for her husband. A dragonwife's life is long, but her daughters are fully human and will live a normal human lifespan unless they, too, marry dragons. And no mother wishes to outlive her children."

"Is it true then," Mudge interrupted, "that there are no female dragons?"

While Edrik hesitated, thinking how best to respond, Grabak answered for him. "It's true. The ability to ascend is passed only from father to son. Dragons' daughters are all human, like their mothers, and inherit the human magic that passes through the female lineage."

Mudge scoffed. "Human women have no magic." He winced slightly as Grabak drew the thread tight.

"None but a human woman can make another human," Grabak said quietly, "or a new dragon."

"But that's just nature," argued Mudge. "There's nothing magical about that."

"For a dragon, it is natural to ascend. Yet you call it magic."

"But that *is* magic." Mudge's brows drew together. "You change from one form to another."

"A seated human is a different shape from a standing one. Ascending, for a dragon, is much the same."

"No, it isn't," Mudge insisted. "Your anatomy completely alters. Ours only changes its position."

"Either way, Mudge, it is a mere rearrangement of anatomy that already exists. A human woman can construct an entirely new anatomy, separate from herself, and give it life of its own. If that is not magic, I don't know what is."

"No." Mudge was adamant. "There's nothing supernatural about reproduction. Every animal of the field or forest can do that. "

"Only the female ones. It is a feminine magic. That it is common makes it no less magical. You call ascension supernatural because it is a thing outside the nature of humans. But no dragon can create a living being—to do so is outside our nature and therefore supernatural."

Mudge was silent for a moment, thinking. "You say when you ascend your anatomy only rearranges, but that's not true. A dragon in his human form has no wings—not even vestigial ones. I checked. So the wing anatomy is created in the change."

Grabak chuckled. "A human who is standing has no lap. A lap is created when a human sits."

"That's different."

"Perhaps, but only in degree, not in essence; a dragon's wings have no life of their own." Grabak sighed. "I do not think we will agree on this, young Mudge."

Mudge frowned and said nothing for a moment. Then he, too, sighed. "Maybe not." He nodded at Edrik. "I'm sorry for interrupting. Please, go on."

"Right," Edrik said. "Where was I?"

"The queen wants her daughter to marry a dragon."

"Indeed she does." Edrik drew a deep breath. "And the dragons desired the same thing, for the princess was very beautiful and came of a deeply revered line of dragonkind. The princess found herself with many suitors, who showered her with gifts, preened in her presence, and engaged in showy battles to win her admiration. Yet her favored suitor remained her old playmate, the adviser's son. His love for the princess grew with every day that passed, but he began to fear that he would lose her to another suitor. Although he came of a strong dragon lineage himself, he was still young, and a dragon cannot ascend until he reaches his full growth, so he could court the princess only as a man, not as a dragon. At the end of the second year, the king had not returned."

Edrik looked to Grabak. The old dragon's eyes were focused on his work; his mouth was drawn into a frown. He didn't look up, so Edrik went on. "As the third year wore on, and still no word came from the king, the drakes began to murmur among themselves, provoked perhaps (though who can say for sure?) by the old Black Dragon, Nidhaug, eldest of all the drakes."

"*Another* black dragon?" Mudge interrupted again.

"There are only so many colors a dragon can be," Grabak grumbled impatiently. "Nidhaug is the only black at present. Do you want to hear the story or not?"

"Sorry."

Edrik cleared his throat. "The dragons began to murmur among themselves. Perhaps, they said, the king was never coming back. Perhaps he had abandoned his kingdom and his family to live in a cave on some high, lonely mountain, as drakes sometimes do when the years begin to weigh upon them. Perhaps he was dead. Either way, Nidhaug whispered that the adviser must give up the throne, and the dragons must choose a new drake to be their king.'"

That got Grabak's attention. His hands stilled, and his eyes locked with Edrik's.

Edrik gazed grimly back. "The adviser refused to step down. He said the king had given him this charge, and he would not relinquish it until the king returned and released him from his duties. The queen gave him her support, and the humans among the Vanir stood behind their queen. But it is for the drakes to choose the king, not the humans. And Nidhaug challenged the king's adviser for the throne."

Grabak's frown deepened, but still he said nothing.

Edrik looked down at his hands. "They fought," he said quietly, "and the adviser refused to yield. He knew the king would not yield to a challenger, and he felt it his duty, when acting in the king's stead, to do as the king would do. So Nidhaug slew the king's adviser and took the throne. And none dared challenge him."

Edrik stopped, turning his palms up in his lap. Empty. Useless.

"The adviser's son?" Grabak's voice was soft but held a burning thread of iron.

Edrik gritted his teeth and forced himself to look the old Drake in the eyes. "The advisor's son could not ascend, and a child is not permitted to challenge a dragon. Nor is a pinion."

Grabak's eyes narrowed as they scanned Edrik, reassessing.

"He is only late because of his size," he said, a hint of uncertainty tinging his voice. "When he ascends, he will be formidable."

"That's what everyone said." Edrik held the Drake's eyes defiantly with his own. "And perhaps the expectation of such a challenge helped preserve the stability of the kingdom a little longer. But the adviser's son passed his quartermark early in the fourth year."

Grabak looked away, unable to meet Edrik's gaze. Edrik looked down at his hands again.

"What does that mean?" Mudge's voice pierced the tense stillness. "There was nothing about pinions and quartermarks in Grandfather's notes on dragons. I don't understand."

A knot of shame clutched at the back of Edrik's throat, and he shook his head.

Grabak, too, held his silence for a time. Then, quietly, he explained. "It doesn't happen often. And it is not a thing we speak of a great deal. You understand that sometimes a human child is born blind or unable to hear. Or . . . sometimes a human girl may grow to be a woman, plump and beautiful and seemingly perfect, but when she is grown, she finds that she is unable to reach the magic—unable to conceive."

"Birth defects," Mudge said. "And infertility. But what does that have to do with—"

Grabak interrupted. "As Rolf said, a young dragon cannot ascend until he is fully grown. As with humans, dragons reach their adult size at different ages—small dragons will ascend at a decade and a half. Others keep growing and don't find the magic until they have passed two decades. Generally, the larger the dragon, the longer it takes. But if a dragon reaches a quarter century in age—the quartermark—without being able to ascend, the chances that he will ever find the magic are very small indeed."

"So . . ." Mudge hesitated. "It's a birth defect? He can't become a real dragon?"

"A dragon is *always* a real dragon, Mudge." Grabak's voice was sharp. "Whether he can reach the magic or not. Just as an infertile human woman is always a real woman, and a man is still a man whether he can see or not. It does not change what they are, only what they can do."

"All right," Mudge said. "So he's a dragon who's stuck in his human form."

"We call it being pinioned," Grabak said, his voice still tight, but no longer sharp. "Bound, so he cannot fly. But he has a dragon heart and a dragon lifespan. He is *still a dragon.*"

Edrik cut in. "He is weak and broken. And like a child, he may not challenge other dragons or claim holdings of his own, and he must make his living as a human man does." He drew a deep, bitter breath. "And he cannot form a proper bond with a woman, even if he marries her."

"But he is still a dragon," Grabak insisted. "Just as a Drake in an iron collar is still a dragon."

Edrik looked up then, and another long, tight silence passed between them, hanging in the air.

"Are you finished, Stig?" Mudge's voice was soft and small.

Grabak looked away from Edrik, back to his task of stitching up the dungeon keeper. "A little more, Mudge. I'm sorry; I got distracted. Perhaps Rolf will tell us what became of the queen and the princess when Nidhaug took the throne." He took up the needle again and set carefully to work.

Edrik sighed and gathered his thoughts. "Nidhaug's hold on the throne was somewhat tenuous. The dragons recognized his right to rule only because they feared to challenge him; the humans, for the most part, regarded him as a mere pretender, holding out hope that their true king would return one day to challenge Nidhaug and take back the throne. The queen refused to step down—she, too, clung to the hope that her husband would return. She sent messengers out into the lands beyond, seeking news of her husband, but they all returned empty-handed. The pretender had no queen of his own to supplant her, only several unbonded mates, and he feared the Vanir might rise against him if he forced her out. So he bided his time, and he spoke gently to the queen. And still the king did not return."

"What about the princess?" Mudge asked.

"The princess." *Lissara.* Edrik drew a deep breath to steady himself. "The princess wept for her friend, for she still loved him dearly, but her crippled childhood playmate could no longer give her the life she wanted. She found consolation among her many other suitors who could."

A clatter made Edrik look over at Grabak's cell. The old Drake didn't meet his eyes as he retrieved the knife he'd dropped. Mudge's dark eyes, however, bored into him, speculating, and across the aisle, Finn snorted softly.

Edrik tried to keep the bitterness from showing in his voice. "As the fourth year wore on, unrest grew among the Vanir, both humankind and dragonkind. Nerves were raw, and tempers thin, and murmurs of rebellion rumbled throughout the land. Many of the great drakes and even some of the Dragonlords abandoned the Aerie, choosing to remain instead in their own mountain fortresses.

"The new king sent away his unbonded mates and whispered to the queen, telling her how beautiful she was, and how wise. He said her husband must be dead, or else he was a fool, because only a great fool could abandon such a woman as she. He said he had fallen hopelessly under the spell of her charms and would have no other woman while she lived. He whispered that marrying him would help legitimize his claim to the throne and return peace to the land of the Vanir. It had been nearly five years since the Drake went away. And the people needed peace."

A low hiss from Grabak. Edrik glanced over to see him cut the thread and begin gathering up Mudge's tools, his motions stiff and tight. Mudge didn't move.

Edrik went determinedly on. "The queen was not yet ready to give up on her husband, but her hope was dwindling, and she saw the need to settle the matter for her people. So she proclaimed that she would wait one more year. If her husband had not returned by summer solstice in the following year, she would accept that, whether widowed or abandoned, she was free to take a new husband, and she would marry Nidhaug."

Grabak shoved Mudge's bundled tools into the dungeon keeper's lap and rose slowly to his feet. His jaw was tight and his eyes hard as his hands closed around the iron bars, clenching the hot sting of the metal. Edrik rose too, not liking the way the Drake towered over him, and wanting to meet whatever was coming on his feet, like a man. Like a *dragon*.

He finished his tale.

"The princess wept at her mother's pronouncement, for she believed her father still to be alive. She begged Nidhaug and the queen to send more messengers to look for him, but to no avail. So the princess turned to her suitors for help. She said she'd marry the man who found her father and brought him home alive before the summer solstice. The suitors did not want to leave her side, for fear of losing ground to their competitors. They believed such a search would be futile, and they knew that seeking the old king would win them no favor with the new. The only suitor to take up the quest was the princess's old playmate, son of the dead adviser to the old king, for he had nothing left to lose.

"He set out with two faithful friends to seek the lost Drake. They journeyed to the lands where the yotun dwell on the ruined fae coast and sought counsel from the Sisters at the Well of Fate. The Sisters said the Drake still lived, held prisoner in the lands of men. They described the place they saw in the waters of the Well and granted each of the three friends a yot mark to help them in their quest.

"But the adviser's son was a fool. He lost most of his coin coaxing the Sisters to help. He landed his friends in three different dungeons and a cage in a mine shaft before they found the right place. He wasted or lost all the yot marks. He lost his father's sword. He got one of his friends killed. And in the end, it was all for nothing." Edrik set his jaw defiantly and met the hot gaze of the king.

Grabak drew a slow, deep breath. "Mudge," he said, his quiet voice quivering with restraint and heavy with command, "you *will* get us out of here." He didn't look at the boy dungeon keeper when he said it; his eyes were locked with Edrik's. "Immediately."

Mudge shifted slowly, rising and backing away as if from some dangerous wild creature. And Grabak probably *was* rather dangerous at that moment. For a heartbeat, Edrik thought the boy might get away, but then Grabak's hand shot out, closing around the retreating dungeon keeper's wrist. Mudge had the presence of mind to pitch the bundle with the knives to one side as the Drake drew him close and fixed him with his formidable glare. *"Immediately."*

Across the aisle from Edrik, Finn rose slowly to his feet and leaned into the bars, trying to see what was happening.

The boy swallowed hard and looked the old dragon in the eyes. "Stig," he said carefully, "we've talked about this. They would kill me if I let you out."

Grabak pulled the boy in closer. *"I* will kill you if you don't."

Mudge squared his shoulders. "If you kill me, they'll have no reason to let you live. You'll be just as dead as me."

Grabak's jaw worked as he ground his teeth together. "If she marries him . . ." he breathed, his control straining to the breaking point, ". . . if she bonds with that worm, he will have access through her to my magic. With mine and his together, he will be able to compel dragons. It has happened before. I cannot let it happen again."

"Let go of my arm, Stig. This won't end well for either of us."

The quiet calm of the dungeon keeper impressed Edrik; he'd seen great drakes crumble in the face of the king's wrath.

Grabak pulled the dungeon keeper hard against the bars and glowered down at the boy. "Do not mistake me. The Black Dragon *cannot* be allowed that much power. I will die if I must to keep it from happening."

"You don't want to die," Mudge said calmly. "And neither do I. Let go of my arm."

Grabak glared at the boy for one long heartbeat more and then released his hold. Mudge stumbled backward until his back fetched up against the bars of the empty cell across from Grabak's.

"Get us out, Mudge!" the old dragon growled.

Mudge bent to pick up his bundle of tools and, leaving the basin, rags, and copper pot sitting on the floor at Grabak's feet, headed back toward the workroom, moving into the center of the aisle as he passed Edrik's cell.

"You have until the Thane's return," Grabak added. "Or I'll tell them about Kaya."

Mudge froze. His face went ashen. "Where did you hear that name?" His voice trembled slightly.

Clearly, Grabak had hit a nerve.

"Your grandfather was still alive when I came here, remember?" Grabak's voice had gone flat as ice. "I heard him speaking of her to you one night. He was carving a puppet at the time, as I recall. Do you remember what he said?"

From the boy's expression, he remembered very well.

"Stig . . ." Mudge turned slowly to face Grabak. "Kaya's mother jilted the Thanesson for a river man. One of the Rattatosk, Stig. If the Thanesson knew they had a daughter, Kaya would be chained to his bed post before she could turn around. Death would be better."

"If I am still here when the Thane returns," Grabak said relentlessly, "I will tell the Thanesson myself."

Mudge's face flushed dark now. His hands trembled as they clutched the bundle, but his voice was strong and steady when he said, "I should just kill you now and be done with you."

Grabak didn't even twitch. "Kill me or free me, Mudge. Those are your only options."

CHAPTER 8

Two days. Edrik had sat helpless in the rimy, iron-infected bowels of the dungeon for two days since Grabak issued his ultimatum, and precious little had changed. Finn had added muttering to his regular routine of pacing back and forth across his cell—mostly obscenities. Grabak had refused to eat anything for the past two days, perhaps fearing that the dungeon keeper might poison him to keep him from telling anyone about Kaya—whoever that was. And nothing Mudge had said or done in the past two days gave any indication that he might intend to help them escape.

The dungeon keeper distributed wash basins and doled out porridge in the morning and fed the prisoners whatever came down in the pot from the kitchen in the evening. Otherwise, he stayed out of the cell block altogether. He went out twice to run errands, leaving the kitchen boy toasting cheese on a stick over the coals in the workroom—and eavesdropping. Besides that, all Mudge did from dawn to dusk, and into the night by candlelight, was sit behind the big desk calmly copying from one wretched book into another.

For two days!

The dwarrow light dimmed again. Finn paced and swore. Grabak sat by the bars at the front of his cell tying knots in a bit of string he had and then untying them again. Edrik leaned against the rock wall on one side of his cell, trying not to move his ribs and watching the dungeon keeper scratch relentlessly away with his pen until, at last, Ket came with the supper pot. Again.

They were all going to die.

And Lissara would marry someone else.

Mudge was scooping stew into the wooden bowls when another, more frantic, knock sounded at the workroom door. As soon as the key clicked in the lock, Ket burst back into the workroom, eyes wide, cheeks flushed. "Thane's retinue is at the river landing. Master Steward's calling assembly."

Dread rose up like bile in Edrik's belly; the Thane was back—and with him, the questioner. It was too late.

Mudge went very still for a long heartbeat. Then he squared his shoulders. "Best hurry, then." He turned and strode purposefully back to the desk, where he carefully closed the book he'd been copying into and added the book he'd been copying from to a stack of similar leather-bound volumes at one side of the desk.

Ket followed, his young face gone pale now. He laid a hand almost reverently on the stack of books. "These the ones?"

Mudge nodded. "Grandfather's notebooks. The archivist is expecting them. Hurry. You mustn't be late for the welcoming."

The kitchen boy hesitated. "Mudge . . ." He stopped, clearly at a loss.

Mudge rumpled the boy's hair. "Stick with Cook, Ket. Remember what I've taught you. You'll be fine."

Ket nodded, eyes still round, and said softly, "Stars guide you, Mudge." Then he snatched the stack of books and took off at a run.

Mudge stood for a moment by the desk, eyes closed, lips pressed together, then returned to dishing up the stew, moving with a quick efficiency that spoke of purpose. He ordered the prisoners to the backs of their cells before he was finished filling the bowls and practically threw the food down in front of the bars before bolting out the workroom door.

Edrik had hardly begun picking at his food when Mudge bustled back in again carrying a bundle wrapped in a wool blanket.

The boy glared at Edrik and snapped, "Eat faster!" before darting out again and returning with another blanket-wrapped bundle.

This time, the dungeon keeper went to stand in front of Grabak's cell. The old Drake hadn't even moved to retrieve his meal.

"Eat!" Mudge ordered. "It's not poisoned, you great fool."

Grabak scowled up at the dungeon keeper, clearly suspicious, and didn't move.

Mudge grunted impatiently and drew something from his pocket—his string of keys.

"Eat," he said again. "We're in a hurry, and I'm not sure when you'll get another chance. I can't have you fainting from hunger before we even get beyond the wall."

Beyond the wall? Had Edrik heard the boy right?

A slow grin spread over Grabak's face, and he chuckled low in his throat as he rose to his feet. "You had me worried, young Mudge." His voice was affectionately reproachful.

Hope surged through Edrik.

"You deserved to fret a bit," Mudge growled. "You threatened to kill me."

"I threatened worse than that," Grabak said solemnly. "I'm sorry."

"Yes. Well." Mudge fumbled with the keys. "Now we're in a hurry." He crammed a key into the lock on Grabak's cell and twisted.

The old Drake pushed out of his cell and drew the boy into a rough embrace.

"Thank you, Mudge," he said gruffly.

"Stow it, Stig." The boy pushed away, scowling furiously. "You're not free yet. And you're not forgiven." He held the keys out to Grabak. "I need to get some things. Be ready when I come back. Our best chance is during the confusion of the Thane's return." Without waiting for a response, the dungeon keeper hurried out again.

The bundles turned out to contain shirts, trousers, and over-tunics, along with belts, stockings, sturdy boots, and thick woolen cloaks. The dragons ate and dressed as quickly as they could—Finn had to help Edrik with his shirt and tunic—and had been pacing impatiently up and down the cell block for what seemed far too long by the time Mudge returned. The bundle the boy carried this time clattered when he laid it on the floor of the workroom just beyond the rune-carved threshold of the archway.

Mudge straightened and solemnly regarded the three expectant dragons on the other side of the dwarrow magic barrier. He ran a hand into his matted hair; the dark tangles convulsed as the rat shifted its position on the boy's shoulder. Then he drew a deep breath and stepped toward the dwarrow runes on the curve of wall nearest Edrik.

Edrik moved forward too, ignoring the itching, tingling sensation that gathered on his skin as he neared the archway from his side. He stopped, however, when a ringing started in his ears, and the tingling sharpened into pain.

Mudge looked up, meeting Edrik's eyes, and swallowed hard. "You promised not to eat me, Rolf," he said quietly. "Remember?"

Edrik grinned. "And you promised not to stick me with iron." He moved half a step forward; the tingling pain seemed to congeal around him, holding him away from the arch, and the ringing in his head began to throb. He was still a good three paces back from the archway.

Mudge raised a hand, trembling slightly, to the runes. He traced several of them with one finger, then stepped over and bent to place his hand flat in the center of the threshold.

The throbbing in Edrik's head ceased abruptly, and the tingling pain dissipated. He stepped across the threshold into the workroom. His blood surged in his veins, and he turned to share a triumphant grin with Finn. They might make it out of here after all.

The new bundle contained a jumble of bronze knives. As the dragons sorted through the stash, Mudge ducked out again and came back a moment later with a short, bronze-tipped spear in one hand, a sturdy oak staff with a clubbed knot at the end in the other, and a baldric looped over one shoulder from which hung a sword in a scabbard.

Edrik knew that sword. He straightened slowly.

Mudge saw Edrik looking and slowed his approach to a hesitant shuffle. "I took what I could that wasn't iron," he said, propping the spear and staff against the edge of the desk. "And I saw this in the armory and thought it might belong to one of you."

He held the sword out, and Edrik stepped forward to take it.

Edrik kept his face impassive enough as he accepted the sword from the dungeon keeper, clenching his teeth against the stab of pain the motion sent through his ribs, but he couldn't stop a grin from breaking over his face as he carefully slid the blade from its fur-lined scabbard.

The sword was simple in form and beautiful, shaped centuries ago at the height of yotun artistry. The keen-edged blade followed the slight, natural curve of the basilisk bone from which it had been crafted. The hilt and sword-catching quillons were of moon silver, as were the slender, intricately woven vines that made up the pommel, caging a single, perfectly spherical blood-red ruby. A delicate web of yot marks twined over every inch of the sword's surface, engraved on the silver, etched into the bone; even the designs formed by the silver wire that bound the white shagreen grip of the sword formed a part of the lattice of power that flowed around and through the sword, making it stronger than iron, immune to tarnish, and hungry for the blood of its wielder's enemies. Only a few swords like this had ever been made, and the shaping of some of the marks had been lost when the old crafters were massacred.

Edrik touched the pommel to his forehead and felt the faint tremor of power that shivered through the grip and down the blade in answer. He looked up, as he slipped the blade back into the scabbard, to find the young dungeon keeper watching him.

"It was my father's," Edrik said softly, running a caressing hand down the plain leather cover of the scabbard. "I thought I had lost it. Thank you, Mudge."

Mudge looked at his feet, apparently embarrassed.

Edrik began to lift the baldric over his head and nearly dropped it when pain lanced through his chest and up his arm, stealing his breath. He hissed in frustration.

"I . . . could help," Mudge said, his voice soft. "If you like."

The boy's nervous hesitation made Edrik chuckle. He held the baldric out. Mudge took it and swallowed hard before stepping closer to lift the leather strap over Edrik's head and settle it across his chest so the sword hung once more at Edrik's hip. Edrik felt a sudden urge to growl or snap his teeth, just to see the skittish boy jump.

"Mudge." Grabak's voice broke the silence. "Have you eaten?"

The dungeon keeper shook himself as if waking from a compulsion daze and looked around. "I took too much time in the armory." Mudge grabbed his copy book off the desk and strode to the wall the workroom shared with Edrik's cell. A sleeping ledge protruded there, much like the ones in the cells, except this one was furnished with a pallet and several extra blankets. The boy drew a bulging satchel out from under the ledge, stuffed the book inside, and slung it over his shoulder. "Let's go."

Grabak sloshed some stew into a bowl and thumped it down on the table. "Eat."

The dungeon keeper opened his mouth to protest.

Grabak interrupted. "It would take longer to argue about it than it will to eat."

Mudge glared back at the old Drake for several tense heartbeats before he gritted his teeth and walked over to pick up the bowl. Without breaking eye contact with Grabak, the boy wolfed down the stew and slammed the bowl back on the table. "Can we go now, or are you determined to stand here until they come slaughter us all?"

Edrik frowned. "If they're assembling the household for the Thane's return, won't you be missed?"

Mudge rolled his eyes and said wryly, "They generally prefer that I absent myself from gatherings. We need to go." He turned toward the workroom door.

"Aren't you forgetting something?" Finn sounded more than a little irritated.

Everyone turned to look at him.

"The collars!" He stepped closer to Mudge and glared down at him. "You forgot to take off the rimy iron collars."

Mudge paled but squared his shoulders and met Finn glare for glare. "The collars stay."

Finn gaped. "You can't be serious! We can't ascend with them on. You expect us to defend ourselves with a club and a pointy stick? We're dragons!"

The dungeon keeper drew a determined breath. "As long as the collars are on, you need me alive."

"You little—" Finn lunged, catching Mudge with a blow to the face that sent the boy sprawling; his rat squealed as it hit the floor, knocked from its shoulder perch.

Mudge sat up and wiped a trickle of blood from his mouth with the back of his hand, directing a disdainful glare at Finn.

"Been saving that up for a while, haven't you, Other Dragon?"

Finn took one prowling step toward the dungeon keeper, but Grabak intervened, forcing Finn back.

"Enough! Mudge is right. Unless you know a dwarrow who wouldn't rather take your head, we still need him alive. And as you just demonstrated, it's a sensible precaution for the boy to take."

"It itches!" Finn grumbled, still eying the dungeon keeper with a feral gleam.

"You'll live," Grabak said grimly. "Would you prefer the club or the pointy stick?"

Finn shifted his glare to the old Drake, locking eyes for a long moment. Then he relaxed his stance and growled, "Fine. Let's get out of here."

Grabak let go. Finn stalked over to pick up the spear and began pacing back and forth across the workroom, muttering obscenities.

Edrik walked over to offer Mudge a hand up.

Mudge stared at Edrik's hand for a moment, then batted it away. "Are you *trying* to make that rib worse?" he muttered, pushing himself to his feet. He collected his rat and led the way through the workroom door.

Edrik and the other dragons followed the boy up a passageway behind some storage shelves and down a quick succession of eerily deserted hallways and staircases that brought them to an immense stockroom where crates, barrels, sacks, and bins crammed the spaces between low, arching ceiling supports. A slumped stack of dusty crates on the far side of the room concealed a crack in the outside wall that Mudge easily widened by removing several loose stones.

Mudge frowned but said nothing as he watched Edrik hunch his way through the opening with his teeth gritted and sweat beading on his forehead from the pain in his side.

On the outside, the crevice in the wall was hidden by a dense cluster of ornamental shrubs and the uncertain dimness of rapidly approaching nightfall. Beyond the shrubs lay the keep's open bailey, where ranks of armed men dressed in the dun and black livery of Shrike's Keep stood at attention facing the gatehouse as several men on horses made their way beneath the raised portcullis. More uniformed men stood guard atop the crenelated curtain wall beyond the bailey, silhouetted against the darkening sky.

Mudge laid a cautioning finger to his lips and gestured for the dragons to follow him.

Edrik looked over his shoulder a few times as he crept along the wall behind the thin screen of shrubbery. The guards' attention stayed focused on the Thane's party or on the landscape beyond the walls, but Edrik breathed easier when the fugitives had all moved around the corner of the squared-off tower and out of sight of the main courtyard.

The light continued to fade as the boy led them quickly through a kitchen garden and then gestured for them to wait behind a stack of barrels while he made sure the brewery was unoccupied. By the time they'd navigated past several more outbuildings and crawled through a hedge into a small, ornamental park, it was just shy of full dark, and Edrik was glad of the light from the waxing moon. Mudge stopped them inside a latticed bower in easy sight of a small postern gate that was half concealed in the turning of the curtain wall.

"This is the part where we're most likely to get caught," Mudge whispered. "Everyone in the household has been summoned to the great hall to welcome the Thane, but there are still guards at the gates." He produced a leather flask from some pocket in the depths of his robe. "This guard and I have an arrangement. I sneak sage wine out of the kitchen for him, and he fails to notice when I go out at night to collect herbs. Tonight, the wine has more in it than sage."

Edrik grinned. "The stuff you gave me to make me sleep?"

Mudge half raised one shoulder in the dimness. "Not quite so strong. If we're lucky, he'll be awake in time for the watch change, and no one will suspect anything until morning. We can only let him see me, though. You'll have to wait here until he nods off."

Finn started to protest.

Mudge spoke over him in a vehement whisper. "If he sees you, he'll sound an alarm and we'll all be dead."

Finn glowered. "What's to keep you from running off on your own and leaving us stuck in these rimy collars?"

Mudge scoffed. "How long do you think someone like me would last on the road alone? If I wanted that, I would've left you in your cage."

"You might set the guards on us while we wait."

"If they find you out of the dungeon, I'm dead too!"

"What if he doesn't drink the wine?"

"He will."

"We should just kill him and be done with it."

Mudge thumped Finn in the middle of his chest with the heel of one hand. "His wife just had a baby. If you kill him, I'll kill you."

"Enough." Edrik laid a hand on his friend's arm. "We'll wait."

Finn turned his head to meet Edrik's eyes, and the two of them stared each other down for a moment before Finn subsided.

Mudge cleared his throat. "There's one more thing." He scrubbed a hand over the back of his neck, disturbing the rat, which slunk down into the robe's hood and curled up between the boy's shoulder blades. "Stig . . . I need your promise. I need you to swear to me that if they catch us, you'll kill me."

"Mudge—"

"*Promise* me." The boy's whisper was sharp and tight. "If they . . . if they found out about Kaya . . . I couldn't bear it. If you ever were my friend at all, Stig, do this for me."

Silence thrummed in the darkness for a long heartbeat. Two. Three. Then, "Grabak. My name is Grabak."

Finn let out a long, low hiss and turned away, crossing his arms over his chest and staring out into the night.

Mudge shivered and shifted on his feet. "What?"

Grabak reached over to lay a hand on the boy's shoulder. "This thing you ask of me—you should at least know the name of the man you're asking."

Edrik stared at the old Drake. *He'd given the dungeon keeper his name!*

The boy looked down. "So, you'll do it . . . Grabak? You promise?"

"I promise, young Mudge." Grabak grinned and leaned closer. "But let's not get caught."

"Where is this Kaya person, anyway?" Finn muttered. "You'd die to keep her secret, but you're happy to run off somewhere safe and leave her here?"

Mudge snorted. "As if a woman would be safe with a bunch of dragons."

Edrik frowned. "Don't roll all of us dragons in the same hog wallow."

Mudge's chin came up defiantly. "I've arranged for Kaya to leave town. She's as safe as I am right now."

Grabak made an odd noise that sounded like a stifled snort. "Best get moving, eh Mudge?"

"Right." Mudge squared his shoulders, then relaxed and strolled around the corner with a loose-limbed gait that spoke of casual confidence in his privilege of going wherever he chose. Edrik had to admire the dungeon keeper's poise–despite being caught between three dragons who, as far as Mudge knew, might kill him as soon as he was no longer useful and a guard who would kill him if he knew about the dragons, he could still pull off a nonchalant swagger.

All three dragons watched intently through the lattice as the guard rose to meet Mudge, and the two exchanged greetings and engaged in some friendly small talk—at least that's what Edrik guessed from the gestures they made; it was too far to hear what was being said. Finn muttered something about it not being too late to kill the guard, but Grabak hushed him. Mudge produced the wine flask with a flourish, and the guard clapped him on the back and waved him toward the gate with an expansive sweep of his arm.

The guard was as keen on the wine as Mudge had predicted, and before long, he was happily dozing at his post. Grabak waited a little longer, just to be sure, before signaling for Finn to circle around to the right, while he circled to the left, and instructing Edrik to give them a count of twenty before strolling up to the gate, drawing the guard's attention if he was still awake, while the other two came at him from the sides. In the end, though, that precaution was unnecessary because the guard never even stirred as the three of them crept past him and slipped out through the postern gate.

Outside the wall, the edge of the bluff fell away to Edrik's right, rock-strewn and treacherous. Below, the lights of Shrike's Hollow spread out along the rich floodplain carved out long ago by a bend of the Drasil River, which had since shifted its course farther to the north and now sprawled lazily out beyond the docks, gleaming broad in the moonlight.

The fields and orchards that fed the town spread along the bluff, both above and below, and a dark line of trees to the south showed where an arm of the great forest reached out to cradle the Hollow in the crook of its elbow. Edrik thought back to Tait's hastily sketched map of the place, drawn with his finger in the forest loam after he'd returned from a scouting flight.

Tait. It felt wrong to be leaving without him. Edrik never should have let his friends come with him on this fool's errand.

Still, they had found Grabak.

Edrik drew a steadying breath. Ten days lost to the Shrike's Keep dungeon. Twenty-two left before the solstice.

Mudge rose like a shadow out of the tall grass to one side of a narrow path that led away from the small gate and then petered out into scrubby overgrowth.

"This way," he said, gesturing. "There's a stream, but it isn't very wide. You can hop over it if you're careful, even in the dark."

He turned and began to move off but was stopped by Finn's quiet challenge.

"Why?"

Mudge turned back. "What?"

"Why should we keep following you? We're past the wall now, we can go wherever we like. You're not in control anymore, dungeon keeper."

Mudge heaved an exasperated sigh. "Fine. I'm not in control. Why don't *you* lead us to the food packs, then?" He scratched at his neck and muttered, "Assuming they're even there."

Finn's only response was an obscenity, and Mudge turned again and led off, pausing briefly to point out the edge of the stream bank before bounding over it and setting out at a slow lope toward a place farther down where the tree line edged close to the wall.

It was, indeed, a very narrow stream, hardly more than a long stride across, but the extension of his body in the small jump sent pain stabbing through Edrik's chest, and the jolt as he landed nearly brought him to his knees. There was no way he was going to be able to run. He let his fingers rest on his father's sword, reassuring himself that it was still there, and felt the subtle stirring of its magic as he strode off at as fast a walk as he could manage. Grabak and Finn slowed to match his pace.

Mudge waited for them under the first trees at the edge of the forest and took a much slower pace as they moved into the forest proper, stopping now and then to get his bearings in the dark. After a quarter of an hour or so, he murmured, "Over here," and ducked behind the looming, upright roots of a fallen tree. A hunters' blind had been created by scooping away some of the earth under the fallen tree trunk and laying branches along both sides as a screen. Mudge ducked inside and emerged a moment later lugging two packs, which he tossed on the ground in front of Grabak and Finn. A second trip into the blind resulted in one more pack and a traveling cloak for Mudge.

Edrik moved to take the pack, but Mudge shoved his hand away. "You're in no shape to be carrying a pack. You need to let that rib heal."

"You already have your satchel," Edrik pointed out. "And your back isn't in any shape for a pack either. I saw what that whip did to you."

Mudge slung the pack over one shoulder and grunted slightly as he stuffed his arm through the other strap. "Superficial. It hurts a bit, but there's no structural damage. If you make that rib worse, you could puncture a lung, and then where would we be?"

Edrik protested, but Mudge ignored him, turning instead to Grabak.

"Well, Stig, I did what you asked; I got you out. Where do we go now? We need to be as far from here as possible by morning."

Grabak settled his pack on his back and turned his face toward the sky, drinking in the night wind that swayed the tree branches, and the stars that glittered between them.

"West," he said and smiled, his teeth gleaming in the darkness. "West to the Edge of the World, and beyond. We're going home."

CHAPTER 9

A t first, they went not west, but south, cutting through the forest. It was the shortest way off the Thane's lands, and the trees hid them from any watchers on the walls of the keep or town. The going was slow; with only filtered moonlight to guide them, Mudge wasn't the only one who kept tripping over tree roots and slipping on mossy stones.

Once, a squirrel scrabbled up a tree almost at Mudge's elbow and ran out on a branch shrieking an alarm that quickly died into a scolding mutter. It took longer for Mudge's startled heart to stop hammering. Rolf, walking just ahead, paused and half turned, teeth showing in a laughing grin. Double canines. It sent a tingling shiver up Mudge's spine.

Three dragons.

No iron bars.

Nothing but the runed collars between Mudge and the dragon magic.

This was a mistake.

But it would have been a mistake to stay, too. Stig—or rather Grabak (*that would take some getting used to*)—was right; Mudge couldn't hide in the dungeon forever. Time was running out. And surely leaving town with three dragons who only *might* kill or betray their former dungeon keeper was better than what would happen if the

Thanesson found out about Kaya. Still . . . this was a mistake. Mudge could feel the Other Dragon's resentful eyes boring through the darkness from behind. And now he had a spear.

Mudge sighed. Sometimes it seemed *all* of the available choices in life were mistakes.

Pip stirred, wriggling his furry warmth more deeply into Mudge's hood in the hollow between the pack and the back of Mudge's neck. Somehow, his presence made Mudge feel less alone.

It seemed half an eternity before the first light of dawn arrived—a sickly grayish green that oozed half-heartedly between the branches of the trees and seemed to seep into the leaf mold and matted pine needles that covered the forest floor. The pack bumped relentlessly against the bruising from the Thanesson's whip and tugged at the stitches, threatening to tear them through the skin. Mudge's cheek, which the Other Dragon had walloped, was swollen now and throbbed with every step. But Mudge kept going, doggedly putting one foot in front of the other, determined not to be the one to stop walking first.

The sun heaved itself over the treetops, bleeding rose and marigold into the scattered clouds. It was well above the horizon, and the day had begun to grow stickily warm before Grabak called a halt in a small glade where a spring bubbled out from a rocky hillside, cascading down to form a broad, clear pool before it became a tiny brook trickling away into the woods. The travelers dropped their packs against the moldering trunk of a fallen tree, slid their boots off, and clambered down the mossy bank to soak the blisters that came from walking too long in boots insufficiently acquainted with their feet.

A soft grunt from Rolf made Mudge glance over to find him, careful of his injured rib, tugging his shirt off over his head. Sunlight slid over the muscles of his shoulders and down his back. Mudge blushed and looked away. It was ridiculous, of course. Rolf had been wearing nothing but his breeks when Benit brought him to the dungeon that first day, and every day since then up until yesterday. But somehow it was different here, outside the dungeon, in the bright light of day.

Mudge couldn't help hearing the rustle of Rolf's trousers coming off and the sounds of the water as he slipped in, followed by a soft dragon hiss as the cold water closed around his body. Rolf's friend splashed into the pool a few minutes later, and Grabak followed a little more sedately. The three dragons splashed, and laughed, and called out to each other, rollicking about the pool in their smallclothes like children.

Mudge watched them, skin prickling with sweat and envy. As entirely unthinkable as stripping down to smallclothes in front of the dragons was, Mudge couldn't help imagining how good it would feel to let the cold water leach away the pain of all the bruises and lacerations.

Judging by the way Rolf moved, the cool water must be doing his rib some good. He still favored that side, awkward as he bent and twisted in the water, but his laughter was full and free, and the tightness of pain around his green eyes had eased. The line of stitches on his back stood out dark against his pale skin. They needed to be taken out, but just the idea of getting that close to the big dragon made it hard for Mudge to breathe.

Rolf saw Mudge looking and grinned.

"Jump in, Mudge," he called. "It would be good for your back."

The Other Dragon turned, and a malicious gleam came into his narrowed eyes. "When was the last time you had a bath, Mudge?"

His grin wasn't friendly like Rolf's, and Mudge's heart began to pound when the dragon moved toward the bank.

"Leave the boy alone," Grabak snapped.

The Other Dragon stopped. He turned his head to glare at Grabak. Then he turned back, scowling hungrily at Mudge. He seemed to be weighing his options.

Mudge's stomach clenched and turned over. Every muscle tensed— though whether to resist or to run, Mudge couldn't have said.

Rolf's arm arced across the surface of the pool, sending a great sheet of cold water splashing over his friend's shoulders.

The Other Dragon turned to retaliate, distracted from his prey, and the two resumed their boyish rowdiness.

Mudge let out a slow breath and stood. It would be safer away from the water.

By the time the drakes had finished splashing about and sunned themselves dry on the rocks, Mudge had made a fire in a small, rock-lined pit, careful to use well-seasoned wood so it wouldn't smoke, and had set a copper pot over it to boil some spring water for porridge.

Rolf came up from the pool while Mudge was poking through the packs and sat down on the fallen tree to put his trousers back on. Pip poked his head out of the tangle of Mudge's hair, sniffing.

"What are you looking for?" Rolf asked conversationally.

"Just seeing what's here," Mudge muttered. "I was hoping for another water skin or two. And I don't think there's a spoon in here anywhere, so we'll have to use a stick to stir the pot."

From behind Mudge, the Other Dragon scoffed. "You mean we've been lugging these packs around all night and half the day, and you don't even know what's in them?"

Mudge straightened and turned, hands on hips, to face him. "I know what I asked for, but getting it myself would have aroused suspicion. I had to call in a favor."

Pip ducked back behind Mudge's neck.

The Other Dragon opened his mouth to retort, but Grabak strode up, tucking in his shirt. "Let the boy be."

"Why?" The Other Dragon spun to glare at Grabak while jabbing a finger in Mudge's direction. "That little brute kept you locked up for more than five years while your throne was stolen out from under you. Why do you keep protecting him?"

Grabak's face remained serene and his voice even. "Mudge kept me *alive* for more than five years when I would otherwise have been killed."

The Other Dragon went livid. "You think I don't know what kind of human keeps a dragon as a pet?"

Rolf rose and placed a calming hand on his friend's shoulder. "We still need the boy to get the collars off."

"So let's get them off!" the Other Dragon snarled. "Cut off a few non-essential body parts, and the beast will be *begging* to take the collars off. And before you get all self-righteous about it, *Rolf*"—he said the name like an epithet—"remember that it's no more than the Mudge and his questioner had planned for you and me."

"Enough!" Grabak growled. "The boy is my friend. I've given him my name. He is under my protection. And you will treat him with the respect due to a friend of your king."

"King!" the Other Dragon spat. "You're not *my* king. I've sworn no oath to you."

Rolf stepped between the other two, forcing the Other Dragon to look at him. "That's true enough. But you were sworn to Tait under my father, and—"

"And your father is dead." The Other Dragon's hands clenched into fists. "And so is Tait."

Grabak growled low in his throat. "Your liege," he said, speaking with exaggerated patience, "had a lord, who had a son, who—"

"Who is pinioned," Rolf interrupted. His words sounded bitter, and his face flushed with what looked like shame. "So the oaths don't carry." He turned to the Other Dragon. "So . . . what, you're back to being a wilding now?"

"It wasn't so bad." The Other Dragon sulked. Then, under the weight of Rolf's glare, he relented. "All right, it was. But I'd rather be a wilding than bind myself to a tyrant. Or a fool." He drew a deep breath and scrubbed a hand over the back of his neck. "Look . . . I would swear to *you* if I could. You know I would. But—"

"But I'm pinioned and landless and can't take your oath. Is this what's really been eating at you?"

The Other Dragon looked at his feet, face twisted with misery. "Well, I can't swear to . . . to Nidhaug."

"No . . ." Rolf said slowly. "No more than I could." He sighed. "And you don't know Grabak."

The Other Dragon shrugged and glowered. "He'd been gone for two years when Tait found me."

Rolf laid a hand on his friend's shoulder and said gently, "Give Grabak a chance. He was my father's liege lord, and you knew my father; he wouldn't give his oath to a fool."

The Other Dragon snorted incredulously. "He sat in that rimy dungeon for *five years*, even after he knew how to get out. He abandoned his people to Nidhaug's tender mercies. He gave his name to the dungeon keeper. And you tell me he's not a fool?"

"What's five years to a dragon?" Grabak growled. Then his shoulders slumped as if under a terrible weight. "I thought my people were in good hands. And I thought . . ." He shook his head and clenched his teeth against what else he thought.

A loud hiss slashed into the tense silence, and a cloud of steam billowed around the fire pit as the copper pot boiled over.

Mudge lunged to pull the pot out of the fire, using a fold of tattered robe to avoid getting burned—but the damage was already done. A thin, white column of smoke and steam drifted upward in the still morning air.

"Trying to signal our position?" The Other Dragon's vicious kick caught Mudge hard in the shoulder, and Pip, who had been perched on that shoulder, squealed shrilly and pitched through the air as Mudge's thin body was sent sprawling away from the fire.

That was the last straw! If the Other Dragon wanted a fight, he'd get one. Mudge scrambled up and flew at the beast, landing a solid fist to his jaw and another, more glancing blow just under his ribs before the dragon realized what was happening and spun out of the way. The dragon snarled and gathered himself to return the attack, but Grabak caught him from behind. At the same time, Rolf's strong arms wrapped around Mudge.

"Stop this!" Rolf ordered. "Both of you! We can't afford to be fighting among ourselves."

The Other Dragon glared at Mudge.

Mudge squirmed in Rolf's grip and glared back. It wouldn't do to show fear.

Rolf tightened his grip and addressed his friend. "Grabak is my king, even if he isn't yours. And he was Tait's king too. If you can't respect him for his own sake yet, at least put up with him for mine."

The Other Dragon glared back for another long moment before he muttered, "Fine," and shrugged out of Grabak's loosened hold. "We should start packing up."

Grabak's scowl deepened. "Not until we've had something to eat. Why don't you go get some firewood, and we'll—"

"I said I'd put up with you, old man," the Other Dragon growled. "I didn't say I'd follow your orders."

Mudge didn't catch Grabak's response because Rolf heaved a longsuffering sigh and leaned down to murmur, "Are *you* finished, Mudge?" The dragon's breath tickled against Mudge's ear, and his low, quiet voice vibrated through his muscled chest where it pressed against Mudge's back.

A sudden, choking panic made Mudge's, "Yes," come out as an unfortunate whimper. Wriggling free of Rolf's arms, Mudge ignored the other two dragons, who had begun shouting at each other again, and looked around for Pip.

The rat lay at the base of a boulder, crumpled and unmoving. "Pip?" An odd, prickling sensation began at the back of Mudge's skull and rushed outward, turning everything numb and strangely dreamlike. Mudge scrambled toward the rat, moving as quickly as could be managed in choking slow motion. "Pip?" Mudge touched a shaking finger to Pip's tiny ear. Not even a twitch. His head was twisted too far to one side, and he wasn't breathing.

As Mudge scooped up the lifeless body of the little rat, the dragons' voices blurred together into a strangling roar that reverberated inside Mudge's head. Still kneeling, Mudge turned to look at the three dragons, posed like angry statues around the smoking campfire.

The roar worked its way through Mudge's chest and shoved its way out: "You *killed* him!"

Everything fell eerily silent for a moment. Then the Other Dragon took half a step forward, hands balling into fists.

"Killed him? Killed your filthy rat?" He took another slow step forward. "You *butchered* my friend! Cut him up like a feast day dinner. And I'm supposed to feel bad about killing a *rat*?"

He took another step toward Mudge, his breath starting to come in fast gasps.

Rolf stepped in front of him. "Stand down, Finn," he said.

Finn. Was that the Other Dragon's name?

The Other Dragon—Finn?—gaped at Rolf.

"Tait was your friend too!" he bellowed. "Don't you want to see him avenged?"

"Mudge didn't kill Tait," Rolf pointed out calmly. "He hasn't done anything to any of us except feed us, and equip us, and get us out of that dungeon."

"*Grabak* got us out. That ferrous little beast wouldn't have lifted a finger to help us if Grabak hadn't threatened him! He won't even take the rimy collars off! What good is it being free if we can't ascend? And now we're supposed to take him with us and pretend he's our friend?" Finn's voice crackled with incredulity.

Carefully cradling Pip's limp body, Mudge rose, trembling with anger, and snarled, "You can *rot* in that collar for all I care!" Then he turned and started walking—it didn't matter where, as long as it was away from the dragons. Just away. This was all such a horrible mistake.

Back at the fire, the argument continued.

"Mudge could have merely killed me to keep his secret," Grabak said. "Could have killed us all. But he chose to give up everything and risk his own life getting us free instead. And this is how you repay him?"

"It was a *rat!*" Finn roared.

"It was all the family Mudge had left!" Grabak bellowed back.

Mudge felt the hot tears boiling up inside and started walking faster, pushing deeper into the trees as the shouting gradually died away. In the solitude of the forest, the tears surged out, boiling over like the cook pot, and Mudge collapsed among the roots of a great tree, body shaking with silent, wrenching sobs, folding protectively around Pip's tiny corpse. It was ridiculous, really—all this over a dead rat. But Mudge couldn't help it.

When the sobs tapered off into shuddering gasps, Mudge sat up, using one grungy sleeve to scrub away the tears. Rolf was there. Of course. The dragons couldn't let their one means of getting free of the collars out of their sight for long—by leaving the collars on, Mudge had effectively become their prisoner. Still, prisoner was better than dead. And better Stig's prisoner than the Thanesson's. Maybe. Probably.

Rolf, still shirtless, sat on a rock a few paces off, half turned away, whittling a stick with one of the bronze knives Mudge had taken from the armory. The single-minded concentration with which he was engrossed in the task made it seem almost as if he were in a separate space from Mudge—as if he couldn't see the tears and wasn't intruding on Mudge's grief. But then he shifted absentmindedly, and the ripple of the muscles under the skin of his broad back made Mudge abruptly aware of just how present the dragon really was—and that those stitches in his back really should come out soon, now that Rolf wasn't going to die after all.

Keeping a careful watch on the dragon, Mudge drew a long, shaky breath and sat up, laying Pip gently on a cushion of moss in the fork of a tree root. Rolf's hands stilled, and his eyes focused on Mudge.

For a long, slow heartbeat they just looked at each other.

Then Rolf said, "I'm sorry, Mudge."

His voice had that low, resonant quality that had made Mudge wonder, back in the dungeon, if it was the voice he used for compulsion. Could Rolf use compulsion? If a pinioned dragon couldn't ascend because he couldn't reach the magic, then maybe he couldn't use the magic to compel people either.

There was something in Rolf's eyes, an intensity, that made it difficult to meet his gaze, and Mudge looked back down at Pip, stroking one finger over the velvety fur on his belly.

"What will you do now?" Rolf asked after a moment.

It was a good question. It clearly wasn't safe to stay with the dragons. But it wasn't safe to leave them either. A ragged boy traveling alone would be easy prey for bandits. Growing up, Mudge had scrapped and brawled often enough with the stable boys and kitchen lads, and even some of the noble sons on occasion, and could manage well enough against a single opponent of a similar size. But most men were taller and heavier than Mudge, and bandits weren't generally known for engaging in fair fights—or for being kind to women and children and other small, weak creatures. And there were worse things out there than bandits. So Mudge only said quietly, "I'm going to bury my friend."

Rolf didn't respond at first. When he finally did, his voice was solemn and earnest. "You arranged a proper pyre for my friend. I would be honored to help you make a pyre for yours."

"A pyre?" Mudge choked on something that was very nearly a laugh. The dragon must think Mudge was daft. "Rolf, my friend was a rat."

Rolf's expression went warily sheepish, and he half shrugged one shoulder. "So was mine sometimes." His gaze dropped, and his tentative smile turned sad.

"Yes," Mudge said. "Well. A pyre would make too much smoke. And Pip was afraid of fire anyway."

Painfully aware of Rolf's watching eyes, Mudge carefully positioned the rat's little paws and wrapped his tail around the curve of his body as if he were sleeping, then upended a large stone near the base of the tree, letting the centipedes and black beetles living under it scatter, and went to find a stick to dig with.

Rolf got up with a soft grunt and came to kneel on the mossy ground beside Mudge, scooping away the loosened dirt with his hands. Sometimes, as they worked, their fingers brushed against each other, and a shiver ran up Mudge's spine, tugging at the stitches.

When Pip had been properly laid to rest on a bed of moss and pine needles, and a small pile of stones had been carefully arranged to keep the scavengers away, Mudge sat down again, leaning against the trunk of the tree, wishing there was some position that didn't hurt. Rolf settled down by the tree too and went back to whittling his stick. He was so close Mudge could smell him—spring water and clean sweat and that wild something else Mudge had first noticed when listening to Rolf's lungs.

Wait a minute.

When they were preparing to leave the dungeon last night, Rolf hadn't been able to lift his baldric over his head without significant pain, and he'd barely made it through the hole in the storage room wall. But just now, he'd been digging holes and carrying rocks around —small ones, to be sure, but still. Had Mudge been wrong about Rolf's rib being broken? No, Mudge had cleaned up after the questioner enough times to know what a broken rib felt like. Mudge turned just enough to see Rolf's face.

"How is that rib feeling?"

Rolf's hands paused for half a heartbeat, then resumed whittling.

"It's . . . better." Rolf grinned. *Double canines.* "My family line is known for healing quickly."

But his healing hadn't been unusually rapid in the dungeon. Mudge frowned. "May I look?"

"If you like."

Rolf shrugged and shifted so his injured side faced Mudge. The bruising was entirely gone. Mudge leaned forward and touched the place, then probed more firmly. Rolf's skin was smooth and sun-warmed, and his ribcage moved with his breathing. He winced when Mudge pressed on the broken rib, but only a little. It was definitely much better than it had been.

"You see?" His voice rumbled through his chest, vibrating up through Mudge's fingers, and bringing with it that strange sense of intimacy from back in the dungeon. This was definitely too close to be to Rolf outside a dungeon cell.

Mudge leaned away rather too abruptly, back bumping painfully against the tree trunk, scrambling for something to say, a way to change the subject. "Yes. Well. Um . . . thank you for helping with Pip."

Rolf made no response as he moved to place his own back against the tree again and resumed whittling, shaving long, pale curls of wood off the sides of the stick with his knife. He was still much too close, but it was better.

"He's not so bad, you know," he said slowly, as if turning the words over in his mouth to test them before he spoke. "My friend, I mean, not Pip."

"Finn?" Mudge asked.

Rolf winced. "I guess you caught that."

"Oh, ach."

"Is there any way I could persuade you not to use his name until he gives it to you himself?"

Mudge frowned. "What is it about dragons and their names anyway? And not just dragons; the alfkin do the same thing, and so do ogres and some other magical creatures."

Rolf didn't answer for so long that Mudge almost decided he wasn't going to.

Finally, he said, "It has to do with the old magic. The deep magic. There is power in a name. The yotun draw on the naming magic when they craft their marks, but they only know how to name objects. The faekind could draw power from the names of living creatures. The older a name is, the more power it holds, and dragons and alfkin can hold their names for quite a long time." He shrugged. "Of course, there haven't been any fae in the world since the Breaking, but some customs remain. We are still bound by honor, if not by magic, to grant mercy and refuge to those who know and invoke our names."

A long shaving of wood flicked off Rolf's knife and landed on Mudge's lap. Mudge picked it up and began to toy with it, bending and twisting. "So if someone knows your name, you can't hurt them?"

Rolf shrugged one shoulder. "Well . . . just knowing the name isn't enough. It must be *given* you by its owner. But that's the general idea, yes." The way he said *given* made it sound like something more than a casual introduction.

"Mmm . . ." Mudge mused, tossing the shaving aside. "I can see why it might not be a good idea to give your name to an enemy, then, especially one not bound by the same traditions."

"Like a human dungeon keeper." Rolf nudged Mudge's elbow with his own and grinned again. *All those teeth!*

"It surprised me when Grabak gave you his name," Rolf went on more soberly. "His is quite an old name and would grant a fae rather a lot of power over him. Finn's is a lot older than mine, but not nearly so old as Grabak's." He stopped whittling and flipped the knife a few times between his fingers before putting it away.

"Mudge, I would appreciate it greatly if you'd not use Finn's name until he gives it to you himself." He looked soberly into Mudge's eyes and away—disconcerting. "He really is a decent fellow; he's just a bit high strung, and these past few weeks have put him under a lot of strain."

Mudge gave a sour snort. "I'll try to take that into consideration when he slits my throat while I'm sleeping."

Rolf's chuckle sounded bitter. "It's the collar. I'm sure his recent behavior hasn't been the sort that might convince you to take it off, but . . ." He sighed and turned to more fully study Mudge's face. "Finn has always been more comfortable in his ascended form. When he's stuck in his human aspect for a long period of time, he gets testy. For him, not being able to ascend is like not being fully able to breathe. He's slowly suffocating. And . . ." he turned away again and rubbed a hand over the pale fuzz growing back on his scalp before he continued more quietly. "And he is grieving for Tait."

"You miss him too," Mudge said.

Rolf held out the stick he'd been whittling and waited for Mudge to take it. It was a bit rough where the long, slender handle joined the slightly skewed bowl, but it was definitely a spoon. "Best I could do on short notice."

Mudge blinked, surprised. "Um . . . thanks."

Rolf nodded solemnly, then drew a long breath and looked down at his hands. "Finn and Tait were the only ones who stood by me," he said. "After Nidhaug killed my father, and my quartermark passed, they were the only ones." He cleared his throat. "And now, it's just Finn."

Mudge didn't know what to say. When Mudge was a child, Papa had gone first. And then the sickness took Mama. Aunt had only hard words for her sister's illegitimate half-blood child and even harder eyes. And Grandfather was the only one. The *only* one. There weren't any good words for that sort of thing, so Mudge said merely, "There's Grabak now. And . . . and me."

Rolf tipped his head back to rest against the bark of the tree. He was silent a long time. Then quietly, but clearly, he said, "Edrik. My name is Edrik. And you may call on me for refuge should you need it. Even from Finn."

A warm shiver wriggled up Mudge's spine, just as it had the first time Grabak said his name. *Magic?*

Mudge turned to stare at the dragon. His name. He'd given Mudge his name. What could Mudge possibly offer in return? Not a name; there was more than one way for a name to be dangerous. But . . . "Edrik," Mudge began—then stopped. Reconsidered. Twice. And tried again. "Edrik, would you like me to take off your collar?"

CHAPTER 10

All the way back to camp, Edrik's fingers kept drifting up to his throat. It was hard to believe the collar was really gone. He'd grown accustomed to the weight of the iron, but the burning itch of it against his skin had been a constant irritation, and its absence was a pleasure he could almost taste, like honey on his tongue. He was aware that Mudge kept flicking nervous glances at him out of the corner of his eye, but Edrik couldn't help grinning.

When the two of them arrived back at the clearing by the spring, the fire had been knocked down, and Finn and Grabak were eying each other warily across the no longer smoking embers.

As Edrik approached, Finn said, "We need to move; anyone looking for us will be following the smoke."

Grabak looked grim. "We made good time last night. A pursuit wouldn't have been rallied until this morning, so we have time to rest a little first."

Finn rolled his eyes at Edrik. "*Your* king is worried that his pet dungeon keeper won't be able to keep up."

Mudge snorted. "I'm fine. And you know he's right, Stig. We've stayed too long already."

Grabak stepped forward, opening his mouth to protest, but Mudge held up a hand. "We don't know how much of a start we got. They could have missed us right away. They could be right behind us. And that smoke would have been visible for miles."

"You need rest, Mudge," Grabak insisted.

The boy's chin jutted out. "I'm not a child."

"No." Grabak's voice was quiet, solemn. "You're not. But you are human. And you are unaccustomed to travel."

Mudge and Grabak locked eyes for several long heartbeats. Then Mudge loosed a long-suffering sigh and stomped over to kick more dirt on his tiny fire and grind out the embers under his boot. He gathered up the copper pot and several other items that he'd taken from the packs and began tucking them away again. After a moment, Grabak went to help.

Apparently, the matter was decided.

Edrik finished dressing before slipping his baldric over his head and settling his father's sword firmly in place. It would still be a while before his rib was fully healed, but the pain was already much more tolerable, and his range of movement was greatly improved. Glancing over at Mudge again, he saw a flicker of a wince as the boy adjusted a fold of his cloak to lie between the heavy pack and his whip-lacerated back, and bleak determination in his bruised face as he reached for his satchel. He was the smallest member of the party and carrying the biggest load. It wasn't right.

"Let me carry that for you, Mudge," Edrik stepped close, gesturing at the satchel. "Maybe I can't manage a full pack yet, but I could at least—"

"No." Mudge glared at him with suspicion. "It's mine. I'll carry it." He lifted the strap over his head so the satchel swung heavily against one thigh and set his jaw with a defiant scowl as he turned away.

"Wait!" Edrik grasped at the boy's elbow to stop him, then quickly released his grip when Mudge flinched and pulled away.

"Sorry." Edrik held up both hands and took a step back to show he didn't mean to seem threatening. "It's just . . . I can't ascend. I can't take my friend's oath. I can't even carry a pack. Let me do *something* useful."

Mudge stared at Edrik, mistrust warring with utter exhaustion in his expression. Grabak was right; the boy needed rest.

Edrik sighed. "I thought we decided to be friends."

Mudge opened his mouth, seeming about to refuse again, but shook his head instead and lifted the strap back over his head. He hesitated one more time before holding the satchel out to Edrik.

"My life is in here," the boy said grimly. "Keep it safe."

Edrik nodded solemnly and settled the satchel over his shoulder.

Grabak handed out nuts, dried berries, and chunks of hard, white cheese from one of the packs and took the lead, setting an easy pace and angling westward. Mudge stuck close to Grabak, seeming wary of the other two dragons, but glanced back now and then, as if making sure Edrik wasn't doing anything untoward with his satchel. Finn straggled along at the rear, keeping a watchful eye on the forest behind them, face drawn into a dark scowl.

After a while, the trees thinned, and the game trail they'd been following widened into a proper footpath.

Edrik stopped to wait, then fell into step with his friend. "Are you all right?"

Finn hissed. "This isn't how I imagined it would be."

"No." Edrik frowned. "Tait should be here."

"And we should be flying home in triumph with that ice-blasted king of yours, to throw Nidhaug off the throne." Finn growled low in his throat. "Instead, we have this ferrous child of a dungeon keeper, with his rimy iron collars. Do you know how long this is going to take if we have to walk the whole way? We'll never make it before the solstice."

Edrik's frown deepened. Twenty-one days; they would certainly be cutting it close. "Maybe if we take the river . . ." He sighed. "You might be right."

They walked in silence until Finn said, "You're better off without her, anyway."

Misery and irritation clutched at Edrik's belly. "Don't start. I love Lissara. I've always loved her. And she's all I have left."

"You should be with a woman who wants you as you are, not one who is merely willing to condescend to marry you if you meet her impossible demands."

"Enough!" Edrik snapped.

Finn opened his mouth to press his point, but glanced at Edrik's face, frowned, and said only, "At least we found your Grabak. Tait would have been—" He came to a sudden halt.

Edrik stopped too and grinned when Finn reached over to push back the neckband of Edrik's shirt.

"Your collar is gone!" Finn stared. "How?"

Edrik raised his eyebrows. "Mudge. How else?"

"You might have said something."

Edrik shrugged. "You were busy shouting."

"So . . ." Finn frowned. "What? You just asked him nicely, and he took it off?"

"More or less." A sheepish grin forced itself across Edrik's face. "I helped him bury his rat. And . . . and I gave him my name."

"You did *what*?" Finn jabbed a finger up the path toward Mudge. "He locked us up! And you saw what he did to Tait."

"He was doing his job; it wasn't personal. And it wasn't Mudge who killed Tait. Was it?"

Finn closed his eyes, then opened them and said grimly, "No, it wasn't Mudge. It was that ice-blasted hunter with the boar spear." He kicked at a stray pine cone. "But he's a *dungeon keeper*! And there's something off about that boy."

"You're one to talk. What was it you were up to when Tait found you?"

Finn at least had the grace to look uncomfortable. "That was different."

Edrik snorted. "Right. You didn't lock anyone up, you just ate them. You don't think that made you a little off?"

"There wasn't anything else to eat," Finn mumbled.

"Mudge did give Tait a real pyre. He didn't have to do that. And Grabak is right; Mudge could have killed us all when Grabak threatened him, but instead, he helped us escape. We probably owe him our lives. He doesn't want to be our enemy; he's just a boy who wants to feel safe. You should understand that better than any of us." Edrik paused. "And Grabak trusts him."

Finn opened his mouth to protest, then closed it, frowning and started walking again. "He's a human."

"Yes," Edrik said. "But he's not one of the humans who hurt you. Give him a chance."

Finn looked down at his feet, and the two of them walked on in silence.

After a while, Finn grunted. "I hit him. And I killed his rat. Humans don't forgive that sort of thing."

"Some do. Just talk to him."

"I don't know how to talk to a human—not an outsider, anyway. Some of the Vanir . . ."

"Well, you're going to have to learn sooner or later. Try pretending he's a dragon." Edrik chuckled. "Or a pretty girl. Girls are human."

Finn glared at him. "Girls are different."

Edrik grinned. "And it's a good thing, too."

The light was beginning to dim toward sunset when Grabak finally called a halt again. They'd put a fair distance between themselves and the glade with the pool, and even Finn was satisfied that it was safe to stop for the night. They dropped their packs against a protective stone outcropping that jutted up in the middle of a small clearing, and Finn set off to gather firewood while Grabak went to the nearby brook to fill the waterskins.

Edrik slipped Mudge's satchel off his shoulder and went to give it back to the boy. Mudge stood leaning against the outcrop, with his pack at his feet. He looked up warily at Edrik's approach, and Edrik was startled by the raw weariness in the boy's haggard face. They should have stopped a long time ago. What had Grabak been thinking? The muscles of Mudge's jaw clenched with determination when he reached for his satchel, and he staggered slightly when he took the weight of it, but he grimly nodded his thanks and set it down next to his pack. The boy's hands were shaking.

"Firewood, next, I suppose." Mudge's voice sounded hollow, but there was an echo of obstinacy hiding in it.

Edrik shook his head. "You're exhausted. Stay here and watch the packs; I'll help Finn with the firewood."

Mudge's eyes narrowed. He pushed away from the stone and straightened his shoulders. "I can keep going as long as you can." But he swayed a little on his feet.

"No." Edrik frowned. "You can't. You're a human. Dragons are stronger and need less sleep. You'd kill yourself if you tried to keep a dragon's pace for too long."

Mudge glared at him, and Edrik tried to make his voice conciliatory.

"Look, I admire your spirit, Mudge, but don't be a fool. You need to rest." He put a hand on the boy's shoulder. "And someone really should keep an eye on the packs. The last thing we need is rodents or rock gnomes making off with our supplies."

Mudge sidled away from Edrik's touch and mumbled, "Fine," before settling one shoulder against the stone again.

When Edrik came back with his first load of scavenged wood, Grabak was building a fire against the sheltered side of a boulder, and Mudge had fallen asleep curled up against the outcrop with his satchel clutched to his chest. They let the boy sleep while they finished setting up camp.

Edrik took the first watch and then woke Finn for the next before kicking his boots off and sprawling out on the ground next to Mudge with one of the packs for a pillow. He wanted to be close enough to intervene if Finn tried to go after Mudge in the night.

He must've slept hard, lost in his dreams of Lissara, because he didn't wake again until sometime after dawn, when he heard someone stoking the fire and clanking around with the cook pot. He sat up, stretching sore muscles, and looked over to find Mudge crouched by the fire, stirring his customary pot of morning porridge with the crooked spoon Edrik had whittled for him. Grabak crouched on the other side of the fire, cradling a steaming tin cup in his hands. Across the clearing, Finn was rolling out of his cloak and scrubbing at his stubbled face with his fingers.

Edrik stuffed his feet back in his boots and wandered over to the fire. Grabak fished a tin cup off a flat rock on one side of the fire pit and handed it to Edrik. The steam that rose from it had a strange, spicy floral scent to it.

Edrik scowled. "What is this?"

"It'll help with the pain and stiffness," Mudge said in a matter-of-fact tone. Then seeing Edrik's expression, he scowled and pointed, "Your rib. And your boots are as new as mine are. But you don't have to drink it if you don't want to."

Edrik sniffed the stuff again, trying to decide, and then took a small sip. It wasn't bad.

Finn hobbled over, carrying his boots in one hand. "Flying doesn't give you blisters," he grumbled.

Grabak handed him a cup of Mudge's tea.

Edrik turned, sipping his own tea, to scan the trees at the edge of the clearing. Something about knowing someone might be following made it easy to feel as if he were being watched.

Behind him, Finn yelped and then swore. Edrik spun to find Finn sitting on the ground clutching his foot with one hand and smacking his boot against the ground with his other.

"What's the matter?" Edrik asked.

"It bit me!" Finn bellowed. "Rimy, ferrous spider in my boot! I hate spiders. Worse than scale mites!" He smacked the ground again with his boot and then stripped off his stocking and peered at his foot. "You can see the fang marks," he complained. "And it's starting to swell up."

Grabak grunted. "Better have Mudge take a look at it."

Mudge, stirring the pot, glanced up. "I wouldn't worry about it too much," he said. "The spiders around here aren't dangerous." He went back to stirring, then stopped. "Except . . . it's not a great hairy thing, is it—sort of grayish brown with pale yellow markings and black forelegs?"

Finn poked at the spot he'd been whacking and swore again. "Yes. Is that bad?"

Mudge frowned and put down the spoon. "It's . . . unfortunate."

Finn frowned. "How unfortunate?"

Mudge shook his head regretfully and squinted up at the sky. "Very. Most likely be over with by noon."

Edrik's stomach clenched.

"There has to be something you can do," Finn pleaded. "Some kind of herbs, or . . . or something."

"I could cut off your foot," Mudge offered conversationally. "I've never cut one off a live dragon before." He shrugged and shook his head. "Only it wouldn't really make any difference."

Finn looked sick.

"Mudge!" Grabak growled.

Mudge shot the Drake an annoyed scowl and sighed. "Fine." He turned back to Finn. "It's just going to swell slightly and itch for a couple of hours. It's unfortunate only because I would have liked to see you suffer for at least a day or two."

Finn stared at the boy, letting his words sink in. Then, slowly, a relieved grin spread over his face. "It was a joke," he said, making sure.

Mudge shrugged and looked coolly back at Finn. "You deserved it."

Finn shook his head and looked down. "Yes." He upended his boot to make sure nothing else lurked inside before he stuffed his foot in it and stood up. "Yes, I probably did. Look . . . Mudge . . . I'm sorry about your rat." He leaned over to pat Mudge awkwardly on the shoulder, then hobbled past Edrik, toward the nearest trees. Apparently, he'd decided to take Edrik's advice and be nice to the boy.

Mudge watched Finn go, a troubled frown drawing his brows together.

Grabak cleared his throat. "Mudge," he said sternly, "did you put that spider in his boot?"

Mudge turned back and raised an eyebrow. "I'm shocked that you would suggest such a thing, Stig."

Grabak snorted and shook his head. "Don't do it again, Mudge."

"I won't." Mudge gave the porridge a petulant jab with the lopsided spoon. "He's gone and apologized, and that takes all the fun out of it."

"I'm serious." Grabak's voice had gone sharp and insistent. "We're not in your dungeon anymore, and it isn't wise to antagonize a dragon. A Vanir dragon would be bad enough—but at least he'd answer to his liege lord if he harmed you. A wilding—well, he'll get that collar off eventually, with or without you, and when he does, you don't want to be his enemy."

Mudge stared at the old Drake. "I don't think I have much of a choice. Haven't you been paying attention? He already wants me dead."

"He only wants his collar off," Edrik said. "And he would be a lot more useful if he could ascend. He could scout behind us to see how close our pursuers are and fly ahead to find the easiest paths. He could guide us to game, and berries, and clean water, and—"

Mudge yanked the pot off the coals. "And I'm sure that would be very convenient for you, especially since you'd have one less mouth to feed, what with me being dead."

Edrik held up a placating hand. "I'm just asking you to think about it."

"I *have* thought about it." The boy scowled and pushed his fingers into the tangled nest of his hair at the back of his neck, perhaps searching absently for his missing rat. "What kind of monster do you think I am? Do you think I *like* keeping him collared? I see how he frets. He probably feels as if he's become—" Mudge stopped and looked at his feet.

Edrik felt his cheeks flush, but he managed to keep his voice even when he said, "as if he's become pinioned."

Mudge cleared his throat. "Yes. Sorry." He shrugged. "And what if something happens to me while he's still wearing that collar and he can't get it off? Of *course* I've thought about it. And if I thought for a moment that I'd live to see the sun set—" He froze, his face going ashen.

Edrik turned to see what the boy was looking at.

Finn stood just inside the clearing at the edge of the trees, listening, eyes fastened intently on Mudge. When he saw them all looking at

him, he stalked the remaining paces to the fire and crouched down
beside Edrik.

Mudge watched Finn warily, then shifted his gaze to Edrik.

"Look," he said, tossing a sidelong glance at Grabak, "what if I
take off Stig's collar instead? He could scout for us just as easily."

Grabak slowly set his cup down. "You would do that? Now?" He
frowned. "I am not pinioned, Mudge. What makes you think it's safe to
free me?"

Mudge shrugged and looked at his feet. "You said you were my
friend."

"And you trust me?" Grabak pressed gently. "After what I threatened . . . Kaya . . . with, you trust me?"

Mudge's face shifted through a pensive frown to an impish, defiant
grin before he looked up again at Grabak. "Maybe I'd just rather be
devoured by a friend than a stranger. Do you want it off or not?"

Grabak scrubbed both hands slowly over his face. Then he said,
softly but very clearly, "No."

Mudge stared at him. "But—"

"Not yet," Grabak interrupted. "It has been nearly a year since . . .
since Edrik and his friends left home. Much can change in a year. I
have no idea which dragons might stand with Nidhaug and whether
any might still stand with me. And if my wife was in league with him
from the beginning . . ." He stopped, staring into the fire as if he might
find answers there.

Mudge's eyebrows rose. "You think your wife betrayed you?"

Grabak sighed. "I don't like to think it of her, but as I said, we
parted badly. I don't know. I haven't been able to feel the bond since . .
." One hand drifted up to finger the iron collar at his throat, and his last
word died off in a soft hiss.

"But I thought you could only bond with a woman who really
loved you," Mudge said. "Deep magic and all that. If she loved you,
why would she betray you?"

"There is more than one kind of love, young Mudge." Grabak
sighed. "She loved her brother too. He was drunk more often than he
was sober. Ran up gambling debts. Used women like shiny new toys

until he grew bored with them or they broke, and then he discarded them. But . . . she loved him." He looked off into the trees to the west. "Perhaps her ability to love so thoroughly and unconditionally was one of the things that drew me to her in the first place."

Grabak was silent for several long moments until Mudge cleared his throat self-consciously and said, "I still don't understand."

The old Drake's gaze shifted to the fire. "He killed a man." His shoulders rose and fell in a hopeless shrug. "I don't think it was intentional, just two drunken hotheads who took things too far. But the man was still dead. And because the perpetrator was a dragon, judgment fell to me. The victim was a human—the son of an influential Vanir trader. The humans wanted blood. A life for a life. Some of the older dragons saw no reason a dragon should be punished at all for killing a mere human. I wanted to maintain peace, so I . . ." He scrubbed his palms over the stubble on his jaw.

"You banished him," Edrik said. "I remember."

Grabak nodded but didn't look up. "I thought it a good compromise. And perhaps it was, except he hadn't learned his lesson." He sighed. "Mirra was furious with me for sending her brother away. She insisted the man's death was just an unfortunate accident, and I was overreacting. She kept up a regular correspondence with her brother in his exile, making sure to describe to me all the ways he was suffering at my unjust hand. And it wasn't long before he had run up debts again, this time with some unsavory humans in a port town built on top of enough iron to keep him from ascending when they came for him."

"Shrike's Hollow," Mudge murmured.

Grabak inclined his head. "Mirra begged me to pay them and bring her brother home where she could help him stay out of trouble. She pleaded. She demanded. She threatened. I said he wouldn't stay out of trouble no matter where he was, and I was glad he was making it somewhere else for a change because I was tired of having to clean it up. She called me a— Well, we both said things we shouldn't have." Grabak scrubbed at his face again. "I didn't relent on the banishment; as king, how could I? But in the end, I agreed to pay off his debt and make sure he was safe. As her husband, how could I not? But we . . . we parted badly."

The firelight played over Grabak's face in the pale morning light, making old man creases where there were none. After a moment, he went on. "It was a trap. His revenge, I think. He gloated when they caught me. He said he'd planned the whole thing. He said he knew I'd be the one to come because I couldn't let anyone else know I was helping him in his exile. He thought he had everything under control. They killed him anyway. They would have killed me too, but someone had heard the commotion and called the town watch."

He looked up at Edrik. At Finn. And settled on Mudge. "I don't know if she helped form the plan, or if he just used her to get me there, like he used everyone else. I might never know for sure." He looked back into the fire, brows furrowed as if he were seeing something there besides flames and ashes.

Mudge frowned. "But if I took the collar off, you'd be able to sense her, right? You'd be able to tell. After all this time, wouldn't it be a relief to know?"

"Maybe. Maybe not. I'd sense the bond—assuming she still lives. I might be able to sense her general mood, if she were willing. But it would not tell me more than that."

Grabak shrugged one shoulder. "Dragonwives are much better than their husbands at reading the currents of the bond. If you take off the collar, she will know not only my mood, but about how far away I am, and in which direction, and she'll know that I am coming to her. Whether she's complicit or not, I'll lose any advantage I might have gained through surprise. Better to leave it for now, I think." He inclined his head in a way that closed the subject politely but emphatically.

For a time, no one said anything.

It was Finn who broke the silence. "We still need a scout. And I have no bonded wife at home to give away our position."

Mudge snorted. "You'd turn into a dragon and bite off my head the moment you were free."

"He'd do no such thing." Edrik wished he was as sure as he hoped he sounded.

"No? What's going to stop him?" Mudge said. "I can't fight a dragon. You're pinioned. And Grabak won't let me take off his collar."

"I'm already a dragon." Finn smirked. "And I don't like the taste of human."

Mudge glared at him. "That's such a comfort."

Finn's face went serious, and he touched his forehead in a gesture of apology that had not been fashionable for at least half a century; clearly, he'd spent too long in that cave. "Forgive me, Mudge. Please. This is . . . difficult for me." He cleared his throat and tilted his head as his eyes searched the face of his former dungeon keeper. "I heard you say you might be willing to remove my collar. Was it the truth?"

Mudge seemed caught off guard by Finn's change in tone. "If I thought there were enough iron pitchforks in the vicinity to make you think twice about ripping me to shreds."

Finn edged forward, shifting from his crouch onto his knees, eyes still fixed on the boy's face. "Edrik tells me I've misjudged you, and I trust him with my life. I would like to trust you too." His voice took on a formal cadence Edrik hadn't heard since Finn swore his oath to Tait. "It is . . . difficult for me because you have been a dungeon keeper, and I . . ." His shoulders tensed. "I . . . have been the monster in a dungeon keeper's pit." His eyes closed, and his voice became a cracked whisper. "The opening was too high up to reach as a man and too small to fit through if I ascended. And my keepers were . . . not kind." He was silent for a moment.

Mudge cleared his throat. "So when you say you don't like the taste of humans . . ."

Finn opened his eyes. He looked tired. Defeated. "It was not by choice." He leaned forward, his gaze intensifying, the firelight making the predatory planes of his face gleam red in the gray morning light. "What if . . ." He paused, sizing up the skinny boy across the fire. "What if I give you my name?" His voice was soft but fell into the taut silence of the clearing like a stone. "If I give you my name and promise not to hurt you, will you take it off?"

For a long heartbeat, Mudge didn't speak. Didn't move. Just

studied the dragon's face, weighing what he saw there. At last, he said, nearly in a whisper, "All right . . . Other Dragon."

He rose slowly to his feet, and Finn did the same, then stepped around the fire to stand in front of the boy. "Finn." His voice was a trembling rasp. "My name is Finn. And I swear to you, Mudge, I will not harm you if you set me free."

Mudge's hand trembled slightly as he reached up to touch Finn's collar with one finger. The muscles in the boy's narrow jaw worked as he slowly clenched his teeth and looked Finn in the eye for one more long heartbeat, weighing. Then the boy's long fingers splayed out to touch certain runes on either side of the collar's latch point, and Edrik saw something he'd missed when Mudge had removed his own collar —the boy flinched when the latch sprang open, and all the blood drained from his face.

Finn's breath burst out in a joyous laugh as the collar came away, and he stretched his arms toward the sky.

"Not here!" Edrik snapped, just in time. Finn shot him a look somewhere between annoyance and apology before he turned and loped away from the campfire.

He was barely beyond the tree line when the crack of timber and a rumbling vibration in the earth announced his ascension, and a moment later, he sprang into view again, as the great gray wings of his ascended form carved into the sky above the forest. The dragon slowly circled, gaining altitude as he scanned the forest around them. He caught an updraft rising from the sun-warmed earth, and the beat of his wings slowed. Then he stooped toward the ground one last time, sweeping low over the watchers in the clearing, and emitted a low, rumbling hiss before spiraling upward again. Higher he climbed, and higher still, until anyone watching from below might have thought him a hawk or an eagle riding the upper currents, searching for prey. Then he turned eastward, winging swiftly into the sun.

Edrik ached to go with him, to feel the air beneath his wings, the warmth of the sun on his scales, and to see the land rolling away far below. He'd dreamed of it as long as he could remember. But it would never be; he was pinioned. He sighed and turned back to his two earth-bound companions. "No nearby pursuit," he reported. "That's what Finn's signal meant."

"Is he coming back?" Mudge's voice was almost a whisper, and Edrik glanced over to see the boy standing rigid by the fire, clutching Finn's iron collar in his fingers and staring wide-eyed in the direction Finn had taken.

Edrik chuckled. "Of course he'll be back. He's just gone to stretch his wings and scout around a bit."

Mudge blinked and shivered. Then he drew a deep breath and grinned in a way that might have looked genuine if it hadn't been for the shadow clinging behind his eyes. "Well, Stig," he said merrily, "Finn's collar is off. What odds will you lay that I'll still be alive at sundown?"

Grabak sat down on a rock and sipped his tea. "I'll not wager over your life, Mudge."

"No?" Mudge's eyes narrowed. "Isn't that what you did when you said I must kill you or free you?"

Grabak's brows drew together, and he looked down at the cup in his hands. "Mudge," he said, "I . . ." He shook his head.

The boy turned to Edrik. "What about you, Rolf?" he asked. Then frowned. "Edrik, I mean. Would you care to make a wager?"

Edrik ignored the question, instead gesturing at the runed iron in Mudge's hand.

"Did that hurt you?" he asked. "When you took it off, you winced."

The boy's false merriment died away, and he turned to tuck the collar in his satchel. "It isn't meant to be removed when the prisoner is still alive. There are . . . penalties."

"And yesterday, when you took mine off, that hurt you too?"

Mudge scowled down at his feet. "And when I take Grabak's off, it will hurt again. Sometimes things hurt. It doesn't mean they aren't worth doing."

"What about when you let us through the archway back in the dungeon? Did that hurt you?"

"It doesn't matter."

"It does matter," Edrik said. "How's your back? Carrying that pack can't have been good for it."

Mudge's dark eyes met Edrik's in a hot glare. "My back is my own business . . . and none of yours. I'm going to get more firewood." He stalked off into the trees.

Edrik's gaze met Grabak's, and the two of them just looked at each other for a long moment. Then Grabak set down his cup and fixed Edrik with a piercing gaze. "Don't act like Mudge's friend unless you mean to *be* his friend. You will not play games with this one."

Edrik shook his head and muttered, "He does make you *want* to be his friend, though, doesn't he?"

Grabak's frown deepened, but he said nothing.

Edrik shrugged. "It's an odd trait to find in a dungeon keeper. Especially one so young."

The old Drake picked up his cup again and took a deliberate sip of Mudge's tea, seeming to mull over his response. Finally, he murmured, "Mudge is not so odd as you might think. Nor perhaps so young either."

CHAPTER 11

It was well past midday when Finn returned, dropping straight from the sky into the campsite. Heart pounding, Mudge dodged one sweeping wing and leapt up to help Edrik stamp out the sparks blown out of the fire pit by the wind of the dragon's passing.

The great stone-gray beast settled into the middle of the clearing, shifting on his feet as he folded his wings and blew a trickle of smoke from one nostril. Then he seemed almost to melt, shedding a cascade of glittering dust as Finn diminished to his human aspect.

"Sun and stars, Finn!" Edrik bellowed, brushing a cloud of the dust off his tunic and trousers. "Your locus is right over there!" He waved an arm at the forest.

"Sorry," Finn muttered, shaking dust from his own shoulders.

"What is this stuff?" Mudge rubbed some of the dust between thumb and fingers. It was powder fine and slightly warm to the touch, and it shimmered softly through a rainbow of colors, like sunlight on soap bubbles, before going dark and dull like ordinary dust.

"Probably his spleen," Edrik said in a low growl and stomped over to put the fire back in order.

"I said I was sorry." Finn went to help his friend

Stig chuckled softly. "It's dragon dust." Seeing Mudge's blank expression, he explained. "A dragon's ascended form is rather larger than his human aspect."

"Like a cat is rather larger than a mouse." Mudge smirked wryly. "I noticed."

Stig's grin broadened. "You always were an observant child," he teased. Then his voice took on a lecturing tone that reminded Mudge of Grandfather when he was playing tutor. "The additional mass needed for ascension does not merely appear from nowhere; new material cannot be created out of nothingness. Rather, the magic draws tiny bits of material from the dragon's surroundings and incorporates them into his ascended form. When the dragon diminishes back to his human form, his body sheds the unneeded mass. If the material's point of origin is close enough in relation to the dragon, the magic will put it back as it was. For example, a dragon's clothing, being very close to the dragon's body, is usually restored to its original condition. And if a dragon diminishes close enough to the location where he ascended— within the locus—most of the other borrowed material will also be restored. But if its original location is too far away, the material will merely be reduced to its component particles and shed as dragon dust."

Grabak put his hand on Mudge's shoulder, nudging gently toward the fire pit. As the two of them moved to join the other dragons, Grabak continued. "A skilled dragon can draw most of his mass from the air and perhaps from skimming just the surfaces of the ground or nearby objects. It leaves hardly a trace."

Edrik was kneeling by the fire, jabbing irritably at the coals. Finn sat on a stump cradling a water skin. Grabak took a seat on a rounded stone near the fire pit, and Mudge sank down to sit cross legged on the ground nearby.

"A thoughtless or inexperienced dragon," Grabak went on, "will just leave a crater. Either way, it's only good manners to put things back where you found them when practicable." He directed a mean-ingful glare at Finn. "Or at the very least, to dust off away from other people."

Edrik frowned. "Let him be. He was a forsaken; there was no one to teach him. Tait found him up north of the Spine."

"Tait was teaching me," Finn said with a touch of petulance. "I just forget sometimes."

"Forsaken." Grabak frowned. "Forgive me, I didn't know. We all forget sometimes. Even after several centuries."

"What does that mean?" Mudge asked impatiently. "You keep speaking as if everyone knows what you're talking about."

The three dragons looked away, obviously uncomfortable. Then Grabak cleared his throat and said, "Sometimes, a dragon fathers a child with a woman who is not his wife or acknowledged mate and abandons them both—he forsakes them. Often, the child's mother doesn't even realize the man she lay with was a dragon—not everyone's grandfather knows to check the teeth. Such children usually grow up believing themselves to be human, but when a male child reaches his full growth, he gains the ability to ascend, just like any other dragon." He stopped, frowning.

Finn said in a subdued voice, "And then the villagers collect their iron pitchforks."

The awkward silence that followed was broken by Edrik, who asked, "So are you going to tell us what you saw, or not, Finn?"

Finn shrugged. "I circled around and flew over the keep from the east and worked outward from there. There's no real pursuit to speak of. They have the dogs out, but they seem to be leading the hunters in circles."

Mudge chuckled. "Then it worked."

"What worked?" Edrik frowned.

"The rabbits. I cut the rags you washed up with in the dungeon into strips and tied them to the legs of some of the Thane's rabbits." Mudge shrugged. "And then 'accidentally' left the hutch unlatched. The rabbits must have spread your scents all over the forest by now."

An appreciative grin spread across Edrik's face, and Grabak chuckled. "Well done." He gestured for Finn to continue his report.

"Well . . ." Finn said uncertainly, "it seems to me that if we want to get back to the Aerie before the solstice . . ." He glanced over at Edrik with a slight frown. "We're going to need to travel faster than we have been. Flying would be fastest of course, but I can only carry one person, so unless Grabak wants to take off his collar and help, flying isn't really an option."

Grabak said nothing, only scowled deeply at the fire.

Finn went on. "The river seems the next best alternative—faster than walking, and it goes in the right direction. And on the river, we could go through the alfkin wood instead of around it, which would save us a week or more. So I scouted north to the Drasil and followed it west. There's a tributary not far from here that flows into a bend of the main river." He shook his head. "Of course, we would have to . . . acquire . . . a boat. And maybe compel a boatman. That would slow us down and might draw attention or pursuit, but we have no coin to hire either one."

"I do." Mudge's cheeks warmed as all three dragons turned to stare. "A little."

"Keep your coin for starting over, Mudge," Grabak ordered, looking up from the fire.

Mudge met the old Drake glare for glare. "Don't tell me what I can and can't do with my own money. I need a fast way out of here as much as you do."

Grabak held Mudge's gaze with his own for one more long heartbeat, then nodded and turned back to frown at the fire.

Finn continued his report. "If we keep angling southwest, we'll come to the edge of some cultivated lands in another two or three days. There's a village there, edged up against the river."

"Grebe's Landing." A tendril of foreboding took root in the pit of Mudge's stomach.

Finn shrugged. "If you say so. A small Ratatosk barge town is riding at anchor there at present. If we get there before the Toskies leave, we should be able to find a boat to take us downriver. One way, or another."

"Have you been there, Mudge?" Edrik asked.

"No," Mudge admitted. "The Shrike's Keep lands only extend to the far edge of the forest; Grebe's Landing belongs to the March Lord. But . . . um . . . we're not so very far from Shrike's Hollow yet that people wouldn't know me as the Thane's dungeon keeper. And the March Lord would send me back."

"You do have a rather . . . distinctive . . . appearance, Mudge."
Grabak frowned. "And a reputation."

Mudge squirmed under the piercing scrutiny of three dragons' eyes
as they considered. "I like looking distinctive. It keeps people from
looking too closely."

"Distinctive?" Edrik snorted. "Disreputable, I'd say, especially
with that black eye Finn gave you on the way out of the dungeon." He
frowned. "We could clean you up and cut your hair. That would make
you less recognizable." He turned to the other two dragons. "Can
anything be done about his clothes?"

Grabak frowned. "We'll think of something."

There was a brief, uncomfortable silence, and then Finn finished
his report. "There's a run-down apple orchard at the edge of the forest.
The well is still good—I checked—and the cottage roof seems fit to
keep out most of the rain, so it would be a good place to spend the
night and clean up before we go into town."

The others kept talking about the details of the plan and of what
Finn had seen on his scouting flight, but Mudge stopped listening. The
tendril of foreboding in Mudge's gut sent out twisting stems and
branches. And over the next two and a half days, as they walked, the
vine leafed out, blossomed, and bore a panicky sort of fruit that, along
with the pain of the whip wounds, kept Mudge from eating or sleeping
properly. At least Edrik was carrying the satchel. And Mudge's pack
grew steadily lighter as their provisions dwindled, and Finn and
Grabak took on more of the load so Mudge could move faster.

They came to the orchard steading late in the afternoon on the third
day. The cottage was cozy and well built, crumbling a bit at the
corners, but certainly sound enough for their needs. The cider barn at
the other end of the orchard and a nearby storage shed had fared nearly
as well. The steading had probably been abandoned after the last
outbreak of plague, which forced the reduced populations to draw back
closer to the towns for protection.

They cleared the bird nests from the cottage chimney, collected
firewood, and settled in for the night. Mudge was helping Grabak make
stew out of the last of the dried meat from Shrike's Hollow and some

roots they'd dug from the remnants of the cottage garden when Finn and Edrik strolled in, laughing boisterously.

"Hoy, Mudge!" Finn called out with a mischievous glint in his eye. "Did you see the setup out in the cider barn?"

He said it like the setup for a joke, and Mudge's skin prickled, dreading the punchline.

"There's a screw pump to bring in water from the stream for washing the apples." Edrik grinned in a manner that said he was in on the joke. "The wood's starting to rot a bit at the top, but it still works."

"And," Finn added, "there's a trough that runs from the pump to a washtub big enough for scrubbing down a stinky young dungeon keeper who will stand out among decent townsfolk like a pig in a henhouse."

"I do not stink," Mudge grumbled sulkily, still slicing roots for the stew.

Grabak chuckled. "You didn't when we left, young Mudge, but you've spent a few days tramping through the woods without washing up much, and dragons have sensitive noses."

Desperation welled up inside, and Mudge struggled to stuff it back down. "Tomorrow. When the sun is out to help things dry."

Finn's grin broadened. "It's going to rain tomorrow. I could taste it in the air high up when I was scouting yesterday."

Maybe the dragons could be distracted. "Tonight, I should remove the stitches I put in Edrik's back. If they stay in much longer, they'll just make the scarring worse."

"That's a good idea." Edrik grinned. "Right after your bath."

Mudge continued slicing. "It'll be easier if I do it before."

"Nonsense," Edrik insisted. "My stitches have waited this long. A little longer won't make any difference. Besides, we already filled the tub."

"In the morning, I promise."

The dragons weren't buying it.

Finn took a step closer, and his grin went feral. "Circle around the other side, Edrik, I bet between the two of us we can catch him and get the job done."

Mudge slammed down the root and brandished the knife—iron, not bronze—glaring back and forth between Edrik and Finn. "The first one to touch me loses a hand."

The two younger dragons laughed uproariously.

Grabak said sternly, "Mudge!" And then more gently, "It needs doing. You're too recognizable. It'll be all right."

Mudge's heart pounded. They were right, of course. If someone sent word back to the Thane that his dungeon keeper was in Grebe's Landing, they'd all be in trouble. Besides, Mudge was too small to fight off even one of the dragons, let alone all three.

"Fine," Mudge grumbled and set down the knife, noticing with grim satisfaction that all of the dragons relaxed subtly in relief. "But I'll do it my way. By myself."

Edrik held up a placating hand. "Just scrub up a bit, and then we'll cut your hair. We'll find you some better clothes once we're closer to the town. Someone's bound to have some wash hanging out."

"Not if it's raining," Mudge snapped.

Grabak rose to his feet. "I'll walk you down there, Mudge," he offered. "And I'll keep an eye on these two to make sure you're not disturbed." He directed a warning glare at the other dragons.

Mudge collected the satchel and pushed the cottage door open. The sun was just beginning to set, edging the billowy white clouds in delicate shades of pink—colors that were echoed in the carpet of fallen apple blossoms that covered the ground between the trees. It was a lovely spot, but Mudge had a hard time appreciating it while trudging with Grabak between rows of apple trees that stood at attention like disapproving guards making sure the prisoner reached the hangman.

"Are you all right?" Grabak asked.

Mudge shrugged and said nothing. It wasn't until they stood looking down at the half filled wooden washtub that Mudge asked the question. "Do you think Kaya would be safe with them? With Finn and . . . and Edrik?"

Grabak must have heard the tremor in Mudge's voice. His own voice was gentle when he spoke. "Kaya?" He waited until Mudge looked up into his face and then asked, "You plan to let us meet her then?"

Mudge looked down again. "I'm still deciding. Do you think she would be safe?"

Grabak laid a fatherly hand on Mudge's shoulder. "There's only one way to know that for sure. But you must judge for yourself." He squeezed Mudge's shoulder reassuringly once and then went out, closing the door behind him.

Mudge stood by the tub for a long time, just looking at the water.

Kaya.

Until Stig issued his ultimatum, Mudge hadn't thought anyone even knew about Kaya anymore. Except Aunt, of course. Kaya had been Mudge for so long that she rarely even thought of herself as Kaya. Truth told, she rarely even thought of herself as *her*self anymore. She was just Mudge. Being Mudge was what kept her safe. But Mudge wouldn't keep her safe here. And no one would recognize Kaya.

Moving slowly, Mudge stripped off the tattered robe and let it fall to the floor. She'd wash it later and cut it up for rags. She removed the hooked pins from the end of the bandaging that wrapped around her upper torso. That would need to be washed too. Setting her jaw, she began to unwind the long strip, watching in the dim light of the sunset coming in through the small, high windows as, little by little, her body was revealed. A woman's body. Skinny and wiry and wearing a man's breeks, but underneath everything, a woman's body nonetheless. Sort of.

She thought of Vivianne in her scented bath with her golden hair and her soft, pale curves. No amount of binding her chest, no amount of hiding in baggy robes and walking with a swagger would ever make anyone mistake Vivianne for a boy. Kaya would never be that kind of woman. Not the kind men watched at night around the festival fires and crept off with into the darkness. Not the kind a man like Edrik would want. But of course, that didn't matter, because Edrik had a beautiful princess waiting for him to return triumphant with the missing king and save her kingdom from the Black Dragon—just like one of Stig's fae stories.

Mudge still wasn't certain what it was she'd felt when listening to the dragon's lungs or while he sat stonily watching her as she worked. She only suspected she knew what she'd felt watching him swim in the pool at the spring and when his fingers had brushed against hers in the soil of Pip's grave. She was afraid to think about how she'd felt at night as they traveled, staring into the darkness, kept awake by the pain in her back and the excruciating sense of his nearness. But she was absolutely certain of what she'd felt when Edrik spoke of his princess. Raw envy. The hungry gnawing of pure jealousy. And it frightened her. Mudge, of all people, had no business feeling that way.

What about Kaya? The thought came unbidden.

Mudge sighed. Kaya was hardly even a real person anymore.

But she had been, once. She'd been a boisterous little girl with a laughing, indulgent father and a beautiful, merry mother. She'd raced barefoot along the bobbing walkways of the Ratatosk barge town, giddy with the sunshine and the music of the wind in the leaves on the riverbank. At night, when the weather was fine, she'd taken her blankets up to the roof of the shabby blue houseboat and watched the stars roll solemnly across the sky in their grand promenade. Yes, 'twas a time not long past, as the storytellers said, before her world was broken, when Kaya had been a real person, and not just someone a lonely dungeon keeper dreamed of now and then when festival music drifted down the stairs from the kitchens.

And now . . .

What was left of Kaya?

She—Mudge—Kaya—opened the satchel and dug out the small cake of soap. It smelled of rose petals and lavender, and she'd longed for a day when she might actually use it ever since Grandfather had given it to her all those years ago. And now that the day had come, using it seemed decadent—almost indecent.

She laid the soap aside and tugged the neatly-folded clothes out from the bottom of the satchel, where they had been tucked away for nearly as long as the soap, waiting for Kaya to leave the dungeon and stop being Mudge. She unfolded the items one by one and carefully laid them to one side. A soft, pale shift. A blouse and bodice. A long brown skirt. And the ruffled green petticoat that had her life's savings stitched into the hems.

The bodice would be tricky. It was a cast-off from one of the Thanesson's women whom Mudge had tended, and it laced up the back, as was fashionable among women wealthy enough to keep body servants. But a front-lacing peasant bodice would have been harder to acquire without arousing suspicion. So she would just have to manage.

The last thing she drew from the satchel, wrapped carefully in rags to prevent it from breaking, was the shell comb that had belonged to her mother, a gift, she'd been told, from her father. As she turned it over in her hand, sunset light shimmered off the intricately carved surface, and Mudge was, once again, the little girl sitting on the deck at her mother's knee; she could almost hear the echo of her mother's voice as she hummed the river songs and worked the tangles out of Kaya's hair.

She hesitated one last time, gazing down at the still water in the washtub as if trying to scry the future. Then, drawing a deep breath, Kaya shucked off the dingy breeks, clutched her soap tightly in one hand and the comb in her other, like a talisman, and stepped into the chill water.

No going back.

CHAPTER 12

E drik slid the knife lightly down the honing stone a few more times, tested the edge again, and set it carefully aside with the other one he'd already sharpened. As he took up the next, Finn surged to his feet across the cottage's one small room and began to pace.

Edrik frowned. "You all right?"

"It's like another rimy dungeon in here. How long is that ferrous half-blood squirrel of a dungeon keeper planning to take? I'll grant you he was pretty grimy, but there's not that much of him to wash." He stomped toward the door. "I need to get out of here."

As he reached for the latch, a knife—the iron one Mudge had left behind on the cutting board—thumped into the wood of the door, skimming close enough to Finn's hand to leave a bloody line across one knuckle. He stumbled back, clutching his hand as the shock of the iron meeting his blood passed, then swore and whirled to face Grabak, who glowered back at him from beside the hearth.

"You'll stay here until Mudge comes back," the old Drake growled.

"Or what?" Finn snapped back. "I'm the only one here who can ascend. I could—"

"Finn." Edrik made his voice stern. "Don't say something you'll regret."

Finn turned his hot gaze on Edrik and opened his mouth to say something.

Edrik cut him off. "Could you have a look at this one?" He held out a bronze dagger with a blade nearly the length of his forearm. "It's slightly bent, and you're much better at straightening these things out than I am.

Finn closed his mouth and scowled, then stomped over to slump down next to Edrik, leaning his back against the wall. "I should have put that snake in the washtub."

As Finn took up the dagger and sighted down the blade, Edrik's gaze drifted to Grabak, who nodded a grim thanks.

They all started when the latch rattled, and the door swung open a crack, stopped, then opened wider. A young woman hesitated in the shadows outside, peering into the cottage with dark, nervous eyes.

Finn tensed and reached for his bronze-tipped spear.

Edrik set down the honing stone and reached for his sword; she might not be alone.

Grabak rose slowly to his feet, a delighted grin breaking across his stern face. "Kaya!" he exclaimed, his voice rich and welcoming. He laughed and stepped toward the woman, beckoning with one hand. "Well, come in and let us have a look at you."

So this was Mudge's friend—the one whose secret Grabak had threatened to expose in order to get Mudge to help them escape. Edrik's hand relaxed slightly on the hilt of the sword, but he didn't put it down. She wouldn't be traveling without an escort of some kind, and they might not be kindly disposed toward dragons, especially the dragons who'd threatened Kaya and forced her from her home.

The woman's lips pressed together in an expression of grim determination, and she scowled as she stepped across the threshold. "Don't make a fuss, Stig," she mumbled.

Something about her soft, alto voice was familiar to Edrik, though he couldn't quite place it. Her eyes flickered over to him and Finn, and the soft honey bronze of her cheeks paled in the firelight before she looked away again and down, letting her sleek black hair fall in front of her face. She strode across the room as if she knew the place as well as they did and swung a satchel off her shoulder, dropping it next to Mudge's travel cloak. Edrik frowned. It was Mudge's satchel—the one he'd taken with him down to the cider barn. Kaya shifted a wad of dark fabric out from under her other elbow and turned back toward the hearth, her slender form lithe and graceful, firelight playing over the angles of her thin face. Now that she was facing the other direction, Edrik could see the half-healed bruise that blotched her cheek and ran a dark line up under her eye.

Her gaze flickered over to Edrik once more, catching him staring. A familiar impish grin tugged at her mouth, and she laughed. "Do I still look disreputable, Edrik?"

Edrik felt his mouth drop open. "Mudge?"

Beside him, Finn burst out laughing. "Sun and stars, Mudge! You make *us* look disreputable." He stood up and stepped over to inspect the young dungeon keeper. "You even smell like a girl. How did we not see it?"

"Soap. I smell like soap." Mudge—or rather Kaya—shifted half a step closer to Grabak and folded her arms across her chest, which in the fitted blouse and bodice looked anything but boyish. "And people mostly see what they expect to see."

"It does explain a few things." Finn circled around her, eyes scanning her as if still not certain what he was seeing, mouth shifting from grinning laughter into a serious frown. He stopped when he faced her again and reached a tentative finger out to brush against the bruised side of her face as he spoke. "I know what it is to have to hide what you are. I should never have hit you. I'm sorry."

Kaya batted Finn's hand away and scowled fiercely. "Touch me again, and I'll cut your hand off." Somehow the threat seemed less menacing coming from a pretty girl than it had from a grungy dungeon keeper. Still, this was the same person who had cut up Tait and bitten off that other man's finger.

Finn's thoughts must have traveled a similar path because he grinned and backed away, palms held out in a gesture of surrender. "I've given you my name, Mudge . . . er . . . Kaya. I'm not going to hurt you."

Kaya glanced nervously over at Edrik again and then away. She shook out the wad of dark fabric she'd held tucked under her arm—

which turned out to be her old dungeon keeper's robe—and headed for the hearth. They all watched as she spread the damp robe out in front of the fire to dry. Then she straightened self-consciously and looked around at all of them. She cleared her throat. "Is that stew ready yet, Stig?"

Grabak chuckled and shook his head as he knelt and began spooning the stew into tin cups. "You look lovely, Kaya," he said in a gently paternal tone. Then his face went sad. "You were right; the Thanesson wouldn't have been pleased to find you'd escaped his attentions all these years. Can you forgive me for threatening to tell him?"

Kaya sat down on the edge of the hearth and studied the old Drake's face. "I needed to leave anyway. Someone would have figured it out soon—even a half-blood boy should have started growing a beard by now." Then she looked down at her hands in her lap. "But . . . if you knew . . ." She glanced up at him again. "If you knew all that time, why didn't you threaten me sooner? You'd have been home a long time ago."

Grabak looked at her, his face serious. "Would I? I could never decide from one day to the next if I thought you more likely to free me or slit my throat in my sleep."

Kaya laughed. "Surely I haven't managed to seem so formidable as all that."

"Mmm . . ." Grabak mused. "Perhaps more unpredictable than formidable. I spent those last two days in the dungeon wondering if I'd wake up enough times to find out whether I could hold out long enough to die of thirst or if I'd give in and eat the poisoned food first. But here we are." He chuckled softly.

"There were other reasons to stay, though." His eyes shifted to the fire, and he frowned. "Home is complicated. My wife might have conspired to kill me. She may do it again, for all I know. Part of me doesn't want to know. None of me wants to tell her that I watched her brother die. And if it can be proven that she was part of the plot against me, I'll have to sentence her to death for treason. It was easier to stay in the dungeon."

He looked back up at Kaya, and his grim face slid into an affectionate smile. "And I didn't want to threaten you. I couldn't help seeing my daughter in you and wondering how she would fare in the same circumstances. I knew if the guards found out they would not be gentle with you." He looked away again and shrugged helplessly. "But I didn't know about your mother and the Thanesson. My threat held more than I intended. I am truly sorry, Mudge."

Kaya was quiet for a long moment, studying the side of Grabak's face. Then she reached out to touch his hand. "You're forgiven."

Grabak nodded a silent but respectful thanks and went back to dishing up the stew.

Edrik studied the young woman as she sat on the hearth combing her fingers through her long black hair, fanning it out to finish drying in the heat of the fire. He couldn't see much similarity to Grabak's daughter. The two women might be about the same age. *"Mudge is not so odd as you might think,"* Grabak had said, *"nor perhaps so young either."* Edrik frowned—that made Mudge closer to his own age than he'd realized.

But Lissara was tall and fair, with golden hair and inviting curves. Mudge—or rather Kaya—was dark and slight with a slender, willowy figure. Lissara's emotions were always on the surface, flitting across her face like butterflies in sunshine. Kaya's feelings were as guarded as the Shrike's Keep dungeon. And Lissara would certainly never have dissected Tait, bitten off a man's finger, or drowned a courtesan in her bath. Edrik frowned. No, if Lissara were in Shrike's Keep, she'd have been in the Thanesson's bed, a fate Kaya had managed to avoid for . . . "How long?" He didn't realize he'd said the words out loud until Kaya frowned and looked up at him. He cleared his throat. "How long were you hiding in that dungeon?"

Kaya's hands stilled for a moment as she looked at him. Then she looked away and began gathering her thick, black hair together, twisting it slowly into a clumsy braid. Edrik had seen Lissara work her hair into an elegant, complicated plait much more quickly and neatly than that; but he supposed Kaya didn't have much practice arranging her hair into anything but a nest for her rat.

"I'm not sure," Kaya said quietly. "I was six when my mother died.

I remember that. But time was confusing in the dungeon, and I lost track. Grandfather used to lie about my age in order to give me more time before people became suspicious." She shrugged.

"You've lived in that dungeon since you were six years old?" Finn sounded appalled. "Who would do that to a child? How did it happen?"

Kaya looked over at Finn and smiled—an impish Mudge smile that was disconcertingly charming on Kaya's face. "'Twas a time long past," she said softly. Then she sighed, tugged her braid undone, and tried again, telling her story as she twined the dark locks between her fingers.

"Grandfather was not always a dungeon keeper. He was a tutor for a long time and then an ambassador for one of the northern kings. He traveled a great deal and made careful notes about all the places he went and the people he met. But there was a war, and his kingdom fell. The king's enemies wanted to kill Grandfather too, so he went into hiding. His wife renounced him and went back to live with her father, taking their two daughters with her. And Grandfather found refuge working as a dungeon keeper for the Thane of Shrike's Hollow, who had been one of his favorite pupils in the early days.

"As time went on, Grandfather's wife arranged what seemed like suitable marriages for both of their daughters. The elder daughter married a landed knight, and the younger daughter was to marry the heir of the Thane. But my mother fell in love with one of the Rattatosk boatmen who were transporting her family to Shrike's Hollow for the wedding. When my Grandfather warned his daughter about the Thanesson's true character, she went to her boatman for help, and they ran away together."

Kaya stuffed her hand into a pocket in her skirt and tugged out a piece of frayed string, which she used to tie off the end of her clumsy braid. "And then there was me. And we were happy. But it didn't last very long." She accepted a tin cup of stew from Grabak and poked at the chunks of root and bits of meat with the tip of her knife as she continued.

"Papa went first. I was very young, so no one told me what happened, but I think someone killed him. Mother took me and ran. We went to her sister's house first. Aunt was . . . not happy to see us. She told my mother she should take her Tosky half-blood get down to the river and drown me immediately so she could start over. Mother would hear nothing of it and would have taken me away again, but she fell ill. She sent word to Grandfather and managed to live long enough for him to get there. Grandfather wanted Aunt to raise me along with her own daughters, but she wanted nothing to do with me. She said I would be a blot on her family's honor." A nostalgic smile softened Kaya's face. "Grandfather said that a little slip of a thing like me couldn't possibly be a blot on anything; I was hardly even a smudge." Her smile deepened. "Only by then, Grandfather had no teeth, and when he said, 'smudge,' it came out 'mudge,' and I giggled. So he took to calling me Mudge after that to make me smile."

She fell silent, remembering, until Grabak prompted, "So he took you back to his dungeon with him?"

Kaya shrugged. "He had nowhere else to go. But he knew the Thanesson was still angry about being jilted, and he knew it would not be safe for my mother's daughter to be anywhere near the man. So I learned to be a boy, and the Thanesson had to settle for keeping my mother's son in his father's dungeon and humiliating me now and then when he remembered I was there." She sighed. "It was better than being on the street. Grandfather loved me. I learned to read and write and made friends with the archivist and the herb woman. And I was happy enough as I was."

"You never had silk ribbons," Grabak said softly.

Kaya blinked. "What?"

Grabak looked sheepish. "That night I heard your Grandfather speaking to you of . . . of Kaya, you were coveting silk ribbons." He shrugged. "You'd been watching a feast day dinner from one of your spy holes and admiring the ladies' dresses."

A soft smile spread over Kaya's face. "I remember. He didn't speak of it often. It was too dangerous. We thought you were asleep. He was carving a puppet for one of Aunt's girls, and I was dissecting a foal that was born too early to live. I told him to give the doll silk ribbons like one of the ladies wore to the feast—deep green like pine needles in the winter. And he put the puppet down and said," her voice went gruff and deep, "'You chould haf hathe filk ribbonge, Kaya. Filk ribbonge and a belbet dressh.'" She smiled at her own imitation and then her face went sad. "I was so jealous of those ribbons." Her fingers drifted to the frayed string that tied her braid, and she sighed. "I miss him."

Into the silence that followed, Edrik said softly, "Where will you go now?"

For a long moment, Kaya looked at her hands in her lap. Then her dark eyes turned up and met Edrik's. "You said I could go with you." She studied his face. "Did you mean it, or were you just trying to get me to let you out?"

Edrik's face warmed under the intensity of Kaya's eyes. "I meant it," he said, then dropped his gaze. "But it isn't safe. There's no guarantee that we'll win the throne back. And if we fail, anyone who helped Grabak will be in great danger."

Kaya laughed merrily. "I've never been safe in my entire life. I see no point in starting now." But there was something wistful behind her eyes. She saw him notice it and turned away.

"Some music, Stig," she commanded, "It's getting terribly dull in here. And I need something to listen to while I remove Rolf's stitches." She directed her impish grin at Edrik. "Take off your shirt, Rolf."

Grabak handed the cup he was washing to Finn and went to pull his small bone flute from a pocket in his cloak while Edrik shrugged out of his tunic.

Abruptly, Finn guffawed. "For someone who doesn't believe in human magic, Kaya, you're terribly good at using it."

Everyone froze, and Edrik felt suddenly uncomfortable in his thin white shirt with his tunic in his hands.

Kaya scowled at Finn. "What are you talking about?"

Finn grinned defiantly back at her. "You have the king of the Vanir and a son of the Nine jumping to your whim without so much as a by-your-leave. Do you think every human woman can do that?"

Kaya's face flushed, and her scowl deepened. "There's no magic involved. I just asked them, and they—"

Grabak burst into a fit of laughter as well. "He's right, Mudge. I didn't even notice you doing it."

"Doing what?" Kaya seemed genuinely mystified.

Grabak explained. "All magic has two sides to it—the tangible and the intangible. Dragons ascend and compel. For alfkin, it's transformation and glamor. Dwarrows and the yotun use runes to bind their intangible magic to tangible things. And humans—"

"Have no magic," Kaya insisted.

Grabak smiled and held up a conciliatory hand. "Among dragons, it is said that the magic of humans consists of creation and fascination. But only the women can wield it."

Kaya frowned. "Creation is reproduction. We've been over all that. What is this fascination meant to be?"

Grabak shrugged. "It's difficult to describe. There's something in a woman that pulls a dragon in. Human men too, I suppose. It's a subtle draw, but powerful. Some men experience it as an attempt to dominate them and might resist or retaliate—especially if they are particularly insecure about their own strength of will. And perhaps some women wield their power that way on purpose. But most women use it to sustain and heal, and in most men, it instills a strong desire to please the woman and protect her. Just now, I would find it quite delightful to play for you, and I imagine young Edrik is rather looking forward to having his stitches out."

Edrik frowned. He had been. Now it felt . . . awkward. As if he'd somehow been disloyal to Lissara.

Kaya snorted. "That's nonsense. I can't make men do things. If I could, why would I have stayed in that dungeon?"

Grabak's brow furrowed as he considered how to explain. "It doesn't work by force; it isn't compulsion. Fascination works . . . I don't know . . . in some other, subtler way. A man can resist it or ignore it if he chooses, but most don't want to. It . . . feels good. In a way that nothing else does.

"Some women are stronger in the magic than others, and some learn to control it better than others, even if they don't believe in it. Some women bludgeon a man over the head with their power, and some can wrap it so cobweb fine that a man doesn't even notice." He twirled his flute between his fingers and pointed it at Kaya. "And as our friend Finn just pointed out, *you* are quite insidiously artful when you channel your magic." He frowned. "And when you don't. A woman who isn't actively withholding her magic gives off a quiet sort of power all the time, and men like to be near her—husbands, brothers, sons, lovers . . ." he raised an eyebrow meaningfully, ". . . cooks, archivists, kitchen boys, dungeon guards . . ."

Kaya scoffed. "That is the most superstitious, nonsensical—"

Grabak's laugh cut her off. "Maybe so. Shall we agree, once more, to disagree? Just tell Finn how happy it would make you if he finished washing up. Then I'll play, and young Edrik can enjoy your ministrations, and all three of us superstitious dragons will find ourselves most abominably content." He grinned.

Kaya stared at him another moment, then rolled her eyes and sighed. "You are impossible, Stig."

Finn snorted. "I'm going to go scout around." He smirked impudently at Grabak as he deliberately dropped the cup, unwashed, into the basin they'd brought in from the equipment shed, and went out, slamming the door behind him.

Grabak shrugged and whistled a flourish on his flute before settling into the swaying melody of a ballad.

Kaya directed an aggravated glare at Edrik. "You still have your shirt on." She stomped over to her satchel and dug out her kit of medical tools.

Edrik hesitated, then told himself he was being ridiculous. Even if Finn was right, there was nothing improper or disloyal about having his wound tended to by Kaya—no more than if she were his mother, or his sister, or some village herb woman. And it wasn't as if any woman could have the same draw for him as Lissara. He loosened the laces on his shirt and pulled it off over his head, watching Kaya from the corner of his eye as she watched him do it.

Kaya had Edrik turn so the firelight fell on his back at a better angle and then knelt behind him, studying her work. He felt her presence like the expectant thrum in the still air before a storm.

"This is more healed than I thought it would be," she said. "The stitches are going to scar. I'm sorry." Her fingers brushed against the healing wound, and her other hand landed lightly on the back of his neck, sending a pleasant tingle down Edrik's spine. He shivered and inched away from her touch.

Kaya laughed, a sad sound too quiet for Grabak to hear over his flute, and whispered, "I told you it would be easier to do this before I cleaned up."

She was right. Before, it would have been merely Mudge checking his wounds. Now . . . Edrik swallowed hard. "I don't mind a scar or two. Just take the stitches out."

"Right." Kaya's hands moved off Edrik's skin for a moment, leaving him feeling both relieved and strangely bereft, and then returned as she carefully cut each stitch and tugged it free. The knife she used to cut the stitches left a slight, stinging burn each time it brushed his skin; it must have had an iron blade. But Kaya's hands were careful and steady and warm against his back, and she never pierced his skin.

When she finished, she sat back on her heels, and Edrik half turned to look at her. "Thank you." It came out gruff.

She looked down at her hands. "I should check your rib too," she murmured. "If that's all right with you."

He nodded, and she directed him to stand and hold out his arms if he could. He did, and she probed the bone with her fingers from behind, then slipped under his arm to stand in front of him and poke at it some more from there. "The bruising is gone," she said. "And the bone is . . ." She pushed on it again and, when he didn't flinch, looked up into his face. "You're a remarkably fast healer, Rolf."

Edrik grinned. "I told you, it's a family trait."

"Yes. Well. You're going to be fine." Abruptly, Kaya looked down and stepped away from him.

She'd done that the first time she checked his rib too, back in the dungeon. And when she'd helped him with his baldric as they were leaving. Then, Edrik had thought it a boy's fear of a dragon, but now he saw it for what it was: a woman's fear of a man. Something clenched in his chest. He didn't want her to be afraid of him. She wasn't afraid of anything—she'd cowed the human murderer, and stood up to the Thanesson, and punched Finn square in the face knowing full well he was a dragon and bigger than her. How could Edrik show her he was a friend?

She didn't look at him as she bent to retrieve her tools.

"Kaya," he said quietly, "someone should check your stitches too. Carrying that pack can't have been good for them."

She stilled, just for a moment, then finished tying the thong on her rolled-up toolkit and straightened. "My stitches are fine," she said, still not looking at him.

She began to move away, but he stopped her with a hand on her elbow. "Kaya—" He cut off when she looked at him with her dark, frightened eyes. There was something in her face . . .

She pulled away before he could tell what it was. "We're going to need more firewood." Her voice rasped, and her face flushed as she dropped her tools next to her satchel and pushed out through the door without looking at him again.

Grabak's music stopped abruptly, and Edrik turned to find the old Drake scowling at him. "What did you say to her?"

Edrik looked at the door and back. "Nothing. I just . . ." He held his hands out, palms up; empty.

Grabak cleared his throat and raised an eyebrow. "Whatever it was," he said dryly, "fix it."

Edrik blinked at him. "Right." He reached for his shirt.

CHAPTER 13

Kaya stalked along the border between the orchard and the forest, peering into the shadows cast by the full moon as it rose over the trees until she spotted a fallen ash tree that looked as if it had been there a while. The dry crack with which the wood snapped when she stomped on one of the thinner branches told her it was well seasoned and would burn cleanly. She propped the broken end of the branch against the trunk and stomped on it again, snapping it in two. She dragged one broken end up onto the trunk and repeated the process until she had broken the whole branch into pieces short enough to carry easily. Then she knocked another branch free and set about breaking up that one too.

The effort of smashing wood and the satisfying, splintering crunch with which the branches broke began to wear away at the dark irritation that tangled through Kaya's mind. Irritation at herself for getting caught up in all this. Irritation at Finn for his talk of magic. Irritation at Stig for being so burning smug. Irritation at Edrik for . . . for caring. She stomped another branch free of the trunk.

It wasn't fair. She shouldn't be feeling this way. He had a princess waiting for him. She propped up the end of the branch. Not that Edrik would even notice Kaya. Not in that way. *Stomp!* And Kaya wouldn't have known what to do if he did. *Stomp!* But the way he'd asked about her back had made her want to figure it out. And she couldn't stop her heart from pounding when he looked at her like that—like she was a woman. *Stomp!*

Somehow, it had been easier when he thought she was a half-mad adolescent boy. When she didn't have to acknowledge even to herself just how much she was feeling for him. Maybe she should have gone on being Mudge. Nobody ever looked at Mudge like that. But she had given up her secret, and there was no taking it back.

As she propped the next branch against the trunk, she heard a soft thump behind her. Had Stig come for her, or was she going to have to deal with Edrik? She pretended not to notice whichever of them it was and stomped, then bent to shift the branch again, ignoring the stinging tug of the stitches in her back as she did.

A soft chuckling sound behind her made Kaya whirl around, heart pounding. The thing behind her was neither Grabak nor Edrik. But she recognized it.

"Clever shuman." The alfkin nymph spoke with a rasping wheeze, shuffling closer on its short legs and knobby elbows. It tilted its head, examining her carefully. "Hidesh itsh schent."

Kaya staggered back a step, blood turning to ice in her veins, fingers fumbling numbly in her pockets for a knife.

The alfkin slowly advanced. "Followed from shtone village." It tilted its head the other way, and its insect-like mouthparts quivered as if it were tasting the air. "Sheeking," it added softly in explanation.

"Stay away from me!" Kaya gasped. She stumbled backward until she collided hard against the broad trunk of a tree, and the whip wounds sent a sudden shock of pain stabbing through her body.

The thing chuckled and shuffled forward again. It was taller than Kaya and close enough now for her to smell the rank musk of it. "Brave shuman," it grated. "Shtrong deshtiny."

One long arm shot like lightning toward Kaya. She raised her knife to meet it—but not fast enough. The creature's bony finger brushed Kaya's forehead.

A soft warmth folded gently around her, like spring sunlight playing over the leaves at the top of the forest canopy. Her vision sharpened and deepened. The sounds of the forest around her crystallized into strands of melody that refracted off each other and wove themselves together into an elaborate, twining lace of music.

The alfkin moved closer. Its intricate face bent toward her like a lover, and the retractable claws at the tips of its fingers left tingling trails behind as they stroked the soft skin of her throat and drifted down toward her belly, drawing Kaya deep into herself. Where she was safe. Where she had always been no one but Kaya.

The knife dropped from her fingers with a distant thump.

A shout slashed through the music, harsh and angry, like blood against snow. There were words, but Kaya couldn't decipher them.

The alfkin turned its head, and Kaya's heart ached for the loss of its faceted gaze. Its body gathered around her, strong and protective as its voice rumbled a new thread into the web of forest music. "Mine."

And she was.

The shout came again, closer and more insistent. Kaya's eyes refocused past the alfkin. A white sword threaded a silent, silver descant into the woodland chorus. Ruby light bled hungry patterns up the blade from the stone in its hilt and down over the hand that held it, twining around the body of . . . of Edrik.

A discordant longing clashed against the music in Kaya's mind, and the alfkin snapped its insectile gaze around to recapture hers.

The music surged.

With a rustle of undergrowth, Grabak loomed into view, brandishing his clubbed staff—larger somehow than he seemed, as if trailing smoke-dark wings and unseen, but deadly, teeth and claws.

"Mine," the alfkin insisted, and the truth of it prickled through Kaya's insides.

"*Mine*," Edrik snarled back. And that was somehow also true.

The white point of the bone sword appeared between Kaya's face and the alfkin's, and Kaya could see the quick pulse of the blood-red runes flowing over its surface.

"No!" This time, the alfkin's frayed voice tore ragged holes in the lacework of melodies. "Deshtiny!" The threads tangled and splintered. The crystal clarity of vision faded; Grabak was just Grabak. And the runes on Edrik's sword were only etched.

Fear engulfed Kaya, hot and raw.

"Stop!" Kaya's voice was a stinging gasp. Her hands plucked frantically at the spindly arms that pinned her to the tree, but the loose, dry skin kept sloughing off under her fingers, and she couldn't get a solid grip.

The alfkin hissed, long and sharp and bitter, and let go of her. It backed a step away, making a dry, rattling sound in its throat, then shifted from foot to foot in agitation for a moment until Edrik raised the point of his sword a fraction. Then, in a sudden rush, the creature leapt into the air, caught the lowest tree limbs with its clawed fingers, and flung itself higher, then higher still, into the branches. It leapt, arcing through the air with an odd sort of grace, into the next tree over, then into the next, long arms reaching and pulling, until it disappeared into the darkening forest.

Kaya's body turned to water and folded in on itself. Edrik caught her as she fell, held her close with one arm while he sheathed his sword, then swung her up to cradle her against his chest. He wasn't wearing his tunic, only his shirt, and the warmth of his shoulder seeped through the thin fabric where her cheek rested. No one had held her like that since her mother died. It felt foreign. And frightening. And indescribably comforting. Distantly, she felt her body begin to shake all over.

"Is she all right?" Grabak's gruff voice.

"She's shivering. We need to get her warm." Edrik adjusted his hold, and Kaya's cheek shifted to lie against his broad chest. Through his shirt, she heard the rush of his deep inhalation and the slowing rhythm of his heart—*lovers' sounds*. Her own heart began to pound a rapid counterpoint to the steady beating of his. His strong dragon heart that would risk everything to win the woman he loved.

A woman who was not Kaya.

Who never would be.

CHAPTER 14

While Grabak went to make sure the alfkin nymph was really gone, Edrik carried Kaya back to the cottage. She wriggled free of his grasp as soon as they were inside and went to get her cloak. It wasn't until Edrik reached to stir up the dying fire for her that he noticed the dark smears and blotches that gleamed wetly red against the white sleeve of his shirt where Kaya's back had rested.

He looked sideways at her when she came to kneel beside him on the hearth, pulling her cloak around her shivering shoulders and edging close to the fire.

She didn't look at him at all.

He put another stick on the fire and said softly, "There's blood on my sleeve. Did that creature hurt you?"

She shook her head. "The bath softened my s-scabs. And I b-backed into a t-tree. That's all."

"Still." Edrik shrugged. "You're hurt. We should do something about that, don't you think?"

She drew a deep breath and closed her eyes. "It doesn't m-matter."

"It does matter." Edrik turned to look at her more fully. "Mudge, you're not alone anymore. You have friends. Grabak. And Finn." He reached to touch her hand. "And me."

She pulled away from his fingers and pressed the heel of her trembling hand to her forehead. "Why am I so c-cold?"

Edrik frowned. "It's probably a reaction to severed magic. You have a strong mind. I think you broke free of the enchantment before the alfkin released you." The idea made him uneasy; it meant she could probably break a dragon compulsion too—not that he could compel her himself anyway, but it would have been nice to think someone else could if it became necessary. He shook his head. "Don't change the subject. You're bleeding."

"I'm fine," she insisted. "It only needs to be cleaned and salved."

Edrik nodded. "I can do that." He put some water in the copper pot and set it by the fire to warm. Then, following Kaya's reluctant instructions, he added a pouch of herbs from her satchel and set out some clean rags and a small clay pot of greasy salve.

When all was ready, Edrik knelt beside Kaya once more. She closed her eyes and turned her face away. "This is a bad idea."

Why was she still afraid of him? "I'm not going to hurt you. I promise." Edrik rested his hand gently on her shoulder. "And I already know you're a girl. I'm your friend, remember? Just let me do this for you."

She closed her eyes and pressed her lips tightly together, then shrugged as if defeated, and nodded.

Carefully, Edrik undid the laces at the back of her bodice—and paused when he saw the blood-soaked blouse beneath. Kaya kept her face turned away from him as she removed the bodice and shrugged out of her blouse, leaving only her shift covering her torn back. Then, hugging her cloak to her chest, she loosened the drawstring at the neck of her shift, pulled her arms from the sleeves, and let the shift slip down to her waist.

Edrik bit back a hiss. The bruising from the four whip strokes was healing well enough, and the raised welts had faded into long purple streaks, but some of the stitches Grabak had put into the two long slashes had torn through her skin—maybe days ago, from the look of it. Layers of scabs caked the area, and where they'd cracked and pulled away, the wounds seeped blood. She should not have been carrying that pack. Shame clenched at Edrik's gut; she'd done it to spare him.

Except for the constant shivering, Kaya didn't move as Edrik worked —didn't flinch, didn't cry out. His frown deepened. Living as she had, she must have learned to hide her pain. And any other sign of weakness. In her world, weakness meant discovery and death—or worse. A memory nudged its way into his mind. Lissara had pricked her finger on the thorn of a rose in the gardens and had squealed, and fussed, and pouted prettily until Edrik dabbed the single drop of blood from her white skin with his pocket handkerchief and kissed the spot to make it well again.

Kaya was nothing like Lissara.

And a kiss couldn't fix this. Not that he would kiss Kaya. Edrik gritted his teeth and focused on his work.

It wasn't until he gently nudged her shift a little farther down to catch a stray trickle of blood that Kaya moved. Her whole body went rigid, and her hand flashed around to clutch at his. "Stop," she hissed. But not before he saw what else she was hiding.

Edrik stared at the mark that marred Kaya's smooth brown skin just below her waistline; it was a rune, red and blistered, charred at the edges, burned into her skin as with a branding iron. It couldn't have been more than a few days old; it had happened while they traveled. He glanced up to find her glaring defiantly back at him over her shoulder, dark eyes hot and angry.

"Leave it," she commanded.

He felt the push of her magic behind her words. He let it flow past him and swallowed hard. "No." He set his jaw defiantly and held her gaze. "Let me see. Let me help you."

She met his eyes a moment longer, weighing; then something shifted in her expression. She drew a deep breath and released his hand, watching him closely over her shoulder as he nudged the fabric down a little farther.

There were three runes at different stages of healing branded into her skin—a large one near the base of her spine and two smaller ones above it, making a row up the middle of her back. "What are these?" His voice came out hoarse.

She hesitated. Then, "Penalties."

He thought back to what she'd said when he asked if removing Finn's collar had hurt her.

"Penalties for freeing us?"

She let one shoulder rise and fall. "The big one is from the archway. The others are from the collars." A sigh. "I didn't mean for any of you to know."

Edrik brushed his finger lightly, almost reverently along the healthy skin next to the burns. "Which one was for me?" he asked gruffly.

"The one in the middle."

His finger stopped next to it, careful not to touch. He'd thought only of freeing himself and his friends, without ever considering what that might cost the dungeon keeper. And this was the price she had paid. For him.

"Kaya . . ." he whispered and then stopped, not knowing what to say.

Kaya laughed softly and reached back to pat his hand. "It's not your fault, Rolf, it's just the way the magic works. I knew the price when I chose to pay it." She sighed and turned away. "Please don't tell the others."

When Edrik finished tending Kaya's wounds, he waited outside the cottage while she changed back into her old dungeon robe, and then the two of them washed the blood from her clothes and hung them near the fire to dry. By the time Grabak returned, Kaya was curled up on the hearth, wrapped in both her cloak and Edrik's, and the shivering had finally stopped.

The old Drake paused in the doorway, his gaze moving from Edrik to Kaya's drying clothes and back again. He frowned as he stepped into the room. "Finn and I checked the forest. No sign of the alfkin. We'll keep a watch for it for a few days, though."

"Still no pursuit from the keep either." Finn pushed through the door behind Grabak. "I think they've given up. I was on my way back when I heard all the yelling." He grinned. "Tait's right, Edrik. You always find trouble as soon as the grown-ups turn their—" He stopped, taking in the drying clothes and Kaya resting by the fire, and his grin broadened. He snickered suggestively. "And what have we been up to back at the cottage?"

Edrik felt the blood rise to his face. "Her back was bleeding."

Finn shrugged and winked at him. "Well, I've heard worse excuses."

From the hearth, Kaya called, "Don't think I can't hear you, Finn!" She added more ominously, "And I know where you sleep," before pushing herself to a sitting position.

Finn strode over and crouched down to warm his hands at the fire. "I was only joking, Mudge," he said to Kaya in a stage whisper. "I just like to make our Edrik blush. With all that fair skin, he goes red all over."

He glanced meaningfully at Edrik over his shoulder, and to his annoyance, Edrik felt his blush deepen.

Finn grinned and went on. "Edrik would never betray his princess —even if she's not actually *his* princess."

Kaya snorted. "Well, we'd better get him back to her then, eh, Finn? Before someone else runs off with her."

"Indeed. Or with *him*." Finn grinned and raised an eyebrow, leaning closer to Kaya in mock confidence. "Although, frankly, I think it would be good for Edrik to be run off with at least once in his life."

Kaya rolled her eyes and began to disentangle herself from the cloaks. She stopped when she noticed the avid interest with which Finn was watching. With a defiant tilt of her chin, she turned her back on him, then looked coquettishly over her shoulder as she slowly lowered her cloak, revealing the tattered black dungeon robe beneath.

Finn snorted.

"Well, what did you think I was wearing, you great beast?" Kaya gave him a very unwomanly smack on the shoulder as she stood and stepped past him to return Edrik's cloak.

Finn shrugged unapologetically. "A fellow can hope."

Kaya dropped her cloak next to her satchel by the wall and went back for her pack.

Edrik got there first and hefted the pack, ignoring the twinge of pain in his rib. "Where do you want it?"

Kaya scowled at him. "I can carry my own pack."

"So can I," Edrik said, and when she drew a breath to argue, he added quickly, "I've seen your back, Mudge. And you've seen mine. Which do you think is better able to bear a pack?"

He slung the pack over his shoulder to prove his point.

She scowled. Then her expression turned thoughtful, and she folded her arms across her chest. "It's because of your sword, isn't it?"

Edrik blinked. "What?"

"Your sword. It heals you." She put her hands on her hips and took a step closer. "You could barely lift your sword when we left the dungeon, and today you carried me in from the orchard. It's too much, too fast."

Edrik waved a dismissive hand. "Dragons heal more quickly than humans, that's all."

"You didn't heal so quickly in the dungeon."

Edrik shrugged. "There was a lot of iron in the dungeon."

Kaya shook her head. "The iron might explain some level of physical weakness for a dragon, but not the speed with which you're healing in its absence. It has to be some form of magic. And you can't reach the magic, even if there isn't any iron, because you're pinioned. Right?" Her eyes dared him to disagree.

"Kaya," Grabak said sternly, "it is both impolite and unkind to remind Edrik of his—"

"The point is, it's not dragon magic," Kaya interrupted with an irritated wave of her hand. "So it has to be something else. And the only thing that's really different between the dungeon and now is that Edrik is carrying his sword."

Edrik tried to think of an alternate explanation to offer but came up empty.

Seeing his hesitation, Kaya pressed her point. "Your sword is made of bone. Bone doesn't hold a good edge. And if you tried to block a metal sword with it, the bone would shatter." She tipped her chin up defiantly. "It's crawling with yot marks, and when I held it in the armory it seemed. . ." She frowned, thinking. "It seemed . . . almost alive. Somehow." She shook her head. "There is magic in that sword. And it heals you. Tell me it doesn't."

"Does it matter?" Grabak's voice was calm but held a warning.

Kaya turned and met the Drake's eyes for a long moment, then backed down and turned toward the fire, bending to pick up a stick. "Maybe not." She poked hard at the fire, sending a shower of sparks spiraling up the chimney. Then she shifted restlessly, drew a deep breath, and met Grabak's stern gaze. "But maybe it does. Maybe it means Edrik isn't pinioned after all."

Edrik froze.

Finn slowly rose to his feet.

Grabak scowled. "What do you mean?" It was more a demand than a question.

Kaya squirmed under the weight of three pairs of dragon eyes. "It's only a theory," she said uneasily. "I might be wrong." Her eyes darted among the three of them for a heartbeat before settling on Edrik.

Edrik slid the pack off his shoulder and dropped it.

"Tell me." His voice sounded strange, even to himself—hollow and cold.

Kaya cleared her throat. "When the alfkin touched me, everything went . . . I don't know how to describe it. But I could see things. And hear things. I don't know if it was real or just an illusion spun with the alfkin magic, but . . ."

Grabak cleared his throat. "Some kinds of alfkin enchantment involve a sharing of the senses. You might have seen, in part, the way an alfkin sees." He shrugged. "Or it might have placed a vision in your mind to distract you so it could slit your belly open and read its destiny in your innards."

Kaya looked uncomfortable and lowered her gaze to the fire. "Yes. Well . . . I saw the sword." She paused and scrubbed at the back of her neck with one hand, remembering. "The ruby in the hilt glowed like a hot coal, and the light from it ran up along the blade and made a sort of living web with the yot marks."

Edrik frowned. "The ruby anchors the sword's magic."

"I figure the magic must preserve the blade." Kaya met Edrik's gaze. "Keep it from breaking."

Edrik studied the woman's face for a long heartbeat, then nodded. "Something like that." *Among other things.*

"Does the silver on it tarnish?" Kaya asked.

"No." Edrik's frown deepened.

"Well . . ." Kaya drew a deep breath. "The web of magic wasn't just on the blade. It ran up your arm and . . . and made a sort of shield around you."

Edrik nodded. Once. Grimly.

Kaya looked around at the group again and propped her stick against the side of the fireplace. "It's just . . . if the magic preserves the sword, keeps it from breaking . . . from changing . . ." She cleared her throat and looked back at Edrik. "Maybe it does the same thing to you." She raised one shoulder almost apologetically and lowered it again. "Keeps you from changing. Fixes what it sees as damage. Preserves you."

"Yes," Edrik said. "But what does that have to do with being pinioned?"

Kaya spread her hands as if offering something to the dragons. "Maybe it sees whatever change happens when you become able to ascend as damage to be prevented or repaired."

Something hard and hot settled in Edrik's belly. "No," he said grimly. "This sword has been passed down in my family for generations. It hasn't stopped anyone from ascending before."

Kaya's brow furrowed. "Was it passed down before your ancestors reached maturity, or after?"

After. Always after. Edrik stared at Kaya. *It couldn't be.*

"Because if the wielder was already a dragon—I mean, if he could already ascend—the sword might not see the transformation as damage. But if he seemed only human when he began carrying the sword, might it not work to keep him that way? To preserve him as he was?"

The thing in Edrik's belly began to claw its way up into his chest, strangling his heart.

"Did your father give you the sword before you reached your quartermark," Kaya asked, "or after?"

Edrik had inherited the sword after his father's death at Nidhaug's fangs—*before* his quartermark. He rose slowly to his feet. "So . . . you think I should get rid of my sword." His voice shook when he said it. "The sword that has been passed down in my family line since before the Breaking."

Kaya held his gaze and half shrugged one shoulder. "Sometimes you have to give up a thing you value in order to gain something of even greater worth."

He moved a step closer to her. "The sword that is all I have left of my father."

Kaya held up her hands and edged away. "It's only a theory. I could be wrong."

"That is all I have left, *period*, because a cripple cannot challenge Nidhaug for my father's place among the Nine." It came out louder than he intended. "Or recover my family's holdings. Or take a liegeman's oath. Or marry the woman I love." He took another step toward Kaya.

"Forgive me," she said, ducking her head. "I shouldn't have said anything." Her tone was submissive, almost obsequious.

It was the same tone, Edrik abruptly realized, that Kaya had used with the Thanesson in the dungeon. He had frightened her again. He backed off, scrubbing his hands over his face. *What if she was right?* But the only ways to unlink the sword from himself were distance or linking it to someone else. The silence was broken by the slow tapping of rain on the cottage roof. He let out a low hiss of frustration.

Kaya was watching him, but when he met her eyes, she ducked her head again and reached for the pack. "I'm sorry."

"Stop." Edrik stepped toward her. "I'll carry that." He drew a deep breath and slipped his baldric off over his head. "You will carry this." He held the sword out to Kaya. Her gaze flitted from his face to the sword and back again, eyes cautious as if she suspected a trap. "Please," he said. "Before I change my mind. You might be right, and there's only one way to know."

Slowly, Kaya reached for the sword. "I might be wrong." Her voice rasped slightly.

Edrik reached out to touch her shoulder, but she flinched away and he let his hand drop. "You might be. But you should always say what you think." He steadied himself with another long breath and added, "Touch the ruby to your forehead; that will link it to you instead of me. It'll help your back." He reached for the pack. "Where did you want this?"

She pointed, and he moved the pack, and everyone started breathing again. Grabak brought out his flute, and Finn started sharpening his knives, and Kaya settled down to put her satchel back in order. Edrik put some more wood on the fire and stepped outside to get some air, huddling under the cottage's generous eaves to stay out of the rain.

Stars . . . what if Kaya was right?

CHAPTER
15

The journey from the abandoned orchard steading to the village of Grebe's Landing should have taken less than a day, but the relentless rain turned the road into a river of boot-sucking mud and the grassy verge into a slippery, matted mess. As Kaya slogged along, she had to admit she was grateful not to be carrying the pack anymore. With the satchel slung over one shoulder and Edrik's sword banging against her hip on the other side, only the weight of her damp wool cloak pressed against the healing wounds on her back. And with Finn's report that the Thane had given up pursuit, Kaya's heart felt nearly as light. The day's travel might almost have been pleasant if not for the rain. And the mud. And the dragons.

All three of her traveling companions were behaving strangely. Grabak kept offering her his arm every time her foot slid on a slick tuft of grass. Finn stopped muttering obscenities under his breath and started humming jaunty drinking songs and poking occasional fun at the other dragons. And Edrik, who had been cheerfully friendly even in the dungeon, turned sullen and silent. When they bedded down for the night in the blessedly dry hayloft of a sturdy barn, instead of sprawling out next to Kaya as he had done most nights in the forest, he sat up all night staring out one of the two dormer windows that let in the moonlight. Was he watching for pursuers? Wondering if Kaya was right about his sword? Missing his princess?

The sun had finally broken through the clouds, and Kaya's clothes felt almost dry when they reached the tiny hamlet of Grebe's Landing the following afternoon. The village sat on a low rise in the bend of the Silver Birch River, where a huddle of houses and one or two small shops clung to the legs of a stone watchtower. A tattered patchwork of small farms and orchards spread out from the village like a much-mended skirt.

The Ratatosk barge town Finn had seen, probably also delayed by the storm, still rode at anchor just off the river bank. It was a smaller town than most Kaya had seen from the docks at Shrike's Hollow—only two barges with their attendant houseboats and fishing skims—but the larger towns rarely cared to navigate the narrow channels of the tributaries. This far from the main flow of the Drasil even a small Tosky town drew plenty of farmers, and crafters, and shop men looking for a good trade. A makeshift market had grown up on the muddy riverbank.

Kaya had vague, childish memories of markets like this one, where goods were bought and sold from the backs of wagons and donkeys and from blankets spread out under shady trees, where traders made their careful way along the floating wooden walkways that stretched from the riverbank to the barges while the Tosky town's children scampered around and between them like a school of giggling flicker fish. But after so many years of haggling at the permanent, orderly booths and stalls of the Shrike's Hollow dock market, this chaos seemed like a completely new experience to her.

Also familiar, but at the same time awkwardly foreign, was the way people's eyes followed Kaya as she worked her way carefully through the muddle, trailing behind Grabak. People had certainly looked at her before—she was accustomed to the darting, suspicious glances and disgusted stares her old dungeon keeper guise had drawn. But they hadn't really been looking at *her* then; they'd been eying the ratty hair and soot-smudged brown skin and wondering what gruesome dungeon messes might have caused the stains that smattered the ragged robe. No one had even noticed the girl behind the illusion, let alone paused to really look at her. But they saw her now. They saw her, and judged her, and the men's eyes followed her with a frightening, hungry interest. It made Kaya feel naked. Did they look at all women that way?

She quickened her step, moving closer to Grabak—and nearly collided with him as he turned away from the river and headed uphill. She clutched at his arm and stopped walking, dragging him to a halt. "I thought we were hiring a boat." She looked meaningfully toward the floating wooden walkway that stretched from the riverbank out to the Barge Master's office—an elaborately painted, square-cornered house-boat that rode close to shore.

Grabak smiled rather patronizingly down at her. "In good time, young Mudge. First, we'll need coin to hire it with."

Kaya scowled. "There's enough in that purse I gave you this morning to get us halfway at least."

"We need to go more than halfway. And you'll need your money later if you want to set up as a healer."

"We need to get on the river as quickly as possible. The solstice isn't going to wait for us. And what if someone recognizes one of us?"

Grabak scanned the crowd and shrugged. "The town is full of strangers just now, and you look very different than you did in the dungeon. Why should anyone pay you any mind? The rest of us have never been here, and I've spent the past half decade in a dungeon no one ever leaves alive. Who's going to recognize us?"

"Stig, we need to—"

"We *need* more coin. It would take too long to walk even half of the journey. We can't afford the time it would take to stop partway and bargain for another boat, even assuming another boat is available and we can find a way to earn the coin for it. We need more coin now. And I know where to get some." He patted her hand in what he probably thought was a reassuring manner and strode off as if that settled it.

"Stig!" She called after him, exasperated. He didn't even slow down. She heaved a sigh. "What about horses?" she muttered under her breath to his retreating back.

Finn chuckled, startling her with his nearness. "Obviously, you've never seen how a horse reacts when a dragon gets too close." He placed his hand against the small of her back to urge her forward. Kaya flinched at the stab of pain as his fingers pressed inadvertently against the branded dwarrow runes. She covered the flinch by smacking his hand away and growling, "Don't touch me."

Finn grinned and held his hands out in a gesture of mocking surrender as he turned to follow Grabak.

Edrik saw the flinch and knew what it meant. He put his own hand on her shoulder, holding her back, and turned her to face him. "Your wounds are still hurting you?"

The concern in his quiet voice made Kaya's heart flutter.

She clenched her teeth against the feeling and met his eyes—their pale green looked gray against the overcast sky. "I'm fine."

His eyes narrowed, studying her face. "Are you?" He leaned forward abruptly and skimmed his hand from her shoulder down the middle of her back. She lurched a startled step forward, colliding with his broad chest. She flinched harder against him when his fingers hit the burns at her waist and gasped as his other arm came up to steady her.

She thrashed away from the unexpected near-embrace, breathing heavily, blood rushing to her face, hand fumbling reflexively for the knife in her hip pocket. "Don't you *ever* do that again!"

Edrik folded his arms across his chest. "That doesn't seem fine to me, Mudge."

"Don't call me that!" she snapped. "What if somebody heard you?" The last thing she needed was for one of the townsfolk to recognize her as the Thane's dungeon keeper.

"Sorry." He glanced sheepishly around, checking for eavesdroppers, before his gaze returned to her. "But you've had my sword for a couple of days, it should be better than that by now." He frowned and reached one hand out to brush her cheek. "At least that black eye is gone."

Kaya swatted his hand away, trying not to let her face show how her heart was pounding, and turned to follow the others.

Edrik caught her elbow. "Something's wrong, Kaya." He stepped closer, brows drawn, eyes earnest. "If it's not better by tonight, I want to see your back again."

"I should never have let you see it in the first place!" She stalked away from him, annoyed to find that she was trembling.

He followed, his longer legs easily catching up and keeping pace with her. After a moment, he said softly, "I could tell Grabak about the burns, if you prefer, and he could check them. It doesn't have to be me."

She whirled to face him, putting all the defiance she could muster into her words. "I said I'm fine."

This time when she stomped away, Edrik gave her space. She focused on catching up with Grabak and tried not to think about how it felt to have Edrik's arms around her.

CHAPTER 16

Edrik frowned as he watched Kaya stalk away from him. He found her increasingly unsettling, and touching her had only made it worse. Kaya's frame was smaller than Lissara's and more delicate—that was how she'd managed to pass as a gangly adolescent boy for so long. But the strength he'd felt in her slender body when she stumbled into him had wakened something primal deep inside him—something that had come abruptly, intensely alert when her body shuddered against his a heartbeat later, and her soft gasp sent tingles down his spine to lodge just beneath his diaphragm.

Had he ever felt that burst of sharp awareness with Lissara? Looking at Lissara, touching her, kissing her, always brought a profound sense of wonder, of awe that a creature so beautiful, so graceful, so powerfully magical, would allow him close to her, that she would take him into her confidence and share anything of herself with him. The feeling Kaya had stirred was . . . different. Less civilized. More intense, perhaps. A flash of lightning beside the steady gleam of the full moon.

A soft, traitorous voice in the back of his mind (that sounded suspiciously like Finn) pointed out that after all, he was not promised to Lissara—not truly—and the only promise she'd made to him had been made equally to any other man who brought her father back before the summer solstice.

But he loved Lissara. He had loved her ever since the day he'd found her weeping out beyond the lily pond when she was twelve and he was nearly fourteen. She'd dropped her sugar cake, and when he slipped in through the cellar window and filched another for her from the pantry, he'd experienced the joy, the utter bliss, of knowing that her glorious smile was all for him. Just for him. He loved Lissara. Soon he would be with her again, and this time she would be truly his.

He shook his head and started after the others. Kaya was no more than a small distraction. A reminder that he was still a man, and that it had been too long since he held Lissara in his arms.

Grabak, it turned out, had been heading for the tavern at the base of the Grebe's Landing watchtower, a somewhat untidy-looking establishment built of precariously stacked stone, with a common room downstairs and a second floor that presumably consisted of living quarters. By the time Edrik caught up with Finn and Kaya, the old Drake was already concluding an agreement with the frazzled taverner, both of them shouting to be heard over the noise of patrons irritable with overcrowding and having to wait.

"Oh, ach." The taverner thumped a brimming tankard onto the counter and wiped a hand down the greasy front of his apron. "Meals in the common for you and yourn, and you can pocket your take if ye can quiet this lot and keep 'em from stringin' me up fer not pullin' ale fast enow. But mind, there ain't a bed in the house nor a stick o' straw in the stable loft what ain't already spoke for, so you'll have to find other lodgings fer the night." He thumped another tankard onto the counter next to the first, and the mismatched pair was immediately snatched up and whisked away by a plump girl with a low-cut dress and a harried expression.

Grabak grinned and smacked a hand on the counter. "Done then."

Pulling the tap to fill another tankard, the taverner grumbled, "Good fer business, I suppose, but won't be a moment's peace 'til them thrice-broke Toskies up anchor and shove along." The taverner waved a hand at one of the serving girls and bellowed orders.

Before long, Grabak was seated on a low stool beside the massive fireplace that dominated one end of the common room, and the others were squeezed elbow to elbow onto a bench at the end of one of the long tables by the wall. The Drake rapped his knobby staff loudly on the hearthstone, and the din stilled enough for his booming voice to be heard over what was left.

"'Twas a time . . .," he declaimed solemnly, and the room quieted even further. It probably wasn't often that a storyteller wandered into Grebe's Landing. "'Twas a time long past," Grabak continued, "perhaps before the Breaking—but just as likely after, for there are princes enough in the world even now, and such adventures happen more often than you might expect." His face shifted into a sly, knowing smile, and a quiet, collective chuckle rippled through the common room. "However that may be, the prince who had this particular adventure was the youngest of six sons. His name was Neskonungarmodvitnir, but since even his mother thought that too big a mouthful for everyday wear, everybody called him Boots."

Edrik smiled. The heroes of Grabak's stories were always called Boots and were usually eldest sons or youngest sons. As the sole offspring of his parents, Edrik had once asked Grabak whether only sons ever had great adventures. To his delight, Grabak had replied that they had twice as many, being the eldest and youngest rolled into one. But Edrik had learned since then that adventures are generally more fun to hear about than to live through, and now the thought of twice as many only made him envy middle sons, whose lives were apparently more or less routine.

"With so many older brothers," Grabak was saying, "Boots never expected to rule the kingdom, but one brother died heroically in battle, and another was lost at sea. The third was taken by a water nixie, the fourth was eaten by a dragon, and the fifth fell off a ladder while valiantly attempting to rescue a princess from a very high tower—though there was some doubt later as to whether the lady was truly in need of rescue or had just been placed in the tower to deter young men from climbing in her bedroom window, which may or may not have been a recurring problem."

A titter rippled through the crowd like a wave through water, and

Grabak leaned back on his stool, grinning while he waited for it to pass. He had them now, and he obviously knew it.

Edrik reflected that perhaps middle sons were no safer from adventure than anyone else after all.

Grabak continued, "When the old king died, Boots found himself in the enviable position of inheriting the entire kingdom. And he also found himself in immediate need of a bride, for with such an accident-prone family, he needed heirs as soon as soon might be. He set off to visit a nearby king who was rumored to have two beautiful and accomplished daughters, hoping to find one of them to be a suitable bride. But alas, he fell afoul of a band of ogres, who robbed him, and beat him, and left him for dead in the forest.

"One of the castle kitchen maids happened to be picking berries in the forest and stumbled upon Boots. Because he was handsome, as all princes ought to be if they can possibly manage it, her heart was moved, and she took pity on him. Because he was also rather large and heavy, and she decidedly was not, she was unequal to the task of carrying him home with her. With great effort, she managed to drag him rather unceremoniously into a nearby cave, where she tended his wounds and wrapped him in her own rough cloak.

"Every night when her kitchen work was finished, the maid went back to the cave to tend to Boots. She brought him food, and cleaned his wounds, and sang to him until he fell asleep. Boots, quite naturally, fell deeply in love with the kind woman, but since she only came at night, he never saw her face. However, when the ogres had robbed Boots, they had failed to notice a secret pocket in the waistband of his trousers, in which he had hidden a golden ring intended as a gift for his bride. One night, when the kitchen maid came, he told her of his love for her which, fortunately for him, she returned, and he slipped the ring onto her finger.

"When he was well enough recovered, Boots left the cave and made his way to the castle. When the kitchen maid saw that Boots was the long-awaited king, she was too frightened to speak to him. But he was received with great joy by the princesses, who were both more beautiful than the rumors had said. When they heard his story, each of the princesses claimed to be the woman who had come to Boots in the darkness of night—but of course, neither had his ring. The elder said it had slipped from her finger as she walked by the river and a fish had swallowed it. The younger said a rock gnome had snatched it as she played in the garden. Since Boots had never seen the face of his rescuer, he could not be sure whether one or the other was telling the truth, and he knew it was unwise to accuse a king's daughter of deceit."

Kaya shifted restlessly on the bench next to Edrik, and he glanced over at her. She looked sick. And her dark eyes were riveted on something near the door. He shifted in his seat so he could follow her gaze. A tall, bearded man in a smart gray uniform leaned against the wall beside the door, listening to Grabak's story. Edrik reached under the table to touch Kaya's hand, drawing her attention. "Someone you know?"

Kaya nodded almost imperceptibly. "Thanesson's man. He keeps a small guard of his own, separate from the Thane's. At least it's not a dungeon guard."

"He won't recognize you." Edrik kept his voice low and tried to sound reassuring. "But you're less likely to draw his attention if you keep your head down and look at Grabak like everyone else. I'll keep an eye on your friend."

Kaya swallowed hard and turned reluctantly toward Grabak, who went on with his story, unaware.

"It happened at this time that another princess was visiting the same castle. Some say she was a fae from Falia in the north. Others claim she was a daughter of the Woodland King. Whichever she was, fae or alfkin, her magic showed her how matters stood. But Boots was very handsome, and she desired him for herself, so instead of revealing the truth, she declared that if Boots could tell a true princess from a false and choose the woman who had rescued him, he might marry her. If not, she would take Boots as her own and carry him away with her. None dared defy her, for she commanded powerful magic."

The man at the door turned to look outside. His hand raised slightly, then fell. A greeting to someone passing by? A signal?

"Boots, being clever as well as handsome, devised a plan. He invited all the princesses to visit his palace, and while they prepared for their journey, he went ahead to make ready. When the princesses arrived, he disguised himself as a poor, sick beggar and sat beside the road.

"Whichever of the princesses took pity on me before will surely do so again, he thought, *and then I will know her."*

A second man in gray stepped through the door, eyes scanning the tavern's common room before coming to rest on Grabak. Edrik nudged Finn under the table with his boot and flicked his eyes toward the door.

Finn followed his gaze and frowned slightly. "Must've gone down the river," he muttered. "There was no one in the woods."

"The elder princess passed by on the other side of the road, holding her kerchief to her nose. The younger princess kicked over the beggar man's tin cup and said she'd have him locked in a dungeon if he bothered respectable people again. The third princess merely smiled slyly as she passed, more certain than ever that Boots would be hers in the end."

The second man went out again, and the first one smiled as he leaned back against the wall.

"As Boots was sorrowfully resigning himself to his fate and preparing to go back to the castle, the princesses' baggage train passed. Among the servants was the kitchen maid, whose kind heart was filled with pity for the beggar's plight. The only thing of value that she had to offer was the ring Boots had given her, which she wore on a string around her neck to keep it from the other servants' eyes. She drew the ring out and placed it in the beggar's cup, saying he had more need of it than she."

The second man returned, bringing a third and fourth with him. Finn shifted uneasily on the bench, and Edrik elbowed him.

"When he saw the ring, Boots demanded to know how she had come by it. The little maid told how she had found a man dying in the woods and nursed him back to health. She'd fallen in love with him, she said, but he turned out to be a king, and far above her station. And since he was to marry one of the princesses, she was just as glad to be rid of the ring, for it only made her sad to look at it. As she spoke, Boots's heart sang with joy, for he well knew the sound of her voice. He took her back to his castle, and before his folk and all the guests, he removed his disguise and declared that he had found his true princess and made his choice. They were married immediately, of course, and lived, so far as I have heard, in happiness all their days."

A murmur of approval rippled through the tavern.

The men at the door spread out, giving each other room to move; they were preparing for a fight.

Edrik's hand strayed to the long knife at his belt. He should never have given his sword to Kaya.

"And so we see"—Grabak grinned at his audience, his eyes lingering for a moment on Edrik—"that it is well to be kind to servant girls, for every maid might be a princess." His sweeping gesture took in the serving girls who worked their tired way between the tables; two of them turned sunny smiles on him. Grabak winked back and rose from the stool, drawing his tin cup from a fold of his cloak. "And it is better to be kind to beggar men, for every beggar might be a king." He presented the tin cup with a grand, flourishing bow, and his audience roared with laughter that broke up into a babble of observations about the story and calls for another one. Several coins clattered into the cup, and others skittered across the hearth, tossed at the storyteller by those too far back to reach.

One of the men by the door called out, "And every storyteller might be a dragon, escaped from a Thane's dungeon."

Abrupt, tense silence filled the room, and everybody froze. The Thanesson's men slowly unsheathed their swords.

"Oh, ach, it's him all right," called another voice from the door leading back to the kitchen—and presumably a rear entrance.

Edrik turned to see three more gray-clad men drawing their swords. A fourth man, the one speaking, wore the dun and black livery of the Thane. "That drake the Mudge kept down the dwarrow hole. Seen 'im down there oft enow. Still got his collar on and all."

"That one *is* a dungeon guard," Kaya muttered darkly.

There was a general rumbling, shuffling sound as the tavern's patrons flocked to the door, abandoning food and drink in favor of a chance at escape before the obviously impending fight broke out. The Thanesson's men let them go, staying focused on Grabak and fanning out around him like wolves stalking dangerous prey.

"They haven't recognized you yet," Edrik murmured to Kaya. "You could slip out with the rest."

"Stig is my friend." She shot him a venomous glare and leaned across Edrik to poke Finn hard in the elbow. "Can't you ascend and eat them, or roast them, or something?"

Finn raised both eyebrows in mock surprise. "You wouldn't object to me killing them this time? Do none of them have sixteen children and an aged grandmother waiting for them back home?"

Edrik elbowed Finn hard in the ribs again and explained quietly to Kaya, "Finn is not particularly precise. If he ascended here, he'd take out half the wall and bring the entire tavern crashing down on our heads. And if, by some miracle, that didn't happen, breathing fire in a space this small would roast everyone in it, including us."

"What about compulsion, then. Can't he compel them not to attack?"

Edrik shrugged. "Not so many. Not from here."

Kaya snorted. "Useless. I should have left his collar on."

The tavern was almost entirely empty by this time, and Edrik didn't want to be trapped behind the table when the attack came. He rose to his feet, slipping the long knife free of his belt.

The movement caught the attention of the livery-clad dungeon guard. "Hoy!" he bellowed. "Ain't that the drake what jumped Egil down by the delvers' quarters?"

All eyes shifted toward Edrik. And toward Finn, who was rising to his feet beside Edrik, tugging his short spear free of the looped rope he used to secure it across his back.

One of the Thanesson's men swore. "And that's the one we brung in from the north woods. I guess it does pay to check the river towns." He chuckled.

Kaya half rose and braced both hands against the table top as if preparing to scamper over it into the fray. Edrik's sword thumped uselessly against the edge of the table, swinging in its scabbard at her hip.

Did she even know how to use a sword? Probably not. She was going to get herself killed. The thought twisted in Edrik's belly, turning to stone, then ice. He couldn't let that happen. He clamped a hand down on her shoulder and pushed her back into her seat. "Stay out of this, Mudge."

She flinched, and he realized what he'd just said.

So did the dungeon guard. "Mudge?" The guard raised his eyebrows and took a step closer to the table, squinting hard at Kaya. "Is that you, Mudge?" A barked laugh. "You're a *woman*!" His face broke into a leering grin.

Kaya rose slowly to her feet again and leaned forward, eyes narrowed, palms pressed flat on the table. "Hello, Tavit." Her voice was wry and mocking. "You're a weasel."

The guard hawked a sputtering snort and spat on the floor. One of the gray-clad men shouted something, and the rest sprang into action. Finn leapt lightly onto the bench and then surged over the top of the table, spear flashing. Edrik swore and snatched his sword free of its scabbard with one hand and, with the other, pressed Kaya firmly back into her seat.

"Stay here." He put every drop of command he could muster into his words and willed her to listen for a change. "Don't move."

He touched the ruby to his forehead, and the sword hummed in his hand as it always did in battle, pulsing with the rhythm of the fight. Edrik flew into the dance, letting the fierce joy of the sword's magic wash through him as the white blade caught iron and shunted it away, then flashed toward the belly of a gray-clad guard. Two of the Thanesson's men went down in the initial rush—one on the point of Finn's spear and one under the onslaught of Edrik's sword. But the other five were well trained, and well armed, and held their own. The dungeon guard hovered at the edge of the fight, dodging in only occasionally to strike a blow. Kaya, for a wonder, stayed in her seat behind the table, hands still splayed against the wood, eyes wide and frightened in her ashen face.

Grabak cracked one guard hard enough in the skull with his staff to lay the man out on the floor. His next blow caught the edge of the fireplace, and the wood smashed to splinters on the stone. The Drake flung the ragged end away and dodged, drawing a knife.

Edrik spun away from his attacker to protect his king, catching a sword just before it struck home. Another blade hissed behind him, and he twisted in time to knock it away and open the man's throat, spattering blood. Before the body hit the floor, Edrik ducked another blow and lunged, just missing his target.

The melee broke apart, as both sides stepped back to take stock. Two gray men, and the dungeon guard formed an arc between the three dragons and any possible escape. The dragons slowly shifted away from the hearth, angling their defense to better include Kaya, who still sat frozen behind the table. Edrik had his sword, but Grabak was down to a knife and so, Edrik realized, was Finn, his spear abandoned where it had lodged between the ribs of a gray man writhing on the floor beyond the others. The knives didn't allow enough reach to get past a sword, and even a scratch from an iron blade could incapacitate long enough for a kill.

A soft gasp made Edrik turn his head to glance at Kaya, and the guards charged, catching him off balance. Both of the Thanesson's men went after Edrik while the dungeon guard held Finn and Grabak at bay, not attacking, but feinting with the iron sword whenever either made a move to help. Edrik spun and twisted, blocking and dodging too fast to strike a blow of his own, fighting back a growing fear that it was only a matter of time until he tired or made a mistake, and one sword or the other had him.

But Kaya moved at last, breaking free of her daze and leaping onto the bench and off the tabletop like a springing cat. She caught one of Edrik's attackers by the hair on the way down, yanking his head back while she drew a knife across his throat with her other hand. The last gray man disengaged, shouted at the dungeon guard, and both of them sprinted for the door.

Edrik watched them go. Grinning, he turned to Kaya and raised the sword's pommel in salute. "Thank you."

Kaya's angry fist caught him hard under the ribcage. Air exploded out of Edrik's lungs as his diaphragm spasmed, making it impossible to draw breath; his legs buckled, and he fell to his knees.

Kaya glared furiously down at him, shaking hard. Her breaths came in ragged gasps as she jabbed an accusing finger at him. "If you ever c-compel me again, you had b-better kill me as well, Edrik, because I s-swear to you I will c-cut your tongue out and feed it t-to—"

"Compel?" Edrik choked out as the spasm began to ease. He sucked in a strained breath. "I didn't." He gaped at her. "I can't."

Grabak laid one hand on Kaya's shoulder and tipped her chin up with the other, studying her face. "Are you all right, Mudge?"

Kaya shook him off. "I'm f-freezing. And I c-can't . . ." She sat down hard on the floor next to Edrik and put her head between her drawn-up knees. They all stared at her. After a moment, without looking up at them, she said, "You made me s-sit there and watch while they almost k-killed you."

"No," Edrik said, rubbing at his gut with one hand. "I couldn't have. I'm pinioned."

Kaya, still shivering violently, snorted a derisive laugh. "You're n-not pinioned. You're just s-stupid."

Edrik stared at her. His breath was coming more easily, but his mind whirled. "Stars," he whispered. "I told you to stay there."

"You s-said, 'Don't move.'" Kaya pinned him with an accusing scowl. "And then I c-couldn't."

"It's too soon. Even if you're right about my sword, I've only been without it for a couple of days."

She shrugged one trembling shoulder. "And all those d-days in the dungeon."

"And a few days before that when you left your sword with Tait and me," Finn put in quietly. "We should get out of here; they might be coming back. With friends." He moved to where he could keep a watch out the door.

Grabak draped Kaya's cloak around her shoulders. "Well, *someone* certainly compelled her. And she broke it. Look at her." He sounded like a proud father.

Kaya tugged the cloak closer and buried her forehead in her knees again. "You're s-stupid too," she muttered. "I b-bet you didn't even notice when T-Tavit picked your p-pocket."

CHAPTER 17

"How could I not have noticed?" Grabak grumbled as they neared the make-shift market, moving with the crowd and trying to be inconspicuous while keeping an eye out for guards.

"He's very good at it. Haven't you been paying attention all these years?" Kaya sighed, tugging her cloak tighter. The shivering had mostly subsided, but she couldn't seem to get warm all the way through. "It's what Tavit does—starts a tavern brawl and then goes through everyone's pockets while they're busy thrashing each other. It's why the other guards won't drink with him. If it makes you feel any better, he got two of the Thanesson's men as well."

"That does not make me feel better," Grabak muttered. "I'd prefer to have their purses myself." He poked through the small assortment of coins he'd picked off the hearth at the tavern and pilfered from the fallen gray men. "Not enough to hire a boat. But we can resupply a bit."

"We won't get there before the solstice without a boat," Kaya pointed out.

Finn heaved a sigh. "Would that be so bad?"

"The princess wouldn't marry Edrik."

"Then she doesn't really want him, and he's a fool to marry her anyway."

"And," Kaya said, "if the queen marries the Black Dragon, he'll steal Stig's magic and be able to compel—"

"Hush!" Finn hissed. "Are you *trying* to get us killed?" His eyes darted around the market as if searching for hidden pitchforks and iron fishing gaffes. "Besides, that's nonsense. Nobody can compel a dragon. Grabak just said that to get you to let us out of the dungeon."

"No," Grabak said, "it's the truth. Ofnir the Drake swore us to silence so others would not be tempted, but I was there when it happened. The husband went slowly mad. Even chained in iron, he was a danger and had to be put down. The lover . . . the second husband . . . bond mate . . . whatever he was to her..." Grabak sighed and scrubbed a hand over his face, as if to erase the memory. "Well, he was a power-hungry fool who made rather a mess before he was . . . stopped."

"And by stopped," Kaya said uneasily, "you mean killed."

Grabak nodded, mouth set in a grim line. "There aren't many left who remember. But Nidhaug does. We have to get there before the solstice."

They walked in silence for a few minutes. Then Finn said, "We could compel a boatman."

"Long enough to get to the Edge of the World?" Grabak snorted. "You'd break his mind and sink us to the bottom of the Drasil. Not to mention undoing decades of hard work improving relations between the Ratatosk and Vanir."

"Why don't we just fly there?" Kaya put in. "I mean, if Edrik can compel, can't he—"

"Flight takes practice," Grabak said. "And we don't have time for that."

"You could have Kaya take your collar off," Finn growled. "Then we could—"

"No." Grabak's tone left no more room for argument.

Edrik stopped and pretended to examine the goods laid out on a plank held up by two stools. He hadn't said anything since the tavern. And he hadn't so much as looked at Kaya. He must be furious with her for hitting him and saying he was stupid. And maybe for breaking his compulsion. Would that make a dragon angry?

She adjusted her satchel and brushed a finger against the ruby pommel of Edrik's sword at her hip. She had expected him to take it back from her as soon as he could reach the magic. He *should* have taken it back. It was all he had left from his father. And it was a part of him, too, somehow. In the fighting, Edrik had wielded the sword with a deadly, fluid grace that was breathtaking to watch, as if the blade were a natural extension of his body. It felt wrong to take it from him, like an unnecessary amputation—a thing the questioner might do.

But he hadn't kept it. While Finn recovered his spear from the body of the dead gray man, and Grabak scavenged for coins, Edrik had wordlessly cleaned the white sword and, without meeting Kaya's eyes, touched the pommel to her forehead and slid the blade slowly into the scabbard that still hung at her hip. With him standing there almost, but not quite, touching her, Kaya had experienced a dangerous urge to burst into tears and wrap her arms around him. She'd wanted to apologize for calling him stupid. For hitting him. Only, the words got tangled up in the wild, dragon scent of his nearness and the pounding of her heart, and before she could sort them out, he'd turned grimly away.

But what difference does it make, really, if he hates me? It might even make things easier. He is, after all, still going home to his princess.

The thought made Kaya ache with envy. And yet, it was only right. Edrik loved Lissara. That was clear in the way he spoke of her. He had come on this mad quest in the first place so he could be with her. It would be more wrong to separate Edrik from the woman he loved than it was to separate him from his sword. And somehow, the aching, twisting, longing part of Kaya that wanted Edrik for herself wanted even more for him to be whole and happy. So she would help him get back to Lissara—before the solstice. Maybe seeing them together would make it easier to let go of him. Of the *idea* of him. Which, after all, was all she'd ever really had.

She pushed past the others and started walking fast, needing to get where she was going before she changed her mind.

"Mudge!" Grabak hurried after her. "Stop. Where are you going?"

His fingers caught at her elbow, but she pulled away.

"I'm going to hire a boat."

He snorted. "With what? I just told you, we don't have enough coin."

Kaya heaved an impatient sigh. "We're friends, Stig . . . of a sort. But do you really think I'd give you everything I have, all at once? Besides, sometimes there are other ways." She tugged her arm free of his grip and continued down the muddy path toward the river.

THE SINGLE, LONG ROOM OF THE BARGE MASTER'S HOUSEBOAT OFFICE was not crowded. A small group of men and women stood to one side dickering over the details of a trade. Four or five young men spoke together in low voices near the doorway. A couple of burly, dark-skinned Tosky men, probably there to keep order when trade disputes grew heated, lounged against one wall, bored. At the far end of the room, the Barge Master himself, a tall, spare man with skin the same shade of brown as his massive walnut desk, frowned over a long roll of parchment that lay on the desktop. He looked up when Kaya strode into the room followed by the three dragons.

"Yes?" His tone said he resented the interruption and would tolerate no nonsense.

Kaya drew a deep breath and squared her shoulders. "I am the daughter of a Free man. I've come to claim refuge among my father's people."

The Barge Master's eyes scanned her from head to foot and flicked back to take in her companions. "Is that blood on your clothes?"

Kaya tipped her chin up defiantly. "Thus my need for refuge."

The man tapped an absentminded finger against the parchment as he considered. "You're a halfblood," he mused. "Married?"

Kaya raised her eyebrows. "Does it matter?"

A smile spread across the Barge Master's face, and he settled into the large, high backed chair behind the desk. "Not to a claim of refuge, no; half is enough Free blood for that. But it might affect the terms if you seek to join our town." He glanced to where the group of young Tosky men had stopped chatting and were eying Kaya with interest.

Did this town have a shortage of available young women?

If that became too big of a problem, a barge town's young men might stir up trouble by courting women belonging to the kingdoms along the riverbanks. Or turn disperser and leave the town altogether in search of better prospects in other Tosky towns.

She cleared her throat. "I seek only passage downriver for myself and my friends."

The Barge Master frowned and shook his head. "Your friends are not of the Free People; we can't shelter Landers from Lander justice. And I'm sorry, but we can't spare a boat to carry passengers anywhere at present. But we can offer you refuge with us until we reach a port that's safe for you."

The man was clever. Keep her in the town and eliminate competition for her attention, and she might settle down with one of the town's young men and have lots of little brown Tosky babies. There was some appeal in that, she had to admit. Sometimes she ached for the life she'd had with her parents. But that life was over for her long ago.

She cleared her throat. "I can't leave my friends."

"Yes, you can." Behind her, Edrik's voice was terse. Almost bitter. "You don't owe us anything, Kaya. And we'd be able to travel faster without you." He was trying to get rid of her. Was he really that angry?

She turned to face him. "Not as fast as you could travel on the river."

"You'd be safer here," Edrik said.

"It would have been safer to stay where I was and just let them kill you." She folded her arms defiantly across her chest. "But I started this, and I'm going to see it through whether you like it or not." She turned back to the Barge Master. "I'll pay half a crown for passage to the Edge of the World."

The Barge Master's eyes narrowed, moving from Kaya to Edrik and back. "Half a crown? Therrish or Vagandian?" Then he shook his head. "Either way, it's not enough. Any boat that could make that run would get twice as much in half the time running furs up to Plover."

"Gorian," Kaya said—and watched the Barge Master's face as that sank in; fae coinage was becoming increasingly rare. "I can pay half a silver crown now and another half crown when we get to the Edge. But we need to leave right away."

The Barge Master's frown deepened, and his eyes narrowed. He was tempted. "Show me."

Kaya hesitated for only a moment. Then she tugged a knife from a pocket and lifted the edge of her skirt, revealing the layered ruffles of her dark green petticoat. Her fingers tested the edge of one of the ruffles until they found what she was looking for. Then she made a small slit in the ruffled hem and extracted two small, silver half moon coins, which she displayed on her palm. Everyone stared.

"Kaya . . ." Grabak scowled like a disapproving parent. "Where did you get two Gorian half crowns?"

Annoyance flared up, hot and tight, in Kaya's chest. How dare he question her in front of the Barge Master! She bit down on her temper and arranged her face into the kind of suggestive simper she'd seen courtesans use. "Oh, you know," she said sweetly. "Trading favors."

The look of shocked outrage on Grabak's face as he demanded, "What kind of favors?" was terribly satisfying.

Then Kaya's gaze flickered in Edrik's direction, and their eyes met. His face went carefully blank, and Kaya's heart sank. Would it always be like this between them now? She turned back to Stig, and her tone was more subdued as she explained. "A few years ago, an Eastland nobleman and his wife were visiting . . . my former patron . . . when the wife was brought to bed with an unusually long and painful labor. When the midwife found that the baby was too large for the birth to end happily, she sent for me; we had an arrangement. I made an incision in the mother's abdomen, through which the midwife delivered the baby, and then I stitched the mother up. It's a chancy business, but better than just waiting for both of them to die. In this case, both the mother and the child survived, though both were a bit worse for wear. The man gave me a half crown for saving his wife and another for saving his son." She cleared her throat. "Not that it's any of your business, Stig."

Grabak harrumphed.

The Barge Master shifted in his seat and smiled. "A tidy tale. Perhaps in a week or two we can arrange something. But at present, as I said, I haven't got a boat to spare."

No, he had a town full of unattached young men. Kaya's gaze drifted to the cluster of young Toskies by the door.

One of them saw her looking and quietly detached himself from the others. "I'll take you." His voice was quiet, but firm.

Kaya's brows rose. "What?"

The young man smiled shyly. "Your name is Kaya?" When she nodded, he continued. "I'm Nik. I'll take you to the Edge." He shrugged one shoulder. "I'm headed downriver anyway, and I could use the coin."

"My friends, too?" Kaya asked. Something didn't seem quite right here. Why would he contradict the Barge Master?

"Of course,"—Nik flashed her a smile, teeth white against his russet skin—"so long as they don't mind bunking on the deck with me, since my boat currently has only the one cabin, which would be reserved for my paying guest." He tilted his head respectfully toward Kaya. "I can include meals if you don't mind simple fare, but I regret other amenities are somewhat limited. It's a houseboat, not a passenger cruiser, and I'm . . . in the process of renovating." He grinned. "Perhaps you can give me some suggestions from a woman's perspective."

Kaya looked a question at the Barge Master, who frowned and released a tired sigh.

"Disperser," he said darkly. "Passing through. I can't stop you from going with him, but I also can't vouch for his character." His tone said he wasn't impressed with the young man, but that might just be because he put ideas into the heads of the other young men. And if he was a disperser, that would explain why he didn't feel obliged to abide by the Barge Master's decision.

Kaya shrugged. "You can't vouch for my character either." She ran her eyes over Nik, weighing his lean, muscular frame and tidy home-spun clothes. He looked respectable enough, but looks didn't always tell the whole story, and there was something in the confident way Nik looked at Kaya that made her nervous.

"How soon can you get us there?" she asked.

"Ah." Nik rubbed at the back of his neck. "As to that . . ." He glanced at the young men by the door and back to the scowling Barge Master. "I am short a few crew members." He met Kaya's eyes again and squared his shoulders. "In fact, it's just me at present, so we'll have to tie up at the riverbank at night. But I can still get you there faster than walking. Say . . . twelve days?"

That would be cutting it much too close. There were only fifteen days left before the solstice. If it took twelve just to get to the Edge, that left only three to get from the Edge to the Aerie and make whatever arrangements they could for allies. And Grabak had said it would take two just to get from the Edge to the Aerie. A boat that could travel at night would cut some time off the trip, as would one with sails. But right now, that wasn't an option.

She glanced at Grabak, who offered a scowling nod.

Kaya frowned. "How soon can you be ready to leave?"

Nik's grin broadened. "I'm always ready."

CHAPTER 18

E drik leaned against the railing that edged the platform of Nik's
houseboat and watched the trees on the river bank glide past.
The light was dimming toward evening again, and soon they'd have to
stop for the night.

The first few nights, when they'd moored just off the riverbank, the
view had been a patchwork of farmers' fields and muddy cow tracks.
After the Silver Birch joined the main flow of the Drasil, they'd begun
to pass small fishing villages from time to time, but everyone agreed it
was wise to avoid being seen. They may be out of the Thane's jurisdic-
tion, but that hadn't stopped the Thanesson's men from coming after
them in Grebe's Landing. And now he knew which way they were
headed. And he knew that Kaya was a woman. So Nik had picked
secluded moorings, waiting until it was nearly dark to tie up on the
riverbank each night, and they'd all stayed on the boat and out of sight.

Yesterday, they'd passed the large port town of Kingfisher, which
crouched on the Drasil's northern bank at the edge of the forest. They
still had to stay out of sight whenever another boat passed them on the
river—particularly when the boat came from behind, pushed downriver
faster than the current by teams of pole men or tacking into the wind
on the wings of their sails. But there were no towns along this stretch
of the Drasil—at least, not human towns. For all anyone knew, there
might be whole cities of alfkin back behind the thick curtain of green-

ery. None but the alfkin were permitted in this forest, except on the river or the road. There was only one road, and traveling it was risky even for well-guarded trade caravans. Even the eyes of a dragon in flight couldn't penetrate the high canopy of the old trees.

A breeze blew, pleasantly cool against Edrik's skin, and the glare of the sun dropped behind the tree line, turning the few stray clouds from white to goldenrod. He should just relax and enjoy the evening, he supposed, but in spite of the whimsical lights of the spark flies that were beginning to gleam among the shadows at the forest's edge, knowing they were passing through the realm of the Woodland King set Edrik's teeth on edge. He shifted, restless.

Somewhere on the other side of the boat, behind the boxy, unfinished structure—it could hardly be called a house yet—that dominated the center of the rectangular platform, Finn and Grabak were arguing again. Edrik could hear the peevish tones of their voices but couldn't make out their words.

Kaya and Nik were nearer; they'd been standing together beside the tiller in the back corner of the platform when he passed them a moment ago. A stack of raw lumber hid them from Edrik's view, but now and again, their quiet words carried over the sounds of the water and the soft chuckling of the chickens that wandered the deck between the neatly arranged barrels of soil and sprouting greenery that constituted the beginnings of Nik's cottage garden.

Ostensibly, Nik was teaching Kaya how to steer the boat—and to be fair, some of the conversation certainly tended in that direction.

Nik had just finished explaining with great pride that the two rudders, one on each of the twin hulls that supported the platform, bore yot marks that made each rudder mimic the other's action, allowing him to steer with great precision from either tiller. But it was clear that Nik had an ulterior motive. Or, perhaps, just an additional motive—he wasn't exactly being subtle about it. Nik was a disperser in search of a wife, and while he was careful not to frighten Kaya off by moving too fast, he certainly wasn't trying to hide his interest in her.

He'd spoken with her often, as they traveled, of his plans for the future and of the pleasant life and extensive family that waited for him back in the Tosky town he'd come from. And he listened with rapt attention when Kaya recalled little details about her first childhood home and of work she'd done as a healer. She never spoke to Nik of the dungeon, though—at least, not that Edrik ever heard. And Nik never pressed her with questions she didn't want to answer. It was obvious to everyone that their easy friendship was growing increasingly intimate.

A lull in their conversation at the tiller dragged on too long . . . and then perilously longer. *What were they doing?* Edrik was not spying on them. He wasn't. But maybe someone should make sure the Tosky wasn't taking advantage of Kaya. After all, living as she had, she couldn't have much experience dealing with men's advances. And Tosky men had a reputation. Stars, Kaya's own mother had run off with a Tosky boatman.

Edrik leaned forward just a little bit over the rail, turning so he could peer past the lumber. Kaya stood at the helm, gripping the arm of the tiller in both hands. She held her bottom lip lightly between her teeth as she focused all her attention on the river ahead. Nik stood a little behind her, watching with pleasure as she steered the boat without him but ready to step in with help if she needed it.

As Edrik watched, the tiller bucked slightly, and Kaya's mouth made a startled little "o" of surprise. Nik grinned and put one steadying hand behind her to rest on the tiller. Kaya twisted to look up at him as she laughed softly at herself. For half a heartbeat, as their eyes met, both of them went very still. Then, cautiously, Nik stepped closer and placed his other hand on the tiller in front of Kaya, enclosing her in the circle of his arms. The smile melted from Kaya's face, and she blinked up at Nik. The Tosky released one hand and drew back slightly, offering Kaya an escape if she wanted it; when she didn't move, Nik brought his hand up to her cheek in a gentle caress and tilted his face toward hers.

Edrik's heart spasmed, and his feet moved before he had quite given them permission. Nik and Kaya jumped when, with a stumbling scuff, Edrik appeared around the edge of the lumber pile. Kaya twisted in the curve of the Tosky's arm to face Edrik, and Nik stepped back—but not very much. Both of them looked expectantly at Edrik.

Edrik didn't quite know what to say; he hadn't exactly planned this. He'd been wanting to talk to Kaya since they boarded the boat. He needed to explain. To apologize. To find a way to repair their friendship. But he could never find her alone.

She was most emphatically not alone now—was, in fact, clearly engaged in an activity that did not require a third person. But . . . well, he did have her attention.

"I'm sorry to interrupt," Edrik began. As he said it, he knew it was a lie. He wasn't certain what he felt, but it definitely wasn't sorry. He cleared his throat. "Kaya, could I speak with you?"

Her brows furrowed, and she hesitated. What if she refused? What if she laughed at him? What if this only made things worse between them? His heart began to pound in his throat, and his quiet, "Please?" came out hoarse and a little shaky.

Kaya turned a wordless glance back on Nik and gave his hand an awkward pat, and then she left him standing at the tiller looking after her with a troubled frown as she walked over to where Edrik stood.

"What is it?" she whispered, too quietly for Nik to hear.

Edrik looked at his boots, unable to meet her eyes. "I owe you an apology. Maybe now isn't the best time,"—he shrugged—"but there hasn't been a good time. I just need to—" He looked up as Kaya's fingers landed lightly on his forearm, sending a warm shiver through his skin that reminded him of his reaction when she stumbled into him back in Grebe's Landing. His pulse quickened.

Kaya looked over her shoulder at Nik, hesitated, then slid her fingers down to nestle in Edrik's hand.

"Come with me," she said.

She led him through the framed part of Nik's small house, which was crammed with barrels, and boxes, and building materials, and through the door of the only finished, or at least mostly finished, room in the place—when Nik had said he was renovating the boat, what he'd meant was he was still in the process of building the thing. It was Nik's cabin, but he'd given it over to Kaya for this trip. Maybe it was out of courtesy for the only woman on board. Or maybe he hoped she'd like it enough to want to live there permanently.

The room was small, but neat and homey. High windows maintained privacy while letting in what was left of the light. Shelves and cupboards were built into the walls, along with a bench and a wide platform bed that were clearly intended for two. Wooden steps led down into one of the boat's twin hulls, where the cupboards and desks of a private double study were beginning to take shape amid a stack of lumber and a scattering of tools and wood shavings.

Kaya released Edrik's hand as she pushed the door closed behind them. Without turning to face him, she said, "I've wanted to speak with you, too. I just didn't know how." She leaned her forehead against the back of the door. "I thought you were angry with me."

Something in the tone of her voice wrenched at Edrik's gut. She'd been *afraid* to talk to him. And who could blame her if she thought she'd angered a dragon.

He tried to make his voice gentle. "Not angry. I was ashamed. I . . . I betrayed you, Kaya. Called you Mudge right in front of those guards. I didn't mean to, it just came out. I'm sorry. It won't happen again."

She turned to face him, brows raised. "They would've figured it out on their own sooner or later."

He scrubbed a hand over the fuzz on his scalp. "And then I compelled you. You showed me how to reach my magic, and the first thing I did with it was turn it on you. You must despise me."

She coughed a small, incredulous laugh. "I don't despise you. I didn't much enjoy being pinned behind the table, but I don't think you did it to me on purpose."

A cautious sense of relief began to work its way through Edrik. "No," he hastened to agree. "That wasn't on purpose either. I didn't even realize I could do it. I hadn't compelled anyone before, and I didn't know what it felt like. I'm sorry, Kaya."

She studied his face. "So . . . does this mean you're not pinioned anymore? You can compel people whenever you like and turn into a . . . I mean . . . you can ascend?"

"Well, yes. In theory. But it doesn't seem wise to attempt ascension on a boat." The weight in his belly lifted a little when she grinned at the idea. But he still looked at his feet when he added. "And there are rules about compulsion. I shouldn't have done what I did to you. I just . . . didn't know I could. And I didn't want you to get hurt. That sounds so foolish now—trying to keep you safe by paralyzing you during a fight. What if one of them had gotten past me to you? You wouldn't have been able to defend yourself. And . . ."

Kaya made a small sound—Edrik wasn't sure if it was a laugh, or a sigh, or a quiet snort of incredulity.

When he met her eyes, she said, "That wasn't the worst part. The worst part was watching you . . . watching all of you . . . fighting for your lives and not being able to help. You're my friends. I didn't want to lose you. And I don't like feeling helpless." She looked down and shrugged one shoulder. "I shouldn't have gut punched you, though. I was angry, but that was unfair. And you're not stupid."

"Yes I am. Regularly."

She looked up, startled.

He grinned. "Just ask Finn."

Kaya giggled. She *giggled*. Had he ever heard her giggle before? It was certainly not the sort of thing she'd have done in the dungeon. In the dungeon, even her laughter had to be guarded. How had she lived like that for so long? What other little quirks were going to surface as she relaxed into her new life? The thought intrigued him—probably more than it should. What was wrong with him?

"I just wanted to keep you safe."

She studied his face seriously. "I don't need you to rescue me, Edrik."

"I know. But that doesn't keep me from wanting to." Edrik looked at his boots. "It's a sort of obsessive urge I have, I guess. Rescuing people."

Kaya laughed. "Well, then you're going to need this." She lifted his baldric over her head and held the white sword out to him. "I think it misses you."

Edrik hesitated. "How's your back?"

"My back is fine."

"Fine like it was in the orchard cottage or fine like it was in Grebe's Landing?" He frowned. "You always say it's fine, and it never is. Has someone checked it for you recently?"

The smile left Kaya's face. "Who would I have check it? If Stig knew about the burns, he'd hesitate when it was time to take his collar off, and that could be dangerous for all of us. Finn would make it seem scandalous. And Nik . . . well, I don't know how to act around Nik even when I'm fully clothed." She looked away and scrubbed a hand across the back of her neck.

Edrik frowned. "The stitches probably need to come out."

"It doesn't matter."

"Show me."

For several long heartbeats, Kaya just stood there looking up at Edrik. Then she laid the sword on the bench by the wall and began undoing her bodice laces. Edrik's heart skipped a beat, and he had to swallow a lump that suddenly formed in his throat.

"You'll need a knife from my toolkit to cut the stitches," Kaya said, not looking at him. "My satchel is in the chest at the end of the bed."

By the time Edrik had found the rolled-up leather tool case and selected one of the bone-handled iron blades, Kaya had removed her bodice and blouse, and was loosening the drawstring at the neck of her shift.

Her fingers were trembling.

Edrik cleared his throat. "It might be easier if we sit."

Kaya glanced around at him, dark eyes examining his face. Then she moved to sit sideways on the edge of the bed. "The light's probably best over here."

Edrik eased himself onto the bed behind her. The mattress was soft —feathers, probably. Kaya clutched the front of her shift modestly to her chest and let the back slip down, exposing the whip wounds. The layered scabs were gone, the wounds were closed and well healed, and the stitches should have been removed a long time ago. She'd always bear scars, but they would fade with time. In fact . . . he'd missed it before in the fire-lit cottage, but the fading daylight revealed several lines of slightly paler skin crisscrossing the light brown of her back.

She'd been beaten before. Probably more than once. A flash of hot anger seared through him and settled into a slow burn deep inside. He would make sure it never happened to her again.

Several wisps of her long, black hair had escaped her clumsy braid, and as he reached a careful hand to move the strands out of his way, one finger brushed against her skin. She twitched slightly at his touch, and her movement sent a tingling thrill racing through him.

He cleared his throat and focused on his task. Laying a steadying hand against Kaya's bare shoulder, he began to pick at one of the stitches with the tiny knife blade.

"If you weren't angry with me," Kaya asked after a moment, "why did you try to get rid of me?"

Edrik frowned. "What do you mean?"

Kaya's half shrug almost made Edrik cut her with the knife. "All that business in the Barge Master's office about me staying in the Tosky town because you could move faster without me."

Edrik picked out two more stitches before he replied. "I just wanted to make sure you knew you didn't have to stay with us if you didn't want to." He picked out another stitch. "You would be safer without us. Your father's people would welcome you. I thought it would be a good place for you to start a new life."

Kaya made an impatient sound. "I can make my own decisions about what to do with my life, Rolf. I managed just fine before you ever showed up in my dungeon." She twisted a little to look at him over her shoulder. "I don't need you to take care of me."

The look on Kaya's face awoke a mischievous little something deep inside Edrik that wanted to hear her giggle again, so he flashed her a sly grin and said, "No, you have Nik for that now."

Instead of giggling, Kaya blushed furiously and looked away. "Actually," she said, "I was glad you interrupted when you did. I—I think he might have been about to kiss me."

Edrik stared at her. "Of course he was about to kiss you. Didn't you want him to?"

She sighed, still not looking at him. "I don't know." One thin shoulder rose and fell. "Nobody ever wanted to kiss me before, and I

. . . I don't know. This is all new. People treat me differently now that they see me as a woman. They have different expectations. Even Stig. It's confusing. Like trying to learn a new language. I can't always read the cues, and it takes me too long to figure out how to react."

She laughed wryly. "Things were clearer in the dungeon. I mean . . . I don't miss worrying about lice for fear I'll have to let someone close enough to pick the nits. But I could tell when a man wanted to cut my throat—that was easy—and I got pretty good at telling when a man was cheating at dice, but . . . well . . . I'm never quite sure what Nik wants from me." She sounded miserable.

It wasn't at all what Edrik had imagined she'd been feeling, there in Nik's arms.

"You'll figure it out," he said gently. "Give yourself some time."

He brushed a hand down her arm, trying to offer comfort, and she started, turning to look up at him, eyes wide, lips slightly parted as if a question had begun to form but had been frightened away. Edrik felt a sudden urge to kiss her himself. To wrap his arm around her slender waist and pull her close. To hold her body against his and teach her not to fear being touched.

It was her magic, he realized—the magic she didn't believe even existed, coiling through his mind and body and pulling him in. He drew a deep breath to steady himself and let it slowly out. This felt very different from Lissara's magic. Lissara had no doubt of her power; she wielded it with skill and intent, a nudge here, a tug there, playing one suitor against another, calculated and . . . cold, Edrik realized. Kaya's magic was warm and earnest, with a fierce undercurrent that stirred his blood in ways Lissara's never had. But she wasn't directing it at him on purpose. It was only the remnants of whatever she'd been sharing with Nik.

He cleared his throat. "Before you worry about what Nik wants," he said, "you should probably figure out what *you* want." That would help her focus her magic, even if she didn't accept that it was real.

She laughed—a strange, bitter sound—and turned away from him again. "What I want doesn't matter."

Edrik blinked. "Of course it matters, Kaya. You're not in the dungeon anymore."

She made an impatient noise and shook her head. "Not everyone gets to become un-pinioned, and reclaim their family fortunes, and marry the person they love." She drew a deep breath, then went on in a more measured tone. "What I want already belongs to someone else. Trying to take it would only hurt people I care about. So I will have to learn to want something else."

"Like Nik?" Edrik teased gently, trying to lighten Kaya's mood.

Something surged in the flow of her magic. Something hot and wild, that flashed through him and was gone, drawing the rest of her magic away in its wake and leaving Edrik slightly breathless.

"Please," she whispered, "just take the stitches out."

Edrik brushed the stray locks of Kaya's dark hair out of the way again, noticing this time how soft her honey brown skin felt beneath his fingers. How warm, and real, and present she was.

I love Lissara, he reminded himself reflexively.

But he shouldn't have to remind himself of that. Was he certain it was even true? What if it had just become a habit to think he loved Lissara? Maybe he had been so determined to fulfill her quest and win her hand partly because so many people had said a pinion would never have her. Maybe he was just trying to prove he wasn't worthless. The princess was beautiful, and intelligent, and accomplished, and he had years of memories with her to draw upon. But she wasn't his wife. He wasn't even promised to Lissara.

He gave himself a mental shake. Of course he loved Lissara. It had just been so long since he held her that it was beginning to feel like a dream, and Kaya was interesting, and unexpected, and . . . well . . . here. That was all.

Or maybe you're beginning to love Kaya too, Finn's voice whispered in the back of his mind.

The thought troubled him—but in a way, it was also exhilarating.

Kaya's beauty wasn't as ostentatious as Lissara's, but she *was* beautiful—and intelligent, and kind, and strong in ways Lissara could never begin to imagine. He had known Kaya only a short time, but he felt the draw of her. Even when he'd thought her no more than a peculiar young dungeon keeper, Kaya had intrigued him, and he'd wanted to be her friend. Coming to know her as a woman only added deeper dimensions to that desire, and perhaps to the tentative friendship that had been growing between them.

Edrik carefully cut the last stitch and eased the thread free. "That's all of them. I just need to check the burns."

He slid his hand lower, letting his fingertips trail down the soft skin over her spine. She shivered but didn't move away from him. It would be so easy to bend forward, just a little more, and kiss the back of her neck. But he didn't. He only nudged the edge of her shift down until he could see the branded runes. And frowned. "Kaya . . ." He swallowed hard. "These aren't healing."

"They are." She pulled away from him, sliding her shift up over her back in one smooth motion and tugging at the drawstring. "Just not as fast as the whip wounds. It doesn't—"

"Don't tell me it doesn't matter." Edrik heard the impatience in his voice and silently berated himself. In a more measured tone, he said, "It matters to me, even if it doesn't matter to you. You should keep the sword."

"No." Kaya tugged her blouse on and reached for her bodice. "I don't think your sword likes my dwarrow runes. I think they'll heal faster without it."

She had a point. Dwarrow magic and yotun magic might look similar on the surface, but they weren't the same, and might in some ways interfere with each other.

He sighed. "All right. You're the healer. We'll do this your way." He watched her a moment longer as she worked at her bodice lacings. Then he rose and went to reclaim his sword from the bench where she'd set it aside. When he touched the ruby to his forehead, the sword thrummed in recognition and welcome; Edrik smiled as he slung the baldric over his shoulder.

Kaya was still struggling with her lacings when he looked around at her again. Edrik had always wondered how women arranged the things so tidily behind their backs where they couldn't see. He'd asked

Lissara once, and she'd laughed and said that was what ladies' maids were for. Of course, Kaya didn't have a lady's maid. What did women without them do? Practice, he supposed—and Kaya didn't have much of that either.

"Let me help," he said.

Kaya's only response was a frustrated grunt, but she moved her hands out of his way when he began unlacing the one that had skipped a loop, and evening out the ends. When Edrik finished tying off the laces and stepped back, Kaya turned with a sheepish grin.

"I'm not very good at this," she said. "Maybe I should just go back to being a grubby dungeon boy. I'm so much better at that."

Edrik frowned and studied her, pretending to consider. "I think I like you better as a woman. Besides, a grubby dungeon boy would have no use for my present, and I would hate to think I traded a good knife for nothing."

Kaya's brow furrowed. "Present?"

Edrik shrugged. "Well, it's more of a peace offering, really. I saw them in the market at Grebe's Landing on the way to the Barge Master's office and thought they might make you more inclined to forgive me." He grinned. "Hold out your hand."

Her eyes narrowed, and she studied his face as if seeking for a catch, or the punchline to a joke. Then she extended her hand, cautiously, palm up, tensed as if ready to snatch it back if he handed her a toad or stuck her with a knife.

Edrik reached under his tunic and drew the two carefully folded hair ribbons out of his shirt pocket with one hand, placing his other hand under hers to keep it from escaping.

She stared at the ribbons when he put them in her hand, and for several long, pounding heartbeats, she said nothing. Then, "Silk ribbons . . ." It came out a choked and breathless gasp.

Edrik grinned. "Deep green," he pointed out. "Like pine trees in the winter."

Her eyes moved from her hand to his face, wide and startled, like a night creature caught in torchlight. "You remembered," she whispered.

Edrik felt his grin dissolve into something more serious. "I hope they're the right color." It felt like a stupid thing to say, but in that moment, it was all he had.

She stared up at him a heartbeat longer, then looked down. "I don't . . . Edrik, I . . ." She turned away from him, holding the ribbons out to catch the dying light, turning them this way and that to make the silk shimmer. "They're beautiful. But—" She looked back at him, and now her eyes held a sort of quiet desperation. "Nobody ever gave me a present before. Except Grandfather. I don't know what to do. What do I say? How do I—" Her voice caught in her throat, and she looked away from him again.

This was not at all the reaction Edrik had expected. Lissara would have laughed at him. Ribbons. How droll. But then she would have thanked him prettily and kissed him anyway, and that would have set Edrik's heart pounding for a week.

He had been such a young fool.

Grabak had been right to warn him not to play games with Kaya. She didn't know the rules. And in some ways, she was so very fragile, even though in others, she was deadly.

Drawing a deep breath to steady himself, Edrik stepped closer to Kaya and put a gentle hand against her elbow, turning her to face him. When she looked up into his face, he had to clench his teeth against the sudden urge to kiss her. This was not a game she was playing. She wasn't being coy or flirtatious; she was just being . . . Kaya.

He cleared his throat and forced a smile. "You just say, 'Thank you, Edrik,'" he said. "And, 'I forgive you.' And then you smile, and we're friends again, and I . . . go away and let you be." *Before I do something else to frighten you,* he added in his mind. No, this was not a game at all.

"Thank you, Edrik," she whispered. "I forgive you."

She smiled, but her smile was a lie. He could tell.

CHAPTER 19

When Edrik left the cabin, he found Nik outside, leaning against one of the vertical supports of his skeletal house, obviously waiting for Kaya. The Tosky's expression was polite but impassive, and he only nodded at Edrik as he passed—but his eyes were as hard as black iron.

Nik would be a good choice for Kaya. The man was attentive and protective toward her, but he gave her space and let her keep her secrets. He had a life to offer her as well—a half-constructed new beginning, ready for her to step in and make the other half her own. And she would certainly be safer with Nik than in the snake pit of quarrelsome drakes the Aerie had become, especially if Grabak failed to reclaim his throne.

Still, the thought of Nik touching Kaya, the thought of Kaya weaving warm strands of her fierce magic around this man and curling up beside him in that vast feather bed, made Edrik's gut clench.

Edrik nodded back, as coldly polite as Nik, and ducked between the open wall supports and around the corner of Nik's cabin where he was at least out of sight of the Tosky. He could hear Finn still arguing with Grabak; maybe he should go make sure neither was going to rip out the other's throat before they reached the Edge.

The sound of the cabin door opening stopped him. Had Kaya come out, or was Nik going in? The silence lasted just long enough for Edrik to tell himself that what Kaya did with Nik was none of his business—and then Nik asked, "Are you all right?"

Kaya's voice was cheerfully dismissive when she answered. "Of course. Why wouldn't I be?"

But she must have been giving Nik the same smile she'd offered Edrik because Nik wasn't convinced either. "You asked the Barge Master for refuge, Kaya," he said solemnly. "There must have been a reason. Now, I'm not asking what it was, and I'm not going to ask; I just want to make sure you know you can tell me if you ever want to."

Kaya's, "I know. Thank you, Nik," was so quiet Edrik almost didn't hear it.

He could hear Nik quite clearly, though, when he said, "And I need to make sure you know what those men are, and that you're with them because you want to be. Because if you need help—"

"They're dragons," Kaya interrupted. "They're my friends. And I know what I'm doing. But I appreciate your concern."

"Friends." He sounded skeptical. But then, Toskies were always a suspicious lot. For a moment, Edrik thought Nik would press his point, but apparently, the river man could read Kaya's currents well enough to know when he was about to hit a snag because he only said, "All right. Well, you look like you could use some cheering up. Do you swim?"

Kaya's laugh sounded genuine enough. "Not since I left my papa's boat. But I have so longed to!"

"Good! We've moored in a nice shallow backwater without much current. It'll be a bear to pole out of in the morning, but . . . well, it was at hand when it came time to stop."

He sounded sheepish, and Edrik suspected Kaya could tell as easily as he could that what Nik really meant was that he'd taken the first safe mooring he came across after Kaya left him at the tiller to go off alone with Edrik.

"And it'll be good for a swim," Nik added. "Race you!"

Kaya laughed. "That would hardly be fair. You don't have bodice laces."

"True," Nik said with mock solemnity. "That is a problem. I guess I'd better help you with those first."

Edrik had never interfered with any of Lissara's other suitors. They'd all been jealous enough of each other, to be sure, but they knew the princess toyed equally with all of them, and they played along with her little games with a sort of friendly rivalry, knowing that eventually she'd pick one of them, and the rest would have to shove off and find other playmates to amuse. But Kaya didn't play those games. And what Edrik felt for Nik just now was nothing like friendly rivalry. Just now, listening to Kaya laughing as Nik undid the bodice lacings Edrik had just tied up, Edrik would gladly and gleefully have eaten the other man's liver.

But in spite of her interest in anatomical exploration, he didn't suppose Kaya would much approve of that sort of behavior among her friends, so instead, he stalked off to find Finn and Grabak.

The other dragons were slouched in two of the folding sling chairs Nik had scattered about the deck for his passengers' comfort. As Edrik approached, Finn was snarling, "That's just idiotic. I should—"

He cut off as Edrik dropped into a chair facing the others. "Back off, Finn; we need Grabak alive." He tried to soften the teasing chastisement with a grin, but in this mood, it might have looked more like he was baring his teeth.

Finn snorted. "Tell *him* that. He wants to wait until all the Dragonlords are gathered for the Conclave and then march in, unprotected, right under their noses. He's going to get all of us killed!"

"If we go in any sooner," Grabak argued, "we'll be easy pickings for Nidhaug's toadies. If we wait for the Conclave, we'll have at least a few allies at our backs. Besides, we don't have much choice in the timing. The solstice is in nine days. We've six days still to the Edge unless you know some way to get there faster. That leaves two days to get from the Edge to the Aerie. We'll only have one day to get our bearings as it is."

"There has to be a better way." Finn turned his defiant glare on Edrik. "Tait died for this. We have to make it work."

A shrieking giggle, and the rapid thumping of bare feet cut off

Grabak's response, as Kaya, wearing only her shift, careened around the corner, followed by a grinning, half-naked Nik.

"Careful!" Nik called. "It's not very deep!"

Kaya caught the back of a sling chair with one hand on her way past and toppled it right in Nik's path. The Tosky, stripped to his breeks, laughed and dodged around it, but Kaya was already clambering over the railing at the edge of the platform. She tossed a beaming smile over her shoulder at Nik and flung herself into the air, tucking her legs up just before she hit the water.

She had never smiled that way at Edrik. Something in him began to smolder again.

"Fine!" Nik bellowed, as Kaya surfaced, grinning. "You win." He vaulted lightly over the railing and slid into the water with her.

Finn snorted a laugh, then heaved a mocking, sentimental sigh. "Ah! Young Toskies in love . . . such a heart-warming sight." He grinned. "What do you suppose he'll do with our Mudge, if he catches her, eh, Edrik?" Then he leaned forward conspiratorially. "And how many organs will he lose in the process? Did you see that knife strapped to her thigh as she went over the railing?"

"Stow it, Finn," Edrik snapped. *Why was Finn looking at Kaya's thighs?*

Finn raised his eyebrows and squinted at Edrik.

"Nik is good for her," Grabak said, "though I'll miss her if she decides to stay with him. All those years in the dungeon, and she's become like another daughter to me. I suppose I'd hoped she'd come home with me and marry a dragon—or at least a Vanir, so I could see her children and grandchildren grow up and grow old. But perhaps she belongs with her true father's people after all."

"She hardly knows him," Edrik muttered.

Finn's mouth popped open. "You're jealous!"

Grabak turned his gaze from Kaya to Edrik.

Edrik squirmed uncomfortably under the weight of the old Drake's scrutiny and felt his face warm. "I just think she should take her time and—"

"You are!" Finn exclaimed in an excited stage whisper. "You're jealous!" His eyes gleamed with mischief. "What about your precious princess?"

"Finn—" Edrik began to protest but stopped when Grabak chuckled.

The old Drake leaned forward, resting his elbows on his knees. "Finn, my friend and adversary, Lissara is my daughter and a lovely girl, and I wouldn't blame any man for falling in love with her. But unless she has grown up a great deal since I left, Lissara can be rather spoiled and a bit manipulative as well, and I wouldn't blame any man for looking elsewhere either."

"Well, he does seem to be looking." Finn laughed softly.

Edrik realized his eyes had drifted to where Kaya was playing tag with Nik in the chest-deep water. Nik dodged behind a submerged stone, and instead of chasing him around it, Kaya scrambled up to stand on the stone, ready to pounce if he came close enough. Her shift gleamed pale in the gathering twilight, clinging appealingly to her slender curves. Behind her, the spark flies played among the trees, lending a twinkling, phosphorescent fae light to the scene. Nik stopped dodging and stood smiling up at her for a moment, as entranced, apparently, as Edrik was by the vision. Then he said something too softly for Edrik to hear and held out his hand to Kaya. She hesitated only a heartbeat before putting her hand in Nik's and stepping off the stone into the Tosky's waiting arms. Edrik gritted his teeth and looked away.

Finn and Grabak were both staring at him.

Finn cleared his throat and said solemnly, "It's serious, isn't it?"

Edrik rubbed at his forehead. "I don't know what it is." He glanced over just in time to see Kaya duck under the water and come up outside the circle of the Tosky's arms, laughing and backing enticingly away. At least she was making him work for her. Edrik stood and stretched, tipping his head up to look at the scattered stars that were beginning to show between the long tree branches that arched low over the water here. "Maybe I've just been away from home too long."

Grabak stood too and laid a hand on Edrik's shoulder. "You're a good man, Edrik. You have a strong arm and a faithful heart, and I would be pleased to see you settled with either of my headstrong daughters."

Kaya's laughter pealed out again across the water.

Grabak winked, and added, "If you can catch one." His eyes turned toward the water again, and Edrik followed his gaze to find Kaya dancing from rock to rock, holding on to Nik's upraised hand for balance, as he walked in the water beside her.

She looked over and saw them standing on the platform in the deepening dusk. "Stig!" she called, "Rolf! Come join us!" She turned and put her free hand up to rest on the low-hanging limb of a tree. "And Finn, when was the last time you had a bath?"

Edrik had to laugh in spite of himself, remembering when Finn had asked Kaya that same question at the pool in the forest the first day away from the dungeon. So much had happened since then. So much had changed.

But his laugh died, choked to death in his throat as the tree branch swayed, and the leaves rustled, and something dark and gaunt dropped from the arching branches onto the rock behind Kaya.

A long, bony arm wrapped around her waist. "Mine," rasped the alfkin nymph. "Deshtiny."

CHAPTER 20

Panic welled up in Kaya's throat, and she half twisted toward the alfkin, meeting its faceted gaze as its bony arm pulled her close. Nik's hand clamped down on hers. From the boat, Grabak bellowed wordlessly. Uselessly.

The alfkin's long fingers brushed Kaya's cheek. "Deshtiny." An affectionate whisper this time, meant only for Kaya. Around her, the evening air thrummed and softened. The light of the spark flies seemed to condense as the half-remembered net of crystalline forest music settled like a cloak over the core of Kaya's mind. Safe. Familiar.

Something tugged at her arm, and she frowned.

With one easy swat, the alfkin bent and batted away the clinging thing—nothing to worry about—then paused to lick the blood from its claws before retracting them. It caressed Kaya's cheek once more, trailing its long, dry fingers down the side of her neck. Her skin tingled at its touch. She wanted more.

The alfkin raised its head and looked around, sniffing. "Privashy . . ."

It drew Kaya's unresisting arms around its neck, and she clung there, eyes drifting closed, ear resting against the creature's chest, where she could listen to the steady thump-bump-bump of its heart. Effortlessly, the alfkin swung them both up onto the low-hanging tree branch, then to another and another, flinging them faster and faster away from the river and into the shadowy realm of the Woodland King. Home.

Still, a pale uneasiness worried at the back of Kaya's mind. *Should I be afraid?* a whispering half thought. She opened her eyes. The ground was a long way down, hidden among the shadows of dusk. But the alfkin wouldn't let her fall. There was nothing to fear. Was there?

She didn't have time to think much about it before the alfkin dropped out of the branches again and into a small meadow where one of the great trees had died, leaving a gap in the thick forest canopy. The tree's trunk had been carefully cut back to a broad stump more than twice as high and wide as the alfkin was tall, its surface smoothed and finished like the glossy top of an enormous table or the floor of a room with invisible walls. The tree's massive roots radiated out from the stump, twining across the ground. Steps had been carved into one of the roots, creating a staircase that curved from the ground to the top of the trunk. Around the edges of the meadow, other, smaller trees bowed gently toward the light granted them by the giant tree's absence, stretching branches toward the tree stump like worshipers in prayer.

The creature set Kaya gently on her feet in the center of the stump, where the rings of the tree's expended life encircled the two of them like ripples of water dancing away from a fallen stone, and released Kaya from her clinging embrace. It moved back slightly, using the long fingers of one hand to tip her face up.

"Lovely shuman." The words threaded into the night noises between the rustle of leaves and the hum of insect wings. "Shee me." And she did. She saw him. Not as he was, but as he would be.

He filled her mind, pushing the forest away into darkness as the music dwindled and took on a different rhythm. The alfkin was stunning in appearance, like a human, but taller and more elegant, with high, proud cheekbones, and slightly tilted eyes the color of a robin's egg or a clear sky in the summer, but cold and piercing. She saw him, noble and powerful—a lord among his people, standing at the right hand of the Woodland King himself. His graceful fingers wove intricate enchantments, twining diaphanous threads into delicate patterns, and though Kaya could not understand their purpose, she felt their beauty to the pith of her soul.

"Shtrong deshtiny," he whispered.

The vision shifted. Kaya saw herself. Not as she was, but as she would be. She knelt on the tree stump like an offering on an altar, head bowed, arms spread, as the alfkin's nymph form reverently extended his claws and opened her belly. She saw herself fold backward, and she watched as the nymph's long fingers drew out what was inside her and carefully arranged it around them on the stump. She felt the exultation, the elated triumph as the nymph, too, folded up, bending over Kaya's lifeless form, and she saw his body change, saw his skin swell up and darken to a hard pupal case as the child in him went dormant, waiting to be reborn in magnificence.

"Inshide," the alfkin said, and his hand drifted down to caress the soft curve below her navel.

The alfkin leaned forward, touching his forehead to hers, and the torrent of his emotions flooded through her, hot and exotic, and utterly seductive. He loved her. He loved her desperately. No one would ever love her as the alfkin did. No one could ever need her as he needed her. She belonged to him. Was part of him. And something of her would live in him always, far beyond the paltry lifespan nature had allotted to her as a human. He didn't want to take it from her. He would if he had to, but he wanted her to give it willingly. Because he loved her.

Her legs buckled, and she sank in the alfkin's embrace until she felt the cool pressure of the wood against her knees. She did want this. Wanted to offer him the gift, the destiny, she held inside. His destiny. He needed her. He loved her. And she loved . . . she loved . . .

The music wavered again, and she twitched in the alfkin's grasp. "N-no." Her fingers convulsed, and her hand groped clumsily for the blade that was still strapped to her thigh.

The alfkin hissed softly. Kaya felt his claws extend against her belly, felt the tips of them pierce ever so slightly through her clothing to her skin.

"Mine!" he insisted, and the music surged, winding its strands around her like a spider's web encasing a fly. She was his love. She was his destiny.

"No!" The word tore from Kaya's lips in a harsh, croaking shout.

He was wrong. This was not love.

Kaya's hand closed around the hilt of her knife through the thin fabric of her shift.

She did not belong to him.

She belonged to . . .

She was . . .

The strands of his enchantment frayed. Then shredded.

"*Mine*," Kaya breathed. It was barely a whisper, but the truth of it sank through her body like burning ice.

The knife came free of its sheath.

The alfkin's grip tightened.

CHAPTER 21

E drik was in the water almost before he knew he was moving. His heart pounded against his ribs, and his breath came in ragged gulps as he struggled, nightmare slow, through the water toward Kaya and the alfkin nymph. He could only watch helplessly as the alfkin stroked Kaya's cheek and whispered to her, drawing its enchantment around her like a net.

Nik, standing in the water below Kaya's perch, held doggedly to her limp fingers with one hand, and slammed the other, balled into a fist, against the side of the alfkin's knee, apparently hoping to knock the creature off balance.

The alfkin, absorbed as it was with Kaya, seemed barely to register Nik's blow.

Edrik plowed ahead, trying to move faster, but the harder he pushed, the more the water resisted. He was going to be too late.

Nik pulled desperately on Kaya's arm, trying to dislodge the alfkin's relentless grip. But Nik was only a human, not strong enough. How had Edrik ever thought Kaya would be safer with the Toskies?

Casually, almost without looking, the alfkin struck at Nik with one long arm, flinging the boatman against the rocks.

Too far. Edrik was still too far. The water dragged at his body.

The alfkin turned its attention back to Kaya, crooning softly to her as it drew her arms around its neck. She leaned trustingly in, clinging to her captor like a child to its mother.

Almost there. Edrik's sword pulsed silently in his hand as he drew it from its scabbard. A few more steps, and he could—

The alfkin sprang lightly from the rock to the low-arching tree branch and off again, caught at the higher branches with its gnarled fingers, and swung toward the riverbank, taking Kaya with it.

Edrik twisted sideways around the stone, cursing the water that sucked at his legs, while the alfkin leapt easily to another tree. If Edrik could make it to the bank, maybe he could still catch them. He had to catch them.

Something more solid than water tangled about his legs; Nik floated face down between the rocks. The Tosky stirred weakly. Still alive. Edrik couldn't just leave him there to drown. He grabbed at the man's hair, dragging his face out of the water. Blood trickled between Edrik's fingers from a gash in Nik's scalp—apparently, he'd hit his head on a stone—and the bleeding gouges the alfkin's claws had ripped across his shoulder left dark trails in the water. The alfkin reached the bank and paused, turning to look back at his pursuers. Its face twisted into a leering grimace—was it laughing at them? Then it swung languidly, almost lazily into the darkening alfkin forest. It moved with surprising speed; no wonder it had managed to keep up with the boat.

Edrik started moving again, hauling the disjointedly wriggling Tosky with him by one arm, cursing softly with every panting breath. The alfkin was getting away. It was going to kill Kaya.

Hands caught Nik under the arms. Finn's taut voice said, "I've got him. You go."

Edrik blinked. Slapped his friend gratefully on the shoulder. And hit the riverbank at a run.

It was darker under the trees. Edrik pushed ahead more slowly. His eyes adjusted quickly to the gloom, but there was no sign of Kaya or the alfkin. Where had they gone? Edrik stopped to listen, wasting precious time, and heard only his own heart pounding in his ears until a tree branch creaked some distance ahead. From the alfkin's passing? Or was it just the wind?

It was in the direction they'd been heading when they left the river, and Edrik had nothing else to go by, so he started running again, his footsteps muffled by the mossy ground and thick leaf mulch. His ears strained to hear over the panting roar of his own breathing. Voices? He couldn't be sure. He thought he caught a flicker of movement off to one side, but when he paused to peer into the shadows, nothing was there.

Where were they? What if he couldn't find them? His heart pounded harder, and a prickle of dread welled up from somewhere beneath his solar plexus. A rustle, and a thud, still in the same direction. Was it them? He ran, flinging himself hard against the dying hope that pounded through his veins. It *had* to be them. The prickling dread surged up and flooded through him, drawing . . . something else . . . in its wake; something terrible and dangerous—and exhilarating.

"No!"

It was her. The ragged, frightened voice was Kaya's. He raced toward the sound, fingers clenching around the hilt of the white sword, body tingling with the terrifying, burning flow of . . . of . . . *his magic*!

The trees parted suddenly into a clearing, open to the dusk-dark sky —and she was there! Kaya was there, kneeling with the alfkin atop the broad stump of a dead tree. But Edrik was still too far away to stop what was happening. Time seemed to slow and sharpen, and the light of the dying sun and the newborn stars brought him every detail. The alfkin's claw-tipped fingers splayed abruptly against Kaya's belly. The creature went rigid. Kaya convulsed, bending forward into the alfkin's arms, which clutched at her body. Blood bloomed over Kaya's shift, gleaming dark and wet against the pale fabric.

He was too late!

The magic inside Edrik ignited, racing down his spine and out along his limbs, arching with him as he bent toward the ground and drew in a great breath of air, and earth, and mossy forest, pulsing outward as Edrik reared up on his hind legs, wings stretching toward the night sky, long neck reaching upward as he bellowed an echoing cry of fire and despair, singeing the leaves from the overhanging branches.

Ascended!

Figures began to emerge from the forest, stepping from behind mossy trunks and dropping silently from the tangled branches. Lights flickered into being—the pale blue wisp lights of alfkin magic, floating in the air, their reflections glinting from abruptly naked swords and glittering off the iron tips of spears.

There were too many of them. Edrik might have defeated one or two alfkin, maybe more—especially in his ascended aspect. They were immune to compulsion, not to dragon fire. But there were at least twenty of them in the clearing. Probably more still hiding in the trees with their bows and iron-tipped arrows. And he was forbidden to be here.

He spread his wings and shifted his feet, flicking his tail to make sure they weren't creeping up behind him. His ascended body felt strange—powerful and dangerous—but strange. Unfamiliar.

The alfkin warriors circled cautiously around him. Their leader, a tall, graceful woman with hair the color of spider silk, flicked out silent orders with her long fingers.

Edrik watched them warily as he tested his wings, cupping air beneath the thin membranes, feeling the current of the faint night breeze tingle across the sensitive nerves that now ran in lines down his sides from shoulder to hip. An experienced dragon could fly out of here. Probably. The alfkin were quick and strong, but dragon scales would deflect most of their blows. And although their magic might temporarily transform things from the forest around them into shields or weapons, doing it would wear them down, and their glamors couldn't touch him directly.

Still, Edrik was not an experienced dragon; he'd be lucky to make it off the ground. Even an attempt would make him vulnerable. And the thought of running away and leaving Kaya here in the hands of these savage creatures, even if she was already dead, made him feel sick.

The alfkin circled, closing in, looking for weak spots. Edrik shifted with them, hissing a menacing warning. Something acrid tickled across the back of his throat, and he snorted, blowing white smoke into the clearing. Maybe he couldn't fly away, but he wouldn't just roll over and die for them either. And they would never have Kaya. He was a dragon. He would avenge her. And he would give her a pyre these alfkin would *never* forget.

His eyes flicked in the direction of the tree stump where she lay—and he froze.

Kaya knelt in the middle of the stump, staring back at him, eyes wide and frightened. The alfkin nymph's head was cradled in her lap, and she clutched a bloody blade in her hand. Edrik's vision flickered, and she came into sharp focus; even in the dimness, he could see her trembling. His other senses sharpened too—he could taste, at the back of his tongue, the coppery blood that pooled around the alfkin nymph's sprawled body; he could smell Kaya's fear, hear the rapid pounding of her heart, the shallow gasping of her breath. She was alive!

His voice rumbled up from somewhere deep inside his chest, low and wondering, and worked itself around the unfamiliar shapes of his ascended tongue and teeth. "Kaya!"

Kaya's mouth dropped open. She stared at him a moment longer, confusion and disbelief chasing each other across her face, before she whispered, "Rolf?"

CHAPTER 22

Kaya's heart pounded. For a long, drawn out breath, they all just stared at each other—Kaya, and the alfkin warriors, and the immense, glistening, jade green dragon. The dragon had to be Rolf. Edrik. Had to be. He knew her name. It wasn't Finn; his dragon form was gray and . . . well, smaller. And Stig was still wearing his collar.

The dragon shifted half a stunned step toward the tree stump, and all the alfkin tensed, their attention snapping from Kaya back to the great beast.

"Hold!" the alfkin captain snapped, driving the butt of her spear into the loamy soil. She glanced around the ring of warriors, locking eyes with each of them, and said something in the rapid, singsong language of the forest. Then she said quietly, but clearly, "If he so much as twitches, kill him."

The woman turned and moved with graceful deliberation to the base of the cut-off tree trunk and up the tree root steps, her night dark eyes fixed on Kaya, who still knelt, shivering from the severed enchantment, with the nymph's lifeless head resting in her lap, and its outstretched arms curved around her folded legs.

Kaya was weary to the center of her frozen bones. She didn't know what was coming, but she knew she was too tired to resist whatever it was. Too tired. Too weak. Too cold. She turned her gaze away from the approaching alfkin, away from Edrik's formidable ascended form, and looked down at the broken nymph.

Was she justified in ending this life? In the dungeon, everyone died; it was just the way things were. But this wasn't like the dungeon. The nymph had only been trying to take what he needed to live. And if he had lived, he would have been *magnificent*. Kaya reached with her free hand—the one that wasn't wrapped around the hilt of the knife through her blood-soaked shift—to touch a careful, shaking finger to the nymph's strange, insectile cheek. He would have been beautiful. And wise. And powerful. And she had taken all of that away. All the long eons of an alfkin life. His face blurred, and Kaya scrubbed the back of her hand across her face, smearing tears and spattered blood down her cheeks.

"Are you weeping for my son?" The voice was precise, and musical, and utterly incredulous.

Were Kaya's tears for the alfkin nymph? She wasn't sure. "He was only a ch-child," she murmured, shivering harder as the nymph's blood cooled on her shift, sticking it to her skin.

She looked up when the alfkin woman knelt beside the nymph's body and checked it for signs of life. She wouldn't find any. Kaya had felt her blade slip up underneath the ribcage and puncture the creature's heart—the heart she'd heard pounding triumphantly as they swung through the trees with her ear against his chest. The alfkin woman was achingly beautiful, her pale hair nearly white in the ethereal blue light of the wisp that hung at her shoulder, but probably merely pale blond in the sunlight. Her large, expressive eyes were set like gems in the ivory face with its sharp cheekbones and arching brows.

She laughed softly, an entrancing sound, like glass chimes in a summer breeze. "He was older than you are, child," she said, "or are ever likely to be." She studied Kaya's face with a musing, puzzled expression. "You humans set such store by time . . . perhaps because you are given so little of it. But it is not a life's duration that gives it value."

The alfkin woman didn't look older than thirty, herself, yet time seemed to cling about her in skeins. Her expression turned wistful, and she looked away from Kaya to stroke a long-fingered hand down the nymph's back.

"I should have liked to see him grow up," she said. "But everything dies in its time. Even alfkin." Her gaze lifted again to meet Kaya's, and she smiled sadly. "My son chose his own destiny and followed it to the end. And that is, after all, what a life is for."

"He d-didn't deserve to d-die," Kaya insisted quietly.

"Nor did you." The alfkin studied Kaya's face. "The Seeking is not about what is deserved; it is about what is needed. Your need as well as his." She tilted her head. "Your need was the stronger."

Her brows drew together, making a tiny crease, and she lifted a cautious hand to Kaya's face, laying her fingers against Kaya's cheek and resting her thumb in the center of Kaya's forehead where the nymph had touched her back in the orchard when he cast his first enchantment.

"He marked you." She smiled at Kaya's confused expression. "So he could find you again. You must have made an impression." Her smile widened when Kaya's confusion only deepened. "Your eyes can't see it, precious one, but ours can. No alfkin will harm you so long as you carry his mark. It is a dark thing to damage another's destiny—especially a destiny strong enough to destroy its object."

Kaya didn't know what to say, so she said nothing, just sat and shivered.

After a moment, the woman's hand dropped away; she sighed and nodded once to herself. Then she gestured out at the clearing, where the rest of the alfkin still surrounded the wary dragon.

"Does that beast belong to you?" she asked Kaya, her tone subtly amused.

Kaya swallowed hard. Edrik had risked his life to come for her. Did he belong to her? No. Not in the way she wanted him to. She drew a deep, shivering breath, and let it out. "He's my f-friend."

And that was all the claim she'd ever have on him.

The alfkin studied Kaya's face once more, jewel eyes disconcertingly intense. Could she see the thoughts Kaya hadn't spoken? She gave no indication, only said, "Then he may live this time, for your sake. But see that he does not come into our realm again uninvited; next time will be the last."

The woman stood and strode down the stairs, leaving Kaya and the dead nymph atop the stump. She signaled silently to her alfkin band, and they backed warily away from the dragon before turning to melt into the shadows.

The dragon folded his great wings and shifted on his feet, his long, curved claws digging into the bare earth of the depression his ascension had left in the meadow turf. He crept closer to Kaya, moving slowly as if being careful not to frighten her, massive muscles rippling beneath his scaly hide. His mouth opened slightly, revealing dozens of razor sharp teeth as the forked tip of his tongue flicked out, testing the air. He looked dangerous. Deadly. Somehow, that was terribly reassuring.

As he drew closer, the starlight glinted off his scales in the dimness, making them shimmer like a thousand smooth, pale green opals. She could just make out the darker green that edged his wings and ran in knobby spikes down the ridge of his neck and back, and the paler marbling that skimmed along his jaw and down his throat. In the dark, he was breathtaking. In sunlight, he would be . . . *glorious*.

Kaya looked away. *He isn't for me*, she reminded herself. Edrik had a beautiful princess waiting for him. He was only Kaya's friend. But he *was* her friend. He had come for her.

The dragon exhaled, blowing warm, musky air around Kaya's shivering body. He nudged the dead alfkin away from her with his nose, and his neck curved around her, tucking her gently against the small, smooth scales of his throat and chest, as he climbed slowly up, winding himself around her, trying and failing to fit his bulk atop the broad, flat tree stump.

His scales were warm—warmer than a man would be. Kaya leaned into the heat of him, letting him absorb the violent shivering, feeling the soft touch of his warm breath down the back of her neck. Her tears came again—great, wracking sobs this time—as the tension and confusion of the long evening drained out of her until nothing was left but quiet, gasping hiccups. She hadn't cried like that in front of another person since she was a small child. Somehow, with Edrik, it felt safe. Maybe because he was a dragon just now, and not quite exactly another person.

A giggle—a strange, cracked thing, but a giggle nonetheless—pushed out of her at the thought. She straightened, squaring her shoulders. "We should go. They'll be worried." She rose and stepped carefully over the dead alfkin and past the dragon's claws, then walked slowly down the dark steps. Behind her, she heard the rasp of scales against wood as the dragon slipped back off the edge of the stump.

Edrik, the man, waited at the bottom of the stairs, seeming almost a different creature than the great beast that had warmed Kaya and comforted her as she wept. He was more distant, beyond her reach, like an ancient god graven of marble and slate, face gleaming pale in the darkness, river-damp shirt clinging to his sculpted shoulders, shimmering softly with dying dragon dust.

He studied her carefully in the dark, his expression solemn. "You killed it, then," he observed softly.

She didn't quite know what to say. There were no words for what had happened. So instead, she murmured, "You ascended."

His face turned shyly down and away. "I did."

Then he moved closer and his eyes came up again to search her face. "Is any of that blood yours?"

The way he looked at her . . . hurt. So she forced a grin, drawing her impish dungeon keeper mask over her features. "Of course not, Rolf," she teased, "I told you; I don't need you to rescue me."

A small, sympathetic smile toyed with his lips in the starlight; he knew what she was doing. But he played along. "And I told you,"—he laid a hand on her shoulder—"that doesn't stop me from wanting to." His fingers slid down her arm to her hand, sending warm tingles up her spine. Gently, he tugged her clenched fingers away from the hilt of the knife she hadn't realized she was still clutching and pulled it carefully the rest of the way through the hole it had made in her shift when she stabbed the nymph.

He said nothing else, just casually tucked the knife in his belt, drew her hand into the warm crook of his elbow, and led her back through the forest toward the river. It made her feel strangely like a lady being escorted by a handsome gentleman. Like a princess.

But Kaya was not a princess.

And Edrik did not belong to her.

Nine days. And then, the solstice.

CHAPTER 23

Beyond the alfkin forest, the banks of the Drasil fell gradually away, and the river spilled out over the flatlands, making it more a vast, shallow lake than a river. As the current slowed, silt settled out of the water, creating an ever-changing maze of submerged sand bars and small, transitory islands before the water slipped indolently over the knife edge of the granite cliff at the Edge of the World and fell in a thundering white curtain into the estuary waters at the bottom of the Crevasse. The spray flung up by its impact hung in the air, giving the light an otherworldly quality and making sounds seem somehow both louder and more muffled than they should have been.

As they neared the Edge, Edrik stood at the deck railing, the fingers of one hand tapping a rapid beat against the painted wood, impatient with the lazy pace at which Nik's boat drifted between the floating markers that indicated where a safe channel had been dredged to the docks on the river's northern bank. They were almost home. Gazing out at the horizon beyond the Edge of the World, beyond the Crevasse, where the mountains of the great islands loomed through the mist, his eyes searched the peaks of Vanahir, the northern isle, for the spires of the Aerie. If not for the mist, he might have seen the tallest of them rising above the craggy ridge line. Perhaps the view would be better once the boat reached Topside, the Vanir trading town that sprawled along the northern shore of the delta lake.

Behind Edrik, Grabak paced back and forth across the deck, perhaps even more impatient than Edrik with the slowness of their progress. Through most of their journey, the old Drake had maintained a calm impassivity, but now that their destination was in sight, he grew more agitated and irritable by the hour.

In fact, everyone's tempers seemed to be fraying at the edges since their encounter with the alfkin. Grabak hadn't quite forgiven Finn for threatening to ascend and sit on him if he tried to follow Edrik into the forest after Kaya. Finn was exasperated because Grabak refused to acknowledge that if he'd gotten himself killed by minions of the Woodland King, their whole quest would have been in vain, Tait would have died for naught, and the Vanir would have been doomed to live forever between the tyrannical teeth of the Black Dragon. Nik was furious that Finn had compelled him to sit on the riverbank and wait instead of letting him stagger uselessly around the forest half addled from hitting his head on that rock and dripping blood from the shallow gashes the alfkin's claws had left across his chest and shoulder. And Edrik . . . well, Edrik had to admit, if only to himself, that he was out of sorts mainly because for the six and a half days that had passed since that night, Kaya had spent all her time with Nik.

Not that he could blame her.

Nik had needed Kaya. And Kaya . . . well, she seemed to need Nik. She'd gone to Nik as soon as she and Edrik had arrived back at the riverbank that night, calmly evaluating Nik's injuries while Edrik waded into the shouting match that raged between Finn and Grabak and made them both back down. When they reached the boat, Kaya cleaned Nik up, and tucked him into his great feather bed, and then spent the night perched on the edge of the bed holding Nik's hand and dabbing at his head wound with cool, herbed water. Well . . . most of the night, anyway.

The first time Edrik went into the cabin to take her a basin of fresh water, she was sitting there. She responded to his questions with one-word answers and wouldn't meet his eyes. Edrik had asked Grabak to take the next basin in and later a bowl of fish stew. Both times, he reported she was still sitting in the same place. But when Grabak fell asleep, and Edrik went in to give Kaya a cup of tea a little before dawn, he found her curled up on top of the blankets next to Nik, sound asleep, still wearing nothing but her blood-stained shift.

The sight had set Edrik's magic roiling in his gut. He had never wanted so badly to rip out a man's throat with his teeth. Finn was right; Edrik was jealous—stone-frozen, star-cursed jealous. His body still held the memory of Kaya curled up against his ascended form weeping hot tears into his scales and shivering as if her bones might shake apart while her wild magic twined around him, weaving into his sinews. Into his soul. He wanted to take her in his arms, as a man, and hold her again until the haunted shadows faded from her eyes.

But she hadn't seemed to want that after she climbed down from the tree stump altar; she had barely been able to look at him. Maybe *he* was what haunted her. Kaya had seen him in his ascended form; she'd heard his desolate bellow and seen the gout of fire he'd spat at the sky when he thought she was dead. And although very little seemed to frighten the former dungeon keeper, she was certainly sensible enough to fear an ascended dragon in a rage.

Or maybe she wasn't afraid of him. Maybe she just didn't find him interesting now that he wasn't pinioned. Maybe she didn't want to be friends with someone who could compel people. Lissara hadn't wanted someone who couldn't reach the magic; maybe Kaya didn't want someone who could. Or maybe she just wanted to be with someone who was human, like her. Like Nik.

Whatever the reason, Kaya had been distant since then. And if Nik was what Kaya wanted, if Nik made Kaya feel safe, Edrik wouldn't interfere. But he had allowed himself the decadent luxury of moving a stray lock of hair out of her sleeping face and trailing his fingers ever so softly down her cheek before he quietly draped her travel cloak over her slender body and left.

The next morning, Nik emerged from his cabin first, looking tired and a little dazed—and about as pleased as a man ought to look after waking to find Kaya in his bed. Edrik seethed with envy, but there was not a thing to be done about it. His mood eased only slightly when Nik said Kaya was still asleep, and he thought it best not to wake her.

When Kaya joined them an hour or so later, she had scrubbed away the blood and was fully dressed. She examined Nik's injuries again and, with a worried frown, informed Nik that he needed to rest for at least another day and shouldn't exert himself too much until he could do it without getting dizzy. Nik protested that he had paying passengers and only five and a half days left of the twelve he'd promised for the journey to the Edge. He'd be lucky to get them there on time even if they left right that moment and didn't run into any more problems along the way.

A short argument ensued, which ended with the dragons wielding the push poles to maneuver the boat out of its backwater mooring, and Nik sitting in a sling chair beside the helm, supervising Kaya while she operated the tiller. Edrik would have liked the arrangement much better if it hadn't involved Kaya spending so much time perched jauntily on the grinning Tosky's knee, but Nik seemed quite pleased with his situation. In fact, Edrik rather suspected Nik of exaggerating his symptoms slightly over the next few days in order to keep Kaya close.

Edrik's only comfort was that Kaya had moved out of Nik's cabin after that first night, insisting that he take the bed because he needed his rest in order to heal. She said she had fond childhood memories of sleeping under the stars on the houseboat roof and dragged her satchel and a few extra blankets up the ladder to the section of Nik's flat, unfinished roof that had a railing along the edge. Every night since then, Edrik had lain awake, swaying in his hammock, listening to the soft scuffing sounds she made as she moved around up there, until she lay still, wrapped in her blankets. Was she warm enough?

On the seventh morning, the last before the Edge finally drifted into sight, Edrik didn't sleep at all. Kaya stayed awake late into the night, padding softly back and forth across the roof. It was well past midnight before she settled into her bed, and Edrik was almost certain he had heard her crying softly for a while after that—but with the river noises, it was hard to be sure. Then, in the gray hours before dawn, Edrik twisted fitfully around to lie on his other side and discovered Kaya's bare brown feet dangling over the edge of the roof. He debated with himself for a little while before climbing up the ladder.

She didn't look up when he reached the rooftop, but when he asked if he might sit with her, she nodded. Neither of them spoke as they watched the sun rise out of the forest, which had dwindled behind them to a dark smudge across the flat horizon. Edrik didn't know what to say. Kaya's magic pooled about them, drifting in gentle eddies that soothed Edrik's rumpled spirit and quietly shored up his determination for the coming days—so different from Lissara's magic, which always left him feeling pleasantly drained and a little off balance. He didn't know what Kaya was feeling, but he sensed that she had reached a delicate equilibrium that might shatter at the touch of a careless word. So . . . he said nothing.

Behind Edrik, Grabak muttered, "We could fly there now and be home for supper."

The sweet memory of sunrise crumpled under the present weight of the waning forenoon. Edrik stood at the railing again, watching the docks at the Edge creep slowly closer.

Finn snapped, "We'd sink the boat. We have to wait until we get to shore."

"*You* would sink the boat," Grabak growled. "I can draw from wind and water."

"If Finn didn't sink it, I would." Edrik sighed. "And I can't fly anyway."

Grabak shot him a sullen glare, and Edrik raised his voice, speaking slowly and clearly as if Grabak were a particularly slow-witted child—or maybe half deaf.

"I can't fly yet," Edrik repeated, "and if you take your collar off so *you* can fly, they will know you're coming. Even if the queen didn't betray you intentionally, her reaction would give us away. Nidhaug's lackeys would fly out and take you down as soon as you went over the Edge. You wouldn't even make it to the walls of the Aerie. Finn could fly you there, but he can only carry one person. Kaya would still be here, and you wouldn't be able to get your collar off. You'd be outnumbered and unable to ascend. They'd only have to kill you and Finn, and the few people unfortunate enough to have seen you, and no one would know you were ever even there. No. We have to walk there.

We have to go together. And we have to wait until the court is gathered to honor the sun, so it can be a clean challenge, and not an ambush."

Grabak hissed. "I know that. It was *my* plan, remember?" He clenched his fingers around the railing, as if strangling it would fix everything. "But time is short. The river took too long. It will take the rest of today and all of tomorrow to get there, and we'll only have until noon the following day to get everything in place. If we went now, we would have two days to plan and gather allies. Except, of course, you're right—Mirra would sense our approach, and we'd be picked off before we even got there." He sighed. "But she is so close, Edrik. I need to know if she betrayed me. I need to know if she . . ." He stopped and turned away. "And I *could* be home for supper." He strode off down the platform again, scattering squawking chickens.

Edrik's gaze followed the old Drake to the back of the boat—where it snagged on Kaya and Nik. The Tosky stood close behind Kaya at the tiller, bending to speak softly, but earnestly into Kaya's ear. He raised one hand to stroke her shoulder as he spoke, and Kaya closed her eyes for a moment and swallowed hard before murmuring a response. Edrik wished desperately that he were close enough to hear what they were saying.

"You should see your face. It's exactly the face a man ought to wear when another man is making time with the woman he loves." Finn chuckled softly and leaned back against the railing next to Edrik. "You never made that face over Lissara."

"Stow it," Edrik growled. "I love Liss—" he began reflexively. And stopped. Did he? Had he ever, really? Did he even really know what love was?

Nik reached around Kaya to put his hand on hers, steadying the tiller, and circling her with his arms. His lips moved again.

Edrik turned his back on them, looking out instead at the approaching docks. He didn't know whether to wish the boat could go faster or hope it got caught on a sandbar. "This is different," he said.

"That was my point," Finn said wryly. He cleared his throat and turned to face forward as well, leaning his shoulder against Edrik's with a companionable nudge. "I'm sorry." He sounded as if he meant it. "Is she staying with him, then?"

"I don't know." Edrik looked away again.

Finn thought about that for a moment. "You didn't ask her when you climbed up there this morning?"

Edrik shrugged.

"You need to talk to her. She deserves to know she has options." Finn picked at the wood of the railing with one fingernail. "And you need to give her a reason to choose you."

"She doesn't want me."

"You don't know that. If you don't ask her, you'll never know."

Edrik glared at Finn. "What do you care? You don't even like Kaya; you punched her in the face and tried to talk Grabak into torturing her until she took the collars off. And you think marriage is pointless, and love is a lie, and a man should just take whatever affection and companionship he wants from a woman for as long as it's still fun and then move on."

"I like Kaya fine. It was Mudge I didn't care for." Finn shrugged. "I'm not sure I would want to bed a woman who can gleefully bite a man's finger off and who is as likely as not to put spiders in his boots and blister nettle in his wash water if she isn't pleased, but I'm not the one making that face." He grinned again at Edrik's discomfiture. Then he turned away and looked out over the water. "As for the rest of it . . . people sometimes speak ill of things they have sought desperately and failed to obtain. It's easier to pretend love is worthless than to admit that I have not been worthy of it." He drew a deep breath and turned to pin Edrik with a serious gaze. "Talk to Kaya."

The intensity in Finn's eyes unsettled Edrik. He focused his gaze on the approaching docks. "What about Lissara?"

"Don't be a fool," Finn muttered under his breath. "You don't owe Lissara anything."

"But what if everything changes again when I see Lissara? I've loved Lissara—or thought I did—almost as long as I can remember. What if I discover that I only feel this way about Kaya because I was lonely, and she was there? I can't hurt Kaya like that. She needs a man who can give her his whole heart, with nothing held in reserve."

"Like Nik? Edrik, what if she stays with Nik?"

Edrik stared out over the river with its floating channel markers and wished someone would mark a clear path between the treacherous sandbanks and scrubby islands that crowded his mind. And his *heart*.

"Kaya can make her own decisions about the kind of man she needs," Finn said. "But she should know her options. Talk to her—before she chooses Nik and it's too late. It's the kind of might-have-been that can break a man." He pushed away from the railing and went off to harass Grabak on the other side of the house.

Finn was right. Edrik didn't know what Kaya was thinking, and he shouldn't be trying to make her decisions for her. And if he didn't tell Kaya what he felt for her, and she stayed with Nik, Edrik would always wonder what might have happened if he'd had the courage to speak. He would talk to her; the rest of it would have to be sorted out after. If there was anything to sort out.

The platform gave a gentle lurch as the boat caught a slightly faster current, and Nik began calling orders from the helm. It was time to break out the push poles again. Nik kept them all plenty busy after that until the dock master, who came in his tight little skim to greet them, had been paid off, and all the lines were properly secured to a tiny dock at the edge of town.

Edrik quickly stashed his pole and turned to look for Kaya. He had to tell her now, before it was too late. She still stood at the helm, leaning on the tiller. Her eyes met Edrik's as he turned; she blinked and looked away.

Edrik had only taken a few steps toward her when Nik vaulted lightly over the railing from the dock and landed in front of Kaya. He offered her a flourishing bow.

"The Edge of the World, my lady," he announced grandly, as if he were a street magician and had pulled the place out of his hat just for her. "As promised."

Edrik drifted closer.

Kaya laughed. "Indeed." She fished in a skirt pocket and held out a small pouch purse that looked as if it might have been stitched from clean bandages. "And here is your other half crown, as we agreed."

Nik looked at the purse but didn't take it. When he spoke again, his voice was solemn. "You could keep it . . . and stay."

Edrik's heart leapt into his throat. Too late! He was too late! Nik had the courage to speak. Kaya would choose him. And Edrik would have to walk away and leave her. His stomach clenched, and he couldn't breathe properly. Still, she hadn't chosen Nik yet. She hadn't said yes.

"Kaya?" Edrik's voice came out a hoarse croak.

Kaya's gaze flickered to him, then back to Nik. She drew a shaky breath. "We talked about this," she said. Her voice was as serious as Nik's.

The boatman shot Edrik a poisonous look. Clearly, he didn't like having an audience for this conversation, but he just as clearly wasn't going to let that stop him. He set his jaw and turned his gaze back to Kaya. "I know," he said. "I hoped you might change your mind."

Edrik watched. Frozen.

Kaya stepped closer to Nik and took his hand.

Panic welled up in Edrik, and he stumbled forward a step.

Kaya didn't even glance at him. She drew a slow breath. "Part of me wants to. I miss this life." She pressed the purse into Nik's hand and closed his fingers around it. "But I can't be what you want me to. Not now. Maybe not ever. I have to figure out who I am when I'm not . . . what I was. And I have to see this thing through first—with the dragons."

Nik's other hand caught Kaya's before she could pull it back. "I can wait." His voice was heavy with conviction.

"I don't know how long it will take."

"It doesn't matter."

"Yes, it does." Kaya laughed a soft, bitter sounding laugh. "You'll find someone, Nik. By next spring, you'll be back in your barge town with a pretty wife and a baby on the way."

"Only if you come back to me." Nik looked down at their joined hands. "I'll be here at least a month doing carpentry work to earn money for a sail. Come back to me, Kaya." He let go and looked her in the eyes again. "It doesn't have to be for me. The Free People can always use a good healer. I could help you find a place. And . . . I could wait. You don't have to go with them." He flicked a scornful glance at Edrik.

Kaya's eyes followed Nik's and locked for one heart-stopping moment with Edrik's. Then her gaze dropped to the deck planking. "Nik . . ."

"I know," he said. "I'm sorry. I had to try." The boatman bent forward and kissed Kaya gently on the forehead. Then he turned, shot Edrik one last scalding glare, and strode off, muttering something about seeing if his passengers needed help gathering their things.

Kaya looked up at Edrik, her eyes sad and tired. She scrubbed at the back of her neck with one hand. "We're here," she said. "Let's go."

Edrik could only nod numbly.

FINN LED THE WAY UP THE DOCK AND INTO THE TOWN OF TOPSIDE, which perched on the edge of the cliff, looking out over the Crevasse and ran back along the bank of the sprawling Drasil. Kaya walked close beside Grabak, and Edrik took up a rear-guard position. In theory, nobody knew they were coming, but it didn't hurt to be careful. And Edrik didn't want to let Kaya out of his sight.

She looked back once, past Edrik to where Nik stood on the deck of his houseboat watching them go. Edrik's heart lurched. Grabak saw her glance too and laid a hand on her shoulder, stopping her.

"Mudge," the old Drake's voice was barely loud enough for Edrik to hear, "you don't have to come with us. You know this?"

Finn heard and turned back, scowling.

Kaya said softly, "I know."

Finn flicked a glance at Edrik before he growled at Grabak, "No. We need her. Your collar."

Grabak hissed. "Our plans can change." He turned to Kaya, and his voice went gentle again. "You could stay with him."

Kaya glanced at Finn. Back at Edrik. Looked up at her old friend. "I know, Stig. But it wouldn't be right. I don't feel for Nik what he feels for me. I tried to, but I don't. It's just . . ." She looked away, scanning the river, and the town, and the cliff beyond. "It was nice to feel wanted. What if nobody ever wants me like that again?"

Grabak chuckled. "Then the world is full of fools."

Kaya gave his shoulder a playful shove and started walking again.

Edrik let out the breath he suddenly realized he'd been holding and followed.

Topside was bigger than Grebe's Landing, bigger than Shrike's Hollow, and as they passed beyond the small, outlying docks like the one Nik had paid for and entered the main market district, the tension in Kaya's shoulders visibly relaxed, and she began to look around with interest.

The town had its share of farms and fields, Edrik knew, but the market was the heart of Topside, and the docks and lifts were the veins and arteries through which the life blood flowed. Trade goods from all the kingdoms of men, and sometimes from the fell mountains of the dwarrows beyond, flowed down the branching tributaries of the Drasil to the main trunk of the river and westward down the river to the Edge.

At Topside, the goods were unloaded at the docks and lowered, for a price, safely down the lifts into the Crevasse where ferries carried them across to the town of Firth, which clung to the ankles of the great island of Vanahir. From Firth, channel boats carried cargo down the three narrow waterways, like roots of the river tree, that separated the great islands from the mainland—north through the lands of the Vanir all the way to the ice coasts of Hel, west to the rocky coves and islands where the yotun dreamed their misty dreams, and south through the blasted lands of the other great island, Faehold, where scattered settlements of humans, ogres, and hobgoblins were beginning to find purchase among the ruins.

And trade flowed back the other direction as well. Those goods, too, traveled the lifts of Topside before flowing up the Drasil, where they commanded premium prices in the human markets.

The market in Topside overflowed with exotic foodstuffs: rich textiles and furs; lumber in every size and species; carvings of wood, and stone, and shell; spices, dyes, jewelry, and minor magical trinkets of every description. Edrik watched Kaya take it all in. She ran her fingers through a thick, gray fox fur, stopped to smell some scented oils that were being dickered over by two elegantly dressed young women, and purchased some herbs with coins she extracted from a slit in her petticoat hem.

When they passed a silk merchant who was laying out samples of his wares for the inspection of a handful of potential buyers from the east, Kaya stopped again to skim one hand reverently over a length of heavy, crimson dress silk. She would outshine all the ladies at the Vanir court in that crimson with her bronze skin, black hair, and bright, dark eyes; Edrik longed to buy it for her. The same table held a display of silk ribbons in every color imaginable, showing off the range of dyes the merchant could access for clients who placed orders with him—but Kaya didn't stop to look at them, only smiled slightly as her hand drifted down to rest on one of the pockets of her satchel. Was that where she kept the ribbons Edrik had given her? His heart beat faster. Perhaps there was hope for him after all.

Grabak used some of the coins he'd collected back in Grebe's Landing to buy some sweet, nutty bread and hard white cheese for a midday meal, along with some dried meat and fruit to supplement what they could scavenge in field and forest for the next day. He said there was enough left to pay for a private pedestrian lift and a passenger ferry, if Kaya didn't mind sleeping in a village haystack halfway up the mountain and breakfasting on porridge. Otherwise, the overseers at the massive cargo lifts and ferries were generally willing, with a little persuasion, to trade passage for extra crew hands, and he could pay for rooms at an inn in Firth.

Kaya snorted and said she thought there was still enough dungeon boy left in her for haystacks and porridge, and the closer they could get to the Aerie before nightfall, the better.

The lifts lined the edge of the cliff far enough north of the waterfall for the ferryboats to approach safely after creeping up the Crevasse from Firth. Here, unlike the ragged cliffs on the other side of the

Crevasse, the naked stone had been smoothed and reinforced by yotun stonesmiths to prevent crumbling. A sturdy stone railing at the edge was broken at regular intervals with metalwork gates that swung wide when a cargo platform needed to be loaded or unloaded. The platforms crept up and down the cliff face, swinging gently—huge, slow pendulums suspended from the chains of the massive treadwheel cranes that clung to the Edge of the World like a row of giant carrion birds endlessly peering into the chaos of the Crevasse.

Grabak stopped once so Kaya could watch the arrival of a loaded platform. She was fascinated by the way the two cranes, one at each end of the lift, worked together to raise their load. Each crane was powered by two wheels, like huge barrels, one on each end of the spindle that formed their axis. The wheels were turned by teams of men—or in this case, trolls—three to a wheel, who walked side by side in the same direction on the inside surface of the barrel-wheels, their collective weight providing the force to turn the wheels, winding the chain around the spindle between the wheels and drawing the platform ever higher.

As the platform neared the same height as the cliff edge, the crew at the top tossed ropes down to the platform crew, who fastened them to cleats on the platform. The foreman, perched on a scaffold where he could keep watch on the whole operation, bellowed orders. The crane wheels slowed. Capstans attached to the ropes began to turn, drawing the cargo platform closer to the railing. Crew members on both the platform and cliff top used long poles to help maneuver the load into position. Brakes were set, the gates swung open, and the crewmen began unloading the cargo onto the wagons that would carry it to the dock markets.

Kaya and the dragons rode down on a somewhat less impressive pedestrian lift. The small, partially enclosed platform with smooth wooden benches and a high safety rail was lowered by a single crane with one modest two-man wheel. But Kaya's eyes were wide as the lift descended into the spray thrown off by the falls.

The Crevasse was breathtaking. The sheer cliff on this side was matched by its twin directly opposite, where the crags of the great island of Vanahir pushed skyward. The stone walls made a corridor stretching north and south as far as one could see, until it disappeared in a gentle curve that suggested it might go on forever. The booming roar of the falls echoed off the stone, and the eternal mists churned far below, making this rift in the bones of the world feel bottomless. Grabak led Kaya to the platform railing, where he pointed northward along the narrowing ribbon of blue that was all that was left of the sky.

Edrik joined them and could just make out the spires of the Aerie peeking around the high mountain crag that hid the main body of the fortress from the Crevasse. On tomorrow's tomorrow, they would be home.

Kaya turned in a slow circle, taking it all in. When the mists rose up to meet them, riding the breeze stirred up by the movement of the water, and carrying the faintest taste of the western ocean, she burst into delighted laughter. Grabak raised an inquiring eyebrow at her, and she pushed her wet hair out of her face, shouting to be heard over the thundering water. "It's raining up!"

Grabak grinned and bellowed back, "It's even more fun on the wing! When things at home are settled, I'll fly you down the Crevasse!"

Kaya flung her arms around the old Drake and squeezed before dancing off to the other end of the lift to watch some birds circling in the Crevasse below them. Edrik discovered he had not left his jealousy behind with Nik. He needed to learn to fly.

Later, Grabak took Kaya up to the promenade on the roof of the ferry to show her the rainbows that danced through the spray in the afternoon sun.

As soon as they were out of earshot, Finn elbowed Edrik in the ribs. "You didn't talk to her, did you?" His tone expressed his disgust even more strongly than his scowl.

"I tried."

"And?"

"I have monumentally bad timing."

Finn stared at him. "Bad *timing*? Edrik, you almost lost her to the alfkin, and then you nearly let Nik take her. How many times are you going to—?"

"I know! But she had just finished telling Nik to shove off because she wasn't ready for what he wanted. Do you really think she'd have had a different answer for me? If I press her about it too soon, she'll just . . ." He substituted a vague, one-handed gesture of frustration for the words he couldn't find. "I'll just have to wait."

Finn snorted. "Or you could find out what it would take to convince her she's ready."

CHAPTER 24

F irth was smaller than Topside, and Kaya was surprised to find that it had no market. Apparently, its docks served mainly as a staging area, where cargo was shifted between the boats that traveled the channels and the ferries built to navigate the churning waters near the Edge, while the trading took place in Topside. Kaya and the dragons passed through Firth quickly and without incident and began the hike up the craggy side of the mountain toward the Aerie—and whatever waited there. Restoration? Death?

Lissara.

Would seeing Edrik happy with Lissara help ease the heavy ache in Kaya's gut? Would it help convince her heart that it had to let go? Or would he still walk her dreams at night, as he had on the boat while she slept in that bed that was too big, and too soft, and smelled far too much of Nik? What if she couldn't let go? Would she be able to have a good life among the Vanir if it meant a lifetime of watching Edrik love somebody else?

She could just leave. The world was a dangerous place for a lone woman without friends or connections, but there was something to be said for a clean break and a fresh start somewhere else. Still, Stig was the closest thing she had to family; she didn't want to lose him. And she could be safe among the Vanir if Stig was on the throne.

Of course, she might be just as safe with the Ratatosk. They would accept her for her father's sake, and a barge town protected its own. The few memories she had of her childhood among the Free People were good ones—at least up until her papa had stopped coming home. What had really happened to him? Had he died from the sickness that had swept through the kingdoms as her grandfather had said—or had someone killed him? Why would her mother have run away from her Tosky home if there wasn't some danger there? If her father wasn't safe among the Ratatosk, would his daughter be?

And then there was Nik. If she went to the Ratatosk, it didn't have to be with Nik; she could set up on her own as a healer in a barge town as easily as in a lander town.

But it *could* be with Nik.

Maybe she had been too quick to reject him so entirely. Maybe when her heart was free of the dragon, it would be able to embrace the Tosky. And he had said he was willing to wait for her. Certainly, the life Nik offered her was a good one. He was strong and kind and didn't ask uncomfortable questions. He would teach her to navigate the inner workings of Tosky society with the same patience and humor he'd displayed when he taught her to steer his boat. And his carpentry skills would always keep his family well fed, especially in a barge town. But Nik needed a steady wife who could be his equal partner and a proper mother to his children; Kaya hadn't even figured out how to be a woman yet. She needed time.

Her thoughts chased their own tails around and around in her head as she trudged up the winding, gently sloping road. The Aerie had been their goal ever since they left the dungeon—but what would she do when they got there? When the king was restored to the throne, and the hero won the hand of the princess, and the wilding found a home, the fae tale would be over. The stories never told what happened to the dungeon keeper while everyone else lived in happiness all their days.

The sun was riding low on the horizon when a hand brushed her elbow.

"Are you all right, Kaya?" It was Rolf. Edrik.

Kaya blinked and looked around. She'd been so absorbed in her own thoughts that she hadn't been paying attention to anyone else.

Finn and Grabak were some distance ahead on the road, bickering quietly, no doubt over some triviality.

Kaya glanced sideways at Edrik and away again.

"I'm fine," she mumbled.

He snorted softly. "You always say that, and you never are."

The memory of the last time he'd said that washed over her—it was in the cabin on Nik's boat just before Edrik took her stitches out. The thought of his fingers against the bare skin of her back sent blood rushing to her face.

She cleared her throat. "I was just thinking about how close we are to the end of your quest. Grabak said we'd camp near one of the villages tonight and spend tomorrow night with a friend who lives near the Aerie. And then . . ."

He finished for her. "And then the solstice."

She looked over at him; his face was as somber as his voice. Was he worried they would fail? Afraid Lissara might not have waited for him?

"Are *you* all right?" she asked.

He glanced at her and away. "I was thinking about the beginning of my quest. It's been almost a year since I walked down the mountain on this road—*walked* because I couldn't fly, and I was far too proud and stubborn to allow anyone to carry me."

He looked off to one side of the trail, and Kaya's eyes followed his gaze. Just ahead, the road curved around a stone outcropping and skimmed the edge of the great island, where the mountain fell away into the Crevasse. The cliff on this side wasn't as abrupt as the knife edge across the chasm, but the drop was still breathtaking.

Without looking at Kaya, Edrik said, "Finn and Tait walked with me because they were my friends. And now Tait will never come home." He stopped walking. "So much has changed since then."

Kaya stopped too, and Edrik turned to study her face with his serious green eyes. Their intensity made Kaya's pulse pound in her throat.

"Kaya . . ." He hesitated, as if he feared how she might respond to what he was going to say. "Can I—can I show you something?"

Kaya glanced up the curving road; Grabak and Finn were just disappearing behind the outcrop. She was alone with Edrik. Her heart began to hammer against her ribs. Could he hear it? She had to find a way to stop reacting to him like this.

Edrik saw where she was looking. "Don't worry, we'll catch up to them." He held out his arm, offering to escort her as he had in the forest after the alfkin, and she found that she couldn't say no.

Swallowing hard, Kaya tucked her fingers into the crook of Edrik's elbow and walked with him down a narrow footpath that led away from the road and out to the ragged edge of the Crevasse. Steps had been hewn into the stone there, continuing the pathway downward at an angle across the face of the cliff. Edrik moved in front of Kaya and took her hand in his as he led the way down. He turned once to smile up at her and gave her hand an encouraging squeeze; she felt it down to her toes.

The steps ended at a narrow ledge that curved around the base of a jutting crag. Edrik stepped out onto the ledge and shifted aside, making room for Kaya to step down in front of him. She stumbled just a little as she followed him onto the ledge, and he caught her, winding an arm around her waist and pulling her against him. So close. She could smell the wild, dragonish scent of him. She could have kissed him if she dared.

Kaya's heart seized up completely at the thought, and everything swam into sharper focus—the soft hues of the light from the sinking sun, the water sounds echoing distantly off the stone. And Edrik. Every particle of Kaya's body seemed abruptly aware of every particle in Edrik's, as if she were becoming part of him, absorbed like stone, or grass, or wind into his ascending form, fated to be cast off again as so much shimmering dragon dust when the journey ended and the magic was gone.

Kaya choked on her own breath and swayed, clutching at the stone wall with her free hand. Edrik tightened his grip on her.

"Kaya, are you all right?"

The alarm in his voice cleared her head a little, even as the press of his body against hers turned her stomach to custard. She drew a deep,

Edrik-scented breath, and laughed shakily. "Apparently, I like high places better if there's a railing," she lied. She leaned her forehead against his shoulder and tried to pull herself together.

"You won't fall, Kaya," he murmured. "I'll keep you safe."

Kaya choked on another laugh. She had already fallen. She was only waiting to see what kind of pieces she would smash into when he was gone. She drew a ragged breath and teased, "How? You can't even fly yet."

He shrugged, and his muscles moved against her body. "I could flap awkwardly and keep us from crashing down too hard. And I do know how to swim." Then his voice grew serious again. "But I won't let you fall." He gathered her closer, and Kaya felt his warm breath on her neck when he bent his head to whisper, "Do you trust me?"

And stars help her, she did. She drew a deep breath and murmured, "I trust you, Rolf."

She pushed against his chest, and he slowly released her, eyes studying her face. Then he tipped his head, gesturing forward along the ledge.

"It's just around that corner," he said.

Kaya couldn't suppress her gasp as they rounded the bend and the Edge of the World came into view across the Crevasse. The waterfall was impossible to see properly from Topside, and from below, it was mostly hidden behind a constant shroud of misty spray. But from here, from across the Crevasse and a little to one side, it appeared in all its glory. The full weight and volume of the great river Drasil spread across a vast, slightly curving stretch of granite cliff, tumbling endlessly down in a thin sheet to break into churning froth against the water below. Light from the setting sun tinged the fall a gentle shell pink, and a soft, cool breeze drifted up the Crevasse to caress their faces.

"It's beautiful!" Kaya breathed.

"Wait a moment," Edrik said softly. "It gets better."

He leaned back against the cliff, settling in to wait, and after a moment, Kaya set her back against the stone next to him. From the corner of her eye, she saw him turn to look at her, but she couldn't bear to meet those unreadable green eyes, so she kept her own gaze fixed on the waterfall while he searched her face for . . . something . . . and then looked away again, out across the Crevasse.

Her heart was just beginning to settle into a steady rhythm again when something brushed against her fingers. Edrik's hand folded itself gently around her own. Her breath caught, pounding in her throat, and she almost jerked away. But his thumb caressed the back of her hand, sending shivers racing up her arm to lodge somewhere behind her breastbone, paralyzing her.

Why was he doing this? It made no sense. It was the sort of caress Nik had offered sometimes when they stood together at the houseboat railing looking up at the stars. But Nik had wanted to kiss her. Nik had wanted more than that. But not Edrik. Edrik had a princess waiting. And he was nearly home. Edrik was just being friendly, she told herself. He was trying to help her feel safe so close to the dangerous drop, telling her he wouldn't let her fall. It couldn't mean anything else to him. She couldn't let it mean anything else to her.

She returned the gentle squeeze of his fingers and clamped her teeth tight together, closing her eyes to hold in the hot tears that suddenly wanted to spill over. She breathed deeply several times, drawing the cool air in to quench the hot chaos inside her, and the pulse pounding in her ears slowed and quieted.

When she opened her eyes again, the waterfall was on fire. The sunset light had deepened into gold and crimson, and from this angle, it reflected off the stone behind the fall and back through the water, making it glow like a fall of dragon fire.

"Oh!" It was all she could manage to say in that moment.

Apparently, it was enough, because Edrik chuckled and leaned close to whisper, "It only happens near the solstice." His breath tickled down her neck, and she was intensely aware of how close his lips were to her ear.

"Rolf!" she breathed. Then a nervous giggle bubbled out of her. "Sorry. I mean Edrik . . . this is incredible!"

He didn't respond, and she half turned to look up at him. It would be so easy to kiss him. She hadn't let Nik kiss her—it hadn't felt right

—but she longed for Edrik to do it. Only, he wasn't going to. Not ever. He was going to marry Lissara.

His kissable lips spread into a broad grin. "I like it when you call me Rolf." The soft, throaty rumble of his voice shivered down her spine. Then his smile folded up again into a solemn intensity, and his hand clasped hers more firmly as he turned to fully face her. "Kaya, there's something I need to say to you before—"

"There you are!" Grabak's voice startled them both.

Kaya flinched, accidentally snatching her hand away from Edrik's as if he'd burned her. "Stig!" she snapped. "Don't sneak up on people when they're standing on a cliff! We might have fallen!"

"Don't wander off without telling anyone." Grabak countered. "What if you'd been snatched again?"

"It was my fault." Edrik's voice sounded conciliatory, but there was a tightness around his mouth that seemed almost angry. "I thought we'd just take a quick look and then catch up with you, but . . . well, it was sunset, and I decided she should see the firefall."

Grabak's scowl relaxed a little, then deepened again. "It's a good thing I remembered your father complaining about having to fish you off the overlook every time he took you with him down to the village."

Behind Grabak, Finn cleared his throat loudly. "We should get going. It'll be dark soon, and we haven't even picked out a haystack to sleep in."

Grabak muttered something under his breath and held out a hand to assist Kaya. "Well, come on then. You've seen it."

CHAPTER 25

Edrik cursed silently as he followed the others back up onto the road. He could have throttled Grabak—couldn't he have waited just a little longer? Still, he didn't have long to feel sorry for himself because the lights of the village of Harrows Bend came into view down the road, and Finn signaled for Edrik to take the lead.

They had all agreed days ago that it would be best to avoid the village proper because of the risk of being recognized this close to home—it wouldn't do for word of their whereabouts to get back to Nidhaug and ruin the surprise. Grabak, of course, knew the land around the village better than any of them since it had belonged to him for several centuries, but Edrik and Finn insisted that the Drake stay between them, where they could best protect him in the event of an ambush. And Edrik, having grown up in the Aerie and thoroughly explored the villages that supplied the great fortress, knew a cow track that wound out across the fields and pastures and through a stretch of pine forest before it rejoined the main road well beyond the village.

So it was Edrik who led the way up the narrow track between the stone walls that separated the tenant crofts and edged the communal fields. Now and again, Grabak stopped to inspect places where the walls had fallen into disrepair, where wells had been boarded over, or where farms had been left to the weeds. One of the croft houses was a burned-out shell; no apparent efforts to rebuild had been made even though it looked to have been that way for a long time. Grabak's mood darkened with the night, and the chill that had them all tugging their cloaks close wasn't only in the air.

They were working their way through a narrow place, where the corners of two walls had half collapsed toward each other, when Edrik heard a shuffle and a clank. From behind one of the corners, a figure stepped into their path, tall, lean, and brandishing an iron pitchfork. Edrik's hand went to the hilt of his sword, and he glanced back over his shoulder to find three more dark figures converging on the path behind Finn.

"Hold!" the first man called. "Who are you? What business have you here?"

Edrik pushed the hood of his cloak back from his face; he'd seem less threatening that way. "We're on our way to the Aerie for the solstice." He kept his voice calm and friendly. "We hoped to find a place to stop for the night."

The man took half a step forward, and the pitchfork wavered. "Lord Edrik? Is that you?"

Edrik squinted into the gloom. "Darri?"

The man—Darri—hooted a laugh and gestured enthusiastically toward someone around the corner he'd come from. "Bring the lantern, Master Holfer! It's Lord Edrik and his friends come back to us!"

A stockier figure emerged from the darkness behind the wall, limping slightly and fiddling with a shuttered lantern until a broad beam of light half blinded Edrik.

Holfer's familiar belly laugh rumbled out. "Why so it is! Edrik, my lad, we'd just about given you up for dead." He shoved the lantern at Darri and wrapped Edrik in a beefy embrace. "Welcome home, lad. You and your friends." He turned to squint light dazzled eyes at the others, grinning. "Glad to see you're all three back safe and sound."

He must have mistaken Grabak for Tait; the two were of similar build, and the hood of Grabak's cloak kept his face in shadow. Kaya was right—people mostly saw what they expected to see.

Holfer frowned. "But that slip of a girl sure don't look like the old king to me. Too much to hope for, I expect."

Edrik returned Holfer's enthusiastic greeting. "You old goat! It's good to see you. This is Kaya. She's a healer. Might have something for your gout if you ask nicely and pay her well."

He glanced at Grabak, who shook his head very slightly. It was probably safest to let these men continue assuming Grabak was Tait. Edrik shifted forward, drawing the attention of the villagers—and the light of the lantern—away from Grabak.

"What are you all doing out here in the dark?" he asked.

Holfer's face went solemn. "Been bandits around of late. Village council has set regular patrols."

"Bandits?" Edrik frowned and looked around at the others who had stopped them—all men from the village. "You shouldn't be the ones patrolling; you're not even armed properly. Where are the guards from the Aerie?"

"Ain't no guards coming," one of the other villagers said. "Him up to the Aerie says the guards is for the Fortress, and it's our own lookout if we got bandits."

Edrik frowned. "Perhaps I can have a word with the queen when we reach the Aerie."

One of the men muttered, "Won't do no good. She don't go against what the Black Dragon says."

Holfer shook his head. "Maybe you'll catch him in a good mood. Word is, they're to wed before the Conclave day after tomorrow."

Grabak hissed softly, and several of the villagers glanced at him.

Edrik called their attention back to himself. "I guess we'd best be getting on, then. That sounds like something we shouldn't miss."

Holfer clapped Edrik on the shoulder. "Not tonight, lad. We got to bring anyone we find out here back to the village council. But there's a bit of a romp up at the square tonight, and you can all sleep in my barn loft—which ain't much, but it's better than a ditch. Then you can get on your way first thing."

Edrik quickly weighed the options. If the dragons hesitated too long, the patrol might become suspicious and take a closer look. If they refused to go, the villagers would have to try to force them, and someone was likely to get hurt. He had already been recognized; whatever harm might come of that was already done. But the villagers still assumed Grabak was Tait. If they went to the village, someone might recognize him and send word up to the Aerie that the old Drake had returned. But it was dark, and if Grabak kept his hood down and stayed quiet, their odds were reasonable. People didn't look closely when they were sure they knew what they'd see.

The villagers weren't well armed—they carried iron scythes, and pitchforks, and cleavers—but there were five of them. Except for Edrik, the dragons weren't well armed either. Finn and Edrik could ascend, if they were fast enough, but the villagers were standing very close at this point and might manage to stick one or both of the dragons with their iron implements before the transformation was complete. There were too many of them to compel all at once, and trying it would likely set off a skirmish. Also, Edrik knew these men and didn't want to hurt them. The bandits weren't their fault, and the measures they were taking were only sensible under the circumstances. He glanced at Grabak, who offered a nearly imperceptible shrug.

"Well then, I guess we'd better go see the council, eh, Holfer?" Edrik tried not to let his apprehension show in his grin.

"Oh aye." Holfer grinned back with a touch of relief and motioned for Edrik to fall into step with him as he started back toward the village. The rest of the patrol fell in behind Edrik and his friends, making quite a parade through the pastures. Apparently, they either didn't entirely trust the dragons not to jump Holfer as soon as they were out of sight or didn't want to miss out on the fun.

Whichever the case, Holfer carried on a cheerful monologue as they walked. "Not much changed since you left, lad. 'Course, Darri's married now to Marta—you remember Marta, the swineherd's daughter?"

Edrik did, but Holfer didn't wait for an answer.

"And then old Widow Perdi from over to Stony Hill, she's come to look after her daughter what married the smith. And of course, Gegnir ain't with us no more. Did you know Gegnir?"

Edrik had, though not well, but again, Holfer did not require a response.

"Firebrand, that one. Fetched up to the Aerie when he wouldn't give up more sheep than what he thought good for his flock. Whole flock's gone now." This time, Holfer paused to spit off to one side. "Ah well, maybe more change has come than I like to think of. Still, we've a bonfire, and music, and a good dinner spread—have you eaten yet? Everyone will be at the square, so we'll find the council there and have a bit of fun. Then we'll get you settled in the barn. You think you'll be looking for work again? I could still use another good hand at the butchery. Or if that's not to your taste, I heard the old master candler is looking for a likely young lad to train up. You're older than most apprentices, but that only makes you stronger of arm and steadier in the head . . ."

Holfer nattered on all the way to the square without Edrik needing to contribute more than a sentence or two here and there to the conversation.

There was indeed a good bonfire burning in the village square, and the village's council of elders were all seated together under some trees to one side of it, sipping ale and gossiping. Holfer quickly explained the situation, and since everyone on the council knew Edrik from his visits with his father and from his short stint in Holfer's employ after being declared pinioned, the council only gave him an enthusiastic welcome and an invitation to join in the merriment, with barely more than a cursory glance at his companions.

Holfer shepherded the visitors to one side of the square, where long boards had been set on trestles to create make-shift tables, saying they'd get a "right hearty country feast tonight, for all it was mostly plain fare, times not being what they was under the old king," and then the patrol went off to resume their rounds. It wasn't long before Edrik and his friends were seated on a log bench away from the glare of the fire, sopping hearty stew out of rough-hewn trenchers with good country hearth bread. The villagers cast curious glances at the group, and a handful of them who had known Edrik before stopped by to offer him a quick, "Welcome back, my lord." Clearly, he still made them nervous; but then, nobody ever seemed to quite know how to act around a pinioned dragon, and as far as any of them knew, Edrik was still pinioned.

After one such greeting, Edrik glanced over to find Kaya's dark eyes inspecting him solemnly. He dropped his gaze to his trencher and murmured, "Why are you looking at me like that?"

"I'm not used to hearing people call you 'my lord.' That's all. It caught me off guard."

He shrugged. "It's only a courtesy title because my father was one of the Nine; I've never been lord of anything in my own right. Grabak doesn't call me that because he's the king. And Finn doesn't because he's a wilding and . . . well, he's Finn."

She thought that over for a few minutes before asking, "What should *I* call you?"

Her voice was small; self-conscious. It caught at his heart, and he looked up again, meeting her eyes. Reflected firelight danced in their black depths, mesmerizing him and making his blood pulse faster. He cleared his throat. "I hope you will always call me Rolf."

This time, it was Kaya who looked away.

As the night deepened and the feast wound to a close, a low, throbbing pulse of drum beats worked its way through the hum of conversation. Another drum joined in, higher in pitch and faster in tempo. A third drum began to beat a counterpoint, and the villagers started clapping in rhythm with the building cadence. A flute laid a thin, wailing melody atop the thrumming beat, another added a twining harmony, and slowly, dancers began to weave their way into the circle of light that pooled around the bonfire.

It began with the men, heavy boots keeping time with the drums, stomping and turning, shuffling and sliding, forward and back, as they circled the fire. The women joined in, bending and swaying to the music of the flutes, gliding and stopping, pivoting and stepping, in a circle that revolved in the opposite direction to that of the men.

Finn joined in with enthusiasm, taking advantage of the opportunity to look over the young women the village had to offer while they eyed him in return. There was only one woman Edrik wanted to look at tonight. Kaya watched the dancers, dark eyes rapt, lips slightly parted, fingers tapping absently with the rhythms of the music. He had never seen her look quite so . . . *alive*.

"Dance with me, Kaya."

She jumped, startled at the sound of Edrik's voice, and her eyes snapped toward him, wide and round. "Oh . . . I don't—I don't dance."

On the other side of her, a deep chuckle rumbled from the shadows of Grabak's hood. "But you've always wanted to. Go dance with the boy, young Mudge."

Kaya glared at the Drake. "I don't know the steps."

"You've got a good head. You'll figure it out."

Edrik leaned toward her as if sharing a secret and said, "They all know you must come from somewhere far away. Not knowing the steps will make you seem exotic. Learning them will make you seem friendly. And the more eyes we draw to ourselves, the fewer will be on our friend."

She stared at him a moment, mulling that over. Then her familiar impish grin flashed across her face. "You're right. And if I'm going to die the day after tomorrow for helping you lot, I'm going to die having danced. Let's go." She grabbed his hand, setting his heart throbbing to the rhythm of the drums. He trailed in her wake, grinning, as she practically skipped toward the fire, where she was swept away from him in the current of the dance.

The first time the circles brought them together again, she didn't even notice him; she was carefully watching a smiling girl with chestnut hair who demonstrated the steps for her. The next time she didn't see him either, focused as she was on the steps and the rhythm of the music. The third time, though, her eyes sought his, and caught, and held his gaze. She inclined her head toward him in the firelight, and her smile cut through him clear to the bone.

When that tune ended, another began—one with a cheerful, bubbling melody that tugged the circles together and then burst them apart as the dancers formed pairs and whirled off together in a merry, skipping country dance. Hand to hand, and bend and turn.

Edrik was caught on the far side of the fire, so Finn got to Kaya first; he shot Edrik a rakish grin over Kaya's head as he guided her through the steps. But Edrik caught her for the next dance, and kept her for the one after that, until the music pulled them apart and sent them spinning around the fire again in separate circles.

Edrik lost track of how long the dancing went on. The drumbeat moved his feet, and the stars spun overhead, and sometimes, when he was very lucky, his arms were full of a breathless, laughing, Kaya, and her magic twined around him, wild and throbbing with the rhythm of the flames.

In a moment like that, a perfect, crystalline moment lit by stars and firelight, scented with woodsmoke, and roses, and lavender, the music swirled them to a stop with his hands on her waist and hers on his shoulders, and only a breath between them. She looked up at him, and her smile softened and faded into something deeper. His heart stopped beating. Her magic wrapped them up together in a space just big enough for two. He bent toward her, slid his hands farther around her waist, holding her against him with one arm while he trailed the fingers of his other hand up her spine, careful not to touch the burns.

"Rolf . . ." Her whisper was rough and throaty. He caught it with his lips in a hungry kiss. Tasting her mouth. Inhaling her Kaya scent— roses and lavender. Feeling the tremble of her lips against his. Or perhaps it was him that was trembling. He couldn't be sure.

Kaya's hands moved up his shoulders to cradle his face, pulling him toward her, pressing against him, deepening the kiss.

Edrik's fingers stroked up the back of her neck while his thumb found the delicate edge of her ear; his own magic sang inside him, hot and wild like dragonfire. Oh, how he *wanted* this! He hadn't known how much until this moment.

Abruptly, she gasped, flailed in his arms, shoved away from him. She stood, chest heaving, arms wrapped protectively around herself, and stared at him with wide, frightened eyes. "Wh-why did you do that?" she choked out. "Why would you kiss me? What were you—" Her face contorted in a half sob.

"Kaya . . ." Edrik stumbled a step toward her but stopped when she backed away. "Kaya, I didn't mean . . ." What had he done wrong?

She spun away from him, darting for the shadows that ringed the circle of firelight.

"Kaya, wait!"

He only took two steps after her before something bit into his back just below his shoulder blade, and fire exploded through his veins. His legs buckled, his stomach clenched, and he hit the ground clutching desperately at the agony in his back. His fingers closed on something hard. He yanked it out and gulped air as he stared at the thing in his hand: an iron needle dart. Before he could look for its source, another one thudded into his thigh, and a third caught his shoulder.

Someone shouted, "Bandits!" and the village erupted into a chaos of screams, and grunts, and guttural cursing.

A boot caught Edrik in the gut as the fire of the iron seared through him. He retched, emptying his belly onto the hard-packed dirt of the village square. He tried to twist around to see his attacker, but the heavy links of an iron chain snaked around his neck and pulled taut.

Where is Kaya?

Blindly, he snatched the dart out of his thigh, choking against the stinging iron around his throat, and fumbled for his sword. *Where is she?* A dart buried itself in his calf muscle. Another in his side. Hands clamped down on his wrists, and a knee hammered into his back as he spasmed against the burning chain. His vision swam. The sounds of battle fused and elongated.

For a single heartbeat, Kaya's voice carried above the roar, fierce and angry: "Burn you, Stig! You promised!"

CHAPTER 26

They shackled and chained him and left him retching in the dirt until the farce of a battle was over. When they loaded Edrik onto the cart with Finn and Grabak like so much dead wood, he was too sick and exhausted even to protest. But where was Kaya? She wasn't on the cart. Was she one of the crumpled forms that littered the ground amid the scattered remnants of the fire and the ruin of the overturned tables? Would he ever know? *Stars, please let her be alive. Let her be safe.*

The cart rattled out of the village and into the night. Edrik tried to pay attention to where they were going and how long they had traveled, but the iron burned in his blood, and between fits of retching, he kept drifting in and out of sleep . . . or maybe unconsciousness. The first ashen light of dawn was creeping between the scraggly pines when they reached their destination—one of the many caves that pocked the mountainside below the Aerie. They had all but reached their destination. And on the last day before the solstice.

So close. They had come so close.

The three dragons were hauled from the cart and dragged to the back of the cave, where a grate of iron bars had been installed across an alcove to form a makeshift cell. It wasn't big enough to stand up in, but there was more room here than in the cart. Edrik's squirming managed, at last, to dislodge the last two iron darts from his body, and despite the shackles that pinned his arms behind his back and the heavy iron chain that still burned against the skin of his neck and weighed down his arms, his stomach began to settle and his head to clear.

He managed to work himself into a sitting position with his back braced against the roughhewn rock wall and took stock.

Grabak lay on the floor of the cell, still and silent except for the fitful rise and fall of his chest as he stared grimly up at the dark ceiling. When Edrik asked, the Drake reported quietly that apart from the needle punctures and a few bruises he was uninjured; then he rolled over to stare at the back wall.

Finn lay curled up on his side, twitching weakly. Blood stained his tunic in several places, and a dart protruded from the back of one shoulder, where Finn couldn't reach it with his arms bound up in the chains. Edrik used his foot to knock it loose; Finn sighed gratefully and stopped twitching.

Where was Kaya? The others didn't know either.

Their captors moved about between the cell and the mouth of the cave. Edrik wasn't sure how many there were—at least a dozen, he thought. And they were not bandits. They wore the dun and black of the Thane of Shrike's Keep or the gray uniforms of the Thanesson's personal guard. What were they doing this far from home? Several of the men went out to gather wood for a fire. Others carried in supplies pillaged from Harrows Bend and stacked them against the wall of the cave. Two came back from a nearby stream with full water skins. They said little, and Edrik learned nothing before his exhausted body dragged him down into sleep.

The smell of meat cooking over the fire woke him sometime later. From the angle of the light coming in at the cave mouth, he guessed it was late afternoon. Of the same day? He didn't know. The Thanesson's men crouched around the fire, murmuring quietly as they ate and casting nervous glances toward the dragons at the back of the cave.

There was still no sign of Kaya. Had she escaped capture? Was she dead? That last, fierce cry he'd heard from her bubbled up in his memory. *"Burn you, Stig! You promised!"* Promised what? Edrik's mind filled with an image of Kaya in the garden at Shrike's Keep when she was helping the dragons escape—when she'd demanded that Grabak promise to kill her if they were caught.

No.

No, it couldn't be that. Grabak could not have done that. Could he? Edrik's eyes sought out the old Drake where he still lay at the back of the cell, staring grimly at the wall. It wasn't like him to sulk. A chill of dread shivered through Edrik all the way to his bones. Was Grabak brooding because he'd broken his promise to Kaya? Or because he'd kept it? Edrik could ask him, but he wasn't sure he wanted to know the answer. What he wanted was to get out of the rimy cage and go find Kaya.

She was alive.

She had to be.

Carefully, conscious of the dead ache of muscles wrenched by his violent retching fits, Edrik shifted himself around to place his back against the grate so he could use his bound hands to test each bar for weaknesses.

Finn saw what he was doing and hunched over to the other end of the grate to do the same, muttering, "I swear, Edrik, if you get me locked up one more time . . ."

But the bars were newly placed and securely fastened; the door hinges were encased so the pins couldn't be pushed out; and the lock was beyond the edge of the alcove opening where he couldn't see it. Still, they'd figure something out. Maybe they could grab a guard when he came to feed them. If anyone ever came to feed them. And if they could get out of the shackles and chains.

Finn turned around so Edrik could examine his shackles. The design was basic enough. Two bands of iron had been bent to fit around the back of a man's wrists, and an iron rod passed across the front of the wrists, threaded through holes punched in the ends of each band. One end of the rod had been bent into a loop to stop it sliding all the way through the holes, and the other end had a hole, through which the haft of a padlock had been inserted to keep the rod from sliding back out. The chain that looped up around Finn's arms and circled his neck to prevent him from ascending or using compulsion had been secured in place by sliding the bar of the shackles through a couple of links in the chain. If Edrik could pick the padlock, the whole arrangement would fall apart. From the look of it, the lock was secured with springs rather than pins, and the keyhole might be big enough to get the tongue of his belt buckle through.

Grabak's shackles looked like Finn's, and the lock on Edrik's own shackles felt to be the same. Maybe he could get them out of here. He put his back to the wall to hide what he was doing with his hands and began tugging his belt around to get the buckle in the back where he could work with it.

The sun had shifted a few hands deeper into evening, and Edrik had determined that the padlock mechanism had only a single spring, though he hadn't yet managed to pick it, when they dragged Kaya in, wriggling and spitting.

Alive!

Edrik's heart surged with relief. The bruise that darkened one side of Kaya's face was visible even in the fading light, and her eye was swollen partly shut. Her dress had been torn in several places, and there were smears and spatters of blood on it—how much of it was hers?

But she'd given fair measure for what she'd gotten, too. Four long, bloody gashes had been clawed down the cheek and neck of the guard who yanked her along by the rope that bound her wrists together. The guard with his hand wound into her loose, draggled hair, was limping and had a black eye. The third, prodding her forward with the point of his sword in the middle of her back, had a bloody rag wrapped around his off hand. Several other guards trailed in their wake, apparently just to witness the spectacle. *Vultures.*

"Hoy!" one of them called out. "Look at that. The Mudge really is a girl! Tavit said so, the crafty coot, but that's the kind of thing I got to see 'fore I believe it."

Another guard sidled up alongside Kaya and reached brazenly over to squeeze her breast. He hooted, "It's real! She's a girl, all ri—"

Kaya jerked sideways and twisted, slamming one foot solidly into the man's groin.

The guard with the sword kicked at the back of her other knee, and Kaya crashed to the floor.

The one with the limp snorted, eying his writhing comrade with disgust. "Mudge in a dress is still Mudge, Oskar. Best remember that and keep your distance."

They chained her hands to an iron ring that had been bolted to the floor opposite the dragons' cell—perhaps originally intended for securing livestock—and left her there with barely enough slack in her chain to straighten her back while kneeling.

"Kaya?" Edrik called out uncertainly when the guards were gone.

She clenched her jaw and turned farther away from him. He probably should have expected that; she'd been running from him when all of this started. He was such a fool.

Grabak heaved himself awkwardly up off the floor and worked his way over to lean heavily against the bars. "Are you all right, Mudge?"

Kaya made a sound somewhere between a snort and a bitter, incredulous laugh. "Stow it, Stig. You don't get to talk to me." Slowly, she turned her face to them, squinting angrily sideways through the growing shadows. "You promised. You gave me your name and you promised to kill me if they caught us."

"Mudge—" Grabak began.

She cut him off, her voice growing harder. More biting. "This has been my nightmare since I was six years old. *Six years old*! I practiced being a boy like other children practiced counting, or skipping, or walking a fence rail—so that *this* wouldn't happen."

Edrik's fingers fumbled frantically with the padlock behind his back. He had to get out. He had to help her.

"I started patching up his women when I was nine, Stig." There was a grating edge of resignation in her voice now. "I would wake up at night sometimes and think I heard him breathing in the darkness— that he'd found out and had come for me. When I was older and my blood cycles started, I was terrified he would know—that he would see something different about me, or . . . or smell it on me, and realize that I was a woman. When Grandfather died, I thought . . . I thought . . ."

She sucked in a ragged, choking breath and didn't say what she had thought.

"This isn't over." Grabak sounded grim and determined. "We won't let him hurt you, Mudge."

"Hurt me?" Her incredulous voice shattered into a broken laugh—a hopeless, destitute sound. "He's not going to *hurt* me, Stig. He's going to beat me bloody and rape me over and over until that's not amusing to him anymore."

"Mudge—"

"And then he's going to torture me until I beg him—beg him—to do it again. And I will, Stig. I will beg him. I've seen what happens to his women. And I've seen him work with the questioner. So have you. He delights in it. And he has no reason to hold back with me."

Stars. Edrik's stomach turned over. He had to get her out. But he couldn't quite get the right angle on the rimy lock spring.

"And when he's turned me into a groveling, broken dishrag, do you know what he'll do then? He'll give me to them." She jerked her chin toward the guards at the other end of the cave. "And I'll beg them too." She turned her face away again. "You could have kept it from happening, but you wouldn't."

Grabak cleared his throat. "Where there is life, there is hope, Mudge."

Her head snapped back up, eyes wide and burning. "You think I would hope to live after what he will do to me?" She made a grating, choking sound that might have been the carcass of an incredulous laugh. "Don't you even talk to me!"

She tugged the edge of her green petticoat out from under one knee and buried her face in it. Grabak turned away from her and went to lean his forehead against the cold stone at the back of the cell, giving her as much space without him in it as he could.

For a while after that, no one said anything. Edrik gritted his teeth and worked at the lock behind his back. The shackles pinning his wrists made it difficult to maintain a good grip on both the lock and the belt buckle at the same time. He could feel the spring inside the lock with the tongue of the buckle; it was stiff, but he'd almost tripped it more than once. He could do this. It was just a matter of time.

His hand cramped, and the lock slipped out of his grip. He hissed softly and leaned his head back against the stone while he worked the stiffness from his fingers.

Kaya looked up at the sound, and their eyes met . . . and held.

"We *are* going to get out of here, Kaya," Edrik murmured. He glanced toward the mouth of the cave, making sure all the guards still sat hunched around the cook fire before he whispered, "I can pick the lock on these shackles; I just need to find the right angle. I've almost got it."

She regarded him silently for a long heartbeat before whispering, "And the cage?"

"We'll figure something out." Edrik shrugged nonchalantly, trying to seem more confident than he felt. "One thing at a time, right? But we *are* going to get out of here."

She studied his face. "It'll be too late."

"No." Edrik shook his head, then leaned his forehead against the sting of the iron bars so he could look her squarely in the eyes. "I will not let that happen."

Her bruised face pulled into a wry grimace. "So . . . what . . . you're going to rescue me?"

"It's what I do." He grinned. "Obsessive urge, remember?"

She laughed softly and closed her eyes, turning her face away again.

"Kaya . . ." Edrik's voice sounded hesitant even to himself.

"Mm?" She didn't look up.

"I'm sorry."

No response.

"Back at the village. When I kissed you. I'm sorry. I didn't mean—"

Kaya coughed out another bitter laugh. "Stars, Edrik, I know you didn't mean to kiss me. You said so, right after; you don't need to tell me again. It was only the music, I suppose, and the dancing, and it was late, and you were nearly home. Maybe you had a little more of that ale than you realized, and you just got a little carried away. You're going to marry your Lissara, and that kiss didn't mean anything. I understand. It's all right, I won't tell anyone."

"No!" Edrik stared at her. "Kaya, you didn't let me finish. I didn't mean to *frighten* you. I absolutely meant to *kiss* you. Yes, it was impulsive, but that doesn't mean it wasn't intentional. What kind of spineless profligate do you think I am? I wouldn't go around kissing other women if I was promised to Lissara—no matter how tempting you are when you're dancing. And even if I had, I certainly wouldn't expect you to lie about it for me." He sighed and started working at the lock again behind his back. "Look, I don't know what's going to happen with Lissara. It's been a year since I last saw her. A lot has changed since then, and I—I just don't know. But I haven't broken any promises to her; I'm free to kiss any woman I like." He studied Kaya's bruised profile. "I knew exactly what I was doing when I kissed you. I've been wanting to kiss you for ages."

She turned her head slowly to look at him. "You have?" She sounded skeptical.

"Pretty much since you gut-punched me in that tavern. Maybe before that. I'm not exactly sure."

"But what about . . ." Her brow furrowed. "That doesn't . . . Why did . . ." Her whisper cut off with a ragged intake of breath. Her eyes squeezed shut, and her lips pressed tightly together as she turned her head away from him. "I guess it doesn't matter now."

He answered her anyway, as much as he could. "I needed to sort out my feelings for Lissara. And there was Nik. I thought . . . Well, I didn't want to lead you on. I didn't want to hurt you. But I didn't want to lose you either. I didn't know what to do." He drew a deep breath and said more forcefully, "I kissed you on purpose, Kaya. I don't regret it, and given the chance, I would absolutely do it again. I just forgot to take into account how unaccustomed you are to being kissed—and for that I am sorry."

For a moment, he thought she might say something, but a sudden rustle and a barked order from the front of the cave startled them all. Kaya cringed farther back into her corner and buried her face in her petticoat again. Edrik leaned his back against the wall, hiding what he was doing with his hands, but he didn't stop working at the lock. Finn and Grabak whirled into crouching positions, as ready to fight as they could manage under the circumstances. The flurry of movement that had broken out among the guards stopped abruptly as two new figures strode in through the mouth of the cave.

The Thanesson entered first, his stocky figure tense and slightly hunched. He gestured, and a guard handed him a torch, which he held high as he moved toward the back of the cave. The shadows of grim determination on his face flared into ravenous fury when his eyes fell on Kaya, then settled into a look of predatory satisfaction.

The man who followed him was lean and elegantly dressed and moved with the grace of arrogance. Black hair framed the pale, almost translucent skin of his face, from which his penetrating, ice blue eyes gleamed with something like triumphant amusement.

Nidhaug.

Bile rose in Edrik's gut, and his fingers slipped on the lock. He gritted his teeth, adjusted his angle, and began again.

The Black Dragon stopped on the other side of the bars and eyed the prisoners as if sizing up livestock held for auction, totting up the measure and value of each. "Well, Selwin, it seems as if you have indeed recaptured the old Drake."

The Thanesson wedged his torch into a crevice in the cave wall and moved to stand beside Nidhaug. "As I assured you, Magnificence."

Nidhaug turned his head slowly and regarded the Thanesson with the air of a man who'd found a maggot in his meat. "Six years ago, you assured me he was dead."

The Thanesson scowled sullenly. "He *was* dead. Or as good as. I couldn't stop my father from selling him to that lunatic dungeon keeper and his brat, but nothing goes down the dwarrow hole and lives. He should've been dead and butchered years ago."

Nidhaug shook his head and said pointedly to Grabak, "You see what happens, old friend, when we treat them as if they're our equals?"

One hand flashed out, snake fast, to catch the Thanesson by the throat and slam him against the iron grate. "I didn't pay you for almost dead," he remarked calmly, "or as good as dead. I paid you for *dead*."

The Thanesson choked, scrabbling uselessly at the dragon's grip with his fingers, and his face slowly shifted from blotchy red to deep purple before the dragon cast him roughly to the stone floor, where he floundered, gasping like a fish.

Nidhaug ignored the man, turning again to Grabak. "You always were too soft with them. They've forgotten their place."

Grabak growled low in his throat. "And as always, you've forgotten their value. Without humans, there would be no more dragons."

Nidhaug crouched down outside the bars to look Grabak squarely in the eyes. "An excellent point, which you made most convincingly to Ofnir the Drake in the days after the Breaking. And you were right to persuade the king to grant some of the humans protection in the Vanir lands; there were so few of them left in those days. But you are far too sentimental about them, Grabak. Does a fish fall in love with the weeds in which it lays its eggs? Does a farmer grovel before the soil in which his seeds grow? When will you learn to see humans as they are?"

He leaned forward and his voice grew more intense. "In the old times, when I was a youngling, we were their gods. They offered tribute to us—their finest sheep, the firstfruits of their crops, their best wine, and every good thing. They gave their most beautiful women to us as sacrifice, and we used them as we chose. We took what we pleased with no expectation of anything in return except that we allow most of them to go on living.

"And now, because of you, they expect us to protect them from their enemies. They think we should mend their walls, and clear their roads, and feed their children in the wintertime, and"—he cast a disgusted glance at the Thanesson, who cowered against the wall—"they think they can lie to us without repercussion. They have forgotten that we are dragons."

Nidhaug leaned forward, pinning Grabak with his icy gaze. "And so have *we* forgotten. The humans have spread across the plains again, ripe for the harvest, yet most of the young drakes brought up with you on the throne have never experienced the passion of battle or the thrill of a raid. They've never seen the look of worship in the eyes of a groveling supplicant that is their due as dragons! Enough of the Nine agree with your obscene philosophy that I am reduced to courting your castoff doxy and giving her my bond before they will agree to confirm my claim to the throne. My bond, Grabak. The oath of a vassal to his lord, sealed by dragon magic. They would make me vassal to a woman—to a human—in order to claim what is rightfully my own. It is a disgrace." The last word turned into a long, venomous hiss.

"And you will betray my wife," Grabak scoffed, "as you have betrayed me as your liege lord. *You* are a disgrace."

Nidhaug grinned broadly. "That was, perhaps, my intention, I admit —until our friend Selwin showed up on my doorstep a few days ago with news of your survival and escape." He leaned in as if sharing a confidence. "He seems remarkably relieved to have recaptured you before you could work any mischief. Perhaps he appreciates how fortunate he is that you are about to become more useful to me alive than dead."

He paused as if waiting for a response; when Grabak only glowered at him, he went on, apparently thinking an explanation was in order. "Come now, you remember what happened to Halorem when his wife secretly accepted Melrakki's bond—the magic and the madness. Even when the iron cut off the sense of the bond, it was still there, and Melrakki could still reach Halorem's magic through it. And she couldn't release either bond. There are not many of us left who do remember that—which is well because, otherwise, the Nine would demand proof of your death before allowing the queen to marry another dragon. But you were there, and I know you remember; you were the one who wielded the knife at the king's command." He rose to his feet so he could sneer down at Grabak. "I will so enjoy using your own magic to compel your sycophants to confirm my kingship. It's quite a delicious irony, don't you agree?"

"You would make the Nine oathbreakers like yourself?"

Nidhaug spread his arms wide, palms up, and turned his face to the ceiling, as if imploring the stars for patience. "If I must. If you force it upon us, with your rigid refusal to see reason." He turned his icy stare back to the old Drake. "I meant for you merely to die and leave them free to choose me. But you didn't die, so now we have other choices to make, you and I. You may relinquish your hold on them if you like, to spare their honor. But even if you don't release them, you have generously gifted me with another way to obtain their bonds. And their oaths to you will be flimsy things anyway after being left to fray for five years without renewal; they won't even notice the breaking. If I must be an oathbreaker and compel them to be the same in order to restore our dignity as dragons, then I will gladly make that sacrifice. And in a few years, they will thank me for it. We are gods, you feeble-minded fool. Dragons! And we deserve a king who remembers that."

Grabak growled. "I will see you get what you deserve, Nidhaug."

A smile spread across the Nidhaug's thin lips. "I deserve everything you had, Grabak. Everything you wasted. And tomorrow, when the solstice sun is at its apex, I shall take it. Beginning with your wife. It will be a simple affair, out of respect for the memory of the bride's departed husband." He inclined his head mockingly toward Grabak. "All the great drakes and their heirs will bear witness, and the Nine will give me their oaths whether they choose to or no. No one will dare question the legitimacy of my reign after that." His voice grew soft and mocking. "How does it feel, old friend? How does it feel to know she will be mine? And that through her, you will be mine? Such a shame a marriage bond does not degrade over time like a liege bond, is it not? If it did, you might be able to free yourself from it."

"It is forbidden!" Grabak snarled.

Nidhaug laughed. "Forbidden by whom? By Ofnir? He's been dead for centuries. By you? So far as anyone knows, you're dead too. I am the king now, and I take what I want."

"I will see you dead!" Grabak snarled. "I will find a way, and I will see you dead."

Nidhaug ignored the threat. "Selwin." He waited with an air of aggrieved impatience while the Thanesson scraped himself off the floor and offered a low bow.

"Yes, Magnificence?"

"I will return for the old Drake in three days' time. It should be safe to move him by then." He held up a warning finger. "I will expect him to be alive and in good health, Selwin. You have failed me once already. Take care not to do it again."

The Thanesson paled. "Of course, Magnificence." He hesitated. "And his companions?"

Nidhaug turned his pale gaze back to the cage. "His companions." He moved a step forward, considering. "The steward's pinioned pup. Well, we can't have him telling what he knows." Nidhaug glared at Grabak. "Already you have made me an oathbreaker, old friend. Would you make me a slayer of broken children as well?"

His gaze turned to Finn. "And my own wilding get. You showed such promise. I warned you not to get mixed up in this. Perhaps you have had time to come to your senses, and you are ready to take your rightful place among the gods?"

"I would rather die than offer you my oath," Finn snarled.

"Would you?" A thoughtful frown spread across Nidhaug's face. "Ah, but after tomorrow, your oath will be as easily compelled as the oaths of the Nine. And your silence as well." His frown stretched into a scheming smile. "And your pinioned friend can be made to tell how his desperate quest failed when he found the old Drake dead. He will even believe it himself. No one will ever go looking for Grabak again; and no one will suspect he is the source of my power. You see, I can be merciful." He turned to the Thanesson. "I want all of them alive, Selwin. In three days."

The Thanesson bowed. "And the girl?" He cast a malicious glance at Kaya, who so far had avoided the notice of the Black Dragon.

Nidhaug followed his glance and raised one eyebrow. "What does a girl matter? So long as she cannot speak what she knows, do with her as you will."

CHAPTER 27

It had gone completely dark outside the cave when Nidhaug left, anxious to get back to the Aerie before anyone noticed his absence. As soon as he was gone, the Thanesson bellowed for the captain of his guard. The gray-uniformed man who answered the summons was the one whose face Kaya had clawed bloody. He saluted grimly. "My lord?"

"Have they been fed?" The Thanesson jabbed a finger at the dragons.

The captain frowned, and the flickering light from the torch still wedged into the wall crevice made his face look even more disfigured. "N-no, my lord. We thought—"

"Feed them. If they die, you die. And then bring the Mudge to my quarters. We have things to discuss, *she* and I." He stalked out, and the captain began calling out orders.

Edrik went cold. Somehow, he'd thought he would have more time. He *needed* more time. The lock slipped from his fingers again, and he hissed in frustration. He needed to push on the spring and pull on the lock haft at the same time, but the shackles kept him from being able to get a proper grip on both. And he still had to figure out how they were going to get past the iron bars. Maybe when the guards brought the food, they'd take the shackles off so the prisoners could eat, and the dragons could grab one of the guards. But the Thanesson's men just shoved three bowls between the bars and left the dragons to lap up their stew like dogs.

Edrik ignored the food and began again with the lock. If he twisted one wrist just so and slid the shackle as far up the other wrist as it would go, he could almost get the right angle. The iron bands pressed painfully into his wrists, but he gritted his teeth and pushed harder against the burn, keeping his eyes on Kaya. He had to get her out. Now.

The captain of the guard fingered the scratches on his face as he eyed Kaya. She crouched by the far wall with her hands still chained to the ring on the floor, but she was no longer weeping into the hem of her petticoat. Her mouth was set in a grim smirk, and her eyes held a feral gleam. She wouldn't go quietly, and the captain clearly knew it.

"Oskar," the captain barked, "bring the keys."

The guard Kaya had kicked in the groin stomped over from the fire, a scowl darkening his face. "Sir?"

"His lordship wants the Mudge brought to his quarters for . . . questioning."

"Oh ach?" Oskar's face lit up with a spiteful grin. "Serves the lying whore right, that does."

He stepped closer to Kaya and bent to unlock the chain that pinned her to the iron ring. As soon as the lock clicked, Kaya whirled into motion, smashing Oskar in the face with both of her bound fists, and then catching him in the gut with her knee as she sprang to her feet. The guard crashed to the floor, flailing, and Kaya brought her boot heel down hard on his throat, crushing his trachea. By the time the captain's sword flashed from its scabbard, Oskar was already choking on his last breath, and Kaya was squaring up to face the captain.

Edrik twisted harder against the shackles, trying to keep the lock spring depressed while his fingers scrabbled at the haft.

Kaya and the captain eyed each other warily.

"You don't have to do this, Samel," Kaya said quietly.

Samel grimaced. "It ain't personal."

"It's very personal to me."

"Right. I can see that." He flicked a glance at Oskar, who had gone horribly still, and then pinned his wary gaze on Kaya. "Look, Mudge, he only says he wants to talk to ya. That ain't so bad."

Kaya made a disgusted sound. "You know him better than that, and so do I."

Samel gritted his teeth. "Guess I do. Still, I got to do what needs doing so my family can eat."

"Guess you do." Kaya sighed. "But I'll do what I have to do, too. Don't make me kill you."

Samel shifted nervously on his feet. "I'm the one with the sword, Mudge. And I can call the others."

Kaya shrugged. "It's a small space; you can't all come at me at once. And you wouldn't dare rob the Thanesson of the pleasure of killing me."

"Maybe not. But there's enough of us to take you, and you know it. You might kill one or two more, but it will all end the same. And you ain't one to kill without need."

The two of them eyed each other in silence for a long moment, shifting restlessly on their feet, tense and ready.

Edrik pressed even harder against the sting of the iron bands, clenching his teeth against the burn. The haft moved! But not far enough. He stretched his fingers. Just a little farther. He pushed harder—

The squared-off edge of one band broke the skin, and Edrik convulsed, hissing as the iron's poison fire seared up his arm. Distantly, he felt his shoulder slam against the bars, as his back collided with the stone wall, and the lock spun away from his spasming fingers.

"Fine." Kaya's voice cut through the sick fog in Edrik's head. "You win."

What was she doing?

The captain said something Edrik didn't catch as he shoved the shackles away from the seeping wound on his wrist and shook his head to clear it.

"Just let me say goodbye to my friends."

She was giving up. She *couldn't* give up!

"Mudge—" Samel protested.

"Last year," Kaya said, "when your baby was sick with that fever—"

"Don't do that, Mudge. I told you, this ain't personal."

"They're my friends, Samel. I just want to say goodbye, and then I'll go quietly. I won't fight you. I swear."

No! She had to keep fighting! Edrik would spring the lock any moment now, and then . . . then . . . Well, then there would still be the bars. He couldn't do it. Not in time. And clearly Kaya knew that too.

He had failed her.

Samel hesitated one more heartbeat, then sagged and nodded. "Fine. But be quick, right? Take too long and his lordship won't be none too pleased with neither of us." He sidestepped enough to clear Kaya's path to the cage but didn't put his sword away. Kaya kept her eyes on the guard as she edged over to the grate, waiting until Samel made a broad, impatient gesture with his hands before she turned her back on him.

Edrik couldn't bear to face her. He closed his eyes and leaned the side of his head against the bars, savoring the burn of the iron.

Grabak cleared his throat. "Mudge," he rasped. "I'm sorry. I just thought you—"

"Stow it, Stig." Kaya's voice was gentle, despite her cross words. "You did what you thought was best for me. I can't fault you for that forever, so I might as well forgive you now, while I'm still . . . me. That way, when I'm gone, you'll know I really meant it."

When she was gone? What did she mean, gone? She wouldn't do something to hurry her death, would she? Edrik clenched his teeth. She might. She'd made it very clear that she would rather be dead than in the Thanesson's brutish hands. He risked a glance at her face. It showed only sad resignation. A lump formed in Edrik's throat.

Grabak started to reply, but Kaya cut him off again. "Other Dragon." Finn chuckled wryly, and Kaya continued. "I'm sorry about the spider."

"I'm sorry about the rat." He held her gaze until she gave a nod of acknowledgement.

Kaya stepped to Edrik's side of the cage and lowered herself to her knees—only a breath away from him, but completely beyond his reach.

"Rolf?" Her voice was barely more than a whisper. "Are you all right?"

Edrik gritted his teeth against the emotion that flooded through him. She could ask him that? Now? He cleared his throat. "I'm fine."

Her wry smile was oddly knowing. "You say that. But you're not."

He collected himself and straightened, turning to face her. "You're right. I'm not. Not until you are." Leaning forward, he held her eyes with his own. He couldn't compel her, not with this much iron against his skin. But he put all the force of his will behind his words as he whispered, "Don't give up, Kaya. Don't do anything you can't undo. I am coming for you. Don't you give up."

She blinked hard and looked down at the rough stone floor. "Stars, Rolf," she murmured. Then she cleared her throat and looked at him again, a new intensity behind her dark eyes. "You said you'd kiss me again if you had the chance. Did you mean it?"

"Kaya—" Edrik's voice broke, and he couldn't finish.

"It's only . . ." She drew a deep breath and leaned her forehead against a crossbar of the grate. "It would be nice to have one kiss to remember, given in kindness, and know that it really was meant for me." Her eyes searched his face, asking, but too proud to plead . . . and perhaps a little bit frightened.

He would have kissed her anyway, but that was the most unguarded expression Edrik had seen on Kaya's face, and it called to him—to the deepest part of him where he was all dragon and raw magic. He felt the tentative spiderweb touch of her own magic against his as he leaned forward, heedless of the burn of iron against one cheek, and gave Kaya the kiss he ought to have given her first—before that wild, possessive kiss when they were dancing. This kiss was gentle. Seeking. Exploring. Persuading, instead of insisting. Her lips trembled against his as she drew a breath that was half a sob and reached her bound hands between the bars to twist her fingers into the collar of his shirt, pulling him closer, deepening the kiss. Edrik met her intensity with his own, edging closer to the bars, straining against the shackles with arms that longed to wrap around her slender body and pull her against him. This was what he wanted. This slow, deep tenderness. With Kaya. Forever. And he wanted more. He wanted—

Something hard pressed against his lips. Her teeth? No, something else. Something flat and round, like a coin, but lighter and smoother. She tightened her grip on his collar, keeping him from pulling away as she pushed the thing between his teeth and into his mouth. It tasted of wood. Her mouth moved slowly against his one more time, then pulled away.

"I lied to you," she murmured. "I'm sorry."

And she was gone, striding down the length of the cavern with Samel hurrying to catch up and the Thanesson waiting for her somewhere close by. The other guards leapt to their feet as she approached the cave mouth, apparently thinking she was trying to escape, and then, when Samel hollered for them to stand down, most of them fell in around her like some kind of twisted honor guard escorting her to her doom, leaving only one or two distracted guards to watch the imprisoned dragons. She didn't look back.

Edrik slumped back against the wall, fumbling with the lock. He had to get out of the rimy, ice burned cage and find her! The disk in his mouth still held the warmth of Kaya's body. He turned it over with his tongue. One side had been polished as smooth as glass. The other had several curving, interwoven lines etched into the smooth surface. What was it? It seemed familiar. Why had she . . . ?

Realization scorched through Edrik like dragon fire. *Tait's yot mark!* She must have had it stitched into the hem of her petticoat like those Gorian half crowns and the coins she'd used to buy herbs back in Topside. She hadn't been weeping into her petticoat at all, she'd been picking the mark out of her hem with her teeth. But why had she given it to him instead of using it to free herself? Although . . . if she had tried to use it on her own restraints she would probably have burned herself because her hands were chained so close to the iron ring.

Stars. He was stupid! How much time had he wasted trying to get his own shackles off, when it would be so much easier to reach the lock on someone else's?

He shifted the mark to lie between his teeth and the inside of his cheek so he could speak and whispered, "Finn. Turn around. Now."

"What?"

"Stars, Finn, just turn around."

Finn did, and Edrik set to work on Finn's lock. In moments, the padlock was sprung, and Finn was shrugging off his chain. Grabak shifted over to where he could keep a watch on the guards at the front of the cave while Finn worked at Edrik's lock.

"Can you feel the spring?" Edrik prompted as Finn wiggled the belt buckle against the locking mechanism. This was taking too long.

Finn grunted an affirmative.

"You just have to push it against the haft and then keep it pressed in while you pull the haft, so the spring fits through the hole with the haft instead of catching against the case."

"I know."

"Then what's the—"

Finn's fingers jerked and the lock spring thunked softly as the buckle tongue slipped off it yet again. Edrik ground his teeth in frustration.

"Hold still," Finn growled.

"I *am* holding still. Hurry."

"I think you bent the spring when you were—"

"There is nothing wrong with the spring. Hurry up."

Grabak shushed them both, jerking his head toward the front of the cave, and Edrik clamped his mouth shut, cursing silently as he waited. How far was it from the cave to the Thanesson's quarters? Had Kaya gone quietly as she had promised, or had she fought them and bought herself more time?

Please let her be all right.

At last, the lock gave way to Finn's inept prodding, and Edrik's shackles clanked to the stone floor. The guards started trickling back into the cave in twos and threes. The Thanesson must have Kaya. What was he doing to her?

"What about the bars?" Finn grumbled as Edrik wriggled free of his chains.

Edrik slipped the wooden disk from his mouth and pressed it into Finn's palm, then snatched up his belt and spun to work on Grabak's restraints.

Finn froze, staring wordlessly at the thing in his hand. Then he choked. "Tait's mark! Where did you get this?"

"Kaya."

Finn snorted disbelief. "She said she burned it. Back in her dungeon, she—"

"She lied," Edrik said. "You heard her."

Finn chuckled as he moved over to the iron grate. "Are you sure that's what she meant? Maybe she lied about wanting to kiss you. Maybe she just wanted to pass you the—"

"Stow it, Finn." How could he joke around at a time like this? "Just set it up. You do remember how, right?"

Finn grunted and turned to inspect the bars of the cage, looking for a good spot, while Edrik pried at the spring in Grabak's padlock.

Just as the haft slid free, Grabak whispered, "They're coming."

Edrik glanced toward the mouth of the cave. One of the guards had risen to his feet and was peering back toward the dragons, his face an ominous mask of firelight and shadow. His lips moved, but Edrik couldn't hear what he said. The other guards' heads all turned, and one of them jumped to his feet and yanked a burning stick out of the fire to use as a torch. Several others fell in behind him as he started toward the back of the cave.

"Now, Finn!" Edrik shoved the bar on Grabak's shackles back through the holes, freeing his wrists. Grabak writhed out of the chains as Edrik dragged him toward the back wall of the cave.

Finn carefully placed the wooden disk on one of the crossbars of the iron grate. He traced the mark with his finger, murmured its name, and sprang back against the far wall with Edrik and Grabak. As they watched, blue light shimmered in the etched grooves of the mark, pulsed once, twice, and spat out a blue tongue of flame, like a tiny alfkin wisp that perched on the iron bar, nibbling furiously at the wooden disk.

The torch in the wall flickered out.

When the first guard arrived at the cage, the disk had been entirely consumed, and the flame had grown into a pulsing white ball about the size of a man's fist. It had wrapped itself around the iron bar like a spider's egg sac. By the time a knot of men gathered on the other side of the grate, cursing and gesticulating frantically, blue tendrils had sprouted from the ball, crept over the grate, and twined around the bars, throbbing in time with the pulse of the white-hot heart at their center.

The bars started to glow coral red, flared gold and white, and began to drip onto the cave's floor, burning into the stone like hot coals on a blanket. The magic at Edrik's core flared with it, pressing back against the heat of the flames on his skin, demanding release. Finn shifted eagerly on his feet, and Edrik sensed the dragon magic swelling inside his friend as well.

The muttering of the guards flared into a shouted chaos of curses and orders as the entire grate folded in on itself and sank, groaning and spitting sparks, to the pocked floor, leaving the throbbing white heart of the flames still hovering in the air where the wooden disk had been. Finn called out the yot mark's release, and the pulsing ball began to rotate, slowly at first, then faster and faster, drawing the glowing tendrils back into itself like threads on a spindle. The iron of the grate settled, dimmed, froze hard and black, and hazed over with a thin feathering of frost as the ball of fire faded to blue and dwindled until nothing was left but the empty, gaping hole where the iron grate used to be.

The guards broke for the cave entrance.

Finn laid a hand on Edrik's shoulder and grinned. "I'll take care of them. You find your Kaya." He sprang over the broken grate and sprinted after the guards.

Grabak followed him, stopping only long enough to snatch the sword from the guard Kaya had killed.

Edrik's foot caught on a mangled bit of frozen iron; he crashed to the floor, rolled as he struck stone, and flung himself upright again. *He had to find her! She had to be all right!*

Beyond the cave mouth, Finn's triumphant laughter shifted into a savage roar, and a flare of dragon fire lit the landscape outside.

As Edrik dove out of the cave, his own magic unfurled, drawing in stone, and fire, and a great gout of night air, which tasted of woodsmoke and brimstone, pine trees, and the sweet, coppery tang of fresh blood. Part of him triumphed in it—in the power, and the clarity, and the newness of it all. *He was no impotent pinion!*

But the Thanesson had Kaya.

He reared up on his hind legs, stretching out his wings for balance, and released his pent-up frustration in a flaming bellow. Then he drew in a slow, deep breath, searching for Kaya's scent among the currents of human fear that drifted around the mountain clearing. Where was she?

He *would* find her.

A guard staggered out of the darkness, his face frozen into a mask of terror. He shouted something incoherent and hacked at Edrik's exposed belly with his sword. Reflected firelight glinted off the iron blade as it clattered uselessly against Edrik's scales. The faintest hint of roses and lavender caught at the back of Edrik's throat—Kaya! He turned his head, seeking its source. The man with the sword took another swing, and Edrik, distracted for a fraction of a heartbeat, lost the scent. This was taking too long! *The Thanesson had Kaya.*

Edrik batted irritably at his attacker with one foreleg and was annoyed to find that the man's body stuck to his talons. He shook the writhing guard off and shifted on his feet, seeking Kaya's scent again. *There it was.* He opened his mouth to let the trace of her slide unhindered down to the back of his throat, flicked out his forked tongue to capture more of it, and followed it across the clearing, head swaying and bobbing to catch the elusive fragrance.

Twice more he was waylaid as he wove across the clearing and pushed his way into a stand of pines that had grown up in the shelter of the rock face. The first attacker had only a sword and was easily disposed of, but the second had a spear and was smart enough to aim it at Edrik's eyes. Edrik had to spit a small stream of flame at that one and then pause to stomp out the resultant sizzling mess before it started a brush fire. He found Kaya's scent again, buried under the cloying stink of charred human, but it took too long. *Too long!* And all the while his mind churned with thoughts of what the Thanesson might be doing to Kaya.

The pines concealed another opening in the rock face, and there the scent of roses and lavender pooled, along with other, stronger smells. Smoke from a charcoal brazier. The musk of human male. And blood. *Please let it not be Kaya's blood.* Edrik flicked his tongue out, testing and sorting the scents. There had been a sentry. Two. But they were gone now, probably to help with what was happening out in the clearing.

Edrik considered the cave opening. As a man, he could have walked through it easily enough, but there was no way his ascended form would fit. He could probably dig it out, but that would take time Kaya didn't have and might cause a collapse. He bent his head to peer through the hole. The passage inside curved, blocking his view of what lay beyond, but dim light flickered against the wall at the turning, and a murmur of quiet voices drifted out, the words obscured by echoes and the sounds of carnage coming from behind Edrik. A quick yelp of pain stabbed through the murmur—*Kaya!*—and a man's mocking laugh chased it down the corridor.

Edrik leapt from his crouch in a swirl of dragon dust and was already halfway down the passage before he realized that in his human form he had no weapon. It didn't matter; there was no time to go back and look for one. He'd rip the Thanesson apart with his hands and teeth if he had to.

Beyond the curve, the passage opened into a cave, smaller than the one the guards had occupied but much larger than the alcove where the dragons had been penned up. A brazier in the center lit the chamber red, and stalactites dripped from the ceiling at the back, giving the impression of having walked into a beast's gaping maw. The rugs and furnishings of a human lord's hunting pavilion should have looked out of place, but somehow, the folding table and chairs that stood beside the brazier, the iron-bound chests, and the dark wood bedstead with its black netting and blood red coverlet seemed to have been made for this cavern.

The pale fabric of Kaya's shift gleamed against the dimness where she stood, sideways to Edrik, body tensed, leaning her forehead against the tall post at the foot of the bed. Her ankles had been tied, and her hands were bound to the bedpost above her head. Tattered shreds of her clothing lay scattered about the floor. Her shift was spattered with blood and had been sliced down the back from neck to waist, revealing the scars from the whip lashes she'd received in the dungeon and the three branded dwarrow runes. The Thanesson stood on the far side of Kaya with his body pressed against hers and one hand on her belly . . . or maybe her breast; it was hard to tell from Edrik's angle. His other hand held a large hunting knife, the butt of which was pressed into the largest burn on Kaya's back. Was that what had made her cry out?

As Edrik entered, the Thanesson looked up and raised his knife so the point rested against Kaya's neck at the base of her skull.

"Get away from her!"

Kaya flinched at the sound of Edrik's voice, and a dark line of blood trickled from under the knife's point. The muscles in her jaw tightened, but she didn't look at him. Her face wore the dazed, broken expression of a woman for whom a lifetime of nightmares had just come horribly, unbearably true.

The Thanesson's eyes traveled over Edrik, noting his empty hands, and a slow smile spread across his face. "No weapons. Come to watch, have you, boy?" His smile broadened as he ran his hand down the front of Kaya and around to her side where Edrik could more easily see the man's fingers begin to slide the hem of her shift up her thigh.

Edrik's blood boiled over, and he lurched three steps forward.

The knife's blade flashed as the Thanesson tilted the edge of it under Kaya's ear and used the point to lift her chin.

Edrik froze.

The smile dropped from the other man's face, and he bent his head slightly to whisper in Kaya's ear.

"No," she whimpered. "Leave him alone. I'm the one you want."

"Your mother was the one I wanted," the Thanesson growled.

"But you will have to do." He directed a leering grin at Edrik and pressed even closer against Kaya. "You have your mother's eyes." His fingers reached the edge of Kaya's shift and crawled onto the flesh of her thigh like white worms against her soft bronze skin.

Edrik took two steps closer—close enough to hear Kaya's sharp intake of breath and see the dark drop of blood that spattered from the edge of the knife onto the pale shoulder of her shift. He stopped. Then he took one more deliberate step and said, "You're not going to kill her."

The Thanesson raised his eyebrows. "No?"

"No." Edrik took another step. "For one thing, it would spoil all your fun."

The grin spread across the man's face again, but he said nothing.

"And for another"—Edrik stepped closer—"if you did"—he took another step—"I would have no more reason not to kill you."

The tip of the knife slid down the edge of Kaya's jaw, leaving a dark, seeping line beneath the bruise on her cheek. Edrik gritted his teeth and took one more step.

The Thanesson barked a laugh and stepped away from Kaya, directing the knife's blade toward Edrik instead. "You're right, of course. I have plans for this one that require her to be breathing. Still, this was a fun game too, while it lasted—though it would have been more amusing if she'd shown any hope that you might actually rescue her. She hasn't much faith in you, has she?"

He shifted into a fighting stance as Edrik took another step. "Perhaps it will be diverting to find out whether a pinioned dragon can last long enough without weapons for my guards to come back, or if Mudge and I will get to make a private little party out of carving you up. What odds will you lay, eh, Mudge? I hear you were quite a hand with wagers back in my dungeon."

Kaya's only answer was a soft gasping sound that might have been a sob.

"Maybe my friends will get here first," Edrik said.

"Your friends are outnumbered. And my men caught them before without much fuss. I'm sure they'll manage to do it again." He feinted with the knife.

Edrik shifted a little on his feet and didn't point out that this time it was not the dragons who were caught off guard.

The Thanesson grinned and lunged. Edrik dodged aside, then sprang back as the Thanesson flipped the knife in his grip and twisted into a backhand attack. The two men circled warily, each taking the measure of the other.

Then the dance began in earnest.

The Thanesson led, knife blade flashing red in the light from the brazier as he thrust and whirled, bearing ruthlessly down on his prey.

Edrik ducked. Sidestepped. Skipped back, then cut around the Thanesson's overextended reach to jab a fist into the man's side, just below the ribcage.

The Thanesson grunted and staggered back. No longer grinning, he launched a new attack, more cautious this time.

Edrik dodged and spun, watching for another opening. He took it when it came, landing a blow that sent the Thanesson sprawling.

The knife skittered across the stone floor. Both men dove for it, but Edrik was faster and snatched it from under the Thanesson's grasping fingers.

As Edrik adjusted his grip, the Thanesson rolled to his feet, fumbling another knife from the top of his boot. He swore and flung himself back into the fight.

The next time Edrik found an opening in the Thanesson's guard, he drew blood.

The Thanesson staggered back, cursing. As Edrik closed on him, the coward broke and ran for the entrance corridor. Edrik let him go; he had more important things to worry about.

Kaya was breathing in long, ragged gasps, and when Edrik cut the ropes that bound her to the bedpost, she collapsed against him and began sobbing hysterically. He sank with her to the floor, gathering her into his lap. She twisted her fingers into the front of his tunic and burrowed her face into his shoulder.

"You c-came," she choked.

"Of course I came," Edrik stroked a soothing hand down her back, careful not to touch the burns, trying not to notice how little of her the remains of her shift actually covered. This was not a time for that. "I said I would." Strangely, that only made her cry harder.

He pushed sweat damp hair back from her face. Cradled her cheek against his palm.

He had almost been too late. "Why didn't you fight him?"

She buried her face against his chest, muffling her answer in his tunic. "He s-said he'd hurt you."

"Kaya . . ."

A wordless shout echoed from the corridor, followed by scuffling sounds. Then, "Edrik?" This time, the shout was clearly Finn—but he sounded odd.

"All clear!" Edrik hollered back.

"Quick!" Finn called. "It's Grabak!"

CHAPTER 28

Kaya was only vaguely aware of what was happening around her. After that last sleepless night on the boat and the next night spent trying to evade the Thanesson's men, her body was on the verge of collapse and her mind was snarled in a wild morass of careening emotions. The joy of the dance and the baffling rapture of Edrik's first kiss tangled with the terror of flight and capture. The utter elation of kissing Edrik again blurred into the surreal horror of the Thanesson's hands on her body. It was too much, too fast, and reality drifted in and out of a sick, shifting haze.

When the ropes gave way and Edrik's strong arms wrapped around her, something inside Kaya broke too, like an overburdened river dam; everything came flooding out at once, hot and tempestuous, searing her soul and then scouring it bare. Edrik gathered her into his lap like a child, and she clung to him as the storm tore through her. And yet, there was a part of her, a splinter of her broken self, that stood back and watched, untouched, calmly fascinated by the violence of her own disintegration.

That was the part that heard the shouting. And when Edrik scooped Kaya up and set her gently on the bed so he could go see what was happening, it was that splintered part that gathered up the rest of her and made her pay attention. When Finn half carried, half dragged Grabak in from the corridor, the old Drake was convulsing violently and dripping blood from a fresh wound in his side. Only the whites of his eyes showed between his fluttering eyelids.

Stig! Kaya's lips moved, but no sound came out.

Edrik cursed and went to check the corridor for pursuers.

"What happened?" Kaya's voice was thin and reedy, but at least the words came out this time.

"We thought we got them all," Finn said. "So we tracked Edrik here. Grabak went in first while I shifted. The Thanesson was lurking in the passage."

Kaya slipped off the bed and edged nearer, still struggling to get control of herself. "Did you kill him?"

Finn shook his head. "He ran past me before I knew what was happening, and Grabak needed help." He knelt beside the spasming dragon and muttered, "The knife's out, but there must still be iron stuck in him somewhere. Maybe a needle dart, or . . ." He ran his hands rapidly over Grabak's limbs, frown deepening, and then stripped off Grabak's tunic.

As he was opening the bloodstained shirt underneath, Edrik returned. "Ogre knife. Found it in the corridor." He thumped the knife onto the table and went to help Finn.

Kaya went cold. Ogre knives were fat, deadly blades with barbed points designed to detach when the blade was twisted inside a victim and remain behind when the knife was withdrawn. And the point of this one was buried somewhere inside her friend. The detached splinter of herself took over, and before the rest of Kaya's mind caught up, she was already kneeling beside Grabak and sliding two fingers into the knife wound. She had to get that point out of him.

Kaya tested the layers of tissues with her fingers as she felt her way along the path the blade had taken. Skin, fat, layers of muscle, connective tissue . . . how far in had the blade gone? Too far. The wound angled up under the edge of Grabak's ribcage, and blood oozed out past her fingers at an alarming rate—probably not enough to mean a major vessel had been severed, but enough to make her suspect organ damage. His liver?

Her groping fingertips found the embedded iron point and located the protruding key pin that was used to connect the barbed tip to the main body of the knife blade. She pinched the pin between her fingertips as best she could and tugged. Grabak's body curled in a great, arcing spasm, and both of the other dragons struggled to hold him still for Kaya. She tugged at the point again, and this time Grabak vomited as his body convulsed. The bleeding increased a little, but the point didn't budge.

"I can't get it," Kaya muttered. "The barbs are holding it in place, and I can't get a good enough grip. We're going to need to enlarge the hole." She drew her fingers back out of the wound, and Grabak's spasming eased somewhat.

When she looked up, both Edrik and Finn were staring at her.

"I need the smallest knife you can find," she told them. "Or maybe a razor. And water—hot, if there's any to be had. And bandages if you can find them, but bring the other things first."

Finn shook himself. "I think I saw your satchel in the pile of loot from the village."

"Even better. Get it."

While the dragons were gone, Kaya dragged the coverlet off the bed and wrapped it around Grabak. Then she went through the Thanesson's chests until she found a couple of clean shirts that would make much better rags and bandages than the filthy shreds of her own clothing that the Thanesson had flung so gleefully about the floor of the cave.

Edrik got back first, carrying both a full teakettle and a half-filled waterskin, but Finn was not far behind, with Kaya's satchel slung over one shoulder and Edrik's sword hanging from the other.

Kaya snatched the satchel from Finn and tossed Edrik an herb pouch for the teakettle. She dug out her toolkit and some sturdy string on her way back to Stig. She hardly even hesitated, after kneeling beside him again, before she dug out the rag-wrapped glass vial from its padded inside pocket. The syrup inside, mostly poppy and hensbane, was dangerous to be sure, but if Grabak thrashed around too much while she had a knife in his innards, she might do more harm than good. And they had to get that knife point out.

"Hold him," she said.

Edrik grasped Grabak's shoulders, and Finn straddled the old Drake's legs while Kaya carefully dripped a few drops from the vial into the corner of Grabak's mouth.

While she waited for the thrashing to slow and stop, Kaya slid her copy book out of her satchel and examined several anatomical sketches that showed the musculature of that part of a man's body, as well as a detailed drawing of the liver, reminding herself of where the blood vessels she most needed to avoid were located. Then she made a sliding knot in one end of her string, hooked that over the tip of her middle finger, and tucked a thin, flat knife from her kit in between middle and first fingers, before inserting both fingers back into the wound, sliding them up under Grabak's ribs. It was easier to follow the track of the knife without the muscles spasming around her fingers, but she couldn't quite get the loop of string over the knife point's key pin without enlarging the hole at the top just a little.

As she picked the tissue apart with a second knife so more of her hand would fit, Finn stood abruptly and staggered for the corridor with his hands over his mouth. At least he had the sense not to vomit on the patient.

Edrik made an odd noise, and Kaya looked up to see his eyes fixed on her with an expression stuck somewhere between fascination and horror. What must he be thinking to look like that? Did he regret kissing her? Of course he did. She was a half-mad dungeon keeper who cut dead people up for fun. If he'd forgotten that temporarily while they traveled, he was certainly getting a thorough reminder of it now. And he had a beautiful princess waiting at home. Which was just up the road.

Kaya gritted her teeth and focused on Grabak. Her groping fingers managed to loop the knot over the key pin and catch it in the notch. She pulled gently on the string with her other hand, drawing the iron point back out through the wound track while she used the flat knife between her fingers to slice channels for the barbs to follow.

As the knife point came free, swinging loosely on the end of the string, Edrik let out a sigh of relief. "Will he be all right?"

A pit opened up in Kaya's stomach. She had seen men die from wounds like this. But she had seen some live, too. She forced a shrug. "Hard to say. Maybe with your sword?"

He nodded, studying her face with those disconcerting green eyes, and went to get his sword.

She didn't look at him as she cleaned the wound with the herbed water and applied the liniment to prevent festering. But her fingers brushed against his when he handed her the bandages she'd cut from the Thanesson's shirts, and the splinter of calm that was holding her mind together slipped a little. It came unpinned completely when he helped her wash the blood from her suddenly shaking hands. And when he tilted her chin up so he could see her face and asked, "Are *you* all right, Kaya?" the tears threatened to flood out all over again.

She stuffed them back down and pulled away from him. "I'm fine." She clenched her teeth and tried to steady herself.

"You're bleeding."

"Only a little. His knife slipped a few times when he was cutting off my dress. That's all. He didn't get around to . . ." She shook her head. Torture wasn't something she wanted to think about just now. "We should get out of here. He might come back. Or the guards. And Nidhaug knows we're here."

Edrik regarded her solemnly. "Nidhaug thinks we're safely locked up, and as long as Grabak is wearing that collar, the queen can't tell him, even accidentally, when we start moving closer. The guards are all dead. And your Thanesson might be an idiot, but I doubt even he is foolish enough to come back here alone. He'd be daft to go to his master for help, because Nidhaug is as likely as not to kill him for letting us escape, but even if he does, he's on foot and in the dark, so it'll take time. And the villagers will think he's a bandit if they catch him skulking around. We're safe enough for now." He frowned. "Besides, I don't think Grabak is ready for travel just yet."

Kaya turned to look at her old friend where he still lay on the stone floor of the cave wrapped in the Thanesson's bloody coverlet. "We could rig a stretcher." She sighed and scrubbed a hand over the back of her neck. "But you're right. It would be better not to move him tonight." There wasn't much else they could do for him, but they could let him rest.

She needed rest too. She was so tired she could hardly think straight. The adrenaline rush of Grabak's need had pushed back the deluge of careening emotions, but the tide was rising again, and her careful control was starting to crack.

Edrik's fingers brushed softly against the skin of Kaya's back, and she jumped at the unexpected touch. "Sorry," he said, snatching his hand back. "I was just noticing that your burns are looking better."

Her cheeks warmed with the realization that with her shift torn as it was, her back probably wasn't the only part of her he could see. She tugged the tatters closer and looked away from him. "I told you they'd heal over time."

He scowled. "My sword should have healed them faster."

"They wouldn't make very good penalties if you could just erase them with a little yotun magic, though, would they?" Her voice came out sharper than she intended, but if he touched her again she would shatter—and she wasn't sure she could pull herself back together.

"Kaya . . ." He half raised one hand as if to touch her cheek but thought better of it and rubbed at his scrubby hair instead. "When was the last time you ate?"

She shrugged and didn't meet his eyes. She was too tired to be hungry. But her last meal had been back in the village before the dancing began. Before he kissed her. Which he wouldn't be doing again now—she knew horror when she saw it, and she'd seen it written all over his face while he watched her fish that knife point out. Horror and disgust. Maybe seeing her in a dress had made him think for a while that the grubby, ghoulish creature she'd been back in the dwarrow hole was only a disguise she could shed as easily as changing her clothes. But now he knew as well as she did that she was the same person underneath whether she wore a robe, or a dress, or the blood-stained remains of a shredded shift.

In the cave, he'd said he kissed her on purpose. Was that even the truth? Men often said things they didn't mean when they were locked up. She knew that much for sure. And she hadn't met many men who would turn down an opportunity to kiss a girl when they thought they might be about to die. That kiss had felt real. Like he meant it. But what did Kaya know about kisses? Maybe they all felt like that. Was that why so many women had let the Thanesson kiss them? She shivered at the thought.

She supposed it didn't really matter at this point whether Edrik had meant it or not. He obviously found her disgusting now; he couldn't even stand to touch her except to poke at her burns. And he was nearly home to his Lissara. How could Mudge compete with a princess? Maybe someday when she had figured out how to be a woman, she could figure out what to do with a man.

When the silence had dragged on too long, Edrik said, "I'm going to find you something to eat," and headed for the entrance.

Apparently, he didn't even want to be in the same room with her. Well, what did she expect? No hero in any story had ever fallen in love with the ghastly little dungeon keeper.

When he was gone, Kaya roused herself from the insistent exhaustion enough to give her cuts and bruises a perfunctory cleaning with the leftover herb water and slip into the old dungeon robe she'd never gotten around to cutting up. She might as well look her part. Besides, it was the only intact article of clothing she had left. She sighed and gathered up the shredded remains of her skirt, and blouse, and bodice and tossed them onto the brazier. The green strips of petticoat went into her satchel; she'd need those later. She hoped. And after that, the weariness that was seeping through the cracks in her brokenness began to tangle up her arms and legs, making her clumsy. She needed rest.

She was sitting at the table with her aching head in her hands when Edrik returned with Finn. Their voices preceded them down the corridor.

"So you took away his knife and scared him off?" Finn sounded dryly amused.

"More or less."

"Why didn't you just compel him?"

Edrik's silence felt awkward even to Kaya. After a moment, he said, "I guess I didn't think of that. She's right. I'm not pinioned, just very stupid. I could have gotten her killed."

"But you didn't." Finn was grinning when he rounded the corner into the cave. "Don't beat yourself up. The change takes some getting used to."

"I almost got Grabak killed." Edrik's voice had gone very sober.

Finn sighed, and his tone went as solemn as Edrik's. "That can't be helped now. Let it go."

Kaya watched wearily as the dragons tucked Grabak into the Thanesson's bed along with Edrik's sword, then sat down with her at the table. She dutifully swallowed half a bowl of the flavorless stew the guards no longer needed. Had any of them survived? Would Samel's wife be able to feed their baby without him? As the fear drained from her system, a terrible drowsiness settled with the stew into the pit of her stomach, and the voices of the dragons became a buzzing murmur in the back of her head.

She was only hazily aware when Edrik draped a cloak around her shoulders and carried her to a makeshift pallet near the brazier.

She started awake once during the night, half certain she had nodded off while hiding in a ditch or abandoned farmhouse, and the Thanesson was about to find her. Finn looked up from where he sat on a chair beside the bed.

"How is he?" Kaya murmured, rubbing at her forehead to dispel the last fragments of the nightmare.

Finn raised an eyebrow. "If by 'he' you mean Grabak, he's asleep. He roused about an hour ago from whatever you dosed him with and had some broth." His mouth drew into a frown. "If you mean Edrik, he's out scouting around. And I think he . . . Well, he would probably prefer that I mind my own business. Never mind." He shrugged and looked down at his hands.

Kaya blinked wearily, trying to tease an appropriate response out of the sludge in her head and finally murmured, "Wake me if anything changes." She rolled over and pulled the cloak more tightly about herself. It smelled of Edrik and the memory of his kisses.

When she woke again, the pale glimmer of the solstice sun's first light was leaking in around the corner of the passage, and Edrik had just returned. She watched sleepily from under her lashes as he crossed the chamber and sat down at the table, where Finn and Grabak were arguing quietly.

"I still don't like it," Finn grumbled.

"You don't have to like it," Grabak said. "It's just the way things are. There are only two ways to keep Nidhaug from stealing my magic: stop my wife from marrying Nidhaug or kill me. If I go to the Aerie to stop the wedding, the question of the throne will have to be settled as well, and I am not going to just hand it over to that fiend."

"Well, you can't fight him like this," Finn snapped.

"I may not have to fight him at all."

"He's not going to just lie down and die on his own."

"The throne is mine by right. I don't need to challenge him; I only need the Nine to confirm my prior claim. And they will, unless they want to be seen as oathbreakers and risk an uprising of their vassals."

Finn snorted. "Some of the Nine will support Nidhaug. He knows exactly what to promise them. And even if they do confirm your claim, Nidhaug will just challenge you for the throne, and you'll still have to fight him."

"Maybe," Grabak acknowledged. "Maybe not. He and I have fought before to settle other disputes, and he has never been able to defeat me. He won't dare challenge me directly. That's why he lured me away and challenged Edrik's father instead. No, he'll pretend to welcome me home and then rally his forces and bide his time."

"You're wounded. Nidhaug won't pass up easy prey."

"He doesn't *know* I'm wounded."

"How can you be certain? That skunk of a Thanesson may have told him."

Edrik cleared his throat and waited until the other two looked at him. "I tracked the Thanesson up the mountain last night until he went to ground in a crevice. He was too far in to burn him out. And it seemed unwise to shift and go in after him, not knowing if he was armed. So I played monster-in-the-dark all night to keep him from leaving. For all I know, he still thinks I'm out there, but even if he crawled out right after I left, he won't have gotten very far."

Grabak sighed "Well, even if Nidhaug does challenge me, even if he *kills* me, I still win because if I'm dead, he won't have my magic."

Finn hissed. "You'll still be dead."

"That's my risk to take."

"If you're dead, they'll make him king for sure!"

"Is there another way to break the marriage bond?" Kaya asked quietly, and they all turned to look at her. She sat up and scrubbed her hand across the back of her neck. "Besides death, I mean. It's just . . . that way he couldn't use the bond to access your magic. Right?"

Grabak cleared his throat. "The bond is formed with the deep magic, Kaya. It has to be released the same way. Both parties must be present."

"We could just kill you ourselves," Finn grumbled, "and go find a nice cave to live in somewhere else until all this blows over. Being a wilding has to be better than walking straight down Nidhaug's throat."

"We could kill *you* instead, Finn," Kaya said pleasantly, standing up to stretch. She walked over and poked Grabak gently in the side below his injury. "Let me see."

Grabak chuckled and unbuttoned his shirt—one of the Thanesson's, Kaya noted. Blue silk. The bandages had already been removed, and the knife wound had healed into a raw pink scar with a puckered cross-hatch where Kaya had enlarged the wound.

"How does it feel?" She prodded it gently and then more firmly.

Grabak flinched. "Sore. A bit of an ache up under my rib."

"That's because you let your liver get skewered, you old fool," Kaya said fondly. "You're lucky Edrik let you snuggle up with his sword last night."

"It'll hurt worse if you ascend and try to walk on that leg," Finn muttered. "Or fly. Or fight."

Kaya sighed and reached for her satchel. "Normally, I'd tell you to rest at least a few more days and avoid pointy objects and the people who want to stick them in you, but under the circumstances, I think I'll have to just give you something for the pain and hope we're all still alive at dinnertime. When do we leave?"

"As soon as possible." Grabak eyed Kaya up and down. "We need to get you out of that old sack and into a decent dress before you forget you're a girl again."

CHAPTER 29

A steady stream of travelers trickled up the stone-paved road that led to the Aerie and to the town of Vanir's Rest, which clung to the Aerie's ankles. They were mostly peasants from the nearby villages but also landholders, merchants, and gentleman farmers from the other Vanir territories, along with their wives and marriageable children—and their grooms, ladies' maids, messenger boys, and other socially indispensable members of their households.

That was to be expected on the day of the solstice, Edrik knew, especially with the prospect of a royal wedding, however understated that event was intended to be. In fact, these would be the stragglers—even the Dragonlords and the great drakes who didn't make their permanent homes here would have been in residence for days now, if not weeks. Both the town and the palace fortress were undoubtedly already bulging at the seams trying to accommodate all the merry-makers who found it imperative to be in attendance on this sort of occasion.

Edrik had never liked the festival crowds. Even when he was a child, he had avoided them, hiding out on rooftops, or in the stables, or in the darkest reaches of the palace archives, which were off limits to all except the highest ranking of the visitors. Usually, it was Lissara who had tracked him down and teased him out—especially after she told him she'd give him a kiss for every hiding place he showed her. He'd been about seventeen at the time and would have given almost anything for one of Lissara's kisses. In fact, Edrik had spent a decade and more trying to earn Lissara's kisses—trying to win her love.

Over the years, other suitors had risen and fallen in the princess's regard, but Edrik had been the one constant in her life—her playmate, her friend, her confidant. She'd gone to him when she was sad or troubled, and he'd found solace with her after his father died. He had thought it would always be that way. But how much of what he'd felt for her had been because he had won what so many others coveted?

When he was twenty-one, she had said she loved him. She had also said, teasingly, that she wouldn't marry him until he could fight off her other suitors like a proper dragon—but really, she'd only wanted to wait until he could give her a proper dragon's marriage bond. And he couldn't blame her for wanting that. If he'd come into his power when he ought, they would probably be married by now. But he hadn't.

When he was twenty-two, Lissara had gloated about being destined to wed the mightiest dragon born in the last half century because any dragon who took so long to ascend would be wondrous indeed. When he was twenty-three, she still spent more time with him than with any of her other suitors, but she stopped speaking to him of ascension and, gradually, of marriage. Her buoyant enthusiasm faded into uneasy hopefulness, and when he was twenty-four, even that dwindled, and she began to avoid him when she could. She waited until he actually reached his quartermark to end his hopes entirely.

She'd wept then. And truth be told, he'd wept too after she had gone.

When she set her quest, promising to marry the suitor who brought her father home before the summer solstice, it had felt to Edrik like a lifeline tossed to a drowning man. He'd lost so much by then, and the quest had seemed like a way he could get at least the most important part of it back.

And now he was not only returning home with Grabak in fulfillment of Lissara's quest, he was returning home whole and well, a proper dragon at last, able to give Lissara the kind of marriage she had desired and deserved. He should have felt triumphant. He should have felt exultant. He should be hurrying the others along so he could get back to Lissara sooner, planning in his mind what he would say to her when at last they were together again.

But he wasn't.

Mostly, what he felt was a nervous foreboding. And although he did wonder what he would feel when he saw Lissara again, worry about Kaya kept crowding out thoughts of the princess.

Why was Kaya avoiding him? Because she *was* avoiding him, there was no getting around that fact.

She had flinched every time he'd touched her last night and had barely spoken as they ate. This morning, she had chattered cheerily with Grabak over their brief breakfast in the Thanesson's camp and kept herself busily away from Edrik while they gathered up what little they needed for the last leg of their journey. And she'd barely even looked at him since. They had taken up their habitual walking formation as they made their way down the hill and up the dirt cart track to the paved main road, with Finn in front, Edrik behind, and Kaya chatting quietly with Grabak in between. He hadn't seen her so much as glance over her shoulder.

Edrik thought about insisting that they stop so he could take Kaya aside for a private conversation, but there wasn't time; they had to get Grabak to the Aerie before noon if the wedding was to take place during the Conclave. Besides, with the way she was avoiding him, she'd probably refuse anyway, and the whole thing would just end in an awkward mess for everyone. Perhaps it was something best sorted out after everything was settled with Grabak. And Lissara. But the not knowing was eating away at Edrik. What had he done to make her despise him so?

Was she upset because the dragons had killed their captors? Maybe some of the guards had been her friends. She'd called the captain by name and had spoken with him of his wife and child. But surely she had known what would happen when she passed Edrik the yot mark.

And she didn't seem to be angry with Finn and Grabak, who had done most of the killing.

Maybe she was avoiding Edrik because he had kissed her. Back on the boat she'd confided that she found Nik's attentions confusing, and that she hadn't been able to tell for sure whether the boatman wanted to kiss her. Edrik's first kiss must have been entirely unexpected. She'd clearly found it alarming; she'd run away from him. He'd tried to apologize and explain himself in the makeshift dungeon, but now that he thought about it, he'd really only told her that he kissed her on purpose, he hadn't told her why. And what if Finn was right about the second kiss? What if the only reason she'd done it was so the guard wouldn't see her passing Edrik the yot mark? His cheeks warmed at the thought of what that kiss had meant to him—at least until he'd felt the yot mark press against his lips. What if it hadn't meant the same to Kaya? Still, she had kissed him back both times, and it had felt like she meant it, and that thought gave Edrik hope.

But if that wasn't it, what was?

Was she annoyed that he had rescued her from the Thanesson? She had insisted more than once that she didn't need Edrik to rescue her. And he had to admit that she'd always managed to get herself out of the trouble that found her. Maybe his rescue had somehow foiled a plan she'd made to deal with the monster herself, and she resented being cheated out of her victory. It hadn't seemed that way afterward, though, during those brief, heady moments when he'd held her, and she'd clung to him as she wept. What might have happened if Finn hadn't interrupted? If Grabak hadn't been so badly injured?

Kaya had been magnificent then. Lissara would have screamed and fainted the moment she saw all that blood, but Kaya pulled herself together, took charge, and fixed the problem. Her movements had been purposeful and efficient, without any guessing or hesitation. Watching her, Edrik couldn't help imagining the parts of her life in the dungeon that had made sticking her hand into a living body to cut out a cruelly barbed piece of ogre knife seem like such a routine course of action to her.

The idea of such a gentle soul growing up in that place was beyond horrifying. Thinking about it made Edrik long to see her laugh again. Truth be told, it also made him ache to hold her again. To wrap his body around hers so that nothing could touch her, nothing could hurt her ever again, as he had done in his ascended form on the alfkin altar, as he had done in his human form when he rescued her from the Thanesson. When all of this was over, he would hold her again. And he would make sure laughter became as routine for Kaya as blood had been in the dungeon.

If he could fix whatever had gone wrong between them.

Edrik wished Kaya's first view of the Aerie could be from the skyward approach, where the elegance of the graceful archways, the grand colonnades, the soaring towers with their delicate spires, and the exquisitely terraced gardens showed to their best advantage. As a boy, he'd always asked his father to circle an extra time before he landed on the terrace outside their rooms so he could see that breathtaking view. That would make Kaya smile. And he would show it to her.

Someday.

Soon.

After he learned to fly.

If she would let him.

For now, he could only watch her from behind as they walked the last few miles beneath the overhanging branches that shaded the road and blocked the view of the mountaintop. The dense forest of evergreen trees—pines, and firs, and tall cedars—grew up against the stone walls that enclosed the town. Vanir's Rest, unlike most towns, was not surrounded by farms, or pastures, or other cleared, cultivated lands. The Rest was home mostly to tradesmen and functionaries that served the needs of the Aerie, and their provisions came, like those of the palace fortress itself, from the agricultural villages like Harrows Bend that occupied the lands farther down the mountainside and paid tribute to the Dragonlords in exchange for their protection.

They flowed with the current of the crowd through the gates of Vanir's Rest and out into the broad, open market square inside the town walls. Edrik could tell when Kaya first caught sight of the Aerie because she stopped short and clutched at Grabak's elbow.

"Is that . . .?" Her voice was almost lost in the murmur of the crowd.

"Home." Grabak patted Kaya's hand. "We're almost there." He tugged the hood of his cloak farther forward.

"It looks like it's emerging from the mountain!" Kaya exclaimed. "As if it was carved into the stone of the mountain itself."

"It was." Grabak grinned. "The Vanir have long offered protection to the yotun in the west. In exchange, their best stonesmiths come each generation to work their art on our Aerie. I will show it all to you, young Mudge. But there is another place we must go first."

The sun was nearly overhead, and the mass of people in the market were all making their way through the massive archways on the western side of the town. Beyond the archways, broad, tiered galleries had been carved into the stone around the curving sides of a crater created long ago when a star died and fell into the side of the mountain, forming a natural amphitheater.

At the end of the amphitheater, where the crater met the core of the mountain, a high dais had been carved from the naked stone to overlook the immense paved courtyard that formed the floor of the arena. At the back of the dais, in the center, two flights of dragon-sized steps, one on each side, led up to the throne of the Great Drake, Lord of the Vanir, High King Among the Mountains. The dragon thrones of the Nine were arranged on the platform, three directly below the king's throne, and three to each side of those.

More steps led down from each end of the dais to the floor of the arena. On the front face of the dais, an elaborately sculpted archway framed a dark passageway that led beneath the thrones and back into the heart of the mountain.

Edrik and the others moved with the crowd into the amphitheater and edged their way downward and around until they stood directly across the paved court from the great throne of the dragon king. By the time they pushed their way to the front of the crowd on the lowest gallery and pressed up against the waist-high railing that separated the onlookers from the arena, Kaya was openly gaping.

Grabak chuckled and nudged her with his elbow. "A bit larger than the great hall back in Shrike's Hollow, eh, Mudge?"

"I expected it to be bigger," she said. "But I never imagined this." She frowned. "Although . . . I thought there would be . . ." She looked down, shaking her head.

Grabak raised his eyebrows. "You thought there would be what?"

Kaya shrugged sheepishly and looked back up at Grabak. "Well, I thought there would be more dragons."

Grabak smothered a guffaw. His mouth twitched as he scanned the crowded assembly. "How can you tell which ones are dragons, Mudge?" He grinned at her, showing all his teeth.

Kaya opened her mouth to say something, then closed it again and grinned. "All right, Stig, I see your point."

An excited murmur rippled through the crowd, and Edrik looked around to see the first of the Nine emerging from the dark passageway below the thrones. Linngrim was in his ascended form, and the roaring murmur of the assembled masses began to quiet as he prowled up the steps and across the platform before shifting to his human aspect and taking his place as Speaker for the Nine on the central throne in the grouping of three just below the king's high perch.

Fellugand came next, then Hildormur and Eylaug. One by one the Dragonlords took their places, and silence settled over the amphitheater, tense and expectant, as the sun reached its zenith and the slow, sonorous boom of a gong echoed out of the corridor behind the archway, signaling the opening of the Conclave.

Linngrim rose slowly from his seat and stepped to the front edge of the dais.

"It is the Longest Day," he intoned solemnly. His voice was low, but the bowl shape of the amphitheater caught the sound and reflected it, bouncing it back across the tiered galleries so that everyone could hear. "The Sun rides ascendant, and her children have gathered."

From below the dais, the gong sounded again, deep and reverberating.

"This shall be a day long remembered." Linngrim declaimed. "A day of feasting and song. The Sun will smile upon her children, and with her, we will greet the coming darkness with balefire!"

The gong sounded, and a thundering roar burst from a thousand throats and more, a battle cry against the dark that echoed back and forth across the crater, intensifying, reaching heavenward.

Linngrim raised his fists. Triumphant. Exultant. Offering the fierceness of the Vanir people to the Sun to aid her battle against the night. Then he lowered his arms and silence descended once more upon the gathering.

"On this glorious day," Linngrim intoned once more, "the Sun shall consecrate the union of our beloved queen with Lord Nidhaug, her betrothed, and the children of the Sun shall bear them witness!"

This time, when the gong rang out, two figures emerged from the arched passageway, and Edrik heard Grabak's sharp intake of breath. The queen was resplendent. The solstice sunlight gleamed in the folds of her yellow silk gown, danced off the thread of gold embroidery, and shimmered up her pale arms and slender neck to play in her loose flaxen curls and twine around the golden filigree of her ornate crown. She might almost have been an incarnation of the Sun herself. Nidhaug, striding beside her, might have been an incarnation of night in his formal black brocade doublet. The two of them stood before the archway for a moment as a thunder of applause rose once more from the gathered Vanir, then faded into silence. Nidhaug held out his arm to the queen, and she laid her pale fingers against his dark sleeve as the two of them moved forward into the courtyard.

Three new figures emerged from the darkness inside the passageway. The Sun's divine led the way, followed by Nidhaug's right-hand man, Skorpir, who was apparently acting as the bearer of the cord, and by the royal princess, bearer of the cup.

Edrik felt his heart turn over in his chest. Lissara was radiant—starfire beside her mother's sunlight. Her white gown sparked with silver embroidery, and a simple silver circlet crowned her elaborately plaited hair. Her face was solemn and serene, and though Edrik was too far away to see the direction of her gaze, her head turned slightly as she walked, as if she might be scanning the crowd. Was she looking for him? Still hoping he might return and bring her father home?

As if Grabak could hear Edrik's thoughts, the old Drake turned toward Kaya and murmured, "Mudge, my friend, if you are still willing, now would be an excellent time to have my collar off."

Kaya tore her eyes away from the scene in the courtyard and focused on Grabak. He pushed back his hood and unfastened his cloak, then handed it to Finn.

Nidhaug and the queen turned to face the Sun's divine, and the bearers of cord and cup moved to stand beside the bride and groom. On the dais, the Nine rose from their thrones and moved to stand in a line across the front of the platform.

Kaya pushed back the edge of Grabak's blue silk shirt and grasped the iron collar with one hand, carefully placing her reaching fingertips on the necessary runes at each side of the latch point.

Grabak leaned forward and placed a fatherly kiss on Kaya's forehead. "Thank you, Mudge," he whispered. "For everything."

Kaya shrugged one shoulder. "You're my friend, Stig." She closed her eyes and clenched her teeth.

Edrik only saw her flinch this time because he was watching for it, but he knew the penalty she paid. He half reached out to take her in his arms, to hold her as the new dwarrow rune seared itself into the flesh of her back, but he squashed the reflex—if she didn't want to even look at him, she certainly wouldn't welcome his touch.

The collar came away in Kaya's hand, and Edrik followed her gaze back to the courtyard just as the queen started and half turned, swaying a little on her feet as she searched the crowd behind her.

Grabak's breath caught and then he hissed softly.

Kaya said, "What is it? Did she betray you?"

"Shock. Confusion. Hope. Fear." Grabak shook his head. "I can't tell."

His gaze shifted back to Kaya. "Are you all right?"

She smiled. "I'm fine."

That lie came so easily to her lips.

From his place among the Nine, Linngrim solemnly said, "When the Sun and her children have blessed the binding of this marriage, the Nine shall offer oath to their new king."

Grabak searched Kaya's face only a moment longer before he swung himself over the railing and dropped to the paving stones. He took three steps toward the center of the arena, and called out, "What of their oaths to the old king?"

CHAPTER 30

K aya forced her face to remain impassive as she gripped the
stone railing and let the slow lightning of the dwarrow magic
crawl from her hand up her arm to her spine and down to the small of
her back, where it lodged, smoldering like a hot coal, melting the skin
from the inside out and charring it around the edges. She wanted to
scream. She wanted to weep. She wanted to hold on to something real
and solid and feel safe, as she had felt with Edrik's arms around her
after he rescued her from the Thanesson.

But she had learned long ago that showing pain only exposed
vulnerability and invited more pain. And letting herself imagine she
was safe with Edrik had only made it hurt more when she saw his look
of horror, stark and honest, as he watched her tend to Stig—and afterward, when he had distanced himself from her. He hadn't even spoken
to her since they left the cave. Even meeting his eyes felt dangerous
now; what if he looked at her like that again?

So she clenched her teeth, stood up straight, and kept her face
expressionless while she absorbed the burn of the penalty.

This at least was a familiar kind of pain. Wounds like this healed.
Slowly, perhaps, but they did heal. Scars faded. It was that other kind
of pain that frightened her; the kind she didn't know how to mend. The
kind that came from thinking of Edrik's kisses. In those kisses, she had
tasted a fierce yearning that had flung open doors in Kaya's soul that

she'd kept carefully locked and barred so nothing could escape to betray what she was. Listening to his heart in the dungeon had been like listening at the keyhole. Letting him take her stitches out had knocked the bar askew. But kissing him . . . kissing him had broken the bar and smashed the doors to splintered ruins hanging from bent and twisted hinges. And now there was no way to get them closed again. All she could do was stand back and watch the fae tale play out to its inevitable ending.

There was no getting around it. The lost king would reclaim his throne. The wilding would be offered a home. The hero would complete his quest and win the hand of the beautiful princess—and she *was* beautiful; the breathtaking golden-haired, ivory-skinned woman in the shimmering white gown couldn't be anyone but Lissara. Not the way Edrik's eyes followed her.

And the dungeon keeper? Well, with her filthy sack of a robe, and her awkward black braid, and skin that was the color of an old shoe even when it wasn't blotched with bruises, she could hardly compete with the princess. So Kaya supposed the dungeon keeper would do whatever dungeon keepers did when the story was over and everyone else was busy living in happiness all their days. Disappear, never to be heard from again? Plunge to her death from the highest tower? Creep into a crack in the earth and live on lizards and earthworms for the rest of her days while she dreamed of those two perfect kisses?

Or maybe all kisses felt like that. How would she know? Maybe she should have let Nik kiss her after all.

But now she was just feeling sorry for herself. Pathetic. She had known how this would end when she started it; it was hardly fair to complain about it now. She made her fingers relax against the railing and focused on what was happening out in the courtyard.

The queen took a few unsteady steps toward Grabak before Nidhaug's hand shot out and clamped down on her wrist, snagging her like a butterfly in a spiderweb. She turned to look back at him and then toward Grabak, before her knees hit the paving stones with bruising force, and she buried her face in her hands. Lissara leapt to her mother's aid, kneeling beside her and wrapping her arms around the queen to hold her upright.

Edrik stepped into Grabak's place beside Kaya at the railing. His nearness buzzed against her senses.

Nidhaug moved to stand between Grabak and the two women. He held his hands out, palms up, and turned slowly in a circle, his gaze taking in the gathered throng and the Nine Dragonlords standing above him on the dais. "What of the old king's oaths, indeed!" He sneered. "The old king broke his oaths. He abandoned his wife and deserted his people." He turned to Grabak. "And now, after all this time, you come creeping back like a thief in the night. I am the king now! And you shall be cast out as an oathbreaker."

"I abandoned no one." Grabak's voice was calm and pitched to carry above the murmur that rippled through the galleries. "I was unavoidably detained while traveling. In my absence, I entrusted my people to the care of my queen and my very capable adviser. I have not relinquished the oaths of the Nine or released their bonds. I have not been defeated in combat. And now I return from my long journey, not like a thief in the night, but on the Longest Day in the full sight of the Sun and all her children to find that you have slain my regent, and usurped my throne, and seek now to wrest my wife away from me as well with your lies and pretensions. It is you who have broken oath, Nidhaug. I am your king, and I will have my due."

"Is that a challenge?" Nidhaug sneered.

An ominous murmur rippled again through the galleries.

"What's wrong?" Kaya asked. "Why does he sound so smug?"

Edrik hissed softly. "It's a trick question. If Grabak says no, he's backing down. If he says yes, he's acknowledging Nidhaug's claim to the throne."

"And starting a fight he can't win with a half-healed hole in his liver," Finn added.

Kaya frowned and looked back across the arena. "He won't back down."

Grabak snorted a scornful laugh. "Why would I challenge you for what is already mine?"

On the other side of Edrik, Finn chuckled. "He's a sly old snake; I'll give him that."

Did he mean Grabak or Nidhaug?

Nidhaug opened his mouth to respond, but Grabak interrupted. "Think carefully before you speak again, Nidhaug. You are the eldest of us all and have not lived so long by playing the fool. So far, you have earned only exile as an oathbreaker. If you challenge your king, you will die."

"King!" A new voice—new here, but horrifyingly familiar to Kaya —shouted from the galleries near the archway that led back to the town. "You're no king. You're nothing but a lapdog. An ugly girl child's plaything."

Kaya's gut clenched, and bile rose in the back of her throat.

Nidhaug turned slowly toward the voice. "Selwin," he crooned. "Are you still alive?"

There was a scuffle of movement in the gallery, and the Thanesson, tattered and dirty, dropped over the rail to the paving stones. "Yes, Magnificence." He bowed deeply. "Though I barely escaped with my—"

"You failed me, Selwin," Nidhaug's voice was soft but deadly.

"Yes, Magnificence." The Thanesson bowed his head in shamed acknowledgment. "But I have information which I hope will—"

"Come here."

The Thanesson went, cringing like a whipped dog.

"Kneel."

His knees hit the stone harder than the queen's had.

"Speak."

The Thanesson looked around, then leaned forward and murmured softly, gesturing with his hands. Nidhaug leaned closer to hear, then glanced up sharply at Grabak, as the Thanesson finished talking and laid one hand on his right side, just below the ribs. Right where he had stabbed Grabak.

Kaya went cold.

Nidhaug tilted his head. "You will never breathe this to another soul, Selwin," he said, just loud enough for his words to carry to the breathless crowd.

"I assure you, Magnificence—"

"In fact," Nidhaug leaned closer, and this time, his voice held an odd resonance. "You will never take another breath. I do not tolerate failure of this magnitude."

The Thanesson stiffened and brought his hands up to his throat.

Edrik hissed.

Kaya's whispered, "What is it?" fell into the vast, tense silence of the galleries.

"Compulsion," Finn whispered back. "He can't breathe."

Kaya stared at him as horror settled through her along with the memory of sitting behind the table in the Grebe's Landing tavern, willing her body to move—begging her body to move—but frozen helpless while the gray men tried to kill her friends. Compelled not to move.

Out in the courtyard, the Thanesson toppled over, writhing frantically. Compelled not to breathe.

Kaya cleared her throat. "He'll break it, though, won't he? When he gets desperate enough, he'll break it like I did."

"Probably not." Finn chuckled darkly. "Most humans can't. It takes strength of will and the discipline to focus it."

Edrik half reached to lay his hand on hers atop the railing but apparently thought better of it and merely shifted his own grip on the carved stone. Was his disgust for her so great now that he couldn't even touch her hand?

"You have a strong mind, Kaya," he said softly without looking at her.

Nidhaug stepped over the spasming Thanesson and strode closer to Grabak, stopping in the center of the arena. "Forgive the interruption, old friend. I believe you were threatening to kill me." He smirked.

"Release him." Grabak's voice crackled with fury. "You know it is forbidden to kill with compulsion. We are not animals."

Nidhaug stretched his arms out to his sides and tipped his head back, laughing. "No, we're not animals. We are *dragons!*"

The still air cupped in the bowl of the amphitheater stirred as he gathered it into himself and shimmered into a misshapen swirl of smoke and shadow that expanded and darkened under the noonday sun as wings unfurled toward the sky and talons clattered against the paving stones.

The Black Dragon dropped, still laughing, onto all fours. "And I am the king!" he bellowed into the stunned silence that smothered the galleries. "Nothing is forbidden me!"

Grabak's gesture was more subtle, a mere turning up of the palms as a breeze licked around him and his man shape flared like the dancing of a flame into his ascended aspect—a sleek, fearsome creature the colors of merlot and mahogany shading underneath into sunset and fire. "I am king, you arrogant impostor," Grabak roared. "You swore your oath to me, and I will see you answer for your crimes!"

"Clear the arena!" Up on the dais, the dragon who'd been leading the ceremony had also shifted into his ascended form—mottled brown, like an old tree trunk. "This dispute will be settled *now*."

The air gusted and eddied around the bowl as the rest of the Nine shifted form and descended into the arena, where they prowled around the perimeter to take up guard positions around the two dragons that circled warily in the center. Kaya's breath caught as one of the great beasts slunk past the railing near enough she could have touched him, his wheat-brown scales gleaming brassy in the sunlight. In the middle of the courtyard, dwarfed by the prowling Dragonlords, the groom's second helped the queen to her feet, and the cleric offered a steadying arm to the princess as the four moved back toward the dais steps.

"What's happening?" Kaya whispered.

Edrik shifted uneasily. "The Nine have decided to intervene."

"He's going to get himself killed." Finn sounded annoyed.

"We can't let that happen." The grim tone of Edrik's voice made Kaya's skin prickle. She shot him a glance.

Finn muttered, "We can't stop it."

"I can." Edrik scrubbed a hand over his short, pale hair. "Maybe." He boosted himself onto the railing and swung his legs over.

"Don't be a fool!" Finn snapped. "You can't—"

Ignoring his friend, Edrik slid off the other side of the railing and twisted, planting his feet between the balusters in front of Kaya, bringing his face within inches of her own, with only the railing between them. Close enough for kissing. The suddenness of it made Kaya gasp. The intensity in his eyes as he searched her face set her pulse pounding in her throat.

"Kaya . . ." The whisper of her name on his lips sounded like an aching plea. "Forgive me."

Forgive him? For what? For taunting her with kisses that could never become more? For realizing too late that he found her revolting? For going home to the princess he loved? Before she could collect herself enough to ask, he was gone, landing on the paving stones almost under the nose of a great indigo beast—one of the Nine.

"Wait!" Edrik's shout stabbed into the taut anticipation like a dagger. Every dragon's head swiveled in his direction. At the far end of the arena, where the remains of the wedding party were making their way up the steps to the dais, Lissara stumbled and whirled toward the sound of Edrik's voice; she took three steps back down before the cleric caught her arm. An incoherent mutter chased itself through the galleries.

Kaya couldn't move. She could hardly even breathe. *What was he doing?*

Edrik strode out into the arena. "The Black Dragon owes me a blood debt."

Nidhaug snorted smoke. "I challenged your father for the throne, boy," he growled. "There is no blood debt in that."

"The old Drake still lived!" Edrik stabbed a finger toward Grabak. "The throne was not my father's to defend."

The gleaming black beast took a step toward Edrik and lowered his head. "Your father stood as Grabak's proxy in all things."

Edrik didn't back down. "Blood debts and territorial disputes cannot be resolved by proxy, and the question of kingship is a territorial dispute. You slew my father unlawfully. You owe me a blood debt, and it is my right to collect on that debt before you get yourself killed fighting over territory."

Grabak stepped between them, moving with a noticeable limp. "Don't do this, young Edrik," he said. "Your father would not approve."

As he turned, Kaya caught sight of the half-healed scar that ran down Grabak's flank. In this form, the wound from the ogre knife was longer than in his human aspect, and the damage to the muscles and inner connective tissues must also be correspondingly expanded. Even with the accelerated healing from the magic of Edrik's sword, Grabak was in no condition for a fight. Finn was right; if Grabak fought, he would die.

"My father is *dead!*" Edrik's voice was heavy with festering bitterness. He might be doing this to keep Grabak from having to fight, but clearly this was a wound that had been left untended for too long.

Grabak regarded Edrik a moment longer, then turned toward the dragon on the dais. "In the absence of a clear kingship, the Speaker for the Nine holds sway. What is your judgment, Linngrim?"

The dragon on the dais lowered his head and blew a puff of gray smoke. "Blood debts do take precedence over territorial disputes," he said slowly. "That is true, young Edrik. But as a pinion, the settlement of such debts is beyond your reach. I'm sorry."

Edrik spread his arms wide and threw his head back. The torrent of his ascension carved a broad divot in the paving stones and cut into the earth beneath them. A murmur ran through the galleries, swelling into a roar as the enormous jade-green dragon reared up, wings extended, seeming almost half again as large as any other dragon in the arena, and spat a defiant tongue of flame at the sky. "My reach has grown somewhat since I went away. And I have returned to demand the justice I am owed."

Everyone stared.

The princess sank to the dais steps in a billow of filmy skirts. The woman even collapsed elegantly.

The roar of the onlookers rose in both volume and intensity. A low chuckle bubbled beneath its surface, then grew into a great guffaw that echoed around the amphitheater; in the arena, one of the Nine, a lanky, slate colored monster with a scar below one eye, shouted above the tumult, "I say let the boy take his vengeance if he can!"

The indigo dragon lowered his head and hissed like a teakettle. "He is untrained! Look at the size of that crater he left. Pitting him against the eldest would be irresponsible."

"It is my *right*!" Edrik bellowed.

"It is foolish!" Grabak roared in return.

"To first blood, then," the gray one with the scar said.

"Enough!" All eyes turned back to the dais, where apparently Linngrim had come to a decision. "Foolish it may be," he called into the abrupt silence. "Irresponsible, perhaps. Yet it is the boy's right to avenge his father, if he can. And loathe as I am to risk the lives of either our eldest or our youngest, first blood is not enough for a debt of this magnitude." He raised his head. Met and held the gaze of each of the Nine in turn. Nodded solemnly. "To incapacitation," he said. "Or surrender."

The response from the galleries was deafening. Kaya could only exchange worried glances with Finn as two of the Nine escorted the reluctant Grabak to the base of the dais to wait, and a third moved the Thanesson's limp body out of the way.

From beneath the dais, the gong rang out again, and in the arena Nidhaug and Edrik, the Black Dragon and the jade, began to circle each other, heads weaving side to side, tongues flicking out and back, watching, testing, looking for an opening.

Nidhaug struck first, quick as a snake.

Edrik twisted. Caught the Black Dragon's fangs against the dense scales of his shoulder. Whipped his head around and lunged.

Nidhaug reared out of reach. Pounced, talons flashing.

Edrik met him halfway, and the two leviathans crashed together, snarling, writhing, raking scales with teeth and talons.

Edrik was bigger, his reach longer.

But Nidhaug was old and wily. *And quick!*

Kaya's heart pounded in her throat. She couldn't follow what was happening in the tangle of darting claws and flapping wings.

Beside her, Finn let out a long, heartfelt hiss, and Kaya realized the watchers in the galleries had gone deathly silent again.

"Can Edrik beat him?" Her voice sounded small and frightened, as lost as she felt.

"I don't know."

Finn turned a little, and Kaya watched from the corner of her eye as he studied her profile.

"He's going to be all right," he said gently. "He doesn't need to win; he only needs to hurt Nidhaug enough to make him reconsider fighting Grabak. He won't die in this. At worst, he will surrender."

"Or be incapacitated."

Finn frowned and looked back out into the arena, where the combatants had separated and were circling again. Panting. Smeared with blood.

"Or that," he said quietly.

Edrik's back foot caught the edge of his ascension crater, and he stumbled sideways, twisting awkwardly.

The Black Dragon pounced; dark talons raked blood from the pale underbelly.

The jade dragon roared and rolled, teeth snapping.

Nidhaug squirmed away and launched himself into the sky.

Edrik reared up, talons clawing at the hindquarters of his fleeing enemy. Snagged scales but lost hold. He leapt after Nidhaug, flapping clumsy wings . . . and crashed back to the paving stones.

Nidhaug realized he'd lost his pursuer and kited his wings, hanging for a heartbeat, motionless in mid-air. His wings beat once. Twice. Then he roared with mocking laughter. "Stranded, are you, boy?"

Edrik spat a great gout of flame into the sky and bellowed, "Running from a fledgling, Nidhaug?"

Nidhaug's wings folded, and he dove. Straight down. A bolt of black lightning spitting fire.

Kaya couldn't breathe.

Edrik cupped his wings, shielding his vulnerable eyes as the flames slid off his scales. Twisted back and up as Nidhaug struck.

Jade claws snagged in a black wing membrane with a sound like ripping sailcloth, and Nidhaug pinwheeled.

Bone crunched.

Blood sprayed.

Bodies writhed and pitched—then stilled into a snarling heap with Nidhaug pinned beneath Edrik's bulk, and Edrik's teeth clamped down on Nidhaug's throat.

No one in the galleries breathed as Nidhaug wriggled like a fish on a gaffe, his movements growing more frantic as he realized he couldn't free himself, then slowing and finally stopping altogether.

For a long, slow breath neither of the great beasts moved. Then Nidhaug melted, shimmering back to his man shape. Edrik tottered, then caught his balance and stumbled back.

"What's happening?"

When Finn didn't respond, Kaya elbowed him.

Finn blinked and turned to face her. "Nidhaug is surrendering." His face broke into a broad grin, showing all his double canines. "Edrik beat him! Not elegantly, just knocked him down and sat on him, but—" His mouth kept moving, but the explosive roar from the crowded galleries drowned out whatever he was saying.

Kaya grinned and turned back to the arena, where the great jade beast still stood, towering threateningly over the small, black-clad man. Slowly, Nidhaug settled to his knees and bowed his head. Edrik shimmered back to his human aspect, shedding only a little dragon dust as the hole he'd left filled in and most of the paving stones restored themselves to their proper places. The crowd continued to roar as Edrik turned and started walking toward the dais.

Grabak diminished to his human form and strode out to meet Edrik, grinning with pride. On the stairs, Lissara was on her feet again. She wrenched free of the cleric and started running. The queen took one hesitant step back toward her husband and then stopped, frozen on the steps like a gleaming golden statue of herself. What might she be sensing through her bond with Grabak?

The old Drake was only halfway to Edrik, and the princess less than that, when Nidhaug rose from his knees—and kept rising, swirling through smoke shadow into the Black Dragon once again.

And sprang.

Kaya's shouted warning was lost in the roar of the crowd. She didn't know what made Edrik look back over his shoulder—something on Grabak's face, perhaps, or Lissara's—but he did look. His eyes almost met hers before they registered what was happening.

Time collapsed in on itself, forming a throbbing knot in Kaya's belly. The noise of the crowd dimmed.

The Black Dragon's jaws split slowly open, and his forked tongue lashed out, and back.

Edrik's hand crawled toward his sword. *Too slow.*

Nidhaug's mouth gaped wider, and his throat clenched.

The sword slid free. *Too far away.*

Flame burst from Nidhaug's gaping maw like a bright banner unfurling across the courtyard.

Edrik's sword arm swung an arc. The blade spun away from his out-flung hand as he twisted sideways and down. *Too slow! Too unbearably slow!*

Ravening tongues of dragon fire chased each other toward him, engulfing the white sword as it flew tip over hilt toward the Black Dragon.

Edrik slammed into the paving stones. Twisted. Rolled below and beyond the reaching flames.

The ruby pommel glinted blood-red as the sword plunged hilt deep into the Black Dragon's eye.

Nidhaug roared, spitting fire at the sky, rearing back and up, wings wide and beating futilely. Convulsed.

Edrik scrambled slowly backward across the paving stones, staring, as the Black Dragon tilted. Swayed. Crumpled into shadow and ash. And Nidhaug the man, in his immaculate black wedding doublet, slumped to the paving stones.

Silence fell over the arena, and time sped up again as Nidhaug shuddered. And went still.

The clatter of Edrik's sword hitting the paving stones echoed through the galleries.

Hushed murmurs from the onlookers danced around Kaya as Edrik slowly rose to his feet and turned to meet Grabak, who pulled him into a fatherly embrace, then held him at arm's length as if checking for injuries until Lissara pushed between them in a swirl of shimmering white and silver to fling her impossibly graceful arms around Grabak —and then around Edrik.

Kaya sucked a great breath of air into the pit of her belly and said, "So ends the fae tale."

Finn frowned at her. "What fae tale?"

Kaya waved a hand toward the arena, where Lissara pressed her very womanly curves against Edrik's body and tucked her head under Edrik's chin against his chest. Could she hear his heart beating? *Lovers' sounds.*

"The one where the hero rescues the long-lost king and wins the heart and hand of the beautiful princess." Kaya smiled wryly, ignoring the pounding of her own heart. "Isn't that what we came here for?"

Finn sidled half a step closer to her, examining her face. "It isn't what you want, though, is it?"

He could tell?

Her gaze traveled across the arena again, drawn like a lodestone to Edrik. Lissara cupped his face between her hands, tracing the lines of cheek and jaw with her slender fingers and running them into his short, fair hair as if making certain he was really real, really home. Then she wrapped her arms around his neck and drew his mouth down to hers.

Kaya remembered thinking once that maybe seeing Edrik with his princess would ease the ache of losing him. She had been wrong. Seeing Edrik with Lissara seared through her soul like dwarrow magic and lodged, smoldering, behind her breastbone where no healing salve could ever reach it.

She closed her eyes and clenched her teeth against the sudden threat of tears. When she could hold her voice steady, she said, "What I want doesn't matter. He has his princess. True love's kiss, right?"

Finn chuckled. "He kissed you too, remember?"

Kaya snorted. "When has a hero *ever* fallen in love with the dungeon keeper?"

"Kaya." Finn laid a hand on her shoulder and waited until she looked at him. His face was solemn and sincere when he said, "You took Grabak's collar off. Your last prisoner is set free. You don't have to be a dungeon keeper anymore." He held her gaze for a long moment, making sure his words sank in. Then he grinned rakishly. "Just like I don't have to be a wilding anymore. He patted her on the shoulder, handed her Grabak's cloak, and vaulted over the railing to the courtyard below.

"You coming?" He called up to her.

The idea of hiking up her robe, clambering over the railing, and then strolling out into the middle of the arena while everyone stared at her was not remotely appealing. "In this robe? I don't think so."

His grin widened. "I don't mind if you take it off."

Kaya laughed. She couldn't help it. "You're a contemptible cur, Finn."

He shrugged. "Have it your way, then. But this isn't over." He waved an arm down one side of the amphitheater. "If you go that direction all the way to the front, there are steps down into the arena. Come join us."

CHAPTER
31

E drik had barely regained his feet when Grabak yanked him into a crushing one-armed embrace. "You young fool," he rumbled. Then he pushed Edrik away just enough to check him for damage. "How badly are you hurt?"

Edrik shook his head, trying to clear it. "I'm fine." But his head throbbed, and he could feel a bruise developing where the bony ridge above one ascended ear had slammed against the paving stones during his fight with Nidhaug. One shoulder ached abominably and would be stiff in the morning even if he slept with his sword. The gouges Nidhaug's teeth and claws had left on Edrik's chest, belly, and various other parts of his body were not deep, but they still stung and oozed blood into his clothes. They probably needed to be cleaned and bandaged as soon as he could manage it. Would Kaya be willing to forgive him enough, for whatever he'd done, to tend his injuries? He turned to look for her in the crowded gallery—and found his arms rather abruptly full of Lissara.

The princess clung to him, breaths coming in short, hiccupping gasps. "You're home!" she choked. "Oh Edrik, I thought I'd lost you. I thought you were dead, and it was all my fault." She buried her head against his chest and nestled closer. "I was such a fool."

Edrik's arms remembered where they fit in this embrace and slipped around her, cradling the warm, familiar softness of her body.

She felt like memories. She felt like hide-and-seek in the Aerie gardens, like stolen sugar cakes and kisses. And she carried the scent of intrigues and rivalries too, of promises kept and broken, and half-forgotten dreams.

"And you found him! You brought my father home!" She lifted her head, pulling away a little so she could see him better. Her fingers traveled, cool and sure, over the planes and lines of Edrik's face, carefully wiping away a trickle of blood that crept from a scrape on his forehead. "I've dreamed of this a thousand, thousand times," she murmured, "and it never was so grand as this." She slipped her arms around his neck.

He moved his hands to her waist. "Lissara," he said, "I need to—"

She stopped him with a kiss.

Not the teasing, butterfly half-caress she passed out to all her suitors. Not the furtive, mock-shy goodnight kisses she'd offered when he saw her back to her rooms. Not even one of the more serious kisses she'd paid for his secrets with. It was a real kiss. The kiss she'd kept for only him when they thought they would be married. Her mouth was soft, and warm, and familiar. Her kiss was free and deep. Victorious. Claiming him as her own. This was the kiss he'd dreamed about. Hoped for. Worked toward. All the pain, and fatigue, and hunger, and frustration of the long journey, the aching despair, the long days, the cold nights, the blisters, and broken bones, and . . . and Tait—it had all been for this moment and for what was promised after.

Edrik let himself fall into Lissara's kiss, clutching her reflexively close to him. It wasn't what he'd planned to do, but he suddenly realized how much he needed this. He needed all of this. He needed Lissara's gentle caresses and her kind words. He needed her unreserved acceptance and the memories. He needed to savor the sweet taste of what he had so relentlessly pursued all these years. Because he needed to be certain he was making the right choice. That there would be no looking back. No regrets. No more longing might-have-beens. Her mouth moved more urgently against his, and the intoxicating touch of her magic wound around him, sweet and beguiling, offering more . . . *demanding* more. Drawing him further in.

And Edrik was sure.

Certainty settled into the deepest ocean of his dragon soul, and he knew he had chosen right. Because Lissara's kiss was a little too practiced. Her skillful magic lacked the open candor that he yearned for. Her confidence in her ownership of him was a little too self-satisfied. And not all of the memories were good ones.

He pulled away from Lissara, breathing hard, and looked her squarely in the eyes. "I need to talk to you, Lissara. About . . . about this."

A radiant smile lit her face. She laughed softly and dropped him another tiny, teasing kiss. "There will be time for that, my love." She nodded at someone over his shoulder and added. "Right now, I think they're waiting for you."

Edrik turned.

On the dais, Linngrim had resumed his human aspect as well, tall and gaunt, his mouth set in a grim frown. "Lord Edrik." The formal tone and title put Edrik on his guard. This was not over yet. The Speaker for the Nine continued solemnly. "It seems you have not only executed your blood claim, you have slain your adversary."

Behind Edrik, Fellugand, still in his slate gray ascended form, snarled indignantly. "It was a clean kill, Linngrim. Nidhaug broke the code, the boy only defended himself."

"Agreed." Linngrim raised his head to glance at each of the Nine. "Does anyone dispute this judgment?" He waited, but no one spoke. "So be it." He nodded emphatically. "Which raises the question of territory."

Fellugand snorted. "The slaying was lawful. The boy is entitled to the territory of his rival. Where is the difficulty?"

Linngrim smiled wryly. "The difficulty, as so often is the case in recent years, lies with the Black Dragon." He raised his voice to be heard over the babble from the galleries. "Which territory would you say belonged to Nidhaug?"

Fellugand shifted to his human form and spoke as he crossed the arena to stand beside Edrik. "Nidhaug has ruled in the Northlands as long as any of us can remember. No one will dispute that."

"True enough," Linngrim acceded. "Yet of late, he also claimed the Western Reaches as spoils of his battle with the Regent."

"Which Edrik has reclaimed with his successful prosecution of his blood debt." Fellugand laid his hand on Edrik's shoulder to emphasize his point.

"And if he had not slain Nidhaug, I would agree with you, and that would be the end of it. Edrik would have his father's islands, and Nidhaug and Grabak could settle between them which would sit the throne, and which would skulk off to the Northland holdings with his tail tucked."

He paused, raised his hand, and glared sternly around the amphitheater until the uproar among the onlookers quieted. "However," he went on when he could be heard again, "you may recall that Nidhaug agreed to renounce his claim to both the Northlands and the Reaches as a condition of our giving our bonds to him as king and granting him the Aerie and its domains."

This time it was Fellugand who had to quell the roar of the onlookers before he could speak. "No oaths were made. No bonds were given. Nidhaug's claims to the territories were never actually renounced."

"Nor was his claim to the kingship renounced," Linngrim pointed out. "So I ask again; which territory would you say belonged to Nidhaug? What are the spoils of young Edrik's triumph?"

All was silent for a moment. Then Grabak called out, "Edrik inherits Nidhaug's bargain." Everyone turned to stare at him, and both Lissara and Fellugand gave way as the old Drake moved slowly over to stand in front of Edrik facing Linngrim. "Edrik, as victor, becomes heir to Nidhaug's bargain—he holds Nidhaug's territories until he surrenders them in fulfillment of the terms of your bargain and claims the throne you offered Nidhaug."

A soft gasp came from the bottom of the dais stairs, where the queen stood watching, steadying herself with one hand against the sculpted stone façade. Grabak's face went hard, and he glanced at her before he turned his stern gaze back to the Speaker for the Nine.

Linngrim took a step closer to the edge of the dais and studied

Grabak for a long moment before he said, "Again, I would agree, except you have asserted your own prior claim to the throne."

"And that dispute will be settled," Grabak said, grim and determined. "After Edrik receives what is rightfully his."

Edrik's heart fell into his stomach. "Grabak, no!"

"It is the right judgment, Edrik!" Grabak roared. "I may not like it, but the judgment is sound. What was Nidhaug's belongs to you, including his claim to the throne." He stabbed a finger in Linngrim's direction. "This must be settled. Now. Confirm this judgment or offer an alternative."

"No!" Edrik felt sick. "Grabak, I'm not going to fight you for the throne!" It came out shriller than he meant it to.

Grabak spun to face him. "It won't come to that!" His face was pale and clenched as if in pain. "I will not oppose you, Edrik. I owe you far too much for that. I will renounce my claim and be the first to offer you my oath."

A babble of voices broke out. Linngrim raised his hand for silence and met the eyes of each of the Nine in turn. Then he nodded and said solemnly, "Confirmed. The judgment is sound. Lord Edrik's victory has bought him Nidhaug's territories, and Nidhaug's bargain to renounce them for the throne. Do you accept this judgment, Lord Edrik?"

The silence in the amphitheater was almost palpable. Edrik felt it pressing in on him, throbbing with the beating of his heart. The throne? He didn't want the throne. He had never wanted the throne. His head hurt. His shoulder hurt. His scratches were still bleeding. He wanted to work things out with Kaya and then go home and sleep for about a week. And then he wanted to take Kaya to see the ocean. And buy her more hair ribbons. And find her something to dissect. More than anything, he wanted to hear Kaya laugh again. There was no part of him that wanted the throne. But this matter had to be settled so the kingdom could be at peace. The kingship had been in question far too long already.

"I accept your judgment," Edrik called out. His words fell into the silence like fire into dry grass, and the arena erupted with noise.

Slowly, he lowered himself to his knees and looked up at Grabak, waiting while the watchers subsided once more into stunned silence. "I accept your judgment," he repeated. "But I reject your bargain. No claims were renounced. No bonds were given. And I will not exchange my territories for the throne. I renounce my claim to the throne, Grabak, and I offer you my oath." He pressed his palms together and held his hands out.

Grabak hesitated. "You are sure?"

Edrik nodded solemnly. "I'm sure. I didn't bring you home so I could steal your kingdom."

Grabak clasped his hands around Edrik's. "Then I am honored to accept your oath, Lord Edrik of the Western Reaches and the Lands of the North."

Edrik bowed his head and said the words of the oath. "My liege, before the Sun and her children, I offer you this day my fealty, loyalty, and honor; my teeth and my talons; my counsel and my aid. I place my life in your hands and ask you to receive it with kindness." The liege bond was rooted in intent and in magic, but the gestures and the words made the intent concrete, and Edrik felt the stirring of the bond.

"I receive you with gratitude, young Edrik," Grabak said gravely. "And I place my own life in your hands." He bent to touch his forehead to their joined hands, setting Edrik's bond singing inside his chest, and straightened, pulling Edrik to his feet.

The galleries erupted.

Edrik turned to face the crowing throng, searching for a glimpse of Kaya—only to be caught in Finn's startling, back-pounding embrace.

"I still say that was foolish," Finn growled into Edrik's ear.

Edrik grinned. "It came out all right anyway."

Finn leaned his forehead against Edrik's, chin tilted down, and cupped a hand around the back of Edrik's neck. "I want to be your liegeman," he said, just loud enough for Edrik to hear him above the crowd. "I meant it when I said I'd swear to you if I could."

"I'll have you gladly, my friend. I need someone to tell me when I'm being foolish."

Finn backed off and cuffed Edrik in the shoulder. "Not that you listen."

He handed Edrik the white sword, which he'd recovered on his way across the courtyard, then grew more serious and knelt in front of Edrik.

"My liege," he began.

As Finn said the words of the oath, Edrik felt a new bond grow inside him, his magic reaching out to Finn's, creating a new link in the chain mail mesh of magic that bound the Vanir dragons as one.

"I receive you with gratitude, Finn. And I place my own life in your hands." The bond solidified when Edrik's forehead touched their joined hands, and Finn drew a deep, shuddering breath as he rose to his feet with a crooked grin on his face.

Edrik embraced Finn again and looked around for Kaya.

She hadn't come with Finn to meet him. He scanned the railing at the far end of the arena.

He couldn't find her.

He searched again. *Where was she?*

"Lord Edrik—"

He jumped, startled by the nearness of Lissara's voice.

The princess laughed and tucked her hand into the crook of his elbow. "Your king has summoned you."

She steered him up the steps to the platform to stand with her beside Grabak and the queen as, one by one, the Dragonlords knelt and renewed their oaths to the rightful king.

When the last of the Nine rose from his knees, the crowd seemed to let out a collective sigh of relief. Perhaps they'd wondered if one of the Dragonlords might challenge Grabak. Maybe they were just eager to have this over with, so they could get on with the festivities. Whatever it was, the sigh turned into a gasp when the queen, too, sank to her knees on the dais, head bowed, eyes penitently lowered.

"My king and husband, my heart rejoices in your safe return." Her voice was pitched to be clearly heard by everyone in the amphitheater. "I can only express my deep regret at the circumstance that greeted you. Had I but known you lived . . ." Her voice cracked, and she paused, swallowing hard before continuing. "I have no dragon bond to offer. But I wish to pledge to you, before the Sun and all her children so there can be no mistake, my fealty, loyalty, and honor; my heart and my hands; my counsel and my aid." She tipped her head up, searching Grabak's face with her eyes—clear blue like Lissara's, and pleading. She drew a deep breath and pressed her palms together reaching up to him. "I place my life in your hands."

Grabak gazed back at her, his face impassive, his eyes weighing what he saw. What was passing between them through their marriage bond? The muscles in the king's jaw tightened and released before he cupped his wife's delicate hands between his own and bent to touch them to his forehead. He pulled her to her feet and tucked her hand into the crook of his elbow. If Edrik had not been standing so close to the king, he would not have heard Grabak murmur, "We will speak more of this, Mirra. What is wrong between us cannot be fixed by one grand public gesture."

The queen drew a shaky breath. "No. But it's a beginning."

Edrik's eyes wandered back to the railing on the other side of the arena. Where was Kaya?

Dimly, he heard Grabak call for the Conclave to adjourn to the Aerie Council Chamber. Around him, the Nine filed toward the steps. Edrik drifted toward the front of the platform, scanning the galleries.

She had to be there *somewhere*.

Finn appeared at his elbow. "The Conclave awaits, my liege." He sounded almost ludicrously proud to use the title.

"I can't find her."

Finn followed Edrik's gaze back to the galleries. "Kaya?" He chuckled. "Oh, she's too fine a lady now to jump the railing, so she's going around." He gestured toward the side of the amphitheater, where the gated steps led from the galleries down into the arena.

"I need to talk to her."

"You need to do more than talk to her. She just watched you kiss Lissara."

Edrik's pulse quickened. Finn was right. He had to fix this. *Where was she?*

Grabak strode up with the queen's hand tucked into his elbow, and Lissara trailing along behind. "What's keeping you, Lord Edrik?" he asked sternly. "The Nine are waiting. As are the petitioners."

"I was looking for Kaya."

Grabak glanced out at the galleries. "She's right by the—" He frowned. "She's not there anymore."

The queen's brows drew together. "Kaya?"

"A friend," Grabak said, shifting his stern gaze to his wife. "She'll need rooms."

Mirra frowned. "I think all the guest rooms are full at present, but I'm sure we can find—"

"Not guest rooms." Grabak continued to scan the crowd. "Permanent quarters. In the family wing. Put her in the empty apartment on the far side of my rooms. The back parlor opens onto the terrace; she can use it for her work."

Edrik wasn't sure if Grabak failed to notice the way the queen's cheeks flushed and the muscles in her jaw shifted as she inclined her head or if he just chose to ignore it. Either way, the Drake continued. "Find her, Finn. She can't have gone far. Mirra, wait for them in the passageway and get her settled in." His eyes searched the galleries a moment longer, and then he sighed and laid a hand on Edrik's shoulder. "Come, Lord Edrik. We have duties that cannot wait."

Edrik gripped Finn's elbow and murmured, "Stay close to her. We don't know who we can trust."

Finn chuckled. "As you command, my liege. But Kaya can take care of herself."

CHAPTER
32

Kaya was almost there. She could see the phalanx of grim-faced palace guards that stood between the arena gate Finn had directed her to and the murmuring, eddying crowd. Just a little farther.

She hugged her satchel closer to her chest and elbowed her way between a man who looked like a fat merchant and two squawking women who seemed to be glued together at the hip. She was accustomed to people drawing back from her with sneers of loathing on their faces, not merely glancing at her and away, dismissing her as just another skinny country girl wrapped in a dirty travel cloak. It had certainly been easier to navigate a crowd when she'd been Mudge.

Kaya gritted her teeth and reminded herself firmly that it no longer mattered if someone bumped up against what little she had in the way of curves and realized she was a woman. And if she picked up any body vermin, she could wash herself, and comb out her hair, and even ask someone to help her check for nits without fear of discovery. It was an odd feeling—somehow freeing and frightening at the same time.

Up on the platform, the Nine had finished giving their oaths to Grabak and were making their way down the steps to the archway under the dais. The royal family stood grouped at the front of the dais, surveying their people. Grabak looked stern and regal in his stolen blue silk shirt, and the queen was lovely and serene. Beside them, the princess and her returning hero of a dragonlord made a perfectly matched set, both of them tall, and elegant, and golden fair; even their gestures seemed to mirror each other as they looked out over the crowd. They were so obviously meant to be together.

Grabak laid a hand on Edrik's shoulder, and the two dragons walked together down the steps to the courtyard. Lissara and her mother followed, and the four of them disappeared together through the archway below the dais. It was exactly the way a fae tale *ought* to end.

This is a victory, Kaya reminded herself. *Her* victory. She was the one who had gotten them out of the dungeon, and down the river, and out from behind the iron grate in the back of that cave. This was why Mudge had helped the dragons escape from the dungeon in the first place—so Grabak could go home to his wife, Edrik could complete his quest, and Kaya could have a fresh start somewhere new.

And it was *almost* enough. Almost enough to see her friends happy and reunited with the ones they loved. Maybe it *could* have been enough . . . if only Edrik hadn't kissed her.

But no. That was a lie. It could never have been enough. Not since he helped her bury Pip.

And Finn was right. Edrik *had* kissed her.

Twice.

On purpose.

And that changed everything.

Except that maybe it changed nothing. Edrik had still kissed Lissara.

Which was as it should be. Lissara was the reason Edrik had undertaken his perilous quest in the first place. He had risked everything to be with Lissara. And he hadn't made any promises to Kaya. He hadn't even said he loved her. He'd only said that he kissed her on purpose because he wanted to, and that he didn't know what would happen with Lissara.

And now, Kaya supposed, he knew.

Only . . . where did that leave Kaya?

Around her, the press of bodies shifted and began flowing up the gallery steps toward the archways that led back out into the town. Kaya considered allowing the current to carry her out with it. Out of the arena. Out of the town. Away from this place. She didn't belong here. Not really. Grabak was king of the Vanir. Edrik was one of the Nine. Finn was liegeman to a powerful dragonlord. Kaya was just a grubby dungeon keeper. No, not even that anymore. She was nothing. Just extra baggage left over from an unfortunate misadventure. She didn't belong here.

Of course, she didn't belong anywhere else either. And extra baggage or not, at the very least, she needed a place to sleep for the night and eat a good, solid meal while she figured out what to do next. And even if his business was too pressing for him to wait for her now, Stig was enough of a friend not to let her go hungry.

"There you are." Finn's voice next to her ear made her jump. He chuckled as his hand closed on her elbow and he turned her toward the gate again. "Come, my lady," he said grandly. "My liege has grown impatient with waiting and has sent me to escort you to his glorious presence."

Kaya snorted and returned his infectious grin. "Your liege, or your liege's liege?"

This time he laughed outright. "Both, actually. I have strict instructions not to leave your side. And Edrik says he needs to talk to you."

Kaya nearly choked on her heart as it jumped into her throat. Something very like hope fluttered to life in the burned-out hollow behind her breastbone. She sternly told it to go away. Edrik had kissed Lissara. And it had certainly looked as if he meant it. He probably just thought he owed Kaya some sort of awkward explanation. Maybe he did. What did she know of such things? She had to stop reacting like this.

But the fluttery little hope stubbornly didn't go away. It curled up in a soft, warm knot and settled in to wait. Hope was foolish that way. But if the dungeon had taught Kaya anything, it was how fragile a thing hope was. How easily it died. And that feeding it only made its death hurt more. So she ignored it.

Finn tucked Kaya's hand into the crook of his elbow, and the crowd parted around them as he led her through the gate and across the arena.

She shivered under the weight of the onlookers' stares. But as soon as they stepped through the arch out of the bright sunshine and into the dimness of the passageway under the dais, the awkwardness disappeared, swallowed up in a churning ocean of utter befuddlement. The queen waited for them there.

Kaya's feet stopped moving and her mouth went dry. "Finn," she whispered numbly, "I can't—"

Finn grinned conspiratorially at her. "If I can, you can," he whispered back. "Palace people are not so different from dungeon people. He shifted his arm around behind Kaya's back to scoot her forward, and his fingers brushed against the fresh dwarrow burn.

Reflex turned her flinch into a step, and then she kept going, moving ahead into the passageway.

The queen came to meet her, both hands outstretched as if greeting a friend.

"You must be Kaya."

Up close, the queen was even lovelier than she had been from a distance—but her stiff smile didn't quite reach her eyes. Kaya froze as the queen first embraced her, then stepped back to inspect her from head to toe.

Kaya tugged her travel cloak closer, hoping to keep her stained and tattered robe from showing underneath. She couldn't hide the bruises on her face or the narrow cut the Thanesson's knife had left along her jawline. The queen's eyes rested there a moment too long, assessing.

"Kaya," Finn murmured helpfully, "Her Radiance, Queen Mirra, Lady of the Vanir."

The queen waved a dismissive hand. "You must call me Mirra. Grabak tells me we're to welcome you as family. Our daughter, Lissara, has gone in to see to some changes to the dining arrangements, but she is eager to meet you as well."

Lissara. Kaya's mind filled with the image of Edrik's arms wrapped around the princess as she drew his face down to hers.

The fluttery little hope in Kaya's chest rolled over and reminded her that Edrik wanted to speak to her. Kaya told it to mind its own business.

"Shall we?" Mirra gestured down the passageway behind her, and when Kaya began to move in that direction, the queen fell into step with her. Finn trailed along behind as they moved down the corridor, deeper into the heart of the mountain.

"Have you known my husband long, Kaya?"

The queen's question caught Kaya off guard. Life in the dungeon had in no way prepared her for making small talk with other women. "I . . ." She cleared her throat. "We became acquainted a little over five years ago," she said, trying to match the queen's casual tone.

"I see." Mirra's smile went even stiffer. It seemed almost pasted on. "Then you must have us at a disadvantage. I'm sure he has spoken more to you of us than he has to us of you."

How was Kaya supposed to respond to that? Surely the queen wouldn't be flattered to know that until a mere few weeks ago, Grabak had never even mentioned that he had a wife. Carefully, she ventured, "In the time that I've known him, Grabak has always been a very private person."

"Indeed." The queen's eyes narrowed. "And how did the two of you . . . become acquainted?"

This time, Kaya was completely at a loss. Did the queen know where Grabak had been during his absence from home? If not, it certainly wasn't Kaya's place to tell her. "I think . . . perhaps that is a question you should ask Grabak."

The queen's smile froze in place, and they walked in silence for a time as the passage drifted steadily upward, lit at regular intervals by beams of sunlight that entered through long shafts bored into the stone. Kaya studied the queen's profile from the corner of her eye. Had this woman betrayed Stig? Would she do it again?

At the other end, the corridor opened into a vast hall, easily spacious enough to hold several ascended dragons. The vaulted stone ceiling was covered in carved vines with tiny stone birds perched on the looping stems and squirrels peering out from behind the leaves. A row of tall, arched windows formed one wall, and the complex filigree lattices carved along their tops had been designed to cast picture shadows across the smooth stone of the floor—a brook complete with little frogs and fishes hiding in the ripples between the shadowy stones. The walls, except where they were broken by several broad, elaborately carved archways, were covered in sumptuous tapestries depicting forest scenes.

Still smiling her tight smile, the queen led Kaya to one of the archways where a passage curved deeper into the mountain, away from the sunlit windows. A shelf just inside the corridor held a small oil lamp, a bowl of fine sand, and an ornate vase filled with oil-soaked rush lights. The queen selected a long rush and lit the tip at the oil lamp.

"I hope you'll forgive me for taking you down a servants' corridor," she said. "This is the shortest way to the family apartments from here."

The dark passage curved past a number of doors and cross-passages and emerged, eventually, on a high balcony overlooking one end of a room that made the forest hall look small and plain by comparison. Two rows of enormous sculpted stone dragons lined the walls, their rearing bodies forming the support pillars while their curving, reaching wings arched up a full four stories above the floor to become the vault supports of the ceiling. Above the dragons' heads, sunlight dyed in all the colors of flame splintered through a row of tall, mullioned windows set with colored glass. Every finger's breadth of stone in the room was worked into unimaginably intricate patterns— dragon scales, trees, grass and shrubbery, animals and birds. The stone of the balcony railing had been worked to look like tree branches, complete with leafy twigs, a bird nest, and even a tiny stone snail making its eternal journey into a stone knothole.

The queen snuffed her rush light in a bowl of sand set on a shelf and paused to look out over the balcony, surveying the bustle of activity taking place below. Black banners were being pulled down and replaced with burgundy. Tall beeswax candles that had been placed in pairs down vastly long dining tables were being redistributed as trios. And at the high table that sat crosswise on a platform at the end of the room, a bower for two was being hastily dismantled, as additional chairs and place settings were added.

It was a wedding feast, Kaya realized, being hurriedly rearranged to celebrate the triumphant return of the king instead.

Mirra noticed Kaya noticing. Her cheeks colored, and she cleared her throat. "Our great hall," she said. "We shall be dining here after the Conclave. But for now, I'm sure you want to wash and rest after your journey. Your rooms are this way." She set off down the balcony, and Kaya had to hurry to keep up.

Three hallways and a flight of stairs later, a guard pushed open a pair of heavy, ornately carved wooden doors for them, and they entered the wing of the palace that held the royal family's apartments. A tastefully decorated antechamber led into a spacious, but comfortable salon where bookshelves lined the walls between the tall windows, and scattered groupings of tables and chairs invited the room's occupants to converse, or study, or play board games. A pair of doors in the opposite wall stood open, leading to a sunny terraced garden that appeared to stretch along the side of the mountain in both directions, and archways on either side of the room opened into long hallways with doors on both sides.

Partway down the hall to the right, servants bustled in and out of one of the rooms, carrying trunks and bundles. They froze when they saw the queen, but she merely waved for them to be about their business.

"Lord Nidhaug has been staying there," she explained. "But before that, the apartment belonged to Lord Edrik's father. He and my husband were very close."

"Grabak said he was like a brother." Kaya forced a smile of her own onto her face.

"Yes. But he is gone now. And so is Nidhaug." She looked down at her hands. "I've ordered the room cleared out."

Was she missing her lover? They would have been married by now. Had she conspired with him to betray her husband?

The queen cleared her throat. "Lord Edrik will likely want the rooms for himself," she said into the awkward silence. "His old apartment will be too small for him now."

Kaya's heart clenched. Mirra meant that Edrik would need more room when he married Lissara.

The queen led Kaya down the hallway to the left. The king and queen had adjoining apartments with separate entrances on the right-hand side of the hallway, and the princess's rooms were across the hall. Another cluster of servants bustled in and out of the king's rooms, presumably setting things to rights for Grabak, but this time the queen gave no explanation.

Mirra stopped at the next door on the right and paused with her hand on the door latch. "Grabak thought you would like these rooms," she said without looking at Kaya, "because the back parlor opens onto the terrace. But there are others available if you would prefer."

"I'm sure these will be fine." Kaya didn't know what else to say.

"I'll leave you to get settled then. A servant will be along shortly to draw a bath for you and see to anything else you need." The queen pinned her smile in place and pushed the door open, fixing her striking blue eyes on Kaya. Assessing. "I hope you'll be comfortable here."

The servants must have been lying in wait because they arrived only moments after the queen left. Three of them carried a wooden tub through the front sitting room and into the large dressing room just off the apartment's bedroom—which was bigger than the entire cell block back in the dwarrow hole. While a small brigade of servants filled the tub, Kaya had time to explore the room at the back, which was arranged to serve as a parlor or study, with bookshelves, comfortable chairs, little side tables, and a wide writing desk. The mullioned glass windows swung open, letting in a gentle summer breeze, and a door led out into the terraced garden. Grabak was right. She *did* like this room. Hope whispered that it would be a good place to continue her studies.

Kaya turned her back and pretended not to hear.

When the bath was filled, Kaya went back into the dressing room to find that all the servants had left except for one little maid who was nearly in tears. Finn had propped himself nonchalantly in one corner of the dressing room near the bathing tub and was teasing the poor girl by insisting that he had sworn not to take his eyes off Kaya until the king or Lord Edrik came for her. Kaya informed Finn that if he didn't go away she'd teach the maid how to find spiders and what to do with them when she did. He winked at her and laughingly moved his guard post out into the corridor, where he sprawled out on a chair he'd pilfered from the sitting room and told Kaya to scream like a girl if she needed him.

Kaya wasn't certain who was more nervous, she or the maid. She knew proper ladies always had a maid to help them bathe, but she hadn't been unclothed in front of another person since her mother died.

The maid cast anxious, sidelong glances at Kaya and chattered as she laid out combs, and soaps, and scented oils and scattered flower petals in the steaming tub. Hadn't the king's return been *so* exciting? Lord Edrik was *so* handsome and brave. *So* perfect as a consort for the princess. And wasn't it *so* romantic how he'd fulfilled her quest? How soon did Kaya think the wedding would be?

When Kaya laid aside her travel cloak, the girl's animated face clearly betrayed her disgust with the stained and tattered dungeon robe beneath. And she paled at the sight of Kaya's shredded, bloodstained shift. But she didn't stop talking until Kaya slipped out of the shift and the girl caught sight of the whip scars. And the dwarrow burns. And the scabbed over places where the Thanesson's knife had slipped.

Kaya picked up a cake of soap, stepped into the tub, and carefully lowered herself to her knees. A small gasp of pain escaped her lips when the hot water hit the fresh burn—the blistered mess she'd earned by removing Grabak's collar.

Worth the price. All of it, worth the price. She balanced on her knees, keeping the burn out of the water, and started scrubbing. After a few minutes, the maid came to help.

When Kaya was washed and her wounds were salved, the maid wrapped her in a dressing gown made of the softest fabric Kaya had ever touched and then began combing, and twisting, and pinning Kaya's hair. Clothes had appeared from somewhere: a linen shift so fine it was nearly transparent, a silk gown the color of fresh cream, and a voluminous overdress of rich burgundy velvet with bands of pearl-studded gold embroidery at neck, wrists, and hem, and sleeves that belled out from the elbows to nearly drag the floor. There were even matching velvet slippers.

And hair ribbons.

The clothes had clearly been made for someone bigger than Kaya, but the little maid turned out to be quite efficient at cinching laces and pinning pleats, and a belt helped keep the hem from dragging too much on the floor.

When at last the maid held up a mirror for Kaya's approval, the elegant, dark-eyed woman gazing back seemed a stranger. She would have fit in among the court ladies back at Shrike's Keep. But a dungeon rat in velvet was still a rat.

Finn would laugh when he saw her like this. Grabak would think he'd given her a gift. And Edrik? What would Edrik think?

The warm little knot of hope whispered that he might think she was beautiful. And Finn was right—Edrik *had* kissed Kaya too.

The maid's quick tug at a rope hanging from the ceiling in one corner brought the bevy of servants back to empty the bath water down a garderobe hidden behind a sliding panel in one wall of the dressing room and clear away the other bath things.

Not yet ready to face Finn's teasing, Kaya went into the study and closed the door. When the maid rapped to see if she needed anything, Kaya said she only wanted to be alone for a little while. After a few minutes, the bustle died down, the voices stopped, and the footsteps all tromped away. Silence settled around Kaya.

What was she doing here? When she had imagined life outside the dungeon, she had always pictured a little cottage in the country or a tiny herb shop in a town somewhere with a room above it all her own. She had never imagined herself as a lady in a palace. She reached up to touch the complicated plaits of her hair and the ribbons woven into them.

"Filk ribbonge," her grandfather whispered in her mind. "Filk ribbonge and a belbet dressh."

It should have been wonderful. But she felt like one of the Thanesson's women—even down to the scabs and bruises underneath the finery and the lurking suspicion that maybe she ought to run away. The

Thanesson was dead; he could never touch her again. But watching Edrik with Lissara was its own kind of torment.

She pushed the terrace door open and wandered out into the sunshine. The garden was a well-managed maze of manicured shrubs and miniature wildernesses interspersed with intricate stone trellises and statuary.

A gigantic oak stretched its boughs over the paving stones of the tiny courtyard outside the study door, whispering for her to follow the path that wound out into the garden. She decided to go just far enough to look at the elegant purple blossoms where the path turned—she'd never seen that kind before. But from the turning, she could see a family of stone deer grazing in a tiny meadow. The sculptor had carved the stag with his head raised and turned toward the path, as if f he'd been startled by Kaya's footsteps. A closer look revealed astounding detail in the sculpture, even down to a pair of stone flies eying each other warily behind the doe's left ear. It was a fountain after that. And then a tree with white flowers as big as Kaya's head. And an octagonal latticed bower smothered in climbing roses that presided solemnly over a twining intersection of pathways.

A broad meadow separated the garden from the crenelated stone wall at the edge of the terrace, and the tiny deer—or perhaps they were a kind of goat—that grazed there scattered as she stepped from the dappled shade out into the full brightness of the afternoon sun.

The view from the edge of the terrace was breathtaking. She was on the western face of the mountain now, the side facing away from the Crevasse. The Aerie curved like a pale crescent along the side of the mountain. Imposing watchtowers stood guard over the valley below while impossibly delicate spires stretched toward the sky. Layers of terraced gardens transitioned into sharp ridges. Then rolling hills melted into a forested plain stretching into the distance. Out on the horizon another mountain raised its craggy head above the tree line. Beyond that, and beyond the mountains that marched across the great island behind it, lay the endless ocean and the scattered islands of the Western Reaches. Kaya had seen them carefully sketched and labeled on a map Grandfather had copied into one of his notebooks.

Edrik's lands now.

A high, keening wail cut through the stillness from somewhere above—the cry of a horn signaling . . . something. She turned and looked up just in time to see three dragons launch themselves from a tower wall and glide out over the valley—blue, and brown, and brass—winging swiftly out toward the lowering sun. A moment later, two more drakes leapt from the tower, but these arced out and back again to land on the meadowed edge of a terrace below. One of them was gray, like Finn.

Finn.

Had he noticed she was gone? And what if Edrik came looking for her? That horn might have signaled the ending of the Conclave. Or it might just have been a changing of the watch for all Kaya knew. Still, she ought to go back.

She took two wrong turnings on the path and had just backtracked to the octagonal rose bower to try a third time when she heard the voices filtering between the trees.

". . . Can't possibly be anything between them. Bersa says she's as brown as a Tosky and covered in scars. Finn probably picked her up from some barge town fancy house."

Kaya's heart jumped up into her throat and her mouth went dry. The woman was talking about *her*. Her and . . . and Edrik.

"Never let your servants form your opinions for you, Lissara." That was the queen's voice. And it was getting closer. "She's pretty enough in her own way. And she knows when to hold her tongue."

Panic pounded in Kaya's ears. *They can't see me here. They can't know I've heard them.*

The closest trees big enough to hide Kaya were down the path the voices were coming from. The nearest statues were knee-high. The only place to hide was in the rose bower. She ducked inside barely a breath before the two women appeared from behind the trees at the curve of the path. They looked more like sisters than mother and daughter. Kaya supposed she shouldn't have been surprised—Grabak had said that dragonwives, like their husbands, did not age beyond maturity. But what would it be like to be the mortal daughter of an immortal mother, growing old while your mother remained untouched by time. What would it be like for a mother to watch all her daughters age and die? No wonder they wanted Lissara to marry a dragon.

"But she's too young for him," Lissara said disdainfully.

The queen stopped short and coughed out a bitter laugh. "*I* am too young for him, Lissara. He was old when my great grandfather knew him. He remembers the Breaking. The world has changed a great deal since he was young. *He* has changed it. And I am not the first woman he ever loved. I'm not even the first woman he married. He has lost more friends than I have ever known. He has lifetimes of memories that can never be more to me than stories of ancient history. How can I be enough for him?"

Wait. They weren't talking about Kaya and Edrik—they meant Kaya and *Grabak!*

"But he wouldn't just bring her here and expect us to welcome her into the family," Lissara said. "There must be some other explanation. Maybe she—"

"They did it that way in the old times. When he was young, a dragon could keep as many women as he liked." Mirra sighed and wrapped her arms around her middle as if holding herself together. "I sent him away, Lissara. I made him go. I called him a coward—and worse. I said he . . ." She clenched her teeth and tipped her head down, closing her eyes. "And he came back to find me standing before the Sun's divine, a breath away from marrying a man who has been a torment to him for longer than I've even been alive. If he has found some comfort with that girl, I can hardly blame him. If he intends to keep her, I won't object. I've hurt him enough already. And, Lissara, if you love me at all you will be civil to her for my sake, if not for her own or your father's. No matter what you may think of her."

The two women stood silent for what seemed a long time but was probably only three or four pounding heartbeats. Kaya tried not to breathe.

Finally, Mirra reached out to put an arm around her daughter's shoulders. "It will be easier for you," she said. "Edrik is so close to your own age. And he was raised with different expectations than your father."

Kaya's heart clenched. Was it already settled between Edrik and Lissara, then? Hope told her not to give up until she'd heard it directly from Edrik. Kaya told hope to stow it.

A smile spread across Lissara's face. "I can hardly believe he's home. And did you see him, Mother? I always said he would be the mightiest dragon born in the last half century because he was so late coming of age. But did you *see* him?"

Mirra's smile echoed Lissara's, and she laughed gently. "You must let me know when to start planning the—" She straightened. Her face went serious again as her gaze focused on something back along the path Kaya had come down—the one from the meadow at the terrace edge. Kaya followed her gaze.

Grabak stood among the trees a little way up the path. Seeing that Mirra had noticed him, he crossed the rest of the distance to his wife and daughter.

Lissara beamed. "We were just coming to meet you." She wrapped her arms around him, and he buried his face in her golden hair.

"You've grown up, little butterfly," he murmured. Over his daughter's head, his eyes sought his wife's.

The interaction was vastly more intimate and unguarded than anything that had passed among the three of them in the arena, and Kaya was abruptly aware of just how wrong it was for her to be there. She wasn't just eavesdropping on a little awkward gossip about herself, she was intruding on a poignant moment among deeply private people. But she could hardly pop out now and ask them to wait until she left.

Lissara kissed her father's cheek. "Is Edrik with you?" She peered back the way Grabak had come.

Grabak chuckled. "He doesn't fly yet. He had to go the long way around. And I think I saw Linngrim corner him just as I was leaving, so he might be a while."

Lissara spared him another peck on the cheek before she hurried back toward the royal apartments, leaving Grabak and Mirra alone in the garden.

Except for Kaya.

She silently urged them to move off down the path. Any path. But they just stood there, looking at each other.

After a long, throbbing moment, the queen whispered, "I thought you were dead."

Grabak stood where he was, searching her face. "If I was dead, you would have aged. You don't look any older, Mirra."

She raised one hand to her cheek and looked down, face flushing. "No. But I couldn't feel the bond. I . . . he . . ." She stopped and drew a deep breath. Wrapped her arms around herself. "I didn't know what it meant."

"You knew what happens with a double bond." Grabak's voice was rough at the edges. Grating. "I told you because you were the queen, because you could help ensure that it would never happen again." He edged half a step forward. "Mirra—"

"You were *dead!*" She raised her head, eyes flashing defiance. "You were *both* dead. You and my brother. Nidhaug showed me the message before he burned it."

"Mirra—"

"I didn't know what else to do! The Nine were divided. Factions were forming. The unity you built was falling apart. Nidhaug—" She stopped, apparently realizing she was nearly shouting, and lowered her voice. "He was going to be the king anyway; no one else would challenge him. But I didn't think the kingdom would hold together long. And if I was his wife, at least I could . . ." Her voice cracked, and she turned away from her husband, wrapping her arms tighter. "Why didn't you come home? If you were alive this whole time, why didn't . . ." She stopped talking and rubbed at her forehead with one hand.

For a moment Grabak didn't answer, and the silence hung there, taut and heavy. Kaya's heart pounded, loud in her own ears. What if he heard it? What if they found her there? It was her fault Grabak hadn't come home sooner. She was the one who'd bought him and kept him in that dungeon. She was the one who'd put the iron collar on him. What would the queen think of Kaya when she knew?

Slowly, Grabak let out his breath. "Because I didn't want to have to sentence you to death for treason."

The queen whirled to stare at him, eyes wide and frightened.

Grabak's head tilted slightly and the corners of his mouth tightened as his eyes searched his wife's face. What did he sense through their bond?

"Did you know, Mirra?" he asked softly. "Did you know it was a trap? Did you send me there to die?"

She gaped at him. "*No!*" A choking whisper. "Oh, my dearest love, you cannot believe I would . . ." She took a step closer to him—half reached to touch his face. "Grabak, I swear to you I didn't know. It was a mistake. Just a horrible—"

"Some mistakes get people *killed*, Mirra."

Her face paled, and her mouth opened and closed once before she whispered. "My brother. He's really dead."

Grabak nodded gravely. "And Edrik's father. And his man, Tait. And who knows how many of the villagers." He sighed and rubbed a hand across the back of his neck. "And Nidhaug. Did you love him, Mirra?"

The queen clenched her teeth, and tears began to slide down her cheeks. She turned away from him again, huddling into herself. "I did what I thought was necessary. That is all."

Grabak shifted on his feet, studying her back. "I would have been dead too," he said. "If not for Kaya."

The queen pressed the fingers of one trembling hand to her forehead and drew a long, shuddering breath. But she didn't turn to face him. "What is she to you, Grabak?" Her voice sounded hollow and weary. "Have you . . . taken her as your mate?"

Grabak shifted closer to his wife. "Kaya is a dear friend." His voice was gentler now. "She is not my mate."

The queen murmured, "But you considered it."

Grabak shifted closer. "Kaya is strong, and clever, and kind, and—"

"And you love her. I can feel it in the bond." The queen turned to meet her husband's eyes. "You know I cannot share you, so just tell me truthfully—am I to be replaced? I can understand if—"

"Mirra . . ."

The tenderness with which Grabak breathed his wife's name sent chills up Kaya's spine. *She shouldn't be here!*

"I love her like a daughter. Like a sister. Like a friend. And I'll count whoever wins her heart fortunate beyond merit." Grabak reached out a hand to trace the track of one of Mirra's tears. "But you are my *wife*. I gave my oath and bond to *you*. I pledged to you my heart and my hands, my love and my loyalty. My life is *yours*, Mirra." He moved closer to her and brought his other hand up to cradle his wife's cheek. He held her gaze as he spoke. "I was angry. And I was hurt. And I couldn't feel the bond. I sat in that dungeon far longer than I should have. Long after I knew Kaya could get me out. And for that I am sorry. But my oath is not a flimsy thing to be discarded when difficulties arise. And whatever else has passed between us, that part of my heart is far too full of you to make room for anyone else. Can you not feel that in the bond too, my Mirra?"

The queen's face twisted in a choking sob. Her voice was raw and pleading. "I swear I didn't know."

"Hush." Grabak gathered his wife into his arms and rested his cheek against her pale hair. "Hush, my love. I believe you."

She buried her face in his shoulder, and he held her while she wept.

Kaya turned her face away and waited until they were gone.

And this time she chose the right path back.

Her rooms were still and quiet when she crept in through the study. Her satchel was still on the desk where she had left it, but the dressing room had been tidied, and two more dresses hung there. Kaya had never in her life had three changes of clothes to choose from. Several books had appeared on one of the small tables beside the bed, along with a basket of new candles—beeswax, not tallow.

When she pushed open the door from the bedroom to the front sitting room, she could hear the murmur of voices coming from the hall.

"Do you know when she'll be back?"

Edrik's voice!

Kaya's heart jumped, and the little knot of hope unfolded, joyful, reaching tingling tendrils all the way down to her toes. Edrik had come to see her!

Finn answered. "She didn't say."

A smile spread across Kaya's face as she crossed to the door.

In the corridor, Edrik sighed. "Do you think she'll be able to forgive me for kissing her and then choosing someone else?"

Kaya froze with her fingers on the latch. The joyful tingles turned to ice.

So that's what his whisper across the railing had meant.

Forgive me.

Close enough for kissing.

Would it have made any difference if Kaya *had* kissed him?

Would she have known what to do if it had?

Lissara knew *exactly* what to do with Edrik.

Kaya leaned her forehead against the door and heard Finn ask solemnly, "If she couldn't forgive you, would you change your mind?"

"Nothing will change my mind." Edrik's voice had a grin in it. Then it went solemn. "I think I still had doubts until Lissara kissed me, but somehow that made everything come clear."

Finn chuckled wryly. "If you say so. You should find a clean shirt. And have Kaya take a look at those scratches."

"I will." The grin was back in Edrik's voice again. "But I need to see Lissara first and make sure everything between us is settled."

The knot of hope shriveled and hardened into a coiled, venomous thing that wanted to pull out all of Lissara's golden hair. Put blister nettle in her bath. Shards of glass in her bed.

But anything Kaya did to hurt the princess would also hurt Edrik. Edrik loved Lissara. Separating Edrik from the woman he loved would be wrong, an unnecessary amputation, a thing the questioner might do. And the part of Kaya that wanted Edrik for herself still wanted even more that he should be whole and happy.

Hope was a fragile thing. It died *so* easily. Kaya drew a slow breath and ruthlessly crushed it.

She took her hand off the latch and backed away from the door. Her stomach was a hollow ache and her knees felt weak. She couldn't breathe. She had known this was how it would end. She had *always* known it. Lissara was the whole reason for Edrik's quest. So why did hearing Edrik say it out loud make Kaya feel like she'd been gut punched?

She looked down at the velvet gown. She had wanted him to think she was beautiful.

She wasn't beautiful. She would never be beautiful. She was a dungeon keeper.

Except . . . Finn was right. She didn't have to be a dungeon keeper anymore.

And she didn't have to be a prisoner either.

CHAPTER 33

When Edrik returned to Kaya's rooms, Finn's chair in the corridor was empty and the door stood ajar. Voices drifted out from somewhere in the apartment. She must have visitors. Edrik called out, but no one answered. He pushed the door open a little farther. No one was in the sitting room, but he could still hear the voices. Finn. Grabak. The queen. Grabak again.

They sounded agitated. Was something wrong? Had something happened to Kaya?

Pulse quickening, he flung the door open and crossed the sitting room. The bedchamber, too, was still and empty. A stack of books waited on the bedside table—the archivist must have gotten Edrik's hastily scribbled note—and a red dress had been carelessly tossed across the foot of the bed.

Everyone in the back parlor jumped when he entered. The queen stared at him with startled blue eyes. Grabak merely glanced at him and then turned his attention back to a piece of paper that lay on the writing desk. Finn loosed a long, expressive hiss and scrubbed a hand over his hair as he stomped across the room to lean against the doorframe and look out into the garden.

Edrik paused. Scanned the room again. She wasn't there. His heart began to pound. "What's happened? Where's Kaya?"

"Gone." Grabak held the paper out to Edrik. It was a note.

Stig,

*Thank you for your stories—the ones you told me in the
dungeon, and the one we lived together when we left. I wish you
happiness all your days.*
*I've gone to seek a happy ending of my own. Please don't try to
find me.*

Mudge

Edrik's heart beat harder, and his breath caught in his throat. Gone. She was gone. Kaya didn't play courting games. She didn't know the rules. Edrik should have spoken to her first. Lissara could have waited. And now he was too late.

"It's her handwriting." Grabak scrubbed a hand over his face.

Edrik slammed the paper down on the desk. "She can't have been gone long. We have to go look for her."

"She asked us not to." Grabak sounded tired. "We have to respect her wishes."

Edrik turned to glare at him. "She asked *you* not to."

A faint smile tugged at one corner of Grabak's mouth. "I won't stop you. But we have a kingdom to put back together, and after your performance today, you're a key piece of that. You control two of the territories. And I need someone I trust to watch my back. I can't spare you."

"But—"

"The feast begins in a quarter of an hour. You *will* be there." He frowned, eying Edrik's bloodstained tunic. "And you will be presentable." Then he looked Edrik squarely in the eyes. "What else you choose to do with that time is your own business." He picked up Kaya's note and left with his arm around the queen's shoulders and hers tucked around his waist. Apparently the two of them had come to some kind of terms.

Edrik rubbed at the back of his neck, sorting through his limited resources in his mind, weighing his options. "Finn," he snapped.

Finn met his gaze, eyes grim and apologetic. "I'm sorry, Edrik. She told me to wait in the hall while she bathed, and—"

"Find her." Edrik's voice was soft but left no room for argument.

Finn nodded his head in a quick bow. "Yes, my lord." He loped out into the garden.

Edrik headed for his own rooms bellowing for someone to bring him a bath, and some bandages, and whoever was in charge of the contingent from the Reaches. He didn't trust the Northlanders yet, but if there were any men here who had been bonded to his father, they were Edrik's now, and would be loyal enough.

All through the banquet Edrik chafed and fretted, annoyed by the slowness with which the courses were served and the length of the speeches offered by the Nine in honor of the king's return. He started every time the doors opened and silently cursed every maid, every footman, every court musician who entered and was not Kaya.

It can not *end like this!*

But Finn didn't find Kaya. When he reported back to Edrik after the banquet, he had found no one who even remembered seeing her. Edrik's men from the Reaches had made inquiries at all the inns and taverns in Vanir's rest and asked at the food vendors' stalls. No one had seen a woman matching Kaya's description.

Nor did Edrik find her when he wandered, searching, among the bonfires that night, hoping to find her dancing.

It was past noon on the following day, and Edrik was standing at the railing of the dragons' perch atop the highest spire of the Aerie, looking out across the crags and fields toward the Crevasse when Finn found him.

"My lord." Finn knelt and bowed his head.

"Stop that," Edrik said absently. Sometimes Finn took his new status as Edrik's liegeman far too seriously.

"Not until I've told you."

Edrik's attention snapped into sharp focus. "Told me what? Have you found her? Is she all right? Is she here?"

"Edrik, stop. This is hard enough without you doing that."

"Sorry. Stand up."

"No."

Edrik heaved a sigh and sat down on the smooth stone next to Finn. "Fine. Talk."

Finn mumbled, "You don't make it easy to confess." He shifted into a sitting position beside Edrik and drew a deep breath. "I think it's my fault that she left."

Edrik stared at him. "How could it possibly be your fault?"

Finn shrugged. "After you slew Nidhaug and Lissara came to meet you, she said . . ."—he looked sideways at Edrik—"Kaya said the fae tale had ended, and the hero would marry the princess, and that heroes never fall in love with dungeon keepers." He cleared his throat and looked out across the landscape. "And I told her she didn't have to be a dungeon keeper anymore. I meant for her to fight for you. Put crickets in Lissara's bed or something. But maybe she thought I meant she wasn't part of your fae tale anymore and should move on." He closed his eyes and rubbed at his forehead. "Her note said she had gone to find her own happy ending. I think it's my fault. I'm sorry. I only meant to help."

"It's not your fault, Finn. You're not the one who kissed Lissara." Edrik laughed wryly. "I am a fool."

Finn snorted. "That's what I keep telling you—although, technically, I think Lissara kissed you."

"I kissed her back. I thought I was making sure I knew what I wanted." Edrik shrugged. "In my defense, I had hit my head rather hard on the paving stones."

"Maybe I should have pointed that out to Kaya instead of talking about fae tales. But you're sure what you want now?"

"Oh, I am acutely certain. For all the good that does me."

"I thought so. You're making that face again. Did you ever find Lissara?"

Edrik snorted. "Lots of tears and wailing and some very expressive hand wringing. But I'm not sure she believes me. She seems to think I'm just getting back at her for all that time I spent pining over her when she didn't want me, and that when I think she's suffered enough, everything will go back to the way it was. She'll figure it out eventually." He sighed and stared out across the landscape. "I should have gone to Kaya first instead of Lissara. I should be out looking for her myself, but I'd only slow them down. Until I can fly, I'm useless."

Finn stood and offered Edrik a hand up. "Then I'd better teach you to fly." He grinned. "We should start off a little lower, though. If I throw you off this tower, you won't get past the first lesson."

In fact, they started on the ground, and it was still nearly two weeks before Edrik could reliably get into the air and back down again without crashing. It was another week after that before he was able to fly across the Crevasse to search Topside.

That was the last place anyone had seen Kaya. Edrik's trackers thought she'd been back to the caves where the Thanesson's men had held them, though their packs and equipment might just as easily have been pilfered by someone else. The man Edrik sent to Harrows Bend with the relief supply caravan reported that no one there had seen her since the bandit attack. The first real break was when a ferryman from Firth remembered taking a silent young man in a black robe across to the lifts. A young man. They had been inquiring after a woman. Edrik was such a fool. Kaya would want to be invisible, and as a ragged adolescent boy, she was.

A lift operator wouldn't swear to it, but he thought a boy of that description had perhaps asked after a good herbalist. But none of the herbalists or herb vendors remembered anyone of the sort. None of the traders on the docks had seen her either, and the dock master's records showed no boats or barges leaving in the time since the lift operator had seen her. It was as if Kaya had just disappeared.

Edrik wandered the market for hours and even drifted down to Nik's dock to ask if he had seen her. He said he hadn't, but Toskies protected their own, and Edrik thought the boatman looked rather smugly satisfied—though that might have just been because Edrik had not been able to win her either. The trackers watched Nik's boat for a few days, but there was no sign of Kaya.

Finn offered to fly out to Tait's holdings for him, but news like that ought to be given by the lord in person. Edrik's lack of skill and endurance in flight made the journey to the Western Reaches take much longer than it should. And the widow's silent stoicism was almost more heart-wrenching than her grown daughter's inconsolable weeping.

He spent the next several weeks in the Reaches receiving the bonds of all of his father's old vassals and inspecting the villages. The distant cousin who served as steward there was glad to have the lordship back in the family again and made Edrik most welcome, but it seemed a hollow homecoming without Kaya.

After that, a visit to the Northlands was in order. Nidhaug's vassals were a sullen lot, but they offered their liege bonds quickly enough; nobody wanted to fight the jade beast who had killed the eldest. The steward was cagey and suspicious, and a close inspection of his account books showed that the man had been skimming money from the landholder tributes.

When Edrik confronted him, the steward defiantly declared that he'd used the money to fund clandestine schools for the village boys, whom Nidhaug had deemed ineducable, and that he'd do it again given the chance, even if it meant his death. Edrik inspected several of the schools and listened to the boys recite their lessons. Then he told the steward to close up most of the Northland palace, which he didn't plan to use often anyway, and channel those funds into the school project so there would be enough for the girls to be taught as well. It turned out that the steward had several other projects of a similar nature in the works, and when he showed Edrik his real account books instead of the set he'd kept to show to Nidhaug, Edrik decided to let him keep the job. The two were on quite friendly terms when Edrik returned, at last, to the Aerie.

There were no new clues to Kaya's whereabouts. Inquiries made along the banks of the river had turned up nothing. She might be with the Ratatosk; the rimy Toskies wouldn't tell a dragon if she was. But Nik, who had long outstayed the month he'd planned to be in Topside, said he'd asked after her among the barge town traders after hearing she'd parted company with the dragons, and no one had seen her. And this time, he'd looked grim enough when he said it that Edrik believed him. The trackers worked systematically out from Topside, asking among the farms that sprawled inland from the town, scouring the caravan road through the alfkin wood, and checking the river towns east of the forest. They inquired in the few towns that lay scattered up and down the Crevasse and along the channel that separated Vanahir from the other great island.

Summer passed, and harvest time came. The air began to taste of winter in the mornings. The Aerie was again invaded by the Dragonlords and their chief land holders, along with their families and attendants. Winter was the season to renegotiate trade agreements, settle boundary disputes, forge new alliances, and, of course, pursue courtships. Lissara was surrounded by a bevy of suitors, and when it became apparent to the young ladies of the court that Edrik was no longer one of those, he found himself being stalked mercilessly by frothy young beauties and their extraordinarily attentive mothers.

And still there was no sign of Kaya.

On one particularly interminable afternoon, Edrik sat in the family solar absentmindedly staring out the window and waiting for Grabak to take his next move in their half-hearted game of lucky eights. After a tedious morning spent reworking tariff treaties, he had come to have a nice chat with the old Drake, expecting Lissara to be out, as she usually was this time of day. She, however, was most definitely in, and in lively spirits as she entertained a cluster of her ever-present suitors and an equal number of suitable young ladies on the other side of the room under the watchful eyes of the queen. Just listening to all the inane chatter and flirtatious giggles made Edrik feel tired.

"Father," Lissara called, "it must be chilly by the window. Wouldn't you and Lord Edrik be more comfortable here by the fire?" She'd been trying to coax Edrik to join her suitors ever since he arrived. How soon could he leave without seeming rude?

"Thank you, my dear, but we are well enough where we are." Grabak laid another tile.

Edrik studied the board, laid a tile of his own, and looked back out the window. Kaya was out there . . . somewhere.

"She doesn't want to be found, Edrik," Grabak murmured,

guessing the direction of Edrik's thoughts. "Let her have her fresh start."

Edrik looked back at the game board. It was his turn again. And he was losing. "I just want to talk to her," he said just as softly. He placed another tile. "There were too many things I left unsaid. And I need to know she's safe."

Lissara appeared at his elbow. "Would you like a tea cake, Lord Edrik? Father?" She offered a tray bearing an assortment.

Grabak took one that was leaking a thick berry filling and laid his next tile.

Edrik waved an absent hand. "Thank you, no."

He thought Lissara would go away again, but she hesitated beside him. "Come, Edrik," she coaxed, "you have been snappish all afternoon. But we are old friends, you and I, and you always enjoyed the sweet things I shared with you before. Take what I offer, and let it ease your heart." Then, in case he had missed her double meaning, she bent to kiss him lightly on the cheek and whispered, "Have I not been punished enough, my love?"

Edrik pressed his lips together and turned his head to look at her. They'd already had this conversation. More than once. Still, he had no desire to make a scene. "As I've told you before," he said, "my travels have altered my preferences, and I no longer have a taste for the delicacies you offer. I'm sure one of your other friends will prove more obliging."

Lissara's eyes narrowed. "So you're just going to keep chasing a woman who doesn't want you?"

"Apparently." Edrik raised a sardonic eyebrow at her. "Not to worry, I've had lots of practice."

Lissara had the grace to blush, but her eyes sparked fire.

Edrik was spared her response by the door warden's quiet knock. All eyes turned to see who would be admitted, then looked away again when it was only Finn.

Grabak leaned back from the game board. "Pull up a chair, Finn, and tell us why you look so smug."

"Thank you, Majesty." Finn grinned. "But I have only come to inform my gracious lord that I believe I have at last found a remedy for his terrible headaches."

Edrik laid a tile and glared up at Finn. "I don't have headaches."

"Well now, that is a shame." Finn did look smug; Grabak was right. "Because I was down at the Iron Boar just now having a lovely chat with a remarkable fellow from a place called Stone Creek up on the borderlands between Grabak's holding's and Hildormur's, and he says their herb woman has a marvelous remedy for headache."

Something about Finn's tone made Edrik's heart speed up. He cleared his throat and tried to keep his voice even. "Herb woman?"

"Exactly." Finn's grin broadened. "My new friend says she's very good with wounds too, and he'd never have thought such a slight, womanly creature would do so well with blood—although there are rumors that she might be part fae because bad luck follows anyone who tries to cheat her."

A slow smile slipped across Grabak's face. "What kind of bad luck?"

Finn pursed his lips and looked up at the ceiling as if trying to remember. "Well, this fellow says the butcher tried to pay her in bad meat, and a week later, his shop became infested with rats. And the landholder up there, who thought he was too important to pay a mere human herb woman, developed a rash that wouldn't go away until he made it right."

Edrik rose slowly to his feet. "Is it her?" he breathed.

Finn shrugged. "My new friend says it couldn't possibly be her. When the uppity laundress refused to pay for a salve because it was only goose grease and garden herbs and found about a hundred leeches in her washtub the next afternoon, the herb woman had been at the tavern all morning playing pips and pennies with the laundress's husband. So it definitely couldn't be her."

Edrik cuffed him in the shoulder. "That's not what I meant, and you know it. Don't play with me, Finn. Not about this. Is it Kaya?"

"There's only one way to find out."

Edrik grinned. "Suddenly, I find I have the most appalling headache."

By the time Edrik and Finn found the village in the borderland hills, it was far too late at night for an unexpected visit to be anything resembling courteous, so they woke the surly taverner and took rooms, where Edrik stood by the window waiting for the sun to rise. He dutifully ate the breakfast Finn ordered for him, but it might just as well have been dragon dust for all he tasted it. What if it wasn't Kaya? But what if it was, and she was angry that they'd come? What if he opened his heart to her, and she laughed at him? He was such a fool.

The muddy, unpaved streets in the sprawling village weren't well marked and had a tendency to peter out into cow tracks or end abruptly in hedgerows. The dragons had to ask directions three times before they found the cozy little shop with the bundled herbs hanging upside down above the door. Roses and lavender. The scent caught at something primal deep in Edrik's gut and sent his heart leaping up into his throat. It had to be her.

Inside, the shop was bright and cheerful with the sunlight that flooded through the windows, and the scent of the herbs that hung in bunches from the ceiling permeated the air. The walls between the windows were lined with shelves that held books, and bottles, and boxes, and little clay pots. A work table stood at the back, clean and neat, and a curtain covered a doorway in the back wall that probably led to the shopkeeper's living quarters. At the front of the shop, a fire crackled comfortably on a small hearth, and a rocking chair creaked softly as it swayed to and fro with its back to the draft from the door. As Edrik hesitated in the doorway with his heart pounding in his ears, hardly able to breathe, the chair stopped rocking, and the woman sitting there rose to her feet and turned.

She wasn't Kaya. The woman was, as Finn's informant had described her, slight and womanly, but age had given her already slender build a graceful delicacy, and her crown of neatly plaited white hair framed large blue eyes in a face so pale her wrinkled skin seemed almost translucent.

Edrik's heart fell into his stomach, and his mouth went dry. He had been so certain.

Behind him, Finn said, "Forgive us. We're looking for the herb woman."

The elderly woman sized up her visitors, taking in their clothes and bearing. She stepped toward them and offered Edrik a graceful curtsy. "And you have found her. How can I help you, my lord?"

Edrik and Finn just stood there awkwardly until Finn cleared his throat and said, "My liege suffers from headaches, and we were told you had a particularly good remedy."

"He does look a bit peaky." The herb woman smiled as she led Edrik to a straight-backed wooden chair, which she angled to catch the light from a window before motioning him to sit. When he did, she used her long fingers to tilt his chin up while she watched his eyes, brow furrowed. "In which part of your head does the pain occur?"

A loud clatter and a shouted oath from behind the curtain at the back of the shop made all of them jump. The herb woman smiled and straightened. "Are you all right, my dear?" she called.

"I burned it again!" came the irritated reply.

And Edrik's heart began to pound. It was *her*. It was *Kaya*. The chair clattered to the floor as he jumped to his feet and spun.

The curtain fluttered and moved aside. "Mother Agata, how do you keep the milk from—" Kaya cut off as she froze in the doorway, dark eyes wide and startled. Her green dress was elegantly cut, though the fabric was plain and covered by a wide patchwork apron. Her black hair had been expertly plaited and pinned in a manner that flattered her cheekbones and made her mouth seem generous and inviting. And she wore the hair ribbons he had given her. She was so beautiful! He wanted to gather her up, and hold her, and breathe in her scent, and kiss her until she made him stop. But he couldn't move. And she was still angry with him; he could see it in her eyes.

"My assistant," the herb woman, Mother Agata, said into the trembling silence.

"Kaya!" Edrik breathed.

CHAPTER 34

"What are you doing here?" The question fell out of Kaya's mouth before she could stop it. Rude. But really, how dare he come here just when her memories of him were starting to soften around the edges so they didn't cut so deeply when she stumbled over them.

Mother Agata raised her eyebrows. Then smiled knowingly. Nothing got past the old herb woman. "His Lordship suffers from headaches," she explained pointedly, inclining her head toward Kaya.

"Headaches." Kaya frowned.

"Just so." Mother Agata was clearly trying not to laugh.

Kaya scowled and rubbed at her own forehead. "How did you even find me?"

A broad grin stretched across Finn's face. "When you put leeches in someone's washtub, people are bound to talk."

She thought about denying it, but there was no point.

"We've been worried about you," Edrik said. "You left so suddenly. We wanted to make sure you're safe."

Kaya snorted. "I still don't need you to rescue me, Lord Edrik." She dropped a mocking curtsy. "And I did leave Stig a note."

Edrik took a step closer to her, his pale green eyes probing. "Did you find your happy ending, Kaya?" There was something wistful in his voice that made Kaya's heart clench. *How dare he come here and talk to her in that tone!*

"Yes," she snapped. "And you are tracking mud all over it."

He looked down at his boots.

This time, Mother Agata did laugh. "The mud will wash off, Kaya. Perhaps you would like to get Lord Edrik his headache remedy so he can be on his way?" She arched a teasing eyebrow at Kaya. Then she turned to Finn. "Have you ever seen a two-headed pig, young man?"

Finn blinked. "A two-headed pig?"

"Just so."

"I can't say I have."

"Well then, perhaps you'd like to walk with me down to the swine-herd's place while my assistant tends to your friend."

She took her shawl off the peg by the door and waved an impatient hand. Finn stepped up beside her and offered his arm.

"The swineherd has a two-headed pig?" he asked as the two went out the door.

"Oh, I very much doubt it," Mother Agata said, "but we can go and ask him."

Finn burst out laughing and closed the door behind them, leaving Edrik and Kaya alone in the shop.

"Kaya . . ." Edrik began.

Kaya thumped the mortar and pestle onto the table and started gathering the ingredients for a simple headache remedy. She didn't want to talk to him. She couldn't make herself look at him. She just wanted him to go away so she could cry in peace. *Why did he have to come here?*

"Kaya," he said again. "Please. I need to talk to you."

She tossed a generous portion of shredded willow bark into the mortar and added a little skullcap. Then, because she was feeling peevish, she threw in a big pinch of pig yarrow before she started pounding with the pestle. "By all means, my lord. Talk."

He righted the chair he had knocked over and came to stand beside her, leaning against the table while she worked. "I thought we agreed you were going to call me Rolf."

She felt his nearness like a living thing, trapped and panicky. "That was before."

"Before what?" His voice was gentle, coaxing. "Please tell me. I want to try to make this right."

She slammed the pestle against the willow bark and ground it hard, stone grating against stone, gnawing at the herbs, fueling the anger that kept the tears at bay. For now.

"Before . . . everything! Before the dancing. Before the caves. Before the Thanesson stabbed Stig and you realized how disgusting I am. Before you killed Nid—"

"Wait." Edrik straightened, looking at her intently. "Go back. I do not think you're disgusting."

She smashed the pestle down hard. "I saw your face when I fished out that knife point. And afterward, you barely even spoke to me. And you couldn't bear to touch me at all."

"Kaya . . ." He put one hand on top of hers, stopping her pounding. His fingers felt warm and strong. "I wanted to. But I thought you were angry with me, and I didn't want to make it worse."

She pulled away, clenching her teeth against the sudden threat of tears, and went to fetch the kettle from its hook over the fire. He waited, watching silently while she tipped the mangled herbs into a tin cup and poured hot water over them. "It needs to sit a moment," she said, not looking at him.

He reached over to skim his fingers along her jawbone and tip her face up, forcing her to meet his gaze. "Kaya, I think you're beautiful." His green eyes were as earnest as his voice. "I think you're intelligent. I think you're remarkably strong. Disgusting is not a word I would ever use to describe you."

Why was he doing this? She pulled away from him and snatched up the kettle, biting down hard on the threatening tears. When she turned around after hanging the kettle back on its hook, he was still watching her.

"I don't know what my face looked like when you were tending to Grabak. But I know what I was thinking. I was humbled and impressed by your skill. And I was imagining what kind of life you must have had to make it so easy for you to shove your hand inside him, and so difficult for you to laugh. It's not right for anyone to have to live that way." His brows drew together and he frowned, studying her face. It was almost the same expression he had worn in the cave. "Especially not someone as kind as you." He looked down at his muddy boots again. "I'm sorry, Kaya. I never meant to hurt you."

Kaya's belly went hollow and her knees threatened to give out. She was finding it difficult to hold on to the anger, and she turned away from him, facing the fire while she got her expression under control. When she could speak without her voice trembling, she said carefully, "Thank you, Edrik. That's nice to know." She drew a deep breath. "Even if it doesn't really change anything."

He was silent a long moment before he asked, "It doesn't change anything?" The tin cup scraped across the tabletop as he drew it toward himself.

Kaya shrugged and turned to face him again. "Your happy ending is still waiting for you back at the Aerie," she said. "And mine is here. I'm to take over the shop next year. Mother Agata is teaching me to cook things besides porridge"—she smiled sheepishly, remembering the temper tantrum over the scorched milk that Edrik had undoubtedly overheard—"and how to fix my hair properly. I'm figuring out how to be a real woman. It's a good life."

"You've always been a real woman," Edrik said. "Just like I've always been a real dragon. What you wear doesn't change what you are."

Then he smiled. "But your hair does suit you that way. And I like your ribbons."

Kaya felt her cheeks warm. "They were a gift from a friend."

He looked away from her, peering into the tin cup and swirling its contents. "So this is what you want, then?"

It took her a moment to answer. "It's like I told you back on the boat," she said softly, "what I want already belongs to someone else, and trying to take it would only hurt people I care about." His eyes came back up to focus on her. She forced a small smile onto her face.

"So I am learning to want something else. Go home and marry your princess, Edrik. I'm fine."

Edrik stared down into the cup and shook his head. "You always say that," he murmured, "but you never are." He raised the cup to his lips.

"Don't drink that!" Kaya lunged across the room, catching his hand just in time.

He blinked at her, startled. "Why not?"

Kaya laughed. "Because it tastes like troll bile and will turn your urine red for a week. I was angry with you for coming."

A grin spread across his face far enough to show his double canines. He looked into the cup again. "I might deserve that." Then he looked into Kaya's eyes. "I like to hear you laugh, Kaya," he said, making her name a purring caress.

Kaya's heart stopped beating. She tried to snatch her hand away, but he caught it with his free hand and held it while he set the cup back on the table.

"I'm not going to marry Lissara."

She swallowed hard. "You're not?"

"No." He moved closer to her, holding their joined hands against his chest, and reaching for her waist with his other hand.

All the blood in Kaya's body tried to rush out the top of her head at once. She couldn't breathe with him that close. "Why not?" she whispered numbly.

"Because this is not a fae tale," he murmured, sliding the hand on her waist around behind her, careful of the dwarrow runes, and drawing her closer still. "And I've fallen in love with the dungeon keeper."

Kaya drew a gasping breath. "But . . ." Her mind seized up. She couldn't make words form. "But you . . ." Her lungs spasmed, and her breath started coming in ragged, choking gulps. "You *kissed* her." She pushed away from him. Turned her back on him. Wrapped one arm around her stomach as she steadied herself on the edge of the worktable with the other.

Edrik's hand cupped her elbow, offering support, and she felt the warmth of his body close behind her. Too close. "Not on purpose. She didn't know yet. She does now."

"You said k-kissing her made everything come clear."

Edrik drew a sharp breath. "You heard that?"

"I h-heard you in the corridor. I was going to let you in." She couldn't seem to hold her voice steady. "But then you s-said you hoped I could forgive you for kissing me and then ch-choosing her."

"Kaya, no!" Edrik shifted around in front of her so fast it made her dizzy. "I was looking for Lissara. Her rooms are right across the hall from yours."

Tears stung at Kaya's eyes, and she squeezed them shut, turning her face away from him.

"Please, Kaya." His tone was urgent. Imploring. "I was wondering if Lissara might forgive me for kissing her and then choosing *you*. Because when she kissed me, it made me realize how much I would rather be kissing you."

Kaya's eyes snapped open and she stopped breathing altogether as she turned to meet his gaze. "Edrik . . ." She shook her head. She must have heard him wrong.

"I wanted to see her first so I could tell you honestly that I had ended it with her. That everything between Lissara and me was over." He raised a cautious hand. Traced the line of her cheekbone with his fingertips. Carefully laid his palm against her cheek. Whispered, "That you were the one I loved."

Kaya drew a shuddering breath. "But—"

"I tried to tell you when I took you to see the firefall." His fingers caressed the side of her neck and slid into her hair, loosening Kaya's careful plaits.

"You did?" She couldn't move.

"We got interrupted." His thumb slid ever so lightly across her lips. "I tried to tell you again when we were dancing, but I kissed you first. On purpose. And it frightened you." He smiled sadly at her. "I didn't mean to frighten you, Kaya. I never want to frighten you." His other hand moved up her back, sending tingles all the way down to her fingertips.

"Stars, Rolf."

"I made an even worse mess of it in the caves." His face tilted toward hers, and she felt his breath, warm against her cheek as he leaned closer. "And after that, you were avoiding me, and I didn't know why. We were running out of time. I thought I could talk to you after everything was settled. But then you were gone, and I couldn't find you, and—" His breath caught as his cheek brushed against her temple, and she shivered.

For a long, slow heartbeat, they stood like that. Barely touching. Barely breathing. And then he whispered, "I love you, Kaya. Please tell me I'm not too late."

Kaya's pulse beat hard in her throat. She drew a trembling breath and slowly turned her head to press her lips, whisper soft against his cheek.

He drew a sharp breath and leaned back just enough to study her face with those disconcerting green eyes, as if he wasn't quite sure she'd really done it.

She smiled and placed her next tentative kiss on his lips.

He caught it. And held it. Tenderly. Almost reverently. As if it were something rare and unimaginably precious. Then, with a low moan, he leaned into her kiss, deepening it into something more reckless and urgent. His hand cupped her cheek, and his fingers stroked the skin just beneath her ear while his other arm circled her waist, careful not to hurt her, but strong and firm, and . . . and insistent.

Kaya's hands, trapped between them, wound into the front of his shirt, pulling him against her as the muscles of his chest tightened beneath her fingers, and she lost herself in his kiss. Something inside her unfolded and wrapped around him, around them both, brushing against something in him—something hot, and wild, and beguiling. He drew a long, ragged breath, almost like a sob, and buried his face in the side of her neck, folding his body around hers, clutching her to himself as if he would never let her go again.

She slipped her arms around his waist and leaned her cheek against his shoulder, holding on to him until his breathing slowed and calmed. He shifted, loosening his grip a little and straightening. His fingers traced one of the plaits in her hair and tickled the back of her neck as they played with the loose end of one of her hair ribbons. She nestled against him, pressing her ear against his chest so she could hear the calm rush of his breathing and the slowing thump-thud of his dragon heart.

Lover's sounds.

"I love you too, Rolf," she whispered.

ABOUT THE AUTHOR

Amy Beatty grew up in the wilds of Yellowstone National Park as part of an experiment in crossing the genes of a respected research biologist with those of a grammar aficionado. She spent her summers making forts under the sagebrush with her friends and catching garter snakes by the creek to populate elaborate sandbox villages—or holed up in her bunk bed exploring the exotic worlds hidden between the covers of books. She currently lives in Utah with her husband and their two delightfully unconventional children.

ACKNOWLEDGEMENTS

The creation of *Dragon Ascending* has been, for me, a magical adventure. And like all good adventures, this one has been filled with heroes, mentors, allies, guardians, and a shapeshifting trickster or two. I would be remiss if I failed to express my gratitude to those who helped make this story what it is.

First, a special thanks to my family. To my mother, who introduced me to the magic of words and the worlds they can bring into being, and to my father, who taught me the power of the *right* word. To my husband, whose unfailing love and encouragement have kept me going through the dark nights of my writerly soul (and who understands the value of judiciously applied pizza delivery). To my children, who remind me regularly that you can't find out how tall you are until you're in over your head.

To Jen, Lois, and Nichole, my amazing critique partners, thank you for taking a new writer under your wings and sharing your collective wisdom and advice with such kind patience. To Talei Lawson, my friend and cheerful minion, an extra measure of appreciation; your enthusiasm and assistance have been invaluable. Thank you to the crew over at the Life, the Universe, and Everything Symposium for introducing me to the writing community and helping me feel like I belong.

Huge gratitude goes out to my intrepid beta readers for being brave enough to tell me where I had wandered off the path: Julia Despain, Carol and Coralee D'Augostino, Julie Flaming, Mariah Porter, Marilyn Dodson, Bonnie Stone, Andrea Watson, Lyn Gilcrease, Patrice Ashby, Lucille Woolston, Adena Campbell, Laura Rawlins, and Amy and Dan

Fussell. And thanks also to other friends who read for me on a less formal basis; you know who you are. This story is better for your companionship on the journey.

Jo Schaffer, my black-belt agent, thank you for taking a chance on me and showing me the ropes. And last, though anything but least, to James, Jason, Holli, my editor Sarah Hamblin, and the rest of the team at Immortal Works, thank you for your faith in Edrik and Mudge and all the time and effort you have put into making this book a reality.

This has been an
Immortal Production

CPSIA information can be obtained
at www.ICGtesting.com
Printed in the USA
BVHW03s0745130918
527265BV00001B/1/P